## Praise for the
## Chocoholic Mystery Series

"Anyone who loves chocolate—and who doesn't?—will adore JoAnna Carl's *The Chocolate Cupid Killings*. This deliciously fast-paced addition to the Chocoholic Mystery series has more twists and turns than a chocolate-covered pretzel, but this treat won't add any pounds or inches, so you can indulge without guilt!"
—Leslie Meier, author of *Mother's Day Murder*

"Lee McKinney sells chocolates and solves crimes with panache and good humor."
—Carolyn Hart

"I'm proud to stand up and say, 'My name is Charlaine, and I'm a Chocoholic!' "
—Charlaine Harris

"A mouthwatering debut and a delicious new series! Feisty young heroine Lee McKinney is a delight in this chocolate treat. A real page-turner, and I got chocolate on every one! I can't wait for the next."          —Tamar Myers

"Enjoyable . . . entertaining . . . a fast-paced whodunit with lots of suspects and plenty of surprises . . . satisfies a passion for anything chocolate."
—*The Commercial Record* (MI)

"JoAnna Carl's books are delicious treats, from the characters to the snippets of chocolate trivia. . . . [The] fantastic characters . . . have come to feel like good friends."          —Roundtable Reviews

"Delicious."          —Cluesunlimited.com

"The descriptions of the chocolates are enough to make your mouth water, so be prepared. . . . Once again, I enjoyed each page of the book and am already looking forward to my next visit to Warner Pier, Michigan."          —Review Index

"Descriptions of exotic chocolate will have you running out to buy gourmet sweets. . . . A delectable treat."          —The Best Reviews

"Fast-paced and sprinkled with humor. Strongly recommended."
—I Love a Mystery

JoAnna Carl's Chocoholic Mysteries

*The Chocolate Cat Caper*
*The Chocolate Bear Burglary*
*The Chocolate Frog Frame-Up*
*The Chocolate Puppy Puzzle*
*The Chocolate Mouse Trap*
*The Chocolate Bridal Bash*
*The Chocolate Jewel Case*
*The Chocolate Snowman Murders*
*The Chocolate Cupid Killings*

"The Chocolate Kidnapping Clue" (short story)
*Crime de Cocoa* (anthology)

# Chocolate to Die For

## Chocoholic Mysteries

### JoAnna Carl

AN OBSIDIAN MYSTERY

OBSIDIAN
Published by New American Library, a division of
Penguin Group (USA) Inc., 375 Hudson Street,
New York, New York 10014, USA
Penguin Group (Canada), 90 Eglinton Avenue East, Suite 700, Toronto,
Ontario M4P 2Y3, Canada (a division of Pearson Penguin Canada Inc.)
Penguin Books Ltd., 80 Strand, London WC2R 0RL, England
Penguin Ireland, 25 St. Stephen's Green, Dublin 2,
Ireland (a division of Penguin Books Ltd.)
Penguin Group (Australia), 250 Camberwell Road, Camberwell, Victoria 3124,
Australia (a division of Pearson Australia Group Pty. Ltd.)
Penguin Books India Pvt. Ltd., 11 Community Centre, Panchsheel Park,
New Delhi – 110 017, India
Penguin Group (NZ), 67 Apollo Drive, Rosedale, North Shore 0632,
New Zealand (a division of Pearson New Zealand Ltd.)
Penguin Books (South Africa) (Pty.) Ltd., 24 Sturdee Avenue,
Rosebank, Johannesburg 2196, South Africa

Penguin Books Ltd., Registered Offices:
80 Strand, London WC2R 0RL, England

Published by Obsidian, an imprint of New American Library, a division of
Penguin Group (USA) Inc. Previously published in separate Signet editions.

First Obsidian Printing, March 2010
10  9  8  7  6  5  4  3  2  1

Set in Palatino
Designed by Eve L. Kirch

Printed in the United States of America

# CONTENTS

# The
# Chocolate
# Puppy
# Puzzle

*For Norma Hightower,*
*a special cousin and friend*

# Chapter 1

I suppose it wasn't the puppy's fault, but after he handed me the money, everything in Warner Pier seemed to go to pot. Fraud, kidnapping, homicide, theft, trespassing—a real crime wave developed. My romantic life got—well, unromantic. Even the chocolate business became complicated.

The day had started out very well. I was happy as I walked toward the Fall Rinkydink. My favorite guy, Joe Woodyard, was with me. The weather was as perfect as only an October day on the shores of Lake Michigan can be. I may have hummed a hum or skipped a little skip.

Then a chocolate Labrador pup galumped across the Dock Street Park, cut through the buffet line in the picnic shelter, and planted two gigantic feet on the knees of my brand-new tan wool slacks. I nearly dropped a big tray of TenHuis Chocolade's finest truffles and bonbons. The sweets all shifted to one side, and only the extrastrength industrial plastic wrap kept them from hitting the grass.

The dog handed me a large leather wallet with a dirty ten-dollar bill sticking out one side.

That first disaster occurred at the first-ever Rinkydink.

I'm business manager for my aunt's chocolate shop, TenHuis Chocolade, in the picturesque resort of Warner Pier, on the east shore of Lake Michigan. In the summer, Warner Pier's streets—laid out in 1855 for buggies and horse-drawn farm wagons—are thronged with cars, vans, and buses carrying tourists and summer people. The traffic is horrendous.

In the fall, all the tourists and summer visitors go home. The parking problem is over until the next Memorial Day, and traffic is close to nil for six months. Consequently, Warner Pier locals for years have linked the end of the tourist season and the beginning of autumn to the day when our one traffic light becomes a blinker.

All summer the light at Fourth Avenue and Dock Street changes from green to yellow to red—just like a big-city traffic light. On the Tuesday after Columbus Day, the Warner Pier Street Department turns out in force (all three of them) and changes the light to a flashing red on Fourth Avenue and a flashing yellow on Dock Street. For years the merchants in the neighborhood gathered to cheer them on, just as a joke.

It was Maggie McNutt, a close friend of mine and Warner Pier High School speech and drama teacher, who had the idea of making the changing of the traffic light into a fund-raiser for the high school drama club. All the food-related merchants, including TenHuis (it rhymes with "ice"), were asked to donate food for a picnic luncheon, which would be held in the Dock Street Park picnic shelter. Nonfood merchants—the gift shops, antiques stores, art galleries, the hardware store, and the drug store—were asked to kick in items for a silent auction and for door prizes. Everybody in the world was asked to buy tickets.

"It'll be fun!" said Maggie. She had bounced in her chair as she presented the idea to the chamber board. "The chamber ought to have more social events. This one will be a farewell party for those merchants who close up and go south for the winter. It'll be a celebrate-fall party for those of us staying here. And it will help the drama club take students to state competitions."

Maggie had become the speech and drama teacher three years earlier, when she and her husband, Ken, who taught math, were both hired at Warner Pier High School. She had short dark hair and was petite, peppy, and cute—the kind of woman who makes an all-but-six-foot blonde like me feel like a giraffe. But I liked Maggie. Everyone in Warner Pier seemed to like her—with one exception—and Maggie was full of ideas to promote Warner Pier High School drama. Maggie told me she had worked in Hollywood, appearing as an extra or in small roles in several films. But when she'd turned thirty, she'd decided she was never going to make it big in showbiz, so she came back to her home state, got her master's in education, and married Ken McNutt, who'd been a high school classmate. They'd rented a little house in Warner Pier and settled into the community. The previous year her students had taken first place in the state one-act competition. She wanted to make sure they got to go again.

The name of the event, the "Rinkydink," had started as a joke, after somebody remarked that a town with only one traffic light was "pretty rinkydink." Since the small-town atmosphere was what most of us liked about living in Warner Pier, we adopted the term with perverse pride, and the light-changing ceremony was officially christened.

The weather was cooperating for the first Rinkydink, and Maggie hadn't had to move the picnic to the high school gym, as she'd feared she might. The day was sunny, with temperatures just under seventy. The sunlight was creating that autumn effect in which oblique light turns the sky mellow and the air so soft and beautiful you want to gulp big lungfuls of it. The trees were lush with all the reds, yellows, golds, oranges, greens, and browns of a Michigan autumn. The sun glinted off the Warner River. The Victorian houses looked more like wedding cakes than usual. The chrysanthemums were blooming like crazy—bronze, maroon, yellow, rust, and gold. The breeze playfully tossed fallen leaves about.

It was a good day to be alive and living in Warner Pier, Michigan. I had been happy as a clam as Joe and I each carried a big tray of Ten-Huis's fanciest chocolates toward the dessert table.

Joe saw the dog coming. "There's a pup loose," he said. "Some guy is after him."

I turned to see who was chasing the dog. The animal ran right up to me and, as I said, planted his huge puppy feet on the knees of my tan wool slacks. He looked at me with soft hazel eyes. He was holding this big leather wallet in his mouth.

"Hey, fellow! Welcome to the party." I stepped backward, trying to get the dirty feet off my slacks. Of course, the puppy thought this was a game and jumped up on me again. I balanced the tray on my hip, accidentally tipping it. I could feel the chocolates slide as I tried to fend off the pup with the hand I'd freed up. The dog was at that awkward stage of puppyhood, maybe four or five months old. He looked healthy and full of puppy pep, with a lustrous, dark brown coat as smooth and shiny as melted chocolate. He had a tiny spot of white on his chest.

Then the pup nudged my wrist with the wallet. It was a beat-up and moldy-looking brown leather folder, more than twice the size of a standard bifold billfold and more like a passport case than a regular wallet. It didn't look like something a puppy should be chewing on, so I took it away from him. It was covered with dog slobber, of course.

By then Joe had put down the tray of chocolates that he was carrying, and he grabbed the dog.

"Look at the money," I said, showing him the wallet. Five or six odd-sized bills were sticking out. "Somebody's been playing king-sized Monopoly."

"I've seen those big bills in one of the antiques shops," Joe said. "I think they used to be legal tender."

"Somebody's going to want this back."

Joe scooped the puppy up with both arms, and the dog joyously licked his face. Joe laughed. What else can you do when a strange puppy decides you're adorable? Or maybe delicious. Of course, I think Joe's delicious, too. He has not only dark hair, brilliant blue eyes, and broad shoulders; he also has a very sharp mind and a nice personality. Someday I might even set a wedding date.

I took my tray of chocolates to the dessert table and handed it to Tracy Roderick, who was a TenHuis employee in the summer and president of Maggie McNutt's drama club during the school year. Tracy's a nice girl; she could even be a pretty girl if she got a decent hairstyle.

"Hi, Lee," Tracy said. "I'm in charge of the dessert table. As usual, the TenHuis chocolates will be the center of attraction."

"I messed these up," I said. "They nearly landed in the grass."

Tracy brandished a pair of food-service gloves. "I'll straighten them. Your aunt will never know what a narrow escape they had."

The two of us admired the craftsmanship displayed in the chocolates. Swirling patterns of bonbons and truffles filled the two trays, ready to entice Rinkydink picnickers with dark, white, and milk chocolate, each goody filled with an exotic flavor. In the center of each tray was a heap of molded chocolates—squares, small animals, min- iature bars. Joe and I had just delivered two big trays of yummy. To me the chocolates made the cherry pies and coffee cakes a waste of calories.

"Lee, we'd better get this dog back to his owner," Joe said.

Leaving Tracy in charge of her desserts, I fished a large paper nap- kin out of a pile at the end of the serving table and wiped off my hand and the wallet. Then Joe and I walked toward the man who had been running. He'd slowed down after he saw Joe scoop up the puppy.

I waved the wallet. "This yours?"

"Thanks for rescuing it!" The man continued toward us. "And thanks for grabbing Monte!"

As the man approached, I had plenty of time to look him over. He was an older gent, but he was marching along as if he were full of youthful energy. He was wearing an outfit that was just a little too slickly coordinated—neatly pressed jeans, desert boots, and a plaid wool shirt worn over a turtleneck. Gray hair oozed out from beneath a wide-brimmed felt hat that looked—well, Australian. It didn't have one side pinned up, but it should have.

As he reached us, he took the puppy and received a greeting as enthusiastic as the one Joe had gotten. "Monte," he said, "you're a naughty fellow." He looped the puppy's leash over his wrist firmly and put the dog down on the grass. "Sit," he said. Monte sat. Then his owner turned to us, giving a broad, toothy grin. "Thanks for catch- ing him."

"Actually, he caught us," I said. "He's a friendly little guy. Did you call him Monte?"

The man smiled. "Yes. It's short for Montezuma. He's a chocolate Labrador."

"Ah," I said. "The Aztec emperor and fabled consumer of choco- late." I turned to Joe. "According to legend, Montezuma drank choco- late before visiting his harem."

"You're absolutely correct." The gray-haired man swept off his hat, giving me a look at a gorgeous head of hair. I also got a look at the even spacing around the hairline that showed that he'd had an expensive implant job.

"Maia Michaelson invited me to this—is it called the Rinkydink?" he said. "Have you seen her?"

"No." Joe and I both scanned the crowd. I bit my tongue before I could say *She's probably waiting to make an entrance.*

"I'm sure she'll be here in a minute," Joe said. "Is the wallet yours as well?"

I realized that I was still holding the oversized wallet with the big bills. I extended it to the gray-haired man just as a shrill voice called out. "Aubrey!"

"Here's Mae," I said. "I mean Maia." The two names were pronounced almost the same way, but they definitely referred to two different people.

Maia approached dramatically. Back when she was Mae Ensminger, this woman used to simply walk up. But the previous spring Mae had published a romantic novel under the nom de plume Maia Michaelson. According to the dictionary, I'd been told, the two names were pronounced the same way, but Mae called her new moniker "MAY-ah." In her new persona, Maia couldn't just walk up. She approached dramatically.

Becoming Maia Michaelson had changed Mae Ensminger drastically. Mae Ensminger was at least fifty. Maia Michaelson claimed to be only forty. Mae used to wear jeans and T-shirts, like the rest of us. Maia affected solid black from top-to-toe and wore big, clunky jewelry. Mae used to wear her mousy brown hair pulled into a ponytail, not unlike mine. Maia had coal black hair that hung down her back and was heavily teased on top of her head. Mae never wore makeup. But Maia wore lots of it. Mae used to stand with her back against the wall, observing, but not saying a lot. Maia talked all the time, in a voice that varied between too soft to understand and too piercing to bear. Maia theatrically gestured all the time. She hadn't gone as far as placing the back of her hand against her forehead and sighing, "Ah, me," but I wasn't going to be surprised when she did.

Maia—it definitely wasn't Mae—linked her arm through the gray-haired man's arm. "I see you've met Lee and Joe, Warner Pier's most glam young couple," she said.

"I don't know that we're particularly grim," I said. "I mean, glam! We're not very glamorous, and maybe not too young, but I'm Lee McKinney, and this is Joe Woodyard."

The gray-haired man shook hands with each of us. He'd hidden the wallet away someplace before I'd had a chance to ask him where he got the big bills.

He spoke. "I'm Aubrey Andrews Armstrong."

Sure you are, I thought. That name was as bogus as Maia Michaelson's. I spoke quickly to hide my thoughts—too quickly, I guess, because I pulled one of the malapropisms that make me sound like an idiot. "What brings you to Warner Pier, Mr. Strongarm? I mean, Mr. Armstrong!"

He blinked. Then he patted the hand Maia had placed on his arm and started to answer. But Maia spoke before he could. "No, Aubrey! You're not to tell a soul why you're here."

A frown flitted over Armstrong's face. "But, Maia, I know we haven't signed . . ."

"You can tell in a minute. But there's another person I want to hear the news first. That's why I insisted we come to the picnic. Lee, have you seen Maggie?"

Maggie McNutt? That was a surprise. Maia was about the only person in Warner Pier who didn't like Maggie.

"She's helping behind the serving table," Joe said. "I guess we'd better get in line, Lee."

We did so, followed by Maia and her new pal Aubrey. And behind them, I finally noticed, was Maia's husband—actually Mae's husband—Vernon Ensminger. "St. Vernon the Patient," Joe called him. Vernon was a big, bald guy—no implants on Vernon's scalp—who operated a successful fruit farm. His work boots and plaid shirt were so authentic that they made Aubrey Andrews Armstrong look more bogus than ever.

Joe stopped to speak to Vernon, which is typical of Joe. People tended to ignore Vernon, now that he was merely an adjunct to the colorful Maia Michaelson, but Joe had always liked him. I liked him, too. If you had a flat on a lonely road, Vernon Ensminger was the kind of guy who would drop by with a jack.

Maia, Aubrey, and Vernon stepped into line behind us. The puppy frisked up to me again, jumping on the back of my slacks this time. I was beginning to wonder if Aubrey Andrews Armstrong would be good for the dry cleaning bill.

Maia was craning her neck around, talking shrilly. "I do want you to meet Maggie. She's simply delightful. And so talented. This whole event was her idea. Oh, there's her husband. Ken! Ken!"

Ken McNutt had been heading for the parking lot, but he could hardly ignore her summons. He came over, looking as thin as usual. Thin was the word for Ken—thin build, thin hair, thin voice. Like Vernon, he stayed in the background and let his wife star.

Ken nodded to Vernon, then spoke. "Hello, Mae."

Maia didn't introduce Aubrey. "Where is your charming wife?"

"If you stay in line, you'll see her. She's in charge." He moved toward the parking lot again. "Sorry to run, but I have to be back for fifth period."

"Such a lovely young couple," Maia said, dripping condescension. "What my father called 'a teaching couple.' "

Joe seized the opportunity to speak quietly to me. "Why does Mae have it in for Maggie?"

I lowered my voice, too. "They both entered the Historical Society's competition for a dramatic sketch on the founding of Warner Pier. Maggie won."

Joe snorted. "That's something Maia will never forgive."

I shrugged. "Maggie avoids her. But this time she won't be able to."

Maggie had just come into view. She was standing beside the charcoal cooker where Mike Herrera, our mayor and one of Warner Pier's leading restaurateurs, was grilling bratwurst. Maia gave her a tremendous greeting, shrieking out her name.

I had to hand it to Maggie; she didn't visibly wince. She merely waved and picked up a Styrofoam plate, which she held close to Mike's elbow. He began to lift browned bratwurst from the grill to the plate. Maia had to wait until the serving line reached them before she could say anything else. But then she said plenty.

"Maggie! Maggie! Something wonderful has happened, and I want you to be the first to know."

As I say, Maggie was usually peppy as all get-out, but she didn't try to compete with Maia in the energy department. She spoke very quietly. "What is it, Maia?"

"This wonderful man is a Hollywood producer, Maggie! He's buying the film rights to my book! And he wants to shoot the movie right here in Warner Pier!"

Maggie whipped her head in Maia's direction. Her mouth

dropped slightly open, and her eyes grew large. Joe looked amazed, too, and I'm sure my jaw was hanging clear down to my chest. We all thought Maia's novel was awful. And someone wanted to make a movie of it?

Maia gave a triumphant crow. "Yes! A Hollywood producer, Maggie! This is Aubrey Andrews Armstrong!"

Maggie's eyes shifted to Aubrey Andrews Armstrong and grew even wider. She gave a startled gasp. She moved her right hand from under the Styrofoam plate. The plate broke in half and a dozen bratwurst landed in the grass of the Dock Street Park.

# Chapter 2

We humans gasped, but Monte knew what to do. He nabbed one of those brats quicker than a flash of lightning out over Lake Michigan.

"Drop it, Monte!" Aubrey Andrews Armstrong sounded frantic. "It'll make him sick!"

It would take Superman to get a bratwurst away from a puppy as big as Monte, but Aubrey managed to get part of it. Joe and I used paper napkins to pick up the brats that had bounced under the serving table and out on our side, and Maggie picked up the ones that had fallen on her side. Mike Herrera muttered some Spanish word I pretended not to understand and reached for uncooked brats. "More brats in a minute, folks," he said. "If you want chicken, you're all set."

Joe and I decided we'd settle for chicken, though I normally prefer brats, and we moved on down the line. Behind me I could hear Maggie speaking graciously. "I'm delighted for you, Maia. A movie sale is quite a feather in your cap."

Maia introduced Aubrey Andrews Armstrong to Maggie. They exchanged how-do-you-dos.

"Well, well," Aubrey said. "Warner Pier certainly has a pretty little drama teacher. I'll bet the boys fight to get in your classes, Mrs. McNutt. Did I get your name right?"

"McNutt is correct, Mr. Armstrong."

Was it my imagination, or did Aubrey's few words sound not only sexist, but like a taunt? And had Maggie's reply sounded the same way?

Joe and I collected the rest of our lunch—rolls, slaw, potato salad, beans—and went to a picnic table. I found some hand cleaner in my purse, squirted some out, then passed the bottle to Joe. The memory of that dog slobber was fresh.

I was surprised when Armstrong came over. Maia wasn't with him. "May I join you?" he said. "Maia is table-hopping." He tied Monte's leash to the table leg, and told the pup to stay. Monte lay down.

"Monte seems well-trained for such a young dog," I said. "How old is he?"

"Four months. The key is to work with him twice a day, every day."

"I see you're an experienced dog owner."

Armstrong laughed. "You know what they say about Washington, D.C.? 'If you want a friend, get a dog.' That goes double for Hollywood, and I've been around the business all my life. I've always had a dog."

Joe spoke then. "I'm sorry, Mr. Armstrong, but I didn't catch the name of your production company."

"I don't think I threw it. It's Montezuma Movie Productions."

"Then I was wrong," I said. "Monte is named after your company, not after the Aztec emperor."

"No, you were right. Monte's name was inspired by the Aztec connection to chocolate, because he's a chocolate lab. I've always owned a chocolate lab. The company name had the same inspiration."

Joe ignored the chocolate lore. "What films has your company produced, Mr. Armstrong?"

"Call me Aubrey. We're indies, of course. Our current release is *Mimosa Magic*. And *Appaloosa* was a finalist at Sundance."

Joe nodded. "I haven't seen either of those, but I remember the reviews for *Mimosa Magic*. How long have you been a producer?"

Aubrey waved his hand. "Now you're asking a personal question—my age. What's your profession, Joe?"

"I'm Warner Pier city attorney."

Joe's answer surprised me. It was true, of course. But Joe's job advising the city council took him only a few hours a week, and it paid proportionally. His full-time job was restoring antique power boats— a business that was finally looking up financially. He usually identified himself as a boat repairman, ignoring his law degree unless he was doing city business.

Aubrey's eyes widened, just slightly, but if he was surprised to be having lunch with the city attorney, it didn't affect his tongue. He kept right on prattling away about the movies he'd made and the locations he'd used. He dropped names even I had heard—Robert R., Tom H., the C. brothers—and he talked about "the business."

After twenty minutes I'd decided Aubrey was as phony as his hairdo. I didn't make the rounds of the Texas beauty pageant circuit—I mean, scholarship pageant circuit—without learning a few things. When you meet the promoters who are around trying to take advantage of the naivete of the inexperienced girls in those competitions— well, there's a reason contestants are required to have older women as escorts. And I still fell for one of the jerks, the guy who was now my ex-husband.

Of course, putting up a phony front didn't mean Aubrey wasn't a legitimate movie producer any more than it meant all the guys lurking at the Miss Texas Pageant were crooks. It just meant they might be. And it meant they weren't the kind of people I wanted to seek out as friends.

So I was annoyed when Joe announced he needed to talk to the mayor, then got up and disappeared, leaving me stuck with Aubrey and the dog. But his disappearance gave me a chance to ask a question. "Are you a coin collector, Mr. Armstrong?"

He smiled broadly. "Why, no. Do I look like one?"

"I expect they come in all sizes and shapes. I just wondered about the big bills Monte brought me."

I'll swear that Aubrey Andrews Armstrong blushed. If he didn't actually turn red, he squirmed like a little kid, and he laughed weakly before he answered me. "Oh, those were just props," he said. "I really can't say more."

He launched into another tale about the C. brothers, but I was hardly listening. My question might have been a bit nosy, but it was logical. Since I'd seen the big bills, and Aubrey knew I'd seen them, I was bound to wonder.

I shrugged mentally and looked around for Maia. I'd had enough of her tame movie producer, and I was hoping she'd rescue me. She wasn't in view, but I did see Aunt Nettie.

My dear aunt and employer, Jeannette TenHuis, has beautiful white hair, bright blue eyes, and that solid look I associate with a lifetime spent eating substantial Dutch cooking. She was wearing her usual workday garb—a white food-service uniform—topped by a blue sweater, and was carrying bratwurst and potato salad on a Styrofoam plate. I waved. She smiled her sunny smile and came over. "May I join you?"

Aubrey jumped to his feet—not an easy trick when you're sitting at a picnic table—and swept off his outback hat as I introduced them.

"Aubrey's thinking of producing a movie of Maia's novel," I said. "He might film here in Warner Pier."

"How exciting!" Aunt Nettie said. "That would be a real thrill. This is a small town. We don't get a lot of glamour."

Her answer surprised me, since only a few years earlier one of the year's biggest Hollywood productions, starring Tom H., had used locations within ten miles of Warner Pier. Aubrey Andrews Armstrong was not the first producer to discover the beauty of the Lake Michigan beaches, the charm of our lush farmland, and the quaintness of our villages.

"Oh, filmmaking isn't all glamour," Aubrey said. "Your niece says she works in the shop which made those fabulous chocolates I see over there on the dessert table. Now that's glamour! Are you connected with chocolate, too?"

Aunt Nettie dropped her eyes modestly, and I answered his question. "Aunt Nettie is the owner of TenHuis Chocolade."

"We ship European-style bonbons, truffles, and molded chocolates nationwide," Aunt Nettie said. "Lee is our business manager. She keeps our finances in excellent order."

It was as if a light went on behind Aubrey Andrews Armstrong's eyes. He turned the full force of his personality on Aunt Nettie. First, he insisted on trying some TenHuis chocolates. ("I'll be right back. Monte, stay!") Then he gushed over their quality. ("Do you do gift packages? This is exactly what I need to send Meg for her birthday next week. Few people know that she's a slave to chocolate. I don't know how she keeps that great figure.") Then he did his Hollywood producer act for Aunt Nettie, referring once again to Tom H. and Robert R. and Michael D.

The weirdest part to me was that Aunt Nettie ate it up, scarfing up his act along with her bratwurst and potato salad. She even cooed at the dog, scratching him under the chin. "You're as beautiful as the molded pups we have over at the shop," she said. "But I know you can't eat one."

Aubrey beamed. "Good for you. It's amazing how many people don't know chocolate can be poisonous to dogs."

I'll swear Aunt Nettie simpered. "I don't know much about dogs, but I know a lot about chocolate."

I was ready to prick Aubrey Andrews Armstrong with a pin to see if the hot air would rush out by the time Maia finally showed up. But that didn't really help the situation. A second person showed up at the same time: six feet, three inches of redhead with the poetic name of Dolly Jolly.

"Can I join you?" she yelled.

Everything about Dolly is big: her build, which is something like a pro-football lineman; her voice, which could shatter a plate glass window; her hair, which is a vivid natural red; her personality, which is unforgettable. When she sat down at the picnic table I felt as if we'd been struck by a volcanic eruption.

I'd first met Dolly early in the summer, when she'd rented a remote cottage near Warner Pier while she finished writing a cookbook. In September, Dolly had rented the apartment over TenHuis Chocolade, and two weeks earlier she had begun working for Aunt Nettie, learning the craft of making fine chocolates.

To my surprise Dolly wasn't carrying a plate of bratwurst or of chicken. Apparently she wasn't looking for lunch companions. I wondered why she'd joined us.

We introduced her to Aubrey Andrews Armstrong, but she merely nodded to him. To my surprise she turned her full attention—which is like being pinned down by a searchlight—to Maia. Apparently Dolly had come to our table because she wanted to know all about Maia's novel. But because Maia wanted to talk to Aubrey, she didn't want to discuss her novel. This made the resulting conversation pretty nonsensical.

"Loved your book!" Dolly shouted. As I said, Dolly always talks at top decibels. "How much is based on fact?"

"Oh, it all is," Maia said. "Of course, it's been sifted through the artistic process." She turned to Aubrey. "I'm sorry I left you so long. Vernon had to catch up with his deer-hunting buddies. Then I ran into Chuck O'Riley, the editor of our little newspaper. He'll be over to interview you in a few minutes."

"Fine, fine," Armstrong said. "I was just talking to Mrs. Ten-Huis."

Before Maia could acknowledge Aunt Nettie's presence, Dolly jumped in again. "Julia's old father! Interesting character! Really crusty! Is he based on the real man?"

She was too loud for Maia to ignore. "Yes, he is. He was my grand-father, you know. I remember how he terrified me as a child." She turned back to Aubrey. "Nettie's one of our leading entrepreneurs."

Aunt Nettie shook her head. "Entrepreneur is too grand a word for a cook."

Dolly was not to be denied. She was still concentrating on Maia. "The stepmother! Between a rock and a hard place! Felt sorry for her!"

Maia looked surprised as she pulled her attention away from the movie producer and answered Dolly. "It's interesting that you should see that. From Julia's viewpoint, she was a genuine 'wicked step-mother.' But she was my grandmother. Of course, she died young, so I didn't know her."

"She was young! She might have been attracted to Dennis Grundy herself!"

This was apparently a new idea to Maia. She looked a little shocked, but she didn't reply. Instead she looked around the park. "Where's Chuck, I wonder?"

"In Hollywood," Aubrey said. Or I thought he did. Then I realized that he was answering some question Aunt Nettie had asked. At least three conversations were bouncing around that table, and I'd com-pletely lost track of who was talking about what. I was relieved when Tracy Roderick came over and spoke to me softly.

"Mrs. McNutt wants to talk to you," she said.

I was delighted to leave. I went around behind the serving line and called to Maggie.

She came over immediately, and she grasped my arm. "Did Joe leave?"

"He disappeared, but as far as I know he's still here, Maggie. What's wrong?"

"Oh, I can't find Chief Jones. I can't find Joe. I don't know who else I could talk to."

This dithering was most unlike the efficient and focused Maggie. "Why do you need them?"

She made a gesture that was awfully close to wringing her hands. "I don't know. Maybe I don't need them. It's just—Oh, god! Here he comes."

I looked around to see Aubrey Andrews Armstrong approaching.

Maggie spoke loudly. "I appreciate that, Lee. And I'd appreciate it if you'll tell Nettie the chocolates are the hit of the picnic. I'll be by later to thank her personally."

Aubrey and Monte arrived. Aubrey was grinning broadly. "Mrs. McNutt"—he still was making that name sound really odd—"Mrs. McNutt, I think you had a brilliant idea."

"What was that, Mr. Armstrong?" Maggie sounded funny, too.

I moved away as Aubrey spoke again. "This Rinkydink! Such a clever project. . . ."

Their voices faded, and I went back to my picnic table to join Aunt Nettie. I didn't understand why Maggie was upset. Why did she want to talk to the police chief? Why did she not want to talk to Aubrey Andrews Armstrong? She could have spotted him as a phony, of course. But I had, too, and I wasn't incoherent over it. Besides, even if Armstrong was a phony, it was no skin off my nose. If he was up to no good, his target was apparently Maia, not me. Maia had Vernon to watch over her, and Vernon was really good at guarding Maia. I wasn't really worried about Maia. Maggie and Maia weren't exactly friends. Why would Maggie care if some Hollywood-type made Maia look silly?

When I got back to the table, Dolly had gone. Aunt Nettie was alone with Maia. Maia was tossing her artificially black hair and giggling, while Aunt Nettie sat smiling her usual sweet smile.

"Oh, Lee," Maia said. "Guess what!"

"I can't imagine."

"Tell her, Nettie!"

"It's nice, Maia, but I don't want to make too much of it."

I was getting annoyed with Maia. "Make too much of what?"

Maia widened her eyes. "Nettie's got a date," she said. "With Aubrey."

I hope I didn't gasp in amazement. Or dismay. After all, Aunt Nettie had been a widow for more than two years. If she wanted to go out on a date, I really ought to encourage her. I ought to be thrilled for her. And I would have been, if she'd been invited out by anybody but Aubrey Andrews Armstrong.

Because Aubrey might seem like a phony to me, but he was attractive. I didn't doubt that he could, if he wished, cut quite a swath among the single women of Warner Pier. So why had he selected Aunt Nettie? She was full of wisdom and character and loving-kindness, true. These wonderful qualities, frankly, are not known for attracting middle-aged men vain enough to get hair implants. No, those guys are usually hoping the hair implants will attract younger women.

Had Maia promoted this date? If so, why? I'd been under the impression that Maia was thinking of Aubrey as her own catch— perhaps not romantically, with Vernon always guarding her. But I'd have expected her to be somewhat jealous if Aubrey paid attention to someone besides her.

I was stunned. But I had to say something. So I did.

"That's wonderland!" I said. "I mean, that's wonderful!"

Aunt Nettie, who knows about my twisted tongue, shot me an amused glance. Darn her. She always sees right through me.

I didn't have a chance to say anything more. Maia was talking again. "It was all Aubrey's idea," she said. "He invited Vernon and me to go out to dinner at the Warner River Lodge tonight, and he just turned to Nettie and asked her to join the party."

Aunt Nettie was still smiling. "It's not exactly a date. Aubrey simply wanted a companion."

"Don't sell yourself short, Nettie! I can tell that he's quite taken with you." Maia's voice was growing shrill. I decided she might be jealous after all.

"Any intelligent person would be taken with Aunt Nettie," I said. "And the Warner River Lodge is a marvelous place for dinner. It ought to be a nice evening."

Aunt Nettie stood up and collected the debris of her lunch. "I'm looking forward to it," she said. "I guess I'd better get back to the shop."

"We'd both better do that," I said. I gathered my own debris—plus Joe's, since he'd never showed up again—said good-bye to Maia, and followed Aunt Nettie to the trash can. That's when I saw Joe. He was over on the other side of the picnic shelter, talking to Mayor Mike Herrera and Warner Pier's police chief, Hogan Jones.

"I'll just tell Joe I'm leaving," I said.

Aunt Nettie headed toward the shop, and I veered off and walked over to Joe, Mike, and Hogan Jones. Mike and Joe looked solemn, but Chief Jones—a tall skinny guy who could easily find work as an Abraham Lincoln impersonator—formed his craggy face into a big grin as I walked up. "Hi, Lee. What do you think of our Hollywood producer?"

"He's definitely Mr. Personality."

"Ain't he, though. Did he tell you that you oughta be in pictures?"

"No, he saved his charm for Aunt Nettie. He's taking her out to dinner."

Joe whistled, and Mike said that Spanish word I pretend not to understand.

"They're going to the Warner River Lodge with Maia and Vernon," I said. "I first thought it was Maia's idea, but apparently Aubrey came up with the invitation without prompting."

The chief grinned even more broadly. "And you don't like it."

I looked around to make sure Aubrey or Maia or Aunt Nettie hadn't crept up behind me. "I guess I ought to be glad if Aunt Nettie developed a real social life," I said. "She's been much too close to the business since Uncle Phil died. And I think I would be happy for her if . . . well, if we knew a little more about this guy. I'm afraid he's the type who sees himself as a heartbreaker, and she's not exactly up on the current dating scene."

Joe jumped in with, "Don't wo—" but Chief Jones cut him off sharply.

"Now, listen, Lee," he said. "Nettie's a grown woman, and if she wants to have a little fling, you just stay out of it."

I could have kicked him. I'm sure I pursed my lips until they disappeared before I spoke. "Chief Jones . . . Hogan . . . there's nothing I would like better than to see Aunt Nettie get some fun out of life."

"You sure don't act like it. You youngsters think all us old folks are so far over the hill that we can't remember passing the top."

"Aunt Nettie's not over the hill! She's sharper than I am at nearly everything. But this Armstrong—his eyes lit up like he'd hit the jackpot when she said she owned her own business."

Unfortunately for Joe, he decided to join the argument. "Lee, the chief just means—"

"I know what he means! He means I'm aghast. I mean, ageist! Well, I'm not! Aunt Nettie's got tons more brains than I have, but she's never had to deal with a guy like Aubrey Andrews Armstrong."

Before I could go on, a voice boomed out right behind me. "Just stay away from my place! I don't consider leaving a business card under an apple as asking permission to trespass on a man's property."

"But Uncle Silas, he wanted to see the historic site—"

"I don't care if he wanted to see the Statue of Liberty! I don't want to catch another one of those goldurned treasure hunters in my orchard. The next one is likely to get a load of pea shot in his hind end—and I don't care if he's a local kid or some big Hollywood producer!"

# Chapter 3

There was an argument going on behind me, and it was louder than the one I was having with Chief Jones about Aunt Nettie's romantic life.

I heard the second voice again, and this time I recognized it.

"You old silly!" The arch tones could belong only to Maia Michaelson. When I turned around I saw that she was facing an old man who was wearing work clothes even more authentic than Vernon's. Maia laughed merrily and went on. "Don't you know you could make money if they use your property?"

"Make money the way you have? By raking up a scandal? I'd be ashamed."

"What do you mean?"

"Writing about that old story. It doesn't do any credit to the family. Or to you!"

"Why, Uncle Silas! You simply don't have a romantic soul."

"Romantic, my foot! Disreputable! Scandalous!"

Maia smiled, but her smile looked angry. She leaned close to the old man. They were much the same height, the top of her teased hair was even with the dirty baseball cap he wore. "Now, Uncle Silas—"

But the old man wasn't having any. "I don't want to hear any more about this foolishness," he said. He wasn't quite yelling. "It's not women's business! It's sure not the business of stupid women who shame the family!"

Vernon suddenly appeared between the two combatants. "Come on, Mae," he said. "You can talk to your uncle later."

But Silas turned on him. "And I blame you, Vernon. Encouraging her in this silliness! She ought to be in the kitchen canning, not making a fool of herself with this writing nonsense. You should have stopped her."

Vernon drew himself up, and I realized what a big man he was. "I'm proud of Mae," he said. "And you should be, too."

Then he turned away, guiding Maia-Mae in front of him, escorting her for all the world like a bodyguard with a princess.

The old man snorted angrily and walked away in a different direction, crossing Dock Street and walking toward a beat-up old pickup.

I checked to make sure that Maia and Vernon were out of earshot; then I turned to the three city officials I'd been talking to, Joe, Chief Hogan Jones, and Mayor Mike Herrera. "Who's the literary critic?"

Joe laughed, Mike rolled his eyes, and Hogan Jones spoke. "Silas Snow," he said. "He's an uncle to Mae or Maia or whoever she is these days."

"I gather he's not excited about the prospect of a movie of her book being filmed."

Joe answered me. "I guess he's also not excited about having the movie shot on his property. It's the farm at the Haven Road exit. The one with the fruit stand."

"The stand that's all pumpkins right at the moment?"

"Yeah. Not that every fruit stand in the Midwest isn't covered with pumpkins this time of the year. But it's the farm where the real-life story of Maia's book supposedly happened."

"Do you mean that Julia Snow and Dennis Grundy actually existed?"

This time all three of them shrugged. Chief Jones spoke. "You'd have to look up the records to see if there's any truth to her tale. I doubt it happened exactly that way." He walked away, followed by Mike Herrera.

I spoke to Joe. "I knew Maia's book was based on some sort of local legend, but I didn't know it was a family story."

"Every town up and down Lake Michigan has some old tale about Chicago gangsters, you know."

"If all those stories were true, there would have been more gangsters than peach growers around the lake."

"True. But supposedly Al Capone did have a camp of some sort on the Upper Peninsula."

"That's hundreds of miles from here."

Joe nodded. "But back in the twenties and thirties, lots of farmers had little cottages they rented to tourists, just the way a few of them still do. Some of them had docks where cargo could be shifted quietly. And sometimes questionable people rented those cottages."

"Just the way they could now."

"Yeah. Anyway, from what I heard at my grandmother's knee, I'm guessing that Silas Snow's father, Mae Ensminger's grandfather, had a cottage like that back in the woods, with a path down to a creek where it was possible to land a small boat. Apparently old Mr. Snow rented it without asking for references. The story is that a young tough guy from Chicago rented it for a whole summer sometime in the late twenties. Everybody local assumed he was hiding out from the law."

"And the Snows had a daughter."

"Right. An older half sister to Silas and to Mae's mom. That's part of the story. Don't ask me if it was a big romance or something sleazy or nothing at all. I guess there was talk at the time."

"Seventy-five years ago, and it's still an item."

"You knew this was a small town when you moved here, Lee. Part of the story, naturally, is buried treasure. The bank loot—or whatever—is supposed to be hidden someplace on the old farm."

"Now owned by Silas Snow?"

"Right. Going out there and digging around is a Warner Pier High School tradition. Heck, I did it!"

"It's apparently a tradition that annoys Silas Snow. But what became of the supposed gangster? And what became of the farmer's daughter?"

"I don't know. Julia Snow and Dennis Grundy both left Warner Pier, but I don't know if they went separately or together. The Snow family never mentioned Julia after that. Maia thinks the two of them lived happily ever after."

"And Uncle Silas doesn't. And I'm not interested enough to research the matter. I've got to get back to the office."

As I started to go, I saw Aubrey, who now was the center of a group of drama club members. Maggie was not in sight, but seeing Aubrey reminded me of her.

I turned back to Joe. "Did Maggie talk to you?"

"We said hi when you and I went through the line."

"No, this was after that. She acted sort of frantic."

"I'll check with her. And I'll see you later."

As I walked toward the office my mind bounced back to Aunt Nettie and her date with Aubrey Andrews Armstrong. Even more surprising than the date was Hogan Jones's reaction to it. Hogan might be a small-town police chief now, but he'd spent years in law enforcement in a major city. He ought to be wary of people who drop in unannounced and claim to be movie producers. But he thought it was fine for Aunt Nettie to go out with this stranger. He'd accused me of treating my aunt as if she were senile. Or at least too old to have any interest in romance.

Nobody ever gets that old, do they? I knew Aunt Nettie and her friends were still interested. They had coffee klatches in our break room now and then, and snickered over various older gents in Warner Pier. This one was considered too decrepit, that one too much of a dirty old man, another too hung up on his deceased wife.

Oddly enough, the only one they all seemed to approve of was—ta-dah!—Hogan Jones. But Hogan had so far deftly avoided all the invitations of Warner Pier's widows. And if he had himself ever asked anyone out, I hadn't heard about it.

I was trying to refocus my thoughts on TenHuis Chocolade's accounts receivable when Joe caught up with me.

"I'll walk back with you," he said. "My truck's over that way."

"What did Maggie want?"

"Nothing. She said she had solved her problem, and she didn't tell me what it was."

"Good for her. Now I can concentrate on worrying about Aunt Nettie."

"I wish you wouldn't. Like the chief says—"

"Joe, don't start telling me she's a grown woman. I know that. But she's been a big help to me, and I'd be negligent if I stood by and let her get hurt."

"But Nettie's not your responsibility, Lee."

"Of course she's my responsibility! Who else does she have?"

Joe stopped abruptly. "She has herself! You don't have to take care of her! Maybe that's our problem."

"Our problem? Ours! What problem do we have?"

"Getting married. I want to get married, Lee. And I can't get you to set a date. I can't even get you to say that you'll set one eventually."

I closed my eyes and sighed. "How did we get from Aunt Nettie to this?"

"I think you're hiding behind her. You can't even consider getting married and leaving darling Aunt Nettie alone."

"I've never said that! I never even thought that!"

"It's the only explanation I can come up with. You claim you love me, but I can't pin you down."

"Joe, you have lost your mind. I'll plead guilty to the charge of being wishy-washy about getting married, but it has nothing to do with Aunt Nettie. And I'm not going to argue about this in the middle of Peach Street. Good-bye."

I walked away, and Joe stood where he'd been. I didn't look back. I was too mad, and maybe too scared. Because Joe had come up with a new wrinkle in an argument that had been going on since the previous June, when Joe had first told me he wanted to marry me.

Or had he? Frankly, whenever he brought it up, he used the phrase he'd just declaimed. "I want to get married." Somehow that wasn't the same as saying, "I want to marry you."

But this was the first time Aunt Nettie had figured in the argument.

I was ready to admit that Aunt Nettie was special to me. Twice in my life—first when I was sixteen and my parents were getting a divorce and later when my own marriage broke up—she'd stepped in, given me a home, and made me feel that I was a worthwhile person even if my life was in shambles. If I had a shred of mental health, I owed it to Aunt Nettie. And she wasn't even a blood relation; she was my mother's brother's widow.

But the last thing Aunt Nettie would want was to come between Joe and me. She had made it clear that she approved of Joe.

Right at that moment I wasn't sure I did. I walked on, mulling over how quickly my life had changed from happy to horrendous. An hour earlier I'd been enjoying the lovely fall day with nothing on my mind but delivering chocolates to the Rinkydink. Now I was frantically worried about a charmer who was broadcasting phony signals and moving in on my aunt, and I'd had an argument with my boyfriend.

I needed comfort. I resolved not to think about my problems for the rest of the afternoon. I couldn't settle the question of whether or not I wanted to marry Joe while I was upset, and I couldn't risk quarreling with Aunt Nettie by making any overt attack on Aubrey Andrews Armstrong.

As I went in the door to TenHuis Chocolade ("Handmade chocolates in the Dutch tradition"), I breathed deeply to get the full effect of the chocolate aroma. After I've been inside for a little while, I get used to it, so whenever I come in I try to inhale all the chocolate atmosphere I can.

TenHuis Chocolade is my real home, I guess. For one thing, Aunt Nettie and I spend more time there than we do in her hundred-year-old house on Lake Shore Drive, the place where we sleep and store our clothes. For another, it's a friendly place—a cozy retail shop, a shiny-clean workroom, and a comfortable break room.

As I came in I could see Aunt Nettie through the big glass windows that separate our small retail shop from the big workroom where the chocolates are made. She was standing beside Dolly Jolly. I could tell by the color of the substance on the worktable that Aunt Nettie was teaching Dolly to roll uniform balls of strawberry-flavored filling for strawberry truffles ("White chocolate and strawberry interior coated in dark chocolate"). Dolly was sticking out the tip of her tongue, a sign that she was concentrating.

I couldn't hear what Aunt Nettie was saying, but I could see Dolly roll a ball of pink soft filling, compare it to one Aunt Nettie had formed, then set it on a scale. After more than thirty years in the chocolate business, Aunt Nettie can roll those balls for hours on end and have every one come out within a microgram of every other one. This is a trick that the "hairnet ladies," the skilled workers who actually produce TenHuis Chocolade, claim a chimpanzee can do. And maybe a chimpanzee could—once she'd had enough practice. But you have to learn to judge exactly how big to make the little balls. The truffle fillings have to be uniform; we can't sell Customer A one that's larger than the one we sell Customer B.

Dolly Jolly was looming over Aunt Nettie just the way she looms over everybody.

"I think I'm getting the hang of it!" Dolly shouted.

"Those look good," Aunt Nettie said. "It only takes a couple of rolls to get them round. You don't have to handle them a lot. Now you can start rolling them in chocolate."

Dolly took a metal bowl over to the vat of dark chocolate. She used the spigot at the bottom of the vat to drain chocolate into the bowl, then turned to Aunt Nettie, looking quizzical.

"A little more chocolate will make it easier to work with," Aunt Nettie said.

I walked over to them. "Where'd you disappear to, Dolly? I got up to talk to Maggie McNutt, and when I came back you were gone."

Dolly's face turned even redder than it usually is. "I had to get back to work," she said. For once her voice didn't boom. In fact, I could hardly hear her. "Just wanted to meet Maia Michaelson."

"What did you think of her?"

Dolly shrugged. "Glad I'm not part of her family," she said.

"Yeah, being related to Maia is a scary thought," I said.

Dolly didn't seem inclined to make any further comment, so I left Aunt Nettie showing Dolly how to roll truffles and went into my office. My office is a glass cubicle between the shop and the workroom. It's not as homey as the rest of TenHuis Chocolade, I guess, but during the pre-Christmas rush I almost live there. I glanced at the framed picture of Joe standing beside his favorite antique wooden boat. I wasn't going to think about Joe that afternoon, so I laid it facedown.

The chocolate business is seasonal, and the seasons start with Halloween and end with Mother's Day. With October a third gone, we were past Halloween preparations, almost through with Thanksgiving, and well into Christmas. Dolly might be learning to roll truffles, but most of the other employees were molding Santa Claus figures and filling chocolate Christmas tree ornaments with tiny chocolate toys. Toward the back of the room, eight women were standing around a big stainless steel table, wrapping cubes of molded chocolate in gorgeous foils to produce chocolates that looked like tiny little gift boxes.

The scene was giving me the dose of comfort that I needed. I sat at my desk and counted my blessings for a minute. When I'd left Dallas a year and a half earlier, I'd been recovering from a lousy marriage and a mean-spirited divorce. I had finally finished my degree in accounting, but it had been a struggle. TenHuis Chocolade hadn't been in very good shape, either. My uncle Phil had always handled the business side. When he was killed by a drunk driver, the whole thing had been dumped on Aunt Nettie, who made wonderful chocolates, but hated to balance her checkbook. After I'd taken over as business manager, I'd discovered unpaid bills, lousy customer relations, and poor shipping schedules.

Now Aunt Nettie's unconditional love had given me a new sense of my own worth. I'd formed a circle of friends I felt I could rely on—even if my boyfriend was acting like a jerk right at the moment. TenHuis was back on a firm financial foundation, with chocolates shipped on time and all the bills paid. I could honestly say I'd accomplished a lot.

Then I caught sight of our fall display of molded chocolates on the shelf behind the cash register. Aunt Nettie called it "Pet Parade." It featured tiny figures of puppies and kittens in dark, white, and milk chocolate. Some of them were even spotted dogs with lop ears, dark chocolate with white spots, or white chocolate with milk chocolate spots. There were tiny baskets of kittens or puppies. Each little animal was darling. My Texas grandma would have said each one was cuter than a spotted pup under a red wagon. In fact, a five-inch toy red wagon filled with one-inch puppies had been one of our best sellers that fall.

But now those puppies made Monte and his owner flash into my mind.

What if Aunt Nettie really fell for Aubrey Andrews Armstrong? She could get badly hurt. I couldn't stand that idea.

But, as Chief Jones had pointed out, Aunt Nettie was a grown woman. He was right. I had no right to influence her. I'd have to be gracious about Aubrey.

I smiled brightly into my computer screen. "Have a nice evening," I said sweetly.

I might see Aubrey as a real threat, but I had to keep my mouth shut about it.

I stuck to that resolve for an hour. Until Maggie McNutt came into the shop.

# CHOCOLATE CHAT
## IT'S ALL (NOT) RELATIVE

The tree that gives us chocolate was assigned the scientific name *Theobroma cacao* by the Swedish scientist Linnaeus in 1753. *Theobroma* can be translated as "food of the gods," a name that reflects not only the legends of the pre-Columbian Indians as to its origins but also seems to be a comment on its heavenly appeal to the sense of taste.

The dried and roasted seeds of the cacao tree are processed to form cocoa, which is how "cacao" is usually pronounced in American English. Despite the sound-alike, it has no relationship to the coconut palm, *Cocos nucifera*, though products of this plant are sometimes called "coco."

Nor is it related to the coca bush, *Erythroxylum coca*. This plant is used for a tea sometimes utilized to relieve symptoms of altitude sickness. But its greatest use is in producing cocaine.

So, let's get this straight. Chocolate and cocaine are not produced from the same plant. The high chocoholics get from indulging in truffles, bonbons, or plain old solid chocolate is not an illicit form of bliss, and chocolate is not physically addictive. Saying that chocolate is not habit-forming, however, might be going too far.

# Chapter 4

Despite my resolve, I guess I had never stopped worrying about Aubrey. Anyway, shortly after three p.m. Maggie McNutt came in the front door of TenHuis Chocolade carrying two large trays, and as soon as I saw her, the movie producer popped into my mind.

I recognized the trays as the heavy foil ones we'd used to display our donated chocolates, and I went out to the shop to meet Maggie. "Those are just throwaway trays," I said. "You didn't have to return them."

Maggie spoke in a low voice. "I wanted an excuse to speak to you," she said. "I need a favor."

"Sure. As long as it has nothing to do with Aubrey Andrews Armstrong."

Maggie's eyes popped. If she'd been holding another plate of bratwurst, I feel sure she would have dropped it. "Why did you say that?" she said.

"I guess he made quite an impression on me."

"What kind of impression?"

"Oh, he reminded me of a lot of the promoters I met back when I did the Miss Texas pageant. What kind of favor do you need?"

My answer seemed to calm Maggie. "Are you on speaking terms with Maia Michaelson?"

"I rarely have anything to say to her, but I guess we're on speaking terms."

"Well, I'm not. But she needs to be warned about this . . . this Armstrong."

"You make the name sound like a curse." I lowered my voice. "What do you know about him?"

"Not much! I mean, nothing! Nothing at all! I mean, I'm like you. He's the kind of promoter you spot around beauty pageants and talent shows. Some of them are legit. Some are not. They just need to be approached with caution, and Maia seems to be swallowing his act without question."

"Maia's not the only one. Aubrey has invited Aunt Nettie out to dinner."

"Gosh! Can you keep her from going?"

"How? She's a grown-up woman and a lot smarter than I am. If I say anything, it's going to make me look as if I don't want her to get out and have a social life."

Maggie put her elbows on the top of our showcase and dropped her head into her hands. She obviously wasn't looking at the chocolate puppy dogs inside. She seemed close to despair. "What am I going to do?" she said.

She'd barely finished asking herself that when the door to the shop swung open, and of all the people in Warner Pier, who should walk in but Mae Ensminger, also known as Maia Michaelson.

I'm sure I looked guilty. "Oh!" I said. "Hi, Mae! I mean, Maia!"

Maia tossed her black curls and laughed her merry laugh before she spoke. "Hello, Lee. Hello, Maggie. Is Nettie busy? I thought we ought to coordinate our wardrobes for tonight."

Coordinate their wardrobes? Like junior high? "I'll see if Aunt Nettie can come up front," I said. "She's training a new warning. I mean, worker! She's training a new employee."

I slunk back to the workroom. Why does my tongue insist on embarrassing me like that?

At least, I thought, Maggie and Maia weren't speaking, so it seemed safe to leave them alone together. But a minute later, when Aunt Nettie and I came back to the shop, they *were* speaking. And both of them sounded angry.

"More worthwhile than a stupid romance novel," Maggie said.

"Not romance! Mainstream!" Maia countered. "And now a screenplay!"

"Of all the gullible—" Maggie spit out the words, but in midsentence she stopped talking. Her face became pale. I realized she was looking at the door to the shop, and that it was opening.

Aubrey put his head inside and spoke. "Are you nearly ready, Maia? I'm sure that Ms. Nettie and her charming niece can't allow me to bring Monte inside."

Maia's voice fluted. "I'll be right out. Maggie McNutt was just leaving, going back to her sweet little high school students."

Maggie shot Maia a look that would have been lethal to a normal person. Then Aubrey stepped back and held the door open for Maggie. She marched past him without a word.

Maia laughed. "Now, Nettie . . ." she began. I went into my office and did something I rarely do. I closed the door. It was glass, like the walls, so I could still see Maia posturing and posing in the shop. But at least her voice wasn't as loud.

I stared at the computer again, and again practiced seeing Aunt Nettie off on her date. I gave a parody of a smile. "Have a nice evening," I said.

I was truly unhappy about Aunt Nettie being involved for even one evening with Aubrey Andrews Armstrong. But it was none of my affair. She would never interfere with my love life, and I had no right to interfere with hers. Butt out, Lee, I told myself firmly. And keep out of Maia's life, too. She's another grown woman. It's none of your business.

I kept my eyes on the computer screen until Maia left the shop, but when the bell on the door rang again I looked up. That afternoon we had no counter staff, so if anybody wanted to buy chocolates, it was my job to wait on them.

The person who came rushing in wasn't a customer. It was Tracy Roderick, our summer employee—Tracy of the stringy hair, who'd been elected president of the drama club and who had been staffing the dessert table at the Rinkydink.

Tracy rushed over to my office and opened the door. "Can I come in?"

"Sure, Tracy. What can I do for you?"

"My hair! I've got to do something about it."

I stared at her. Yes, Tracy needed a new hairstyle. I knew her mother had been trying to get her to do something about it for a year. But now Tracy was acting as if it were an emergency.

"Why?" I said. "I mean, what brought on this decision?"

"I might have a chance at a part in a movie, Lee!"

"What?"

"You met that movie producer, Mr. Armstrong! I saw you talking to him. Isn't he divine?"

"He's certainly not an ordinary human, so maybe he is divine. What did he say?"

"He told us he's going to hire people in Warner Pier for small roles in the film he's going to shoot. The drama club's going to have a special meeting about it." Tracy clutched her hands together and held them to her chin in a semiprayerful attitude. "Oh, Lee! It could be my big chance! Will you help me?"

I stared at Tracy in utter dismay. I'd just convinced myself that Aunt Nettie and Maia were old enough to take care of themselves, that I should keep quiet about my misgivings about Aubrey Andrews Armstrong.

But now Aubrey had moved in on the high school drama students. They weren't grown-ups; they were young and inexperienced and would be easy for him to exploit. I couldn't stand by and let that happen, but I didn't have the heart to tell Tracy that. And she was waiting for an answer.

"Sure, Tracy," I said. "I'll help you with your makeup, and I'll make an appointment at Angie's for you. I'll go with you, if you like. Angie gives the best haircuts in Warner Pier, and if you need highlights or something, she'll advise you."

"Oh, thank you, Lee! That will be wonderful!" She bounced up and down. "I've got the money I saved last summer. I can take it out of my college fund. I'm just so excited!"

"Angie shouldn't be busy, now that the summer people are gone," I said. "I'll see if she can get you in tomorrow evening. I've got to do some research tonight."

Yes, I'd be busy that evening. I had to try to find out something about Aubrey Andrews Armstrong and Montezuma Motion Pictures. And I didn't want to tell anybody what I was doing. Especially not Joe. Not that there was any reason to expect I'd have the opportunity to tell Joe anything that night. I had the feeling he was as mad at me as I was at him.

So I played business manager until five o'clock, taking orders over the telephone, checking the TenHuis e-mail for more orders, and calling suppliers. In between I worked on the payroll. If business kept improving, I was going to need an assistant.

But closing time finally came. I told Aunt Nettie I was going to grab dinner downtown, then work late. She seemed a bit disappointed that I wouldn't be home to see her off on her dinner date.

"I'll be home by the time Aubrey brings you in," I said. "In case you need a chaplain. I mean, a chaperone!"

Aunt Nettie laughed. "I don't anticipate needing either. But I'm almost sorry I said I'd go."

"It ought to be fun. Aubrey's a charmer."

"I'm looking forward to spending some time with him. And Vernon's a nice person. But Mae has gone crazy."

"You can put up with her for one evening."

Aunt Nettie left. I pulled the shades on the street door and on the show windows, then turned to my computer. That would be the easiest place to start my check of movie producers. I went online, called up Google, and typed in "Aubrey Andrews Armstrong."

An hour later I'd found out something very interesting. Aubrey Andrews Armstrong apparently didn't exist. At least I couldn't find him under that name.

A general search for his highly distinctive name brought nothing. A prowl through the Web site of the Academy of Motion Picture Arts and Sciences found nothing. I'd tried the Web sites of the two films Aubrey had mentioned, *Appaloosa* and *Mimosa Magic*. They seemed to list the entire cast and crew down to the guy who swept out the set, but no Aubrey Andrews Armstrong or Montezuma Motion Pictures was mentioned.

Unfortunately, this didn't prove anything. Aubrey could go by "A. A. Armstrong." Or he could use a completely different professional name. And Montezuma Motion Pictures could have sold distribution rights or done some other tricky thing that made the name not appear on film credits.

Then I tried another tack, and discovered neither Aubrey Andrews Armstrong nor Montezuma Motion Pictures could be accessed anywhere in the country by the biggest telephone information site.

I wasn't ready to give up. I did the whole search of the motion picture sites again, this time using only the name "Armstrong." I found a bunch of people by that name, of course, but none of them was Aubrey or Andrews or anything else that sounded likely.

Things were not looking good for Aubrey, but it was all negative—lack of information didn't prove anything. I rested my head against my computer screen and wondered if I should quit.

Then it occurred to me that Aubrey's new production might have had some publicity around the state of Michigan, so I typed in "Michigan" and "film production." And the Michigan Film Office Web site came up.

"Yeah!" I said it aloud. "I can check with them. They ought to know about film activity all over Michigan."

Yes, there was an e-mail address. I fired off a query. Maybe that would get results.

What else could I do?

Getting some dinner seemed the best plan. I hid the notes I'd written on my fruitless search for Aubrey Andrews Armstrong, turned off the computer, got my jacket, and double-checked the lock on the street door. As I did, I peeked out and eyeballed the windows of the second-floor apartments across the street. Joe had recently signed a lease for one of them, and he'd spent nearly every evening over there painting. My conscience smote me; he was doing all this work because he wanted me to marry him and move in. And old dumb Lee couldn't make up her mind.

But that night, his windows were dark. I turned on the shop's security light, then went out the back door. I zipped the jacket up; nights were already in the low forties in southwest Michigan. Pretty soon, I thought as I climbed into my old minivan, I'd get my annual yen for pumpkin bread.

Pumpkins. The thought of the orange veggie reminded me of Maia's uncle, Silas Snow, who had a fruit stand full of pumpkins. During the argument I had witnessed, Silas had referred to a business card, apparently left at his fruit stand by Aubrey. He'd said something about "sticking a business card under an apple."

That business card should have specific information about Aubrey. If I could get hold of it . . .

I turned the thought over idly, then checked my watch. Seven thirty. Aubrey had planned to pick up Aunt Nettie at seven, so the two of them, plus Vernon and Maia, should be at the Warner River Lodge by now. If I went out to Silas's, which I assumed was near the Ensminger place, there should be no danger of running into them. I turned the minivan toward Orchard Street.

Orchard Street was the quickest way to access the interstate highway and the Haven exit, where Silas's farm and his fruit stand were located. As I recalled the layout of the Snow property, the fruit stand was near the road, and a traditional white Midwestern farmhouse sat a hundred yards behind it. That simply had to be where Silas lived. Silas would still be up. And if I could convince him I wasn't a treasure hunter who was going to dig up his orchard, maybe he'd show me that card.

When I pulled into the fruit stand's parking area, my headlights swept over a sea of pumpkins. Who buys all those pumpkins? During each of the two autumns I'd spent in Warner Pier, these mass invasions of pumpkins had occurred. There were tiny little pumpkins in baskets on the counters, wheelbarrows full of medium-sized pumpkins, and hay wagons loaded with giant pumpkins that needed a forklift to move them into the trucks and vans of buyers. There were rows of pumpkins marked "pie pumpkins." There were washtubs full of pumpkins marked "ornamental pumpkins." There were pumpkins with faces painted on them, pumpkins in arrangements with fancy gourds, pumpkins centering decorations featuring weird squash.

I can understand cooking pumpkins for a few pies and maybe some pumpkin bread. I can see making Halloween and Thanksgiving table decorations out of them. I can grasp using the larger ones to make the front porch look seasonal, with country-flavored arrangements of pumpkins and cornstalks and cutesy scarecrows. I can visualize gigantic jack-o'-lanterns made out of the largest pumpkins. But if every citizen of western Michigan did all those things, there would still be pumpkins left over in the fruit stands.

My headlights showed that Silas Snow's fruit stand was typical. It had a simple shed, open at the front and sides, with three long tables where produce could be displayed. There were baskets of apples along the back wall, and a table loaded with winter squash in the middle. But a majority of the space was given over to pumpkins. Scads of pumpkins. Oceans of pumpkins. Pumpkins galore.

There were so many pumpkins I couldn't find the drive that led back to the house. I could see a light on the porch and one inside the house. But I couldn't figure out how to drive back there. I honked the van's horn, thinking it might bring Silas out onto the porch, but there was no reaction.

"I'll just have to walk," I said aloud. I dug my big square flashlight out of the bin under the passenger's seat, got out, and started picking my way through the pumpkins. It was quiet, since Haven Road doesn't lead to anything but a bunch of summer cottages, and nearly all of those would be empty in mid-October. The interstate was only a few hundred yards away, true, but the trees still had enough leaves to hide the lights of the cars and trucks passing. The traffic sounds were loud, but the silence at Silas Snow's farm soaked them up like a blotter. I told myself that it wasn't really spooky, despite the way my imagination magnified every sound.

I had to keep the beam of the flash right where I was stepping, of course, since I didn't want to break either a pumpkin or my leg. This meant I was keeping my head down and concentrating on the ground right in front of my feet, but periodically I did a sweep of the pumpkin patch, planning a route.

I wasn't making very fast progress, but I eventually got around behind the fruit stand, with the building between me and the road. It was at that point that my flashlight swept over a huge heap of pumpkins. Some of them were smashed.

"Oh!" I guess I said it aloud. "The trespassers have been back!"

After seeing those broken pumpkins, I couldn't deny the spookiness of the situation. If Silas Snow was lying in wait for the treasure hunters who'd been trespassing on his property, I was in danger of getting hit by that shotgun blast he'd promised them. Or I might run into the trespassers themselves, and that wasn't a happy idea.

The Snow farm was not a good place to be in the dark, when neither Silas nor I could see what was going on. I decided I'd better wait until the next day to ask Mr. Snow for Aubrey Andrews Armstrong's business card. I began to turn around, ready to pick my way back through that sea of pumpkins and head for home.

But my flashlight's beam danced over something that wasn't round and that wasn't orange. It definitely wasn't a pumpkin. I moved the beam back to get a better look.

It was blue and oblong and it was sticking out of the heap of pumpkins. And there was something brown on the end of it. I had to concentrate for a long moment before my eyes made the object take a recognizable form.

It was the leg of a pair of blue jeans, and a brown workboot was sticking out the end of it.

"Scarecrow," I said, my voice a whisper. "It's got to be one of those scarecrows."

But what if it wasn't a scarecrow? I couldn't leave without making sure.

I tiptoed through more pumpkins, pushing some aside. Then I knelt beside the leg. I had to touch it. Thank God I was wearing gloves, I thought. Then I realized that was the dumbest thought I'd had in a long time. All I could touch was a boot.

I forced myself to reach out, and I nudged the boot. It moved, just a little. But it didn't move like a scarecrow's foot. It moved like a human foot attached to a very weak ankle.

I didn't scream, though I'm not sure why I didn't. I played the beam of the flashlight around, and now I saw something else sticking out of the heap of pumpkins.

It was a hand. A gnarled, dirty hand—the hand of a farmer who'd worked hard all his life.

Someone was buried under that heap of pumpkins.

Could that person be alive? I pulled my glove off, reached over, and touched the hand. It didn't respond to my touch, and it was cold.

I don't know if I smashed any pumpkins or not, but I ran all the way back to the van.

# Chapter 5

Once in the van, I locked the doors, then looked around inside to make sure nobody had climbed in while I was wading in pumpkins. The backward order of those actions indicated how rattled I was.

Luckily, just across the interstate, maybe three city blocks away, there was a gas station and convenience store. I drove across the overpass, nearly sideswiping a red Volkswagen with a Warner Pier High School bumper sticker in the rear window. It had pulled out suddenly from somewhere. The clerk in the bulletproof booth called 9-1-1, and I waited there. The Haven Road exit is not in Warner Pier; the Warner County Sheriff's Department would be in charge of the situation. But they have a cooperative agreement with Warner Pier, I guess, because Jerry Cherry, one of the three Warner Pier patrolmen, was the first officer on the scene.

I followed Jerry back to the Snow farm and parked on the edge of the fruit stand's gravel lot while law enforcement gathered. Sheriff's cars, Michigan State Police cars, and more Warner Pier cars pulled up, and all sorts of uniforms got out.

Jerry didn't make me show him where the body was; he found the spot from my description. After about twenty minutes, Chief Hogan Jones came over to my van, leaned on my door, and told me the sheriff said I could go home.

"We know where to find you, Lee," he said. "It's probably an accident anyway. We'll have to shift all those pumpkins before we know anything. What were you doing out here?"

I couldn't think of a good lie, so I told the truth. "I was trying to find out something about Aubrey Andrews Armstrong and his company. There was nothing on the Internet. I thought maybe I was spelling his name wrong, and since Silas Snow had mentioned having a business card . . ."

The chief shook his head. "You're incorrigible."

"I'm worried about Aunt Nettie."

"Then you'd better get home and be there when Armstrong brings her home."

He asked Jerry Cherry to follow me home. I assured him this wasn't necessary, but I was glad when he insisted.

As soon as I had gone into the house and had waved Jerry off, I discovered I was starving. Nerves, I guess. I had my head in the refrigerator checking the egg and English muffin situation when I heard another vehicle driving up. I wasn't mentally ready for Aunt Nettie and Aubrey, so I was glad when a glance out the side window showed me Joe's pickup. In fact, it was just plain good to see Joe, even though we had parted on bad terms.

I met him at the back door. "Do we have to settle the plans for the rest of our lives tonight?"

He smiled. He did have a wonderful smile. "Nope. Figuring out the rest of our lives is way too serious a subject for right now. How're you doing?"

"I'm okay. I guess the chief called you."

"He thought you might want some company."

"I could sure use a hug."

Joe obliged. "Have you eaten? I could take you out."

"No, thanks. I want to be here when Aunt Nettie gets home."

Joe frowned, but he didn't say anything.

"She *asked* me to be here, Joe. I was going to scramble myself some eggs. Do you want some?"

He gestured at the eggs and muffins on the cabinet. "I've had dinner, but I might have an English muffin and some of Nettie's peach jam."

"Preserves, you mean."

"Jam," he said. "And maybe sprinkle some pee-cans on top."

Joe and I carry on a joking argument about the proper names of items that are labeled differently in Texas and in Michigan, such as "preserves" versus "jam" and "pecahns" versus "pee-cans." He carries groceries home in a "bag," and I use a "sack." I'll let him settle the "Michigander" versus "Michiganian" controversy.

Joe split and buttered the muffins, then set the table with one place at the head and one on the side. I put on a large pot of coffee so Aunt Nettie could offer Aubrey some if she wanted to, then I scrambled eggs. Two of us moving around made Aunt Nettie's 1910 kitchen even narrower than it really is, but it was comforting to be doing homey things like scrambling eggs and toasting muffins and bumping rear ends.

We didn't talk any more until we were sitting at the table in the dining room, and we kept the conversation light while we ate. I'd just finished rinsing the dishes when I heard an engine. Headlights flashed by the windows, and an SUV parked in the driveway. Our outdoor lights were on, so I saw Aubrey get out and go around to open the door for Aunt Nettie. Then he popped the rear end of the SUV and brought out Monte on his leash. The pup scrambled around in the bushes, undoubtedly giving them a good sprinkling, while Aunt Nettie and Aubrey stood talking. I couldn't make out words, but both of them sounded cheerful. Apparently the evening had gone well. I surprised myself by feeling pleased.

Joe and I retired to the living room, since the dining room overlooks the back door, and the back door is the one everyone usually uses. We didn't know if Aunt Nettie would want to say good-bye to Aubrey there.

But Aubrey came in with her. I heard their voices in the kitchen, then Aunt Nettie called out. "Hello! Do I smell coffee?"

"It may not be as good as the Warner River Lodge's," I said, "but it's there."

Monte frisked into the living room, pulling Aubrey along. Aubrey took the pup off his leash, and once again Monte bounced against my knees, then went to Joe. Joe greeted him, and Monte turned over, obviously ready to have his stomach scratched. He playfully kicked Joe with all four feet as Joe obeyed.

"Did you enjoy your dinner?" Joe asked the pup. "Or did you go along?"

"He went, but stayed in the SUV," Aubrey said. "I don't like to leave him in the kennel too long, though he's patient. But Nettie invited him in."

"There's nothing here a dog can hurt," Aunt Nettie said. I saw that she had put on a dressy blue pants suit. I don't think I've seen Aunt Nettie in a dress since Uncle Phil's funeral.

"I'm going to have a cup of coffee," she said. "Aubrey? Will you have one?"

"Yes, please." Aubrey beamed at her, then turned back to Joe and me as she went to the kitchen. "The restaurant is delightful. Wonderful food! The Lodge might be a great place to house part of our cast— if we're able to shoot here. Did you two have a pleasant evening?"

The question summoned up a mental picture of Silas Snow's boot sticking out from under that heap of pumpkins. I must have turned green, because Joe quit playing with the dog and reached for my hand. "Lee had a bad experience," he said. "We'll tell you about it after Nettie comes in."

Aubrey told Monte to stay, and the puppy lay down calmly. My nerves, however, began to jump wildly. I had just realized that I was going to have to explain the reason I'd gone out to Silas Snow's fruit stand, and I was going to have to explain it right in front of Aubrey.

Yikes! The truth might have done for Chief Jones, but it wasn't going to work now. It would not be tactful to tell Aubrey I'd been spying on him. What was I going to say?

Joe and Aubrey were chitchatting, and I was thinking madly. When Aunt Nettie brought in a tray with two cups of coffee and a dish of bonbons and truffles, I was ready. I don't like to lie, but I sure can sidestep.

"I'm on the Halloween Parade committee," I said, "and we have to round up a lot of punchers. I mean, pumpkins! So after I finished up at the office, I went out to Silas Snow's place. He's got loads of pumpkins." I turned to Aubrey. "The parade is a Chamber of Commerce function, and I'm on the body. I mean, the board! I'm on the chamber's board."

I stumbled on, telling about finding the hand and the foot sticking out from under the pumpkins. "It must have been Silas."

Aubrey's face screwed into a look of incredulous horror. "Are you sure he's dead?"

"Pretty sure," I said. I didn't describe the feel of his hand. "Of course, it might not be Mr. Snow. I couldn't see his face."

Aunt Nettie was looking concerned. "My goodness, Aubrey. Silas Snow is Maia's uncle."

Aubrey's eyes popped. "Not the one who owns the farm where *Love Leads the Way* happened?"

We all nodded.

"My God!" Aubrey appeared genuinely shocked. "Maia and I were out there this morning."

"Silas was angry with Maia. They had a big argument at the Rinkydink," I said.

Aubrey nodded solemnly. "She told me he was eccentric, warned me he might refuse to let us use the property."

"I'm surprised he let you on the place at all," Joe said.

"I guess Maia didn't ask permission. We didn't go to his house. We dropped by the fruit stand as we were leaving, but Maia said since his truck was gone, he must not be there. Maia drove us over there by some back road."

Joe nodded. "Maia probably knows every inch of the property, since it belonged to her grandparents. Besides, the place adjoins Ensminger's Orchards, where she and Vernon live."

"Did Maia marry the boy next door?" I asked.

Aunt Nettie shook her head. "No, both farms originally belonged to Mae's grandfather. Mae's mother died young, while her father was still alive, so Mae inherited that half of the family holdings. Luckily, Vernon was interested in farming it, so they just built a house and moved there."

"Does Silas have children?"

"I'm sure he never married."

"No children to speak of," Aubrey said. He chuckled. Joe and I smiled politely. Aunt Nettie looked puzzled, as if she didn't get the joke. It occurred to me that she was putting on an act; Aunt Nettie may look like a sweet, innocent lady, but she knows what's going on in the world, and I was sure she had caught Aubrey's feeble joke. I wondered what she was up to.

"Silas terrorized Warner Pier kids for fifty years," Joe said. "Not that we didn't deserve it."

"Why was that?" Aubrey asked.

"Snow's orchards were the equivalent of the local haunted house. The legend about the buried bank loot has been around since my mom was a girl—actually a lot longer. We always dared each other to go out there and dig for treasure. Then Silas would chase us off."

"He was threatening to get out his shotgun this afternoon," I said.

Aubrey's eyes got big. "I guess we were lucky to get off the place in one piece."

"I doubt he would have shot at Maia," Joe said.

"He might have if he'd known that—" Aubrey stopped talking in the middle of his sentence and took a drink of his coffee. We all stared at him, but he didn't seem to be planning to say any more.

"Known what?" I asked.

"Oh, nothing. Nothing at all." Aubrey answered in a way that made it obvious "nothing" meant "something."

I started to ask again, but Joe crossed his legs and managed to nudge my ankle in the process. His hint was pretty clear, though I didn't understand why he didn't want me to quiz Aubrey.

Aubrey turned his charm on Aunt Nettie. "Wonderful coffee and wonderful chocolates," he said. He pointed to the plate she'd brought out, almost touching a milk chocolate truffle. His effort to change the subject was transparent. "Now what's this one?"

"Coffee," Aunt Nettie answered. "A truffle covered and filled with milk chocolate that's been flavored with Caribbean coffee. The dark chocolate truffle next to it is Dutch caramel. According to our sales sheet, it's 'creamy, European-style caramel in dark chocolate.' It's a soft caramel—not like Kraft's."

Aubrey was looking entirely too innocent. "Do you ever make any peach or apple flavored chocolates?" he said. "TenHuis Chocolade is in the center of fruit country—or so I judge by my trip to Snow's farm and Ensminger Orchards."

"We make chocolates flavored with strawberry and raspberries," Aunt Nettie said. "I've never come up with anything mixing chocolate and apple that I thought was very tasty. And chocolate seems to overwhelm peach flavor."

"Maia mentioned that you do dipped fruits."

"Yes, but not peaches or apples."

Joe jumped back in the conversation. "How was Maia tonight? Still artsy?"

Aubrey frowned. "She was rather quiet."

"She was Mae tonight," Aunt Nettie said. "Really, it was a very nice evening. You're a perfect host, Aubrey, and Maia was quite her old self. You must have tired her out trotting around Snow's orchards."

"Did you take Monte out to Snow's?" Joe's voice was extremely casual.

"Yes. Of course, I had to keep him on his leash, but he enjoyed running around and doing a bit of digging. He—" Aubrey's voice came to an abrupt halt for a few seconds before he spoke again. "I promised Maia I wouldn't say anything."

We were back to what Aubrey and Maia had found at Snow's place. And I had the idea that Aubrey wanted us to ask about it, whether Joe thought we should or not.

"Okay," I said. "I'll bite. What did you and Maia find?"

Aubrey grinned. "Haven't you guessed?"

I hesitated, but Joe spoke up. "Buried treasure?"

"I'm afraid so." Aubrey produced the big, beat-up wallet—the one Monte had handed me that afternoon—from an inside pocket of his jacket.

"Where was it?" Joe said.

"Right near the old house, the one Dennis Grundy stayed in."

"Don't tell me it was buried in an old mayonnaise jar," Joe said.

Aubrey grinned. "I won't tell you that if you don't want me to, but it was. Actually an old fruit jar with a solid metal top. A cliché, I know. Maia kept the jar and most of the money."

Aubrey laid the wallet and the big bills out on the coffee table, and we all bent over it.

So Aubrey and Maia had found some money that might be part of the legendary bank loot supposedly buried by Dennis Grundy. This was very interesting. It also raised a lot of questions.

"My goodness," Aunt Nettie said. "That was a lucky find."

Joe spoke mildly. "That was an amazing find. You say it was right near the ruins of the old cottage?"

Aubrey nodded, very deadpan.

Joe grinned. "I could have sworn that—during the summer I was twelve—I dug over every square foot of the lot where that house is."

Aubrey grinned back and raised his eyebrows. "Yes, Maia and I were lucky. Of course, we had Monte to guide us. But it almost looked as if one of us knew right where to dig."

I interpreted this as meaning he thought Maia had buried the money herself.

Why? Why would she do that? Why would Maia bother to get hold of some of the old money, then bury it? She would have had to go to a coin and money collector or dealer for the money, then buy an old wallet. And an old canning jar.

I had to admit all those things would be easy to find in a casual crawl of Warner Pier antiques shops. The money might be a little hard to locate, but the canning jar would be a cinch, and the old wallet wouldn't be too hard. The easiest part of all would be burying the treasure. But why bother?

That was a good question. Or I thought it was until I thought of a better one. I asked it. "Aubrey, what attracts you to Maia's novel? I mean, why make it into a film?"

"It's a compelling story," he said.

"Around Warner Pier, I'm afraid *Love Leads the Way* isn't considered great literature."

Aubrey laughed. "I'm afraid it wouldn't be considered great literature anyplace. But that's not the point. The point is that it could make a great movie."

"Why?"

"It's got everything: sex, violence, star-crossed lovers fighting obstacles to be together. An upbeat ending when Julia Snow leads Dennis Grundy away from a life of crime. And it's based on a true story."

"Is that important?" Joe said. "There are dozens of different versions of the Julia Snow–Dennis Grundy romance around here. Everything from 'It never happened' to 'Julia was no better than she should be before she ever met Dennis Grundy.' How do you know Maia's version is true?"

Aubrey thought a moment before he spoke. "Let's be frank. The script we finally come up with may not have much to do with Maia's book, and Maia's book may not have a lot to do with the real story.

But to shoot this 'legendary' "—he traced quotation marks with his hands—"love story in the place where it actually occurred and to base it on a book by a niece of the heroine gives us a publicity hook that's hard to beat."

He gestured at the big bills and the wallet. "So if the treasure we found is just stage dressing, so what? I'm not going to look at it too closely."

"Does Maia understand that?" I asked.

"I think so. I hope so."

"She's sure caught up in the Hollywood grammar," I said.

Aunt Nettie, Aubrey, and Joe all stared at me blankly, and I finally realized what I'd said. "Glamour! I mean, she's caught up in the Hollywood glamour!"

We all laughed, and Aubrey said he needed to be getting back to his B and B. Joe and I cleared away the coffee cups while Aunt Nettie waved good-bye to him, then tactfully went to her room. Not that Joe and I needed privacy. I certainly wasn't feeling romantic, and Joe didn't indicate he was either. I did walk out to his truck with him, and he gave me a good-night kiss before he left.

It was right in midsmooch, of course, that the headlights hit us.

We moved apart, and I looked toward the car that had pulled into the drive behind Joe's truck. The headlights blinded me for a moment, but the driver cut them off almost immediately, and I saw that it was a Warner Pier police car. Chief Jones got out and walked toward us.

"Lee, you didn't see anybody around Snow's fruit stand when you pulled in there, did you?"

"No. I didn't look for anybody, Chief. But it was spooky and there were no lights at the stand, only back at the house. Why?"

"Well, I guess we're going to have to get a complete statement from you tomorrow."

Joe gripped my arm. "What's wrong, Hogan?"

The chief scratched his head and looked more craggy than usual. "When we finally got those pumpkins off Silas . . . well, there was a big bash on the back of his head. And a bloody shovel lying beside the body."

I gasped.

"Yep," the chief said. "Looks like somebody killed old Silas."

# Chapter 6

It wasn't hard to get up the next morning since I'd never closed an eye the night before. Besides, I knew I'd have to make a statement early in the day. Sure enough, Chief Jones was on the phone before I'd washed the breakfast dishes, asking me to come by his office.

The Warner County Sheriff had called in the Michigan State Police, I learned, and they were using the Warner Pier Police Department as headquarters for their investigation into Silas Snow's death. The detective in charge was Detective Lieutenant Alec VanDam. Lieutenant VanDam and I had crossed paths more than a year earlier, when another killing happened in Warner Pier. I'd met Joe because of that crime, but it hadn't been a pleasant experience. I'd just as soon have met Joe at a church social.

I headed down to meet Lt. VanDam. He still had a face like a peasant in a van Gogh painting, and he still had that straight, bright yellow hair that reminded me of a souvenir Dutch doll. He also still displayed that cool politeness that made me nervous. There's no way of telling what's going on behind a polite façade like that. It's more chilling than yelling, snarling, or sarcasm.

I made my statement with only a few verbal faux pas. I did offer the information that I'd seen no sign of a "showman," when I meant a "shovel." But VanDam didn't keep me long; Chief Hogan Jones, who was still hanging around his own police station, was escorting me out the door by nine thirty.

Once we were outside I revealed my deepest wish to Hogan. "I don't suppose VanDam could arrange to arrest Aubrey Andrews Armstrong for homicide?"

Hogan grinned. "We'd all love for Silas to have been killed by an outsider, wouldn't we? And he might have been. But I'm afraid there's not much chance it was Armstrong. He's got a great alibi."

"Aunt Nettie?"

"Partly. But Sarajane Harding—you know, at the Peach Street B and B—was making cinnamon rolls and blueberry muffins in her kitchen from four p.m. until six forty-five. The kitchen overlooks her parking lot. She's willing to swear Armstrong's SUV never moved the whole time. In fact, for about a half hour he and the pup were in her backyard, having a training session."

"And she could see him all the time?"

"Right. He left at six forty-five, and Nettie says he got to her house at seven, right on the button. Not much time to stop and kill someone on the way."

I sighed and went to the office. The first thing I did, as usual, was check the e-mail. I was excited when I saw I had a reply from the Michigan State Film Office. I wasn't so excited after I read it. It was one of those notices that the e-mail recipient was away from her office for several days and would reply when she could.

Then I got a phone call from Tracy, asking about the time of her appointment for a haircut. I fudged on that one. "I wasn't able to get hold of Angie last night," I said. I didn't explain I had forgotten to try. "I'll phone her right now."

"I got excused from English to call you," Tracy said. "I have play practice after school, but I'll try to call again after sixth hour. Or you could leave a message in the office."

I promised to do that, because her call reminded me of a bit of business I wanted to do at the high school. I wanted to ask Maggie McNutt why she had come into TenHuis Chocolade the afternoon before, very upset over something to do with Aubrey Andrews Armstrong. But Maia had come in, and I'd never gotten to quiz Maggie about just what upset her. I suspected that she knew something specific about Aubrey. I was curious. So an hour later I parked in the visitor's slot at Warner Pier High School and Junior High, locked my van, and headed for the front door with two notes in my pocket—one for Maggie and one for Tracy.

Warner Pier is a town of only twenty-five hundred, so our junior high and high school share an auditorium, cafeteria, and gym, with separate wings for the two levels of classes. The building is a standard redbrick, one-story model, with a driveway for buses on the south side. The office, administrative headquarters for both secondary levels, is right at the main door. A student helper took the note I'd written for Tracy—her haircut appointment was at five o'clock—then took the one I'd written for Maggie McNutt.

"I can put Mrs. McNutt's note in her box," the student said. "But if you want to talk to her, this is her free period."

"Good idea," I said. The student used the intercom to make sure Maggie was in her classroom, then told me which way to go, and I started down the indicated hallway toward the speech and drama classroom. But I'd gone only halfway when a voice behind me called my name. I turned to see Ken McNutt emerging from his classroom. He was as scrawny and colorless as ever, but his thin hair, usually oppressively neat, was ruffled.

He spoke abruptly. "Lee, do you know what's eating Maggie?"

"No." I spoke first, thought later. Maybe I shouldn't have admitted I knew anything was bothering Maggie. "She came by the shop yesterday, but we couldn't talk. Why do you think something's worrying her?"

"Maggie and I have known each other since we were the age of this freshman algebra class. We don't usually kid each other. When she begins to use drama techniques on me, I know she's upset."

"Have you asked her what's wrong?"

"Of course I have. She says it's nothing."

"Ken, I don't know a thing."

He snorted. "And if you did, you wouldn't tell me."

"That's what friends are for. But I might urge Maggie to tell you."

He kicked a locker. "Maggie has the attitude that she's going to protect poor old innocent Ken. She hates to give me bad news. But bad news is part of the deal for married people."

"Ken, I'm not getting in the middle of any communications problems you and Maggie may have."

"I know, I know. But she's such a good actress. . . ." Ken shook his head, kicked the locker again, then walked back into his classroom.

I felt sorry for any kid who whispered or passed a note that afternoon. Ken might appear meek and mild, but that day I thought he'd be happy to sentence any freshman who sassed him to a trip to the office and a hundred extra algebra problems.

When I got to Maggie's classroom, she looked as unhappy as Ken had. A box of tissues was prominently displayed on her desk, and a couple of them had missed the wastebasket.

"Hidey, Maggie," I said. When I put on my Texas accent, it always makes Maggie smile, if not laugh, but this time that didn't work. "What's going on?"

Maggie shook her head and looked sadder than ever. She didn't say anything.

I pulled a student desk over close to her and squeezed all six feet of me into it. That didn't make her laugh either. "Okay," I said. "I want to know why you came in the shop yesterday and asked me if I were on speaking terms with Maia Michaelson."

Maggie shook her head, but she didn't say anything. So I asked another question. "And what do you know about Aubrey Andrews Armstrong?

"Oh, no!" Maggie finally spoke. Then she got up and closed the classroom door. "Lee, I'm in terrible trouble."

"What is it?"

"I can't tell you. I can't tell anybody."

"Even Ken?"

"Especially not Ken!"

I sighed. "Then I'll have to help you without knowing why you need help."

Big tears welled up in Maggie's eyes. "Lee, I . . ." She quit talking and reached for the tissues.

"What can I do, Maggie? Tell Maia to jump in the deep end of Lake Michigan?"

"I wish. I've got to warn Maia—I guess I've got to warn everybody—about that so-called Hollywood producer. But I don't know how to do it."

"How about saying something direct? 'Folks, this guy is a stranger. Don't give him any money until we can check him out.' "

Maggie's voice dropped to a whisper. "I don't need to check him out. I know he's a crook."

"Then tell Chief Jones."

"No! No! If I tell—well, Aubrey will tell."

I sat back in my desk. "Oh." Maggie and I stared at each other.

Whoops! So Maggie had some secret in her past, and Aubrey Andrews Armstrong knew what it was. I was speechless with surprise.

On the other hand, maybe I shouldn't be so surprised. The Maggie I knew was efficient and street-smart, the epitome of the gal who knew all the angles. And at thirty-five she'd outgrown the kid stage of her life. But no one is born street-smart. When Maggie was twenty and just as dumb as the rest of us were at that age, she had gone to Hollywood.

Whoops.

Maggie shredded her tissue. "I guess you've figured out that I . . . ran into him when I was in California."

My heart went out to her. And I felt a slight sense of—well, maybe it was pride. Pride that I was the one Maggie turned to when she needed a friend. I couldn't let her down.

"We were all young and dumb once, pal," I said. "You don't have to tell me about those creepy guys who hang around casting offices and beauty pageants. I understand. And, Maggie, I bet Ken would understand, too."

She shook her head violently. "No! Ken's good. He thinks I'm good, too. I just can't tell him I . . ."

A lot of Maggie's sentences were ending in the middle.

"Okay," I said, trying to sound brisk. "Recrimination time is over. Our problem is that Aubrey Andrews Armstrong is a crook, and we need to warn everybody in general, and Maia Michaelson in particular, about him. But we can't tell Maia exactly how we know he's a crook."

Maggie nodded.

"Well, through the magic of the Internet, I may have already solved this problem." I quickly outlined my efforts to check up on Aubrey the night before. "Anyway, he simply doesn't exist on the Internet. And I feel sure that the Michigan Film Office will either know about Aubrey or will know how to check him out. As soon as I can get in touch with the director there."

"After all the state budget cutbacks, I'm sure that's a one-person office, Lee. She's probably scouting locations. Or she could be in New York or California. It may be days before you can reach her."

"True. But in the meantime, I can hint to Maia that all is not right. And I can do it without mentioning you at all."

"Maia will never believe you. This is her dream come true."

I thought another moment. "Vernon! That's the answer. I can talk to Vernon. And nobody could ever suspect that Vernon will shoot his mouth off."

I guess Maggie and I might have hashed the matter over further, but the bell rang. Immediately students began to throng the halls and a group of them thronged into Maggie's classroom. Maggie tossed her tissue in the trash and took a deep breath. I made tracks.

As I paused outside the door, waiting for the crowd to clear, I heard Maggie inside. "Okay, people. Open your speech textbooks to page thirty-two. We'll start with the structure of the larynx." Her voice was clear, resonate, and confident. All traces of the fearful, tearful Maggie had disappeared. I thought of Ken describing her as "such a good actress." He was right.

I left the school and drove toward the shop. I had my assignment. Calling Vernon on the day after his wife's uncle had been murdered might be tricky. If Silas had never married, as Aunt Nettie had said, Mae—I mean, Maia—might be the closest relative. Vernon might be closeted with the police or simply be incommunicado. But I vowed that I'd track him down.

As soon as I got to the office, I called the number listed in the Warner County phone book for Vernon Ensminger. A woman answered, using a hushed voice. When I asked for Vernon, she said he was at the funeral home. When I asked for Maia, the voice said she was resting.

I almost cheered. If Vernon was at the funeral home, and Maia was resting, I might have a chance to catch Vernon away from Maia. Since he followed her around like a puppy dog, this might be a one-time opportunity. I called the Warner Pier Funeral Home and asked if Vernon were still there. He was. I decided driving would be too slow. I ran the three blocks to the funeral home. Then I had to wait, since the receptionist said Vernon was conferring with the funeral director. I sat in one of the visitation rooms. Luckily, no one was in there to be visited. This gave me a few minutes to plan the angle I wanted to use to approach Vernon.

When I heard Vernon's voice rumble in the hallway, I emerged and waited discreetly until he and the funeral director had shaken hands and Vernon seemed to be moving in the direction of the front door. Then I spoke. "Vernon."

Vernon turned toward me. It seemed to take a moment for him to absorb just who I was. Then he gave a little gasp and came toward me.

I held a hand out in his direction. "I'm so sorry about Mae's uncle."

Vernon's giant hand enfolded both of mine. "Lee." His voice almost broke. "I'm so sorry you had to be the one who found Silas. I wouldn't have had that happen for the world."

"I didn't really see him, Vernon. I just saw enough to know I ought to call the police. Can I talk to you a moment?"

The funeral director unobtrusively waved us into the room he and Vernon had just left. It was more like a parlor than an office, but there was a writing table. Vernon and I took two easy chairs, and he waited for me to begin.

"Vernon, first, I hope you'll consider this conversation confidential."

"Sure, Lee. What's wrong?"

"Last night, after you and Mae went out to dinner with Aunt Nettie and Aubrey Andrews Armstrong, I decided to search the Internet and find out what I could about the movies Aubrey has made." I leaned forward. "Vernon, I found all sorts of movie sites, but the name Aubrey Andrews Armstrong was not listed on any of them."

Vernon dropped his head and stared at his feet.

I went on. "So I wondered if you knew any more about him."

"Such as what?"

"An address for his company, to begin with. For example, has he given you or Maia—Mae—a business card?"

Vernon shook his head.

"Did he write her a letter—something with a letterhead?"

"No. He phoned last week, then showed up over the weekend. She hasn't got anything in writing."

I sat back. "I'm worried about Aunt Nettie, of course. If he's not on the up-and-up, he could hurt her feelings, humiliate her. But I don't want to say anything to her if I'm wrong."

Vernon didn't say a word. He just dropped his head even lower. Apparently I wasn't going to get any verbal response.

"Vernon, if you have any more information about this guy—well, I could use it to search the Internet some more. Or to check with the Michigan Film Office. The director should know about any film company considering shooting in Michigan."

Vernon spoke then, but he kept his head down, and his voice was just a mumble. "I'll see what I can find out."

Neither of us moved, but we seemed to have said all there was to be said. Or I had. Vernon had hardly spoken at all. I stood up. "I don't want to smear Aubrey, then find out he's perfectly legitimate. But . . . I just don't see how he can be, Vernon. He mentioned several movies he'd supposedly been associated with. I went to the Web sites for those movies, and he's not listed anywhere. I tried the Academy of Motion Picture Arts and Sciences site. It lists hundreds of people who are in the film business. He's not among them. Anyway, if you find out anything, please let me know."

Vernon nodded again, and this time he stood up. "I'll ask Mae about it," he said. "But I won't tell her why I want to know."

He opened the door to the little conference room and stood back to let me go out. I thought he would follow me. But once I was out in the hallway, the door closed behind me. Vernon was staying in the conference room.

I turned around and stared at the door, surprised. And then I heard a sound from the other side of the door that was even more surprising.

Sobbing. Vernon was sobbing.

## CHOCOLATE CHAT
## AMERICA'S FIRST HEALTH FOOD?

As soon as the Spanish conquerors of the Mayas and Aztecs discovered chocolate, they began to rave about the healthfulness of the native American drink.

One widely quoted conquistador called the drink "the healthiest thing, and the greatest sustenance of anything you could drink in the world, because he who drinks a cup of this liquid, no matter how far he walks, can go a whole day without eating anything else."

Except maybe more chocolate.

European doctors of the sixteenth century still subscribed to many theories derived from the ancient Greeks, including the notion (proposed by famed second-century physician Galen) that all diseases and their cures were either hot or cold and moist or dry. Cacao was deemed "cold and moist" and thus was considered useful in curing fevers.

Mixing chocolate with spices and herbs, doctors warned, changed its efficacy; some spices made it good for intestinal problems, others turned it into an aphrodisiac.

Maybe they'd heard that Montezuma used to drink chocolate before he visited his harem.

# Chapter 7

I walked back to the office slowly. The mental picture of Vernon Ensminger breaking into tears was hard to believe.

But why didn't I believe it? I was being stupid, I told myself. Vernon appeared stolid outwardly, but he still had feelings like anyone else. He'd been through a lot recently—his wife's complete personality change, the invasion of the movie producer, Maia's public quarrel with her uncle, then that uncle's murder. Even if he and Silas weren't close . . . I thought about that one for half a block. Vernon and Silas farmed neighboring property. They must have cooperated, maybe shared equipment. For all I knew they'd been bosom buddies.

Anyway, I'd given Vernon a broad hint about Aubrey, and he'd promised to help me find out more about the guy. And I hadn't had to bring Maggie into it. That was all I could do for the moment. Now I needed to concentrate on my own life, particularly my job.

My goal changed when I entered TenHuis Chocolade, however. My office had been taken over by Aubrey Andrews Armstrong. He was seated behind my desk having an interview with the local press in the person of Chuck O'Riley, editor of the *Warner Pier Weekly Gazette*. Monte was lying down at the foot of the desk.

Aunt Nettie was standing behind the counter in our little retail shop. "What are Aubrey and Chuck up to?" I asked her.

"Chuck wants to do a story about Aubrey's visit to Warner Pier. They set it up yesterday."

"I guess it's newsworthy. By Warner Pier standards, at least."

I could see Chuck leaning forward, apparently lapping up every word that dripped from Aubrey's silver tongue. I remembered my own reaction the night before, when Aubrey had spun his tale for Aunt Nettie, Joe, and me. I'd found myself wanting to believe him. And I remembered how Aunt Nettie had laughed, obviously flattered by his attention.

Then I thought about what Maggie had said about him: "If I tell, he'll tell." That was pure and simple blackmail.

Darn the man! Why couldn't he be legit? He was a charmer. I'd love to believe in him. But after my elementary investigations of him had turned up a suspicious lack of information, and after Maggie had reported knowing him in Hollywood—in a role she didn't want to become public or even private knowledge—I simply had to protect Aunt Nettie and Tracy and all the others who could be humiliated and hurt by him.

I steeled my resolution to resist Aubrey's charm with a Frangelico truffle ("Hazelnut liqueur interior with milk chocolate coating, sprinkled with nougat").

Chuck asked another question, grinning broadly. He was obviously happy with the story he was getting from Aubrey.

Chuck is the latest kid editor of the Warner Pier weekly. The newspaper always has a recent journalism graduate as an editor. A small paper, I suppose, draws newcomers or retirees to its staff. Anyway, Chuck was the only full-timer on the news staff. Three part-timers, all age sixty-plus, filled in the gaps, covering meetings and writing the occasional feature. One ad man and a publisher who also kept the books completed the workforce.

Chuck is five feet tall and five feet broad, a traditional Mr. Five-by-Five. He has dark hair and eyes that snap with interest at nearly everything. He also takes all the *Gazette*'s photos, and as I watched he produced his camera and gestured. I deduced that he wanted to take a picture to go with his story. Aubrey scooped up Monte and came out into the shop.

"Chuck wants to get a photo," he said. "I suggested that we include Monte and one of the real chocolate pups. If that would be all right with you, Nettie."

Aunt Nettie agreed, provided that the picture was posed so that the health department couldn't tell she'd had a dog in the shop. Chuck posed Aubrey, Monte, and a twelve-inch chocolate dog for a close-up. After a series of "Just one more" requests, he put his camera away.

"This has been a great interview, Mr. Armstrong," he said. "The *Gazette*'s readers are going to be fascinated with the plans you have to shoot *Love Leads the Way* here. Especially the part about the money."

Aubrey shook a finger at Chuck playfully. "I never claimed it was part of Dennis Grundy's treasure."

Chuck laughed. "I understand about the antique money. Actually, I was referring to the opportunity for investment."

"Please don't make too much of that. My major backers are likely to be in California."

Chuck turned to Aunt Nettie. "How about you, Mrs. TenHuis? Would you put money in Mr. Armstrong's project?"

Aunt Nettie smiled. "I haven't said no."

Her words sent my stomach into a nosedive. Aunt Nettie is far from wealthy, but she does have Uncle Phil's insurance money salted away. And she needs to keep it salted away in conservative investments to ensure a secure retirement for herself. An independent movie would be far too risky, even if the producer were honest.

Aunt Nettie patted me on the arm. "But I'd never do anything without consulting my financial advisor."

Aubrey and Chuck stared at me. Nobody spoke. Were they waiting for me to write a check? The silence lengthened.

They all apparently expected me to say something. So I did. "I'm only TenHuis Chocolade's business mangler—I mean, manager! I'm business manager for the company, not for Aunt Nettie. She handles her own finales. I mean, finances!"

I'd done it again. My twisted tongue had once again made me look and feel like a complete idiot. Aubrey tried to hide his snicker, but Chuck grinned broadly. Then he left.

I headed into my office, vowing to talk to Aunt Nettie about Aubrey as soon as he was out of the office. After all, if I was warning Maia about him, via Vernon, I owed as much to my own aunt. I sat at my desk, stared at my computer screen, and planned what I'd say and how I'd explain not telling her the night before.

But when Aunt Nettie popped her head into the office, Aubrey and Monte were still standing in the shop.

"Aubrey has invited me to go to lunch down at the Sidewalk Café," she said. "I shouldn't be too long."

She was beaming again. My heart turned over. I dreaded having to tell her Aubrey was a crook. I decided I could put off telling her for an hour. I knew her money was invested in mutual funds and CDs. She couldn't simply write Aubrey a check.

But the whole situation made me so jumpy that I almost fell out of my chair when the phone rang.

I was relieved to hear Joe's voice. "Have you had lunch?"

"No."

"I'd like to consult you about something, and I'm willing to trade a roast beef sandwich for an opinion."

"That's probably more than my opinion's worth. Actually, what I need is a sympathetic ear."

"I'm willing to throw that in. How about meeting me at the apartment in twenty minutes?"

"Your new apartment? Well . . . okay." I couldn't think of any excuse to avoid meeting Joe at his new apartment. It was all of two hundred feet away from TenHuis Chocolade. And I wasn't quite sure why I was reluctant to go.

I hung up, still feeling hesitant. Then it occurred to me that if Aunt Nettie was out to lunch I was supposed to be in the office. Of course, Hazel, her second-in-command, usually handled the lunch duty. I decided to check and make sure Hazel would be there.

I walked back to the workroom and discovered it was largely empty. Four people were at a table in the rear, wrapping Santas. Closer to the front Dolly Jolly was using a parchment cone to put dark swishes on the top of maple truffles.

"Hi, Dolly. Is Hazel here?"

"She's eating lunch in the break room!" Dolly spoke in her usual roar. "Do you need her?"

"No, I just wanted to make sure she was on the premises before I went to lunch. I see they've got you decorating. I could never learn to do that."

"It's just a matter of practice! I learned on my first job! In an ice cream shop!"

"What did you do? Add the curls to the tops of cones?"

"Ice cream cakes! They were our specialty!" She flourished the cone of dark icing and another graceful curve appeared on top of another milk chocolate–covered truffle. "I can write 'Happy Birthday' in any kind of script!"

I laughed and turned to go, but Dolly cleared her throat, a noise something like a bull elephant's trumpet. Then she did something really odd. Odd for Dolly, that it. She whispered.

"That Maia Michaelson—what do you think of her?"

"She's not my best friend," I said cautiously. "What do you think of her?"

"She was only interested in that movie guy. I'd like to talk to her, but it wasn't a good time." She was still whispering. "I was interested in how she writes."

"Oh, yes! You're an author, too."

Dolly got redder than usual and forgot to whisper. "Just nonfiction! All about food! I could never write fiction!"

I leaned a little closer. "Your manuscript was a lot more fun to read than Maia's novel!"

Dolly spoke again, and this time she remembered to drop her voice. "I thought the book was a dud, too. But the family background . . ." She frowned. "The Snows . . . are they . . . well, respectable?"

"You'll have to ask Aunt Nettie. There aren't many of them. As far as I know, Maia's the only quirky one. And I think the book has just gone to her head. She'll probably come down to earth sometime soon. Of course, Silas was a bit crotchety."

I told Hazel I was leaving, then I left. I didn't understand Dolly's interest in Maia's novel, but I wasn't worried about it. I was more concerned about why I was so reluctant to meet Joe for lunch in his new apartment.

Joe was lucky to have that apartment. Warner Pier's quaintness has made the town so darn popular that it's almost impossible for anybody but a millionaire to buy or rent a place to live. That was one reason Joe had spent the past three years living in a room at his boat shop. I think he'd been perfectly comfortable there with his hot plate, microwave, TV set, and rollaway bed until I'd come on the scene. I didn't object to his Spartan living arrangements, but he was so self-conscious about them that he refused to invite me over for more than a pizza. Since I lived with Aunt Nettie in an old house that offered little privacy, Joe and I had been hard put to find someplace to be alone together. And we liked to be alone together sometimes, now that we were engaged. Or on the verge of being engaged. Or going steady. Or whatever our relationship was.

I was almost thirty, and Joe was past it. We'd both been through unhappy marriages and had come out the other end, and Joe was eager for us to set a wedding date. So far I'd been dragging my feet, though I wasn't sure just why. I suspected that Joe thought getting a decent place to live would be an inducement for me to make that final decision and commit marriage.

But he hadn't been able to find anything in his price range until Warner Pier's summer rush was over. He couldn't afford to buy a house, and between Memorial Day and Labor Day every apartment in town is occupied either by tourists, by summer people, or by temporary help—the teachers, college students, and others who staff Warner Pier's restaurants, bed and breakfast inns, motels, and marinas during the tourist season. It had been September fifteenth before Joe signed a lease on a second-floor apartment overlooking Warner Pier's quaint Victorian main drag, Peach Street.

The apartment had two bedrooms, a nice kitchen, and a large living room. The drawback was that it had been thoroughly trashed by four college students who had rented it all summer. Joe got a month's rent free by offering to clean and repaint himself. So for the past three weeks he had spent all his free evenings working over there, and I'd helped him on a lot of them.

But lately he'd been pressing me harder and harder about setting a wedding date. But since I'd found Silas Snow's body, he hadn't mentioned Aunt Nettie or getting married at all. As I crossed the street toward the new apartment, I hoped he'd continue that policy.

The apartment's entrance was a door between a gift shop and an art gallery. It was unlocked. I went inside, then called out as I went upstairs. "It's me!"

"Come on up!"

Joe was in the newly painted kitchen. He had set the secondhand

maple table he'd acquired with his two plastic place mats. I happened
to know he'd scrounged them from his mother; they were patterned
with blue checks. A sack from the Sidewalk Café sat in the middle,
and he was pouring a Diet Coke.

"Roast beef with horseradish sauce," he said. "On thin rye."

"Yum, yum. All that and a dill pickle."

Joe shared out the sandwiches (his was ham and swiss) and piled
chips in the middle of the table.

"I guess I'm starving," I said. "I don't remember much about
breakfast."

"I've got a package of Oreos, if you want dessert."

We ate in silence for ten minutes, and it was comforting. As Joe
swallowed his last bite of ham and cheese, he poured more Diet Coke.
Then he finally spoke.

"Still upset about Silas?"

"Not for the past hour or so. I haven't had time to think about it."

"Something new?"

"Well, yeah." I chewed, swallowed, and decided I still wasn't sure
what to tell him about Aubrey. "But you said you needed advice."

"I need your opinion on some tile for the bathroom."

"Tile? You're putting new tile in the bathroom? I thought the landlord said he wouldn't replace the tile in there, since it's not cracked or
anything."

"I'll buy it myself. You said you didn't like green."

"My opinion doesn't count."

"Sure it does. I don't want to get something that will drive you
crazy." He got up and brought a small box over to the table, then
pulled out several pieces of ceramic tile. "I tried to get light colors. Do
you like the pink? The white? The light blue? Or do you want to go for
the fifties look with the oatmeal fleck?"

"I don't want to pick out tile for somebody else's apartment."

Joe's jaw tightened, and his eyebrows got that thundery look that
means he's mad. He dropped the tile back into the box and stood up.
"That remark makes your intentions pretty plain."

"What does that mean?"

"It means I want to get married, and you don't. At least not to me."

"The bathroom tile tells you that?"

"Well, calling this 'somebody else's apartment' makes it pretty plain you don't think you'll ever live here."

"I don't know that! I just—oh, we've been over this before. I botched things so badly the first time. You know how I feel."

"I'm beginning to think I do."

"Joe, I didn't come over here to make a plan for the rest of my life!"

"Why did you come?"

"You invited me to lunch. Plus I'm just a weakling. I'm upset about Aunt Nettie and I wanted a shoulder to cry on."

"What's wrong with Nettie?"

"Oh, she's gone out to lunch with this nutty guy who claims he's a movie producer."

"So? I thought the chief told you not to worry about that."

"How can I help it? Joe, I know he's a crook."

"How do you know?"

I left out any reference to Maggie, of course, as I sketched for Joe my Internet search and its lack of results. It was better than talking about bathroom tile and all its implications.

"And now he's talking to her about investing in this supposed movie he claims to be making."

Joe grinned. "Lee, you're perfectly right to be concerned, but you really don't have to worry about Nettie."

"I know she's no dummy! I'm not worried about her losing her money! I'm worried about her losing her—her pride. Her self-respect. I'm worried about her friends laughing at her. I'm worried that if a really nice guy comes along, she'll be afraid he's just trying to exploit her like Aubrey the creep."

Joe was grinning more broadly. He took my hand. "Lee, you're a sweetheart. But you really don't need to worry about—"

A loud rapping sounded, and Joe quit talking in the middle of his sentence.

"Is that someone downstairs? At the door?" I asked.

I followed as Joe walked through the living room and threw up one of the windows that overlooked the street. The screens were off, so he stuck his head out. "Hi, Nettie."

I put my head out, too. Aunt Nettie, Aubrey, and Monte were on the sidewalk below, looking up at us.

"Come on up," Joe said.

"You come down," Aunt Nettie said. "Aubrey's offered to take me out to see the site of the big romance, the cottage where Dennis Grundy courted Julia Snow. I knew you wanted to see it, too, Lee. Why don't the two of you come with us?"

# Chapter 8

"Vernon said it would be all right," Aunt Nettie said. "I haven't been out there in years."

Aunt Nettie was sounding a bit urgent. I concluded that she wanted someone to go with her. I agreed; I didn't want her wandering off to remote spots alone with Aubrey. Not after what I'd been told by Maggie.

To cinch the deal, Joe spoke. "I'd like to go. I've never been out there when I wasn't trespassing."

Ten minutes later Joe and I had cleared away our lunch debris and were waiting on the sidewalk when Aubrey pulled his SUV up in front of Joe's apartment. As we got in, Monte gave us a welcoming bark from his heavy plastic traveling crate in the rear deck.

"Chuck O'Riley wanted to shoot some pictures out there," Aubrey said. "He interviewed Vernon at the police station for his news story on Silas's murder, and at the same time he asked if he could take some pictures at the cottage. Newsmen are nervy! I almost thought he was going to ask Maia to come along. I wouldn't have had the courage. Chuck's going to meet us there."

"If Vernon gave Chuck permission then Maia must be Silas's heir?" I asked.

"If Silas had a will, I'm sure it hasn't been read," Joe said. "But Vernon seems to be in charge at the moment. You can't just ignore a farm until the courts act. Somebody has to make sure the stock is fed and the garden watered. It would be normal for a neighbor, especially one who's a relative, to step in."

For once Aubrey didn't have much to say. In fact, we all grew quiet as we reached the Haven Road exit and turned toward Silas Snow's fruit stand. The area was still marked off by police tape, and one lone sheriff's deputy was stationed there. We went west on Haven Road, then turned south when we reached Lake Shore Drive, maybe two-tenths of a mile west of the interstate.

The cottage was at what might be considered the back of Silas Snow's property, since his house was near the interstate. The one-lane road that led to the cottage was less than a mile south of Aunt Nettie's house, which is on the inland side of Lake Shore Drive. The Grundy cottage lane also turned inland off Lake Shore Drive, and the house wasn't far off the road. I'd been by there dozens of times, but the area was so overgrown that I'd never realized any sort of structure was behind the trees and bushes.

"The cottage isn't much to look at," Aubrey said, "but the historical context makes it interesting."

I thought "historical context" was a pretty fancy term for "rented by minor gangster for three months seventy-five years ago," but I kept my mouth shut.

After Aubrey pulled into the sandy drive, we all sat in the SUV and surveyed the cottage. I'd been expecting Dennis Grundy's old cottage to be a ruin, but it wasn't. It wasn't in the best repair, but it was a sturdy little Michigan cottage of the type built around 1920. An ancient coat of white paint still clung to the siding, and rusted screen wire surrounded what had been a sleeping porch where the frame of an old metal cot stood at one end.

The vegetation apparently hadn't been cleared in several years. It was thinner around the house than near the road, but saplings were growing next to the foundation and the grass and weeds in the yard were high. Trees hung thickly above the cottage, and its roof was speckled with patches of moss. It looked lonely and uncared-for, but it wasn't falling down.

"I'd have expected Silas Snow to sell this place," Joe said. "The house isn't worth anything, but the lot is. Walking distance to the lake, after all. It should bring a good price."

"Snow apparently continued to rent the cottage to vacationers up until about ten years ago," Aubrey said. He got out of the SUV, and the rest of us followed his lead.

"It's spooky," I said. "Somehow I wouldn't be surprised if Dennis Grundy's Model A came chug-chugging down the drive."

Aunt Nettie gave a nervous laugh, but before she could hit her third "hee-hee," I heard a strange sound. I clutched Joe's arm and gasped.

It was the chug-chug of an old motor.

Joe laughed. "I believe you summoned up Dennis Grundy's ghost, Lee. Or at least the ghost of his car."

"What is it?"

"I think," Joe said, "that it's actually a Volkswagen."

And sure enough, a red Volkswagen came down the lane from behind the house. It was a real, antique Volkswagen, not one of the new ones. And behind the wheel was Ken McNutt. He stopped when he saw us. The VW was nose to nose with Aubrey's SUV.

Aunt Nettie, Joe, and I all laughed and waved. "I'll have to move the SUV so he can get out," Aubrey said. He got behind the wheel again and backed out onto Lake Shore Drive.

Joe spoke to Ken. "What are you doing here?"

"Oh, I had an hour's break, and I wanted to see this place." Ken nodded toward the cottage. "This is the site of Maia Michaelson's big romance novel, isn't it?"

Joe's voice was curious. "How'd you find it?"

"The high school custodian drew me a map," Ken said. "And now I've got to hurry, or I'll be late for a parent conference."

He drove on out the lane and waved to Aubrey. The VW gave a cheerful beep-beep as it turned onto Lake Shore Drive.

"I'd forgotten that Ken McNutt is a VW hobbyist," Joe said. "I understand he has four of them. At least two are in driving condition."

I stared after Ken. His Volkswagen was shiny and cared-for. It might have come straight off a production line of the late 1950s. The only modern thing about it was the Warner Pier High School bumper sticker in the back window.

Why did that seem familiar?

I caught my breath. I'd seen a red Volkswagen like that one. The night before, right after I discovered Silas Snow's body, I'd pulled out onto Haven Road in a big hurry. And I'd nearly rear-ended a red VW with a Warner Pier High School bumper sticker in the back window. The sticker hadn't been on the bumper. It had been inside the back window, just the way Ken's sticker was, the way people who are picky about their cars' finishes display bumper stickers.

I hadn't gasped loudly, but Joe had heard me. "What's wrong?" he asked.

"Nothing," I said. "I just remembered a prone call—I mean, a phone call! I forgot to call the bank. I'll do it when I get back to the office."

We walked toward the house, but my mind was racing. Was it Ken McNutt's VW that I'd seen the night before, close to Silas Snow's fruit stand? Right after Silas was killed?

If it had been, who had been driving? Ken? Or Maggie? Or was there another red Volkswagen in Warner Pier with a high school bumper sticker in the back window? After all, I hadn't bothered to look at the license plate.

And why hadn't I wanted to tell Joe I'd seen it there? The answer to that one wasn't hard. If I told Joe right at that moment, I'd probably have to tell Aubrey. And I didn't want to tell Aubrey anything that might involve Maggie.

I realized Joe was looking at me closely. He had said something, and I hadn't even heard it. I pulled my mind back to my surroundings. Whatever the reason for the VW being near Snow's fruit stand, I had to forget the whole thing and concentrate on the current moment. I'd decide what to do about the Volkswagen—if anything needed to be done—later.

By the time I gathered my thoughts, Aubrey had parked the SUV again and had taken Monte out of his crate. He pushed a fancy metal stake into the sandy earth near the corner of the cottage and hooked Monte to it by a long leash. I decided Aubrey must have the back of the SUV packed solid with puppy equipment.

Monte seemed content to frisk about, sniffing around under the bushes. Joe, Aunt Nettie, Aubrey, and I began to prowl in much the same way, peeking in the uncurtained windows of the house.

"I don't have a key," Aubrey said.

"I don't think there's anything inside but a thick layer of dust," Aunt Nettie said. "We certainly don't need to go in."

The cottage originally had only two rooms, or so I guessed. There was a living room, with a kitchenette separated from it by a counter, and there was a bedroom. A bathroom now opened off the bedroom, but the fixtures and linoleum were forties-style. And the bathroom stood on piers made of cement blocks. The main part of the house had a solid foundation.

The views through the windows revealed only a few sticks of furniture, and they all looked too modern to have been used by Dennis Grundy.

"I'm sure this place didn't have indoor plumbing when Dennis Grundy rented it," Aunt Nettie said. "The kitchen appliances and that counter you can eat at were added later, too. At least, I never saw a counter like that in a really old house."

"The hole where the pipe from the woodstove would have been is still there," I said. "Up there in the corner."

"It wouldn't have been a bad little cottage for a cheap vacation," Joe said. "In the twenties lots of people still had outdoor plumbing and woodstoves."

"It would have been like camping." I gestured at the metal cot frame on the porch. "The porch might have been a really nice place to sleep. If you had plenty of blankets."

"Where did you and Maia find the money buried?" Joe asked.

"Around behind the house." Aubrey led the way to a little pile of dirt.

"That's probably where the old fence corner would have been," Joe said. He pointed to a stick of wood and a bit of wire. "At least, that looks like the remnants of a wire fence."

"Did you say the money was in a mayonnaise jar?" Aunt Nettie wanted to know.

Aubrey laughed. "I know that's a cliché. . . ."

"What else would Dennis have had to bury money in?" Aunt Nettie said. "Maybe a syrup tin. But he would have had to use something he could get hold of easily."

"Burying the money has always sounded crazy to me," I said. "Why? Why would he bury money anyway? How much was in the jar?"

"Just about a hundred dollars," Aubrey said.

"That wasn't much loot from a bank job, even in 1930. And why was the wallet buried with it? It doesn't make sense."

Joe answered. "It makes sense if the wallet was just stage dressing for the antique money."

Aubrey grinned. "I didn't say that. That's strictly *your* idea, Joe."

We kept wandering around, with me keeping a careful lookout for poison ivy, until another car pulled in and Chuck O'Riley got out.

Aubrey went to meet him, sweeping off his wide-brimmed hat, and Monte barked a greeting. Chuck shook hands with Aubrey, but then, to my surprise, he came toward me. "Lee, I want to talk to you."

"What about?"

"About finding Silas Snow's body. When I saw you earlier I didn't realize you were the one who found him."

I guess I stared. We all took the Warner Pier *Gazette* for granted as a source for local news. But Warner Pier news rarely included crime. The *Gazette* was where I caught up on the school board meeting or the zoning commission. Or about visitors who claimed to be movie producers. I didn't expect to read about murders there. I'd forgotten Chuck would be writing up Silas Snow's murder, even though Aubrey had mentioned Chuck's interviewing Vernon earlier.

I gathered my thoughts and answered Chuck's questions as briefly as I could. I definitely slurred over my reasons for going to the Snow fruit stand in the first place, of course. And I tried to be matter-of-fact about finding the body.

"At first," I said, "I thought the hand and foot must belong to a scarecrow."

"What made you realize it was a body?"

The recollection of how that foot had wiggled sprang into my mind, and I couldn't answer. I put my hand over my mouth and shook my head.

Joe moved in and put his arm around me. "I think that's enough, Chuck."

But I couldn't let Joe protect me. I tried to speak. "I knelt down," I said. "I troweled—I mean, I touched! I touched the boot. It didn't move like a scarecrow's boot would move."

"What did you do then?"

"I ran through those pumpkins like a friend. I mean, a fiend!" I stopped and took a deep breath. "I ran like hell, Chuck."

That seemed to settle Chuck's curiosity. He thanked me and moved on to Aubrey, posing him on the porch of the cottage.

I guess I was still a bit shaken; I wanted to get away from Chuck before he thought of any more questions. So I walked away, following the sand lane further, toward wherever Ken McNutt had been. Joe followed me.

To my surprise, the bushes and trees behind the cottage thinned out quickly.

"What's back there?" I said. Joe and I walked about a hundred feet and came out in an apple orchard.

"McIntosh?" I said.

Joe touched one of the hanging apples. "Looks more like Jonathan."

"I guess we've reached the active part of the Snow farm."

The trees weren't too large. Fruit farmers, I've come to realize, don't want their trees to get very tall. They're easier to prune, spray, and pick if they're shorter and wider.

This orchard stretched on for a long way, hundreds of trees marching along in straight lines, forming squares and rectangles and diamonds. The ground beneath them, of course, was cleared. Most growers mow around their trees. I wasn't sure why.

Joe was a native of orchard country. I turned to him. "Why do fruit farmers mow around trees?"

"Most of them believe tall grass takes nutrients from the trees. Besides, they want to keep the area smooth and even so they can run tractors and trailers down the rows without bouncing fruit around and bruising it."

Now, in October, the fruit trees were still a dull green, but the oaks and maples—the woods around edges of the orchard—were turning brilliant reds and oranges.

"It is beautiful," I said.

"Silas was a good grower," Joe said. "Everything looks neat. Spic-and-span. The only thing I see is one ladder out of place."

He gestured, and I saw it, too. A three-legged ladder, the kind used for picking fruit, was standing beside a tree. But it wasn't an apple tree. It was a taller maple at the edge of the orchard.

"Lee! Joe!" Aunt Nettie's voice came from behind us.

"I guess she's ready to go," Joe said.

"So am I."

We called out, then made our way back down the lane and into the yard of the cottage. Aubrey was pulling up Monte's stake. Aunt Nettie was holding the long leash, and the puppy immediately made for the bathroom "wing," pulling Aunt Nettie behind. Monte crawled under the bathroom, finding an easy path between the cement blocks that held the room up. He began digging around in the sandy dirt.

"Come on, Monte!" Aubrey sounded exasperated. "You'll get mud in the car."

He took the leash and hauled the pup out, over Monte's loud objections. As predicted, the dog was a mess, his chocolate hide covered with gray dirt. Joe held him by the collar while Aubrey brought a towel and a brush—more puppy gear—from the SUV and cleaned him up. Then he led Monte over to the vehicle, opened the rear end, and spoke to the puppy. "Kennel, Monte."

Monte jumped right up, leaping into the SUV and going into his big carrying case.

Aubrey was rewarding him with a dog snack when the shot rang out.

# Chapter 9

I think I was more conscious of a metallic *clunk* than I was of the shot. Which was logical, I guess. The sound of the shot being fired didn't have a lot of significance. The shooter could have been firing in any direction.

But that *clunk* was proof that the shot had hit the SUV. The guy with the gun was firing in our direction.

We all yelled at the same time.

"Get down!" That was Joe.

"Aunt Nettie! Duck!" That was me.

"Heavens! Was that a shot?" That was Aunt Nettie.

"What the hell?" That, of course, was Aubrey.

Monte even began to bark.

The next second the four of us had ducked behind the passenger side of the SUV. Aubrey had to have gotten around, over, or under the vehicle's open rear door, and I've never been sure how he did it. But he did. He was right there with the rest of us, cowering.

Nothing else happened for a long moment. Monte gave one last howl and quit barking. We all looked at each other. None of us seemed to have any idea of what to do next. The moment stretched. No more shots came. Finally Joe spoke. "I don't have my cell phone."

"I don't, either," Aubrey said.

There was another minute of silence before Joe spoke again. "If we had a stick, we could hold Aubrey's hat up and see if it draws fire, I guess."

Aubrey gave a weak laugh. "Just like a B western."

"It worked for Clint Eastwood."

We huddled a few more minutes.

"I don't hear anybody moving around in the bushes," I said.

"I think that was a rifle shot," Joe said. "A guy with a rifle doesn't have to be close. He's just got to be able to see through the bushes and trees."

Aunt Nettie came up with a practical plan, as she usually does. "Do you think we dare open the doors on this side of the SUV and get in?"

"Let's try it," Joe said.

Aubrey opened the right front door. Nothing happened. He started to climb in, but Joe stopped him. "That shot seemed to be aimed at you," he said. "You stay down. Let me drive. At least you've got tinted windows."

I wasn't sure the tinted windows were useful. The guy with the rifle wouldn't be able to see who was in the driver's seat, true, but he was bound to figure out someone was. He might think it was Aubrey and shoot Joe by mistake.

But Aubrey didn't argue, and I didn't, either. Joe got in, followed by Aubrey, who slid in and crouched with his knees on the floor and his elbows in the front passenger seat. I opened the door to the rear bucket seats, and Aunt Nettie and I got in, taking the same prayerful position.

"The back's still open," Aubrey said.

"Can it be closed from inside?" Joe asked.

"I don't think so."

"I can close the kennel," I said. I reached around my seat and did it. At least Monte couldn't jump out.

"Good," Joe said. "I'll back out and drive off gently. As soon as we're a little way up the road, I'll get out and close up."

The plan worked. Joe backed the SUV out onto Lake Shore Drive. Monte barked, maybe trying to tell the stupid humans the rear door was still open. Joe shifted into drive and moved forward, driving slowly for about a quarter of a mile before he stopped. Aubrey started to open his door, but I stopped him. "No, Aubrey. You stay down." I jumped out, slammed the rear door, and was back inside in less than five seconds.

When we moved off again, Joe gunned the motor and dug out. And we all took deep breaths.

"Go to my house," Aunt Nettie said. "We can call the sheriff from there."

That gave me nearly a mile to try to absorb what had just happened.

First, why had we all assumed Aubrey was the target of the man with the rifle?

That was easy. Aubrey had been at the back of the SUV. Joe, Aunt Nettie, and I had all been around on the passenger's side, ready to get into our seats. The shot had come from the driver's side of the SUV. Aubrey was probably the only person the gunman could have seen clearly enough to aim at.

Besides, I admitted to myself, after what Maggie had told me, I was ready to kill Aubrey myself. It was easy to assume that someone else had a reason. Maggie sure did.

At that thought, my heart leaped to my throat, then dropped to the pit of my stomach. I didn't want to involve Maggie in this. But Ken had actually been out in the area. Maybe Maggie had been there, too. Ken was worried about Maggie; he'd told me as much that morning. If she'd told him that Aubrey had threatened her . . . I shoved the idea out of my mind. I didn't want to believe Ken or Maggie could be involved. Besides, how could they have known Aubrey would be there?

Joe pulled into Aunt Nettie's drive, and Aunt Nettie got out her house keys. "That cottage is outside the city limits," she said. "I'll call the sheriff."

"No, wait!" Aubrey's voice was sharp. "I'm beginning to think we're overreacting to this whole episode."

"Aubrey! Someone shot at you!"

"I'm sure it was some sort of accident."

"Even if it was, you can't simply allow people to fire around wildly without complaining about it."

"But why would anybody want to shoot me?"

"Why would they want to shoot any of us?" Joe said. "Let's see if we can find the bullet hole."

We all got out and looked. The bullet hole was high up on the SUV, right at the back, where the roof met the side. Joe got Aubrey to restage the shooting, to stand right where he'd been when the shot rang out. Then he whistled softly. "Aubrey, that guy didn't miss you by six inches."

Aubrey looked a little green, but he stuck to his argument. "It must have been some sort of accident."

"I guess the guy saw the outback hat and thought you were a kangaroo," I said. "Are we going to call the cops or not?"

Joe hesitated, to my surprise, and Aubrey carried the day. Or at least a compromise was reached. Joe said he and Aubrey could drive Aunt Nettie and me back to town, then show the SUV to Chief Jones privately. They'd tell him what had happened without going through the county dispatcher. Maybe, since the dispatcher wouldn't be using the radio to send out a patrol car, we could keep the report quiet.

I thought it was screwy, but Joe was, after all, a lawyer. He was even Warner Pier City Attorney. If he thought that was good enough, I wasn't going to argue. I'd spent enough of my day making statements and being quizzed by detectives. But knowing that some unknown rifleman was prowling around on the Snow farm less than twenty-four hours after its owner had been beaten to death seemed highly suspicious to me.

The SUV was the only vehicle available, so Aunt Nettie and I accepted a ride back to TenHuis Chocolade. As I got out of the SUV, I did reach behind the seat to give Monte's chocolate-colored hide a pat.

The first thing I saw as I walked in the door was more dark chocolate puppies. Dolly Jolly was standing at a big worktable in the front of the shop, molding them.

"Oh, hi!" she said. As usual, Dolly's voice was loud enough to shatter glass. "Lindy Herrera came by to see you, Lee!"

"Did she say what she wanted?"

Dolly didn't answer for a long moment. She was pouring molten dark chocolate into a mold that made a dozen one-inch dogs. The mold was arranged something like an ice tray and Dolly was carefully filling each compartment with melted chocolate she ladled from a big stainless steel bowl at her elbow. This is one of the first jobs Aunt Nettie gives new employees. It looks easy, but when you're learning, it's best to concentrate, and Dolly was doing that. I could tell by the way she was sticking her tongue out.

She put her ladle in the bowl, then tapped the mold gently on the table to remove any air bubbles. Next she picked up the mold and ran a spatula across the top, scraping any excess chocolate back into the bowl. Then she looked up at me and spoke. "All Lindy said was that she'd heard a juicy bit of gossip! But she didn't offer to tell it to me! Said she'd wait for you!"

"A juicy bit of gossip. Hmm. I'll give her a ring."

But first I had another job to do. I'd put off telling Aunt Nettie about Aubrey's lack of credentials as long as possible. I couldn't tell her what Maggie had said, but I needed to tell her at least as much as I had told Vernon.

I turned to her. "Aunt Nettie, could you come in the office a minute. There's something I need to discuss with you."

Aunt Nettie sighed. "Can we put it off? Lee, I should make a condolence call on Maia and Vernon. Can you come with me?"

I must have frowned, because she went on. "After all, I was out to dinner with them last night. I guess I could go alone." She sounded doubtful.

"No, I don't want you to do that," I said. "I'll give Lindy a quick call, then go with you. We can talk when we get back. Do we need to take food?"

"Maybe a plant would be better. We can stop at the Superette."

Maybe I was looking for an excuse not to tell Aunt Nettie about Aubrey. Anyway, I put it off.

Lindy wasn't in her office, so I left a message, and Aunt Nettie and I left on a condolence call I'd rather be shot than make.

Come to think of it, I nearly had been shot. A shiver ran around my shoulders and down my back. Then we got in my van and headed back the way we'd gone earlier, turning off the interstate at Haven Road. Only this time we turned inland, away from Lake Michigan, to reach Ensminger Orchards.

Vernon and Maia's house was nothing special. It was just an ordinary one-story, white frame house with no claim to either architectural or historic significance. Any significance the farm had came from the outbuildings. The house was surrounded by well-maintained barns, machine sheds, and storage buildings. The property gave the impression of prosperity, but it looked as if every cent had been plowed back into the orchard business. The house was unimportant in the overall layout.

I might have blamed Vernon for this, but the yard Aunt Nettie and I parked beside didn't look special, either, and that was usually the farmwife's responsibility. There was no fence or flower bed. The shrubs needed trimming, and one lone tree had been planted smack in the middle of the patch of grass that passed for a lawn. The only other trees nearby were peaches and apples planted in the usual neat rows.

Aunt Nettie got out of the van with the pot of ivy she'd bought at the grocery store. I moved close to her and spoke softly. "From the looks of the yard, we're abandoning this poor ivy to a terrible fate."

"It's only a plant, Lee." Aunt Nettie's voice was sharp.

As we walked toward the porch, Vernon opened the door. "Oh, hello," he said awkwardly. "It was nice of you to drop by."

I expected him to step back and invite us in, but he didn't. He just stood there, blocking the door, as we approached. Then he stepped outside and let the storm door close behind him.

That was certainly not hospitable. But it was surprising.

Aunt Nettie smiled sweetly, just as if he'd strewn flowers in our path. "We wanted to tell you and Maia how sorry we are about her uncle."

"She's resting." Vernon looked back into the living room nervously. "I'll tell her you came by."

"It must have been a real shock to her," Aunt Nettie said. "Are there other relatives?"

"Not close." Vernon wasn't budging from in front of that door. "My sister was down from Grand Rapids for a couple of hours."

There was a long pause. I didn't know what to say, and apparently Aunt Nettie didn't either. Finally she moved toward the porch, holding out the ivy plant. "We wanted to bring this."

Vernon looked panicky. To take the plant, he had to either move away from the door, toward Aunt Nettie, or he had to let her come within reaching distance of him. He stepped forward, still holding on to the door handle behind him. Then he moved back, still clutching the handle. Apparently he wasn't able to decide which of the two alternatives to pick. I stared. It was fascinating. I could almost read his mind. He couldn't decide if he should let go of the door, or if he should let Aunt Nettie come close enough to . . . to what? See into the house?

What was eating big, old, reliable, solid Vernon?

Then I heard a tinkling laugh. It was Maia's phony ha-ha, but it didn't come from inside the house. It came from my left. I swung my head in that direction, and Maia herself came around the corner.

"Oh, you've brought a plant," she said. "Aren't you two darlings?"

"We're very sorry about Silas," Aunt Nettie said.

Maia made a strange little sound, someplace between a choke and a giggle. "Uncle Silas and I weren't close," she said. "But I guess I'm the only relative he had."

"That's what Vernon said."

Maia made that strange noise again. "It's funny. My grandfather had three children, but my mother was the only one to marry. Except for Aunt Julia, of course. The one who ran off with Dennis Grundy. Of course, she was from an earlier marriage. She was a half sister to my mother and Uncle Silas.

"She never contacted the family after she left. If she had children, we didn't know anything about it." She giggled or choked again. "So I was the only child in my generation. And now I've outlived them all. I'm the last of the Snows."

Vernon moved, finally, letting go of the storm door. "I thought you were lying down," he said to Maia.

Was I imagining the challenge in the way Maia looked at him? "I thought I'd take a walk," she said.

We obviously weren't going to be asked inside, so Aunt Nettie began to make motions toward leaving. She handed the ivy to Maia. "We just wanted you and Vernon to know that we're thinking of you. And please call on us if there's anything you need."

I decided I'd better chime in. "Yes, if you need . . . anything, we're here." I turned toward the van, unable to think of anything more to say. I had my hand on the door handle before I was inspired to make another comment. "And thanks for letting us visit the cottage."

Maia didn't say anything, but Vernon spoke. "Don't mention it."

"It's pretty interesting," I said. "I hadn't realized it had been in use as recently as it had. And the orchards behind it—they're beautiful."

Maia did that little giggle business again. "What do you mean by that?"

"Just what I said. The orchard behind the cottage is beautiful. It looks well-cared-for and perilous—I mean, productive! The orchard looks productive."

"Silas was a good fruit man," Vernon said. He moved close to Maia and put his arm around her shoulder. "He could be cantankerous, but he was a hard worker."

Maia giggled, then pressed her fingers against her lips. Aunt Nettie and I said good-bye, then got in the van and drove away. As fast as we decently could.

"Maia's getting stranger and stranger," I said.

"She acted almost normal last night. Subdued, the way she used to act."

We were silent a moment, then I took a deep breath and prepared to tell Aunt Nettie about Aubrey. I began that way. "About Aubrey . . ."

"That really mystifies me," Aunt Nettie said. "Why anybody would shoot at him. But I don't want to talk about him, Lee."

"But, Aunt Nettie, there's something—"

She smiled and patted my hand. "Now, Lee, don't worry. I'm not going to give him any money. And speaking of money, how did we come out on the special order of chocolate-covered Oreos?"

I tried to report on Aubrey once more before we got back to work, but she cut me off again. And during the hour and a half we spent at work that afternoon, she simply refused to talk to me privately. I was completely balked. I had to face it; Aunt Nettie didn't want me to say anything about Aubrey.

When Tracy came in at four, all excited about her upcoming hair appointment, I had to give up on Aunt Nettie. I promised myself I'd talk to her at home.

Tracy was so excited about her new haircut that she had showed up at TenHuis Chocolade an hour early. Aunt Nettie put her to work wrapping Santas until it was time to go, but I'm not sure if Tracy was a lot of help. She was simply bouncing with excitement.

I was relieved when her mom called. "Lee," she said, "I really appreciate you taking Tracy for a haircut."

"I'm glad to hear that. I wouldn't want to do anything you don't approve of."

"I've been trying to get her to cut that stringy mess for two years. And since it's ol' dumb mom suggesting it, she has refused. She'd look so much better with a body perm."

A body perm? None of the high school girls had a perm. I could see why Tracy had dodged her mother. "I'm going to leave it up to Angie," I said cautiously. "She's the hair expert. I have a feeling she'll suggest a blunt cut. It may still be straight."

Mrs. Roderick laughed. "As long as it's not too strange a color. That's all I'm worried about."

I was worried about a lot more than that. Tracy was setting her heart on a part in Aubrey's movie—a movie I believed would never be filmed. On the way over to Angie's shop I tried to warn her.

"Tracy, this Mr. Armstrong—don't forget he's a stranger. Just because he claims to be a movie producer—"

"Oh, Lee! You talk just like Mrs. McNutt."

"Mrs. McNutt and I have been around talent shows and beauty pageants, Tracy. We've learned the hard way. A lot of these guys are not for real. They just want to take advantage of pretty girls."

"Pretty girls?" Tracy's voice was awed.

I pressed the point home. "Young, pretty girls like you, Tracy."

She thought a moment, and when she spoke her voice was slightly subdued. "Mr. Armstrong told me never to go to any sort of tryout without my parents." Then she bounced back. "But I still want a new hairdo."

Poor Tracy. She didn't want her dream punctured, but it was going to be.

Angie's skill made Tracy look a lot more grown-up, as well as more attractive. I hung around and put in my two cents' worth while Angie did her makeup. Then Tracy insisted on taking me out to dinner at the Dock Street Pizza Place. She wanted to show off her new look at the main community hangout. Joe was tied up with a city council meeting, so she knew I didn't have a date. It would have been cruel not to go along.

The result was that by the time I got home Aunt Nettie had gone to bed.

It wasn't late, but her door was shut and there was no light under it. I banged around in the kitchen for a while, but Aunt Nettie didn't come out.

I went to bed and read a book. I read quite a long while, actually. It seemed that every time I turned out the light I heard the *thunk* of that rifle bullet hitting Aubrey's SUV.

Once I got off to sleep, I must have slept soundly. Anyway, when Aunt Nettie came to my room, she had to shake me before I was able to wake up.

"Lee. Lee!" Her voice was quiet. "There's somebody outside."

I sat up. Suddenly I felt wide awake. "What going on?"

"I heard somebody on the porch, right outside my window."

I got up and grabbed a robe and slippers. Then I went to the bedroom across the hall. I looked out the window over the porch roof, trying to see if someone was in the yard. I couldn't see anybody, and I couldn't hear anybody.

"Something slid across the porch," Aunt Nettie said. "It sounded like sandpaper. But when I looked out, I couldn't see anything."

"Did you turn on the porch light?"

"Well, no. I guess I didn't really want to see anything. Or I didn't want whoever was out there to see anything." She sighed. "Maybe it was an animal."

"A raccoon doing woodworking?" I looked at my watch. Six a.m. Which in Michigan in October means it was still dark as a piece of Aunt Nettie's bitterest chocolate.

The two of us crept down the stairs and into Aunt Nettie's bedroom. I peeked through one curtain, and she peeked through another. At first I saw nothing but blackness. But in a moment my eyes grew slightly accustomed to the dark, and I saw something white. It was definitely larger than a bread box. It was about the size of the big packing box my new computer had come in.

"Somebody's put something on the porch," I whispered. "But I don't think anybody is moving around. Let's turn on the light."

Aunt Nettie and I went into the living room, and she flipped the switch beside the front door to turn on the porch light.

Immediately an ungodly noise cut loose.

It was a dog barking.

# Chapter 10

Once the light was on, both Aunt Nettie and I recognized the big white object on the front porch. It was a pet crate. And we could hardly mistake the barking.

We spoke in unison. "It's Monte!"

We rushed out the front door. I expected to see Aubrey's SUV sitting in the lane. It wasn't. I ran around the corner of the house and looked in the drive. The porch light was bright enough that I could see there was no SUV. Where was Aubrey? Why was Monte there, but not his master?

Apparently Aunt Nettie felt the same way. "Where's Aubrey?" she said.

I came back to the porch. "There's no sign of him. It's strange. I can't imagine Monte without him."

"There's a note taped to the kennel."

Aunt Nettie pulled it off and read it, frowning. Then she handed it to me. It was printed in block letters on a scrap of notebook paper.

"I'll be back in a day or two," I read. "Please look after Monte."

Monte had stopped howling, but he was looking out the window in his kennel. He seemed anxious. A large plastic garbage bag sat on the floor beside the kennel. When I looked inside, I saw Monte's belongings: food, treats, toys, and another thing that seemed to be important at the moment. His leash.

Shivering in the predawn chill—the temperature was in the mid-forties and I was wearing a robe and slippers—I took Monte out of the kennel and fastened the leash to his collar. He snuffled happily around the porch and followed eagerly when I stepped down onto the front walk. I allowed him to water the grass a few minutes. Then Aunt Nettie took the leash and led him into the house. I brought in the sack of puppy gear. Monte investigated the living room, and Aunt Nettie and I stared at each other.

Aunt Nettie shook her head. "Where could Aubrey have gone without Monte?"

"And why would he leave the dog with us? We're both at the shop all day. We can't take him there."

"And why did he leave him on the porch, kennel and all? Even if he came in the middle of the night, I'd have expected him to come to the door. We'd better try to call him."

"It's only six a.m."

"He's at the Peach Street B and B. Sarajane will be up fixing breakfast."

"I'll make coffee. I guess it's morning for us, too."

Sarajane Harding is one of Aunt Nettie's brisk, no-nonsense friends. She runs a bed and breakfast inn with four guest rooms, which she handles all by herself. In decor, her B and B simply drips country. Her hat racks are made from garden trellises, the hall is thick with baskets of dried flowers decorated with calico ribbons, the front porch features a watering trough used as a planter, plaster geese march up the stairs, quilts are used as wall hangings. All this contrasts mightily with Sarajane herself, who is a plump sixty-year-old with straight gray hair she apparently cuts with a bowl. She's one of the most efficient businesswomen I've ever run into.

While I made the coffee and kept an eye on Monte, I eavesdropped on Aunt Nettie's conversation.

"Sarajane? Sorry to bother you. I know you're cooking breakfast. But is Aubrey Armstrong there?"

Aunt Nettie paused. "No, I wouldn't expect him to be down yet. But we thought he must have gone out early."

Another pause. "Would you mind checking his room?"

She listened. "No, I'm sure nothing's wrong. But we woke up to find Monte"—Sarajane apparently broke in, but Aunt Nettie went on quickly—"yes, Monte the dog. He was on my front porch in his crate. And there's a note from Aubrey. He says he's leaving town."

I could hear Sarajane's squawk clearly. "Leaving town!"

"He's coming back! Sarajane! Sarajane!" Aunt Nettie looked at me with consternation. "She dropped the phone."

I laughed. "Well, news that Aubrey is leaving town would certainly get Sarajane to run up and check to see if he's there."

"Oh, dear. I do hope he hasn't done a flit. Hogan was so sure it would be all right."

"Hogan? Chief Jones?"

I wanted to ask more, but Aunt Nettie brushed my question aside. Sarajane was back on the other end of the line.

"His bed hasn't been slept in? Oh, dear. But his things are there?"

She listened again. "The note he left out here said he had to leave Warner Pier for a day or two. But it certainly indicated he intended to come back. I can't imagine him leaving Monte. He really loves that dog."

Sarajane spoke. Aunt Nettie nodded. "Yes. If his clothes and luggage are in the room, it means he intends to come back, Sarajane. But Lee and I don't understand why he left the dog with us." She listened. "All right. I'll wait."

She turned to me. "Sarajane's going to check the parking lot."

"I don't think she'll find Aubrey or his SUV there."

"Neither do I."

I put out the toaster, then looked through Monte's sack until I found his food. "Do you know how often Aubrey feeds him?"

Aunt Nettie shook her head. Then she concentrated on the phone. "Oh? I'm afraid I'm not surprised, Sarajane. But don't worry. I'm sure Aubrey will be back. I'm positive that he wouldn't leave Monte."

She hung up. "Sarajane says she didn't find anything in the guest parking area but a bunch of cigarette butts. Aubrey's SUV is not there."

She tapped her fingers on the telephone. "I guess we'd better tell Hogan about this."

I was surprised. "I don't think we can report someone missing just because he went off and left his dog."

"Oh, but Hogan can put out an all-points bulletin or something for Aubrey. I know he doesn't want to lose track of him."

I didn't even ask Aunt Nettie why the police chief would be interested in Aubrey. All I could think of was Sarajane Harding and the Peach Street B and B. Had Aubrey taken off for good? Was he going to leave Sarajane and other Warner Pier merchants stuck with bills? Had he used stolen or phony credit cards?

I'd been worrying about Aubrey fooling Maia, Aunt Nettie, and Tracy. I hadn't given a thought to his cheating my fellow Warner Pier merchants.

Now I did, and the thought scared me stiff. If my friends and business associates lost money because I'd fooled around trying to let Aunt Nettie down easily, trying to protect Maggie McNutt, it was going to be humiliating. It could even leave me open to some sort of legal problems, I wasn't sure just what. And it could cost me some friends, and I need all of those I can get.

Then Monte came into the kitchen, snuffling around as he investigated his surroundings.

Could Aubrey really have abandoned Monte? It was hard to believe he'd leave the pup with Aunt Nettie and me. We had no fence, and we couldn't take him to TenHuis Chocolade for the day.

I could only hope that Chief Hogan Jones would have some suggestion that would lead to finding Aubrey.

I knelt down and scratched Monte under the chin. This made him flop over onto his back for a tummy rub. I complied.

"Monte," I said. "I wish you'd tell us just where your master has gone. I'm not sure I know how to take care of you."

In the garbage bag I found a red blanket covered with Monte's silky brown hair, and I spread it out in the corner of the dining room. Monte sniffed at it, turned around three times in the traditional manner of dogs, then lay down for a snooze while Aunt Nettie and I sat down at the breakfast table. It was then I realized that, for the first time since I'd talked to Maggie McNutt about Aubrey nearly twenty-four hours earlier, I now had a chance to tell Aunt Nettie what I'd learned about him. I sighed.

"Aunt Nettie, I'm afraid I've got some bad news for you," I said. Then I detailed my fruitless Internet search. "Unless I'm looking for Aubrey under entirely the wrong name, I just don't see how he can be a real movie producer," I said.

Aunt Nettie smiled. "Oh, I know that, Lee."

"You do? Then why—"

"Why did I encourage his attentions? Well, there is a reason, but it's not my secret. But don't worry about my giving him any money."

"I know you're smarter than *that*."

Aunt Nettie spread peach preserves on her toast. "It's refreshing for an old woman—"

"You're not old," I said.

Aunt Nettie ignored me. "—for an old woman to feel that she can still be attractive to a man. And Aubrey is—I guess the word is 'likeable,' Lee. I enjoy being with him, even when I'm reminding myself that every word he says is a lie. He's good company."

"I'll admit that. I'm just afraid you're going to get your feelings hurt."

"I might. But even if I do, Aubrey's been fun. He's jogged me out of my rut."

I made a few more attempts to get Aunt Nettie to tell me what had inspired her to court attention from Aubrey if she knew he was moving under false pretenses, but she didn't answer. So I dropped it. But I felt deeply relieved that she hadn't been fooled by him.

We ended our breakfast conversation by talking about Monte and why we were stuck with him. Neither of us had any fresh ideas.

As she left the table, Aunt Nettie shook her head. "I guess I'll take a shower. We've still got to get the shop open."

"I'll do the dishes and try to think of somebody who can babysit Monte," I said. "I guess some people leave dogs in those portable kennels all day, but I don't think Monte's used to that."

"I guess we should give him some breakfast." Aunt Nettie sounded doubtful. "I wouldn't know how much or how to fix it."

I had a sudden thought. "You know who has always had dogs? Lindy and Tony Herrera. I'll give Lindy a ring and ask her about feeding a half-grown pup."

My idea turned out to be an inspiration. Lindy first told me a pup like Monte would normally be fed morning and night, and she described how to prepare the food I'd found among his belongings. Then she actually offered to let us leave Monte in her fenced backyard for the day.

"What will Pinto say?" I asked cautiously. Pinto is Lindy's ancient mixed-breed dog. The three Herrera kids claim she's named "Pinto" because she's marked with big black and white spots like a pinto pony. She's also nearly as big as a pinto pony. Tony Herrera says she's named for the bean, for reasons Lindy won't let him explain. But Pinto rules Tony and Lindy's backyard with an iron paw.

"Pinto's usually good with pups," Lindy said. "Since all the kids figured out where babies come from we've put her out of the puppy business. But she still has some maternal instinct. I'll be home today. I can keep an eye out."

I'd hung up before I remembered that Lindy had promised to tell me some gossip. I made a mental note to ask about it when I dropped Monte off.

It was nearly nine o'clock when I led Monte out to my van and said, "Kennel," speaking firmly, as Aubrey had. The pup jumped right into his crate, and I felt a thrill of accomplishment. I remembered to give him a dog treat before I shut the door.

I had decided to cart the kennel along, for one thing, because Monte was used to being in it while riding in a car. And for another, Lindy might want to use it if the two dogs had to be separated. I also brought Monte's blanket, treats, food, and some of his toys. When I arrived at Lindy's she looked a bit amazed at all the paraphernalia.

"I promise I'll take it all away this afternoon," I said. "But I don't know what you'll need. I can leave the kennel in the van."

Lindy knelt down and gave Monte a good tummy scratch. "If he and Pinto don't get along, I might use the kennel."

I unloaded the van, then went to the backyard with Lindy to watch as Pinto and Monte got acquainted. Lindy's prediction seemed to be right. Monte frisked around, yapping and barking at the older dog. Pinto took it for a few minutes, then gave one deep woof and put Monte in his place. She lay down regally and watched the pup explore her domain. Since Lindy's backyard had a hedge as well as a fence all around it, up the sides and along the alley, Monte had plenty of nooks and crannies to explore.

Lindy and I sat on the back step. "What did you call me about yesterday?" I asked. "I called back, but I missed you."

"I wondered if you wanted to buy a house."

"Oh, Lindy, has your house deal fallen through?"

"It looks like it. Wouldn't you and Joe be interested? Joe could handle a fixer-upper."

"Joe and I—things are too unsettled between us for us to be buying a house, Lindy. But I thought Ken and Maggie were interested in it."

"We thought we had a deal. But Ken called yesterday. He says they might leave at the end of the year."

"Leave! Did he say why?"

"No. In fact, he was extremely evasive. But we need to find another buyer."

"I hope you don't lose the Vandermeer house."

"So do I. But we can't sign on that until we sell this one."

I went to work then, but the conversation had left me feeling low. Ken and Maggie were thinking of leaving Warner Pier? I guess we'd all known that a drama teacher as talented as Maggie would eventually get the call to a bigger school, but they'd seemed happy in Warner Pier. Could Aubrey Andrews Armstrong be the problem? Was Maggie so sure he'd tell about her scandalous past that she was already assuming she wouldn't get another contract?

I spoke aloud. "If Aubrey comes back alive, I'll kill him."

Yes, it was imperative that we find Aubrey. I was glad to discover that Aunt Nettie was already doing something about this when I got to TenHuis Chocolade. She and Chief Hogan Jones were conferring in the break room.

"I've got the sheriff talking to every gas station in the county, and the state police checking up and down the interstate," Hogan said. "If Armstrong used a credit card, we should be able to figure which way he went."

"But he could have gotten beyond Chicago on less than a tank of gas," I said. "Checking the stations looks like a long shot. Besides, what's to stop him from going anywhere he wants to go? He's not wanted for anything, is he?"

Hogan didn't answer. Instead, Aunt Nettie spoke. "I simply can't believe Aubrey took it on the lam. I mean, he might run away, but he wouldn't leave Monte."

Hogan nodded. "That would look like a definite break in the pattern."

I was mystified. "What pattern?"

Hogan hung his head and kicked a chair, but before he could answer the phone rang. I answered on the break room extension. "Ten-Huis Chocolade."

"Hello, Lee." The voice was unmistakable.

"Hi, Maia. What can I do for you?"

"I was looking for Aubrey. I don't suppose you or Nettie knows where he is."

"No. In fact, we're trying to find him." I quickly sketched our discovery of Monte on the front porch and told her we were completely mystified about where he had gone and why he'd left the dog with us. "Lindy Herrera is dog-sitting today," I said.

"Oh, Lindy has a big yard. That's a good place for Monte."

"Yes, we appreciated Lindy's offer. But if you hear from Aubrey, or if you track him down, we'd sure like to know what's going on."

Chief Jones was nearly out the back door when I hung up. "Wait!" I said. "Have you found out anything about that shot?"

"The one that nearly hit Armstrong? Nope."

"Did you figure out where it came from?"

"Not exactly. The sheriff and I took Aubrey's SUV out there and parked it at what Joe said was the same spot. We tried to figure the angle. All we could tell was that it came from someplace off to the north and up high."

"Up high? Like a tree?"

"Or the second story of a house. Or a telephone pole."

"Is there a two-story house or a telephone pole in the right spot?"

"Hard to say." That was the chief's final word, and I realized it could mean either "I don't know" or "I don't want to tell you." Either way, I didn't find out anything.

Warner Pier was up to its small-town tricks that day. The phone nearly rang off the wall with people wanting to know about Aubrey and Monte. At first I was amazed at how fast word had gotten around, but I soon traced the path the information had followed. Sarajane had apparently told the laundry service deliveryman, because we heard from several more B and Bs. Lindy had told her mother, who told her dad, who's an electrician, and he happened to be working at the Superette that morning. And once the news that Aubrey had left Monte on our porch and gone on some mysterious trip hit the druggist at the Superette's pharmacy, Greg Gossip—I mean, Glossop—we might as well have sent a truck with a loudspeaker blaring the news up and down the streets.

I was kept busy answering the phone and telling people we had no reason to believe that Aubrey wouldn't come back to get Monte. I also assured them that I hadn't heard that the state detectives were unusually interested in Aubrey as a suspect in the killing of Silas Snow. A few of the more curious even came into the shop to ask about it. I gave those a hard sell and managed to get some of them to buy a few chocolates.

The morning had been quite hectic, and I wasn't pleased when, at about twelve thirty, the phone rang yet again. It was an effort to make my voice cheerful when I answered, "TenHuis Chocolade."

"Lee! It's Lindy! You'd better get out here. This pup's sick! The dog got hold of some chocolate!"

# CHOCOLATE CHAT
## GOOD FOR WHAT AILS YOU

Chocolate may well help when you have tummy trouble. Intestinal upsets or even a round of antibiotics can upset the balance of lactase enzymes and bacteria needed to digest milk. This produces a form of lactose intolerance. In one study, researchers at the University of Rhode Island discovered that drinking a cup of milk to which 1½ teaspoons of cocoa had been added helped half of their subjects—all of them lactose intolerant—deal with their problem. (In some people, sadly, chocolate can relax the esophageal sphincter muscle and allow stomach acid to shoot up into the esophagus, resulting in heartburn.)

Chocolate is a good source of minerals, since it contains magnesium, potassium, chromium, and iron, and is commonly used as a sort of home remedy for the blues. This is not just self-indulgence. Chocolate actually contains mood-lifting chemicals such as caffeine and theobromine. Mixed with sugar and fat, it produces chemicals that promote euphoria and calm. Some women use chocolate to fight mild forms of PMS.

Last, in animal experiments, some test subjects reduced their intake of alcohol when they were offered a chocolate drink as an alternative. Chocolate martini, anyone?

# Chapter 11

I squealed to a stop in Lindy's drive, ran around the house, and went in the back gate. Lindy was sitting on the back step, petting Monte. He hadn't rolled over to ask for a tummy rub.

As I watched, he got up and sprinkled the grass. Then he gagged once or twice.

"I called the vet," Lindy said. "He said it doesn't sound as if he got enough to be fatal, but he said maybe we'd better take him in. After all, Monte's a valuable dog."

"What about Pinto? She's awfully valuable to your kids."

"She ate chocolate, too, but she's a bigger dog. It would take more to hurt her."

"How do you know the dogs ate chocolate?"

Lindy held up a plastic sack. In it were several of the silvery paper squares from baking chocolate, the same stuff I buy at the Superette to make brownies. All of them were torn and chewed. There were also a couple of the squares themselves, still wrapped.

"Baking chocolate?" I was amazed. "I'd been thinking some kid walked by and tossed the dogs a bite of his candy bar. That looks as if somebody threw a whole package into the yard."

"That's what I think, too. This was no accident. Someone did it deliberately."

"Did you see anybody?"

"No, the dogs seemed to be getting along all right, so I was in the house, trying to get the washing done. I think whoever tossed the chocolate in came up the back alley, anyway. The hedge would have kept me from seeing anybody."

Lindy called her mother and asked her to be there when the kids got home from school. She said she'd already called Tony to tell him what had happened. Then we loaded both dogs into my van and drove the thirty minutes to Holland, where the nearest veterinarian—the one Lindy took Pinto to—was located. The vet's assistant took both dogs right into the examining rooms and directed Lindy and me to the waiting area.

Lindy had gone to the ladies' room when Chief Jones came in.

"What are you doing here?" I said.

"Tony Herrera called and said his dog had been poisoned. That's a crime. I thought the Warner Pier Police Department ought to look into it. The state police are a little too high-toned to investigate a dog poisoning."

"Why would you think the state police might consider being involved?"

"Ever since Silas Snow was killed, it seems as if all sorts of things are happening to animals and people who were hooked up with Aubrey Andrews Armstrong."

I clutched his arm. "Nothing's happened to Aunt Nettie?"

"What could happen to her?"

"I don't know. You just frightened me."

"No, Nettie's all right. Which is more than I can say for Silas. And Vernon says Mae Ensminger is sick. Of course, I ought to bawl out both you and Nettie for making a lot of tracks in your driveway before she called to tell me Monte had been dumped off on your porch."

"We had to go to work. Why shouldn't we have left tracks in the driveway?"

"If I'd seen the drive before you drove out, it might have helped me figure out how the dog got onto your front porch."

"Is there any question about that? Aubrey obviously drove up, stopped in the drive, got the kennel out of his SUV, and put it on our porch."

"Nettie says she didn't hear a car stop."

"I didn't ask her about that. She said she heard somebody on the porch, and I assumed that a car had driven up."

Hogan shook his head. "When I quizzed her about the details, I realized that wasn't the way it happened. All she heard was something—the kennel, I guess—sliding across the porch. No, apparently somebody walked up to the house from Lake Shore Drive. The guy had to carry the kennel and the dog and that sack of stuff. It must have taken at least two trips."

"I guess Aubrey didn't want to wake us up."

"Maybe so. But I wonder where Aubrey would have gotten a wheelbarrow."

"A wheelbarrow? He used a wheelbarrow?"

"Yep. I managed to find bits and pieces of the tracks of a wheelbarrow coming up your lane from Lake Shore Drive. You can see the single track of the wheel, and I even found the places where the back supports rested on the ground not far from the porch."

"But that's an awfully complicated way to put a kennel with a dog on a front porch. Driving up would be much easier. Why didn't he do that?"

"The obvious reason is that he definitely did not want Nettie to wake up and catch him doing it."

"I know she would have told him we couldn't keep the dog, but still . . . I don't understand. Why would Aubrey be *that* anxious not to be seen? And, like you say, where would he get a wheelbarrow?"

Hogan sat back and looked at me, obviously inviting me to think it over. Gradually the light dawned.

"Hogan," I said. "Are you trying to tell me Aubrey didn't drop Monte on our porch? Somebody else did?"

"I can't be sure just what happened, Lee. But it sure seems possible."

"Have you asked Mae about Aubrey? He came to Warner Pier to see her. It seems as if he wouldn't leave without saying good-bye."

"I talked to Vernon. He said he doesn't know anything about Aubrey. And he says Mae is sick in bed. I didn't get to talk to her."

"I admit Mae acted pretty strange when I saw her yesterday. Maybe she *is* sick. But I don't know what that would have to do with Aubrey taking off."

"If he took off."

I finally saw what Hogan was getting at. "You think something's happened to him."

"I don't know, Lee. But you, Joe, and Nettie all swear somebody shot at him yesterday. And nobody's seen him since late last night. Now it seems somebody has it in for his dog. That's what I'd call suspicious."

Lindy came back then, and Chief Jones took the particulars of when she'd found the sick dogs. She handed over the uneaten chocolate and its silver wrappers. Then the chief went away, leaving my head whirling.

Maybe Aubrey hadn't simply left town. Maybe he was missing. Kidnapped? Killed?

But in my scenario, based on Aubrey's status as the invisible movie producer and on Maggie's description of him as a blackmailer, Aubrey was supposed to be the crook. He should be the leading suspect in the killing of Silas Snow, for example. But now it seemed Aubrey might have become a victim.

How was Aunt Nettie going to react to this?

And what was Maia up to? She had called me earlier, trying to find Aubrey, but now Vernon said she couldn't talk to Chief Jones. I felt sure she was simply hiding behind Vernon. I felt impatient with her; she'd attracted Aubrey to Warner Pier with her silly novel and had drawn all of us into this mess. Now she had gone to bed with a headache. Darn her anyway, I thought. First she dragged Vernon around, treating him like a flunky, then she made him cover for her.

Before I had a chance to tell Lindy what I'd learned about Aubrey, the vet came out and told us we could take Pinto home. I was relieved when he asked to keep Monte overnight. At least the pup was safe there. Maybe Aubrey would even show up to pay the bill.

Lindy loaded Pinto into the van, and we drove back to Warner Pier. I started to tell Lindy what the chief had said, but Pinto headed off any confidences by upchucking on the floor of the backseat, as the vet had said she might, and Lindy became so upset over a mess in someone else's vehicle that I gave up trying to talk to her.

I had to wait around at Lindy's while she insisted on cleaning up Pinto's mess and spraying the van with air freshener. By the time I got away I'd nearly forgotten everything but sick dogs.

I remembered my other concerns, however, when I came to the Peach Street stoplight. I was on the flashing-red side and had to come to a stop and wait for a farm truck to cross on the yellow. That farm truck had ENSMINGER'S ORCHARDS lettered on the door and was driven by Vernon. And it was not headed toward his house. Vernon was not on the way home.

I watched Vernon go on down the street. He parked in front of the hardware store, got out of his truck, and went inside.

If Vernon was at the hardware store, then Maia was probably alone at the farm, and maybe I'd be able to talk to her. I simply had to find out if she knew where Aubrey could be. If nothing else, I couldn't be responsible for Monte if someone was trying to harm him.

I abruptly turned left and headed out of town.

Maia and Vernon's place once again impressed me with the attention that had been paid to the outbuildings, in contrast to the slightly neglected look of the house. I parked in front and walked up on the porch, being careful to make noise. It's not polite to sneak up on anybody who lives out in the country.

I had knocked three times and had nearly given up when I heard a horn honk behind me. I whirled to see a sedan turning into the road. The car was a sedate tan, but it was being driven as if it were a bright red, souped-up sports model. I saw Maia's mop of black hair behind the wheel.

She skidded to a stop on the gravel drive, throwing up a cloud of dust, then jumped out of the car. "Lee! Have you found Aubrey?"

Maia looked awful. Her hair was matted, her makeup was streaked. She wore her usual black pants and shirt, but they looked as if she'd slept in them. She'd left off her clunky jewelry, and instead of her usual black ballet-type slippers, she wore tennis shoes.

She trotted up onto the porch. "Where is he? I must find him!"

"I haven't heard from Aubrey," I said. "I came here hoping you knew something."

"Drat the man! A plague on him!"

A plague on him? Hmmm. "I wondered if he gave you any kind of hint as to where he was going."

"Come in, come in!" Maia pushed past me, opened the unlocked door, and led me inside a living room that was as bedraggled as the outside of the house. She staggered over to a tired-looking plaid couch and sat down. "I went over to the Peach Street B and B to see if he was there."

"Sarajane told Aunt Nettie it looked as if he hadn't come in last night. You know he left Monte with Aunt Nettie and me."

"I heard that—from somebody. Was it you?" Maia's eyes closed. "But you palmed him off on Lindy Herrera."

"Just for the day, Maia. Lindy was keeping him while Aunt Nettie and I were at work. But somebody fed the poor thing chocolate."

Maia licked her lips and gave a giggle. "Chocolate sounds good."

"It's good for people. But it's poison to dogs."

"I know." Her eyes took on a crafty look. "Is Monte dead?"

"Monte? No. The vet says he'll be all right. But I need to tell Aubrey what's happened to him. Are you sure he didn't give you any idea of where he was going? When did you last talk to him?"

Maia got up and paced around the living room. "I haven't seen him or talked to him since Tuesday night, since we all went to dinner at the Warner River Lodge." Her voice took on a singsong quality. "I came home about four. I took a long, soaking bath. I lay down and rested for half an hour. I got dressed. Aubrey and Nettie came around seven, and we went out to dinner. Afterward, they dropped us off. They didn't come in. Vernon and I went straight to bed. Vernon was here all the time."

It was a rather peculiar answer, but none of Maia's comments were making too much sense. I tried a new tack. "Maia, when did you first hear from Aubrey?"

"First?"

"Yes. When did he first call about buying the movie rights to your book? Last week? Last month?"

"Sometime." Maia ran her fingers through her hair, or at least she tried. They got stuck in some of the tangles, and she gave up and simply pulled the fingers loose. "Aubrey called the day before he showed up," she said. "That was Monday. He drove in Tuesday morning. Why does it matter?"

"If I could track down some of his associates, maybe they know how to find him. He must have a secretary." Or he would if he were a genuine movie producer. I left that unspoken.

Maia puffed herself up like a bird on a cold morning. "If he has a secretary, it isn't I," she said.

"I know that."

"Everybody keeps asking me about Aubrey, just as if I was his secretary."

"Everybody?"

Maia made another try at tossing her matted hair. "People."

She flopped back onto the couch. Her getting up and sitting down and pacing back and forth was beginning to make me as nervous as it apparently made her. I decided I was wasting my time. One more question. "Did Aubrey give you an address for his California offices?"

"No!" Maia laughed, but she didn't sound pleased. "Aubrey's a man of mystery. I'm beginning to realize that."

"Thanks for letting me ask you all these questions, Maia. I'll go now." I turned toward the door. But before I could open it I heard footsteps outside. They were approaching swiftly. I opened the door and saw Vernon trotting up the steps.

His face was screwed up. With anger? That wouldn't have surprised me. But when he spoke his voice didn't sound angry. I wasn't sure what emotion it had, but it didn't seem to be anger.

"What are you doing here?"

"I wanted to talk to Maia, but I shouldn't have bothered her."

Vernon came in the front door. "Maia! Where did you go?"

"Just over to the Peach Street B and B, Vernon." There was an undertone of guilt in Maia's voice.

"You should have taken your medicine." Vernon shifted his stare from Maia to me. "Why did you want to talk to her?"

"I'm still trying to find some black gown on Aubrey." Vernon's jaw dropped, and I felt like an idiot. "Background! I mean, I'm trying to find some background about Aubrey."

I went on quickly, determined to change the subject to one that wouldn't make me feel nervous. "By the way, Vernon, I grew up in farming and ranching country, you know, and I want to tell you how impressive your layout is."

"My layout?"

"Ensminger's Orchards. The barns and storage buildings just sparkle. The equipment looks great. The orchards are neat as a pin. How much help do you have?"

I asked a few more questions. This seemed to thaw Vernon. He began to look calm, then even to show a bit of enthusiasm. I tried another question. "Did you grow up on a fruit fly? I mean, farm! Did you grow up on a fruit farm?"

"No, I didn't know a thing about farming before Mae and I got married. Everything I know about orchards I learned from Silas."

"Then his death must have been a double shock to you, Vernon."

He nodded. But he didn't say anything.

I tried to look understanding. "I know. The police inquiry and everything. It's dreadful."

Vernon sighed. "Mae and I have been over it and over it. We came home about four. Mae took a bath, then laid down for a while. I worked on my crop report. Then I took a shower. We got dressed and went out to dinner. Aubrey and Nettie picked us up at seven."

Vernon was answering a question I hadn't asked. And we seemed to be covering old territory. I headed for the door. "I'm sorry I bothered you all. Maia needs to get some rest."

"She will. I'll see to that."

I paused in the doorway and asked one more question.

"As you can tell, I'm not familiar with fruit growing. There's one piece of equipment that's always stumped me. The three-legged ladder. Why is it better than a regular ladder?"

Maia giggled. I stared at her, but Vernon ignored her. "It's really just a stepladder," he said. "It rests against the branches. But the leg keeps the weight of the ladder and the picker off the tree. Besides, the leg can snake through the branches and keep the ladder steady."

Maia shook her tousled head. "Forget the ladder," she said. "I don't want to talk about any ladder."

Vernon and I stared at her. She giggled vigorously. "I'm just a secretary. Maybe an answering machine."

She was repeating the comment she'd made a few minutes earlier. I decided to try for information.

"You mean being asked to take messages for Aubrey? Who asked you to do that?"

"That newspaper guy."

"Chuck O'Riley? What did he want?"

"Nosy. Jus' nosy."

Vernon's face looked as if he'd been kicked. It reminded me that he had sobbed at the funeral home. When I said good-bye, he mumbled an answer. Then he walked out on the porch and watched until I drove off.

I certainly hadn't gotten any real information from Maia. But she had sparked an idea. The more I thought about it, the more I liked it.

As soon as I got to my desk I called Chuck O'Riley.

# Chapter 12

alling Chuck may have been my intent, but life intervened. My
working life, that is. I'd been gone most of the afternoon, but
TenHuis Chocolade had been rocking along. Before I could call anybody I had to go through a pile of messages Aunt Nettie had taken
while I'd been gone. Most of them could wait, but I had to call the
bank, then do an invoice for five pounds of crème de menthe bonbons that would adorn the pillows of the new Gray Gables Conference Center. Aunt Nettie had already boxed them up. I'd deliver them
on my way home.

When I finally called Chuck, he sounded harassed. "You barely
caught me," he said. "This is supposed to be my day off."

"I guess I knew that, Chuck, since the *Gazette* came out today. But
I'll trade you a half pound of TenHuis's best for the answer to a
question."

"What's the question?"

"Have you looked into the background of Aubrey Andrews
Armstrong?"

There was a long silence. Chuck cleared his throat. Then he spoke.
"Why do you ask?"

"I tried to look him up on the Internet, just out of curiosity. And I
couldn't find him there. I wondered if you had better sources."

"I hadn't tried to find out anything about him until he disappeared. I couldn't find out anything on the Internet either. So I called the Michigan Film Office."

"I e-mailed them. The director was out of town."

"She still is, but someone should call me back pretty quick."

"Did Aubrey give you a business card? Or anything in writing?"

"No. Lee, why do you want to know this?"

"I need to find Aubrey. I guess you've heard that he dumped his dog on Aunt Nettie and me."

"I also heard the dog was poisoned. I wasn't going to do the story today, since I can't get it in the paper until next week, but what's the deal on that? A dog poisoner would be worth a story."

That was something I didn't mind talking about. I told Chuck all about it. When I'd finished, he spoke. "What are you going to do about the dog when he's well?"

"I hope Aubrey will be back by then."

"Chief Jones seems to think something has happened to the guy. What do you think?"

"I haven't the slightest idea. I hope Aubrey has taken off on some sort of trip. And I also hope he'll be back soon to take responsibility for Monte. That's why I was asking if you had some contact information for him."

"I interviewed him, of course. Anything I learned about him is in today's *Gazette*, Lee."

I began to wonder if the *Gazette* had information on other topics. "How complete are your files, Chuck?"

"We've got all the back issues. Either bound or on microfilm."

"How about files on people?"

"You mean, like Lee McKinney is named business manager of TenHuis Chocolade? Or Joe Woodyard takes job as city attorney? Yeah, we've got stuff like that."

"Do you let the public look at it?"

"Sure. You're welcome to come by the office and look at our files. But not today. Tomorrow morning. Okay?"

I could hardly ask Chuck to stick around on his day off just to satisfy my curiosity. I agreed to wait until morning. Then I hung up and gave myself a pep talk about getting my own work done. That resolve lasted about ten minutes, until Dolly Jolly appeared in the door of my office.

Her voice boomed. "Lee! I wanted to talk to you before I left!"

I tried not to grimace as I looked up. After all, I was supposed to be running the paycheck and health insurance side of TenHuis Chocolade. I couldn't refuse to speak to employees.

"What can I do for you, Dolly?"

Dolly lowered her voice to a low roar. "It's sort of private."

Oh, gosh. It was something important. Or personal. Did she need time off? Was she sick? I hoped she hadn't already decided she hated the chocolate business; Aunt Nettie was really pleased at how quickly Dolly was catching on.

My uneasiness grew when Dolly came in and closed the door, isolating the two of us in the glass cubicle. I waved her to a chair. "This looks serious, Dolly."

"It's serious to me," she said. Dolly's freckled face was getting red. She didn't go on immediately, but took several deep breaths before she spoke again.

"This Mae Ensminger," she said. "Do you think she's mentally ill?"

I was astonished. Why on earth would Dolly ask such a question? And why would she ask me? Anyway, the answer popped out.

"How the heck would I know?"

Then I felt terrible, because Dolly looked more miserable than ever. She had obviously wanted something more than a smart-aleck answer.

"You've been around her a lot," she said. "You're a smart person. I'm just asking you for your opinion, not for a diagnosis."

"Why do you care?"

Dolly looked down and did something I'd never seen her do before. She mumbled. "I guess I don't really have a good excuse," she said. "I just wondered if insanity runs in her family. Her uncle was kind of odd. And if her real grandfather was like the one in the book . . ."

This was certainly the strangest conversation I'd had in a long time. But it was very serious to Dolly. I didn't want to give her a brush-off, but I didn't know what to answer.

"Dolly, I never heard that any of them were hospitalized for mental problems," I said. "You could ask Aunt Nettie. Or Hazel. They're the natives here."

"I thought I could ask you, and you wouldn't tell anybody I wanted to know."

"I won't mention it if you don't want me to."

"I just wanted your opinion."

Dolly was still keeping her voice very low, an action that forced her to concentrate. She was naturally a loud person, and speaking in a low voice was hard for her. So I knew this was very serious to her. I tried to give her an intelligent assessment of the Snow clan.

"As for Silas," I said, "Judging by the one time I saw him and by what Vernon said about him, I think he was old-fashioned and cantankerous. But that's a long way from being mentally ill. When it comes to Maia—or Mae—I don't understand what's going on at all. But I think that having that book published went to her head. It certainly changed her personality."

"You think she was okay before this book deal came up?"

"She certainly became a different person. Mae was always colorless. She struck me as really dull. Now . . . it's as if she's working to be a caricature of a novelist."

I had an inspiration. "Listen, Dolly, tomorrow morning I'm going to the *Gazette* office to look up some information. Maybe they have some files on Silas. I'm sure they'll have some on Maia. I'll see what I can find out there."

"I'd appreciate it."

Dolly stood up and moved toward the door. I allowed myself to think that our interview was over.

Then she turned around again. "It's just hard to figure how Maia could get so excited over a vanity book."

After dropping that bombshell, she opened the door and left the office.

I had to take a minute to absorb what she'd said. Then I was out the door after her. "Wait a minute, Dolly! Come back in here."

She came. This time I was the one who closed the door and dropped my voice.

"A 'vanity book'? Are you saying Maia *paid* to get her book published?"

"She must have, Lee."

"How do you know?"

"I wrote a regional cookbook, remember? I talked to every publisher in Michigan—and you'd be surprised at how many there are. That particular publisher told me they do only 'author participation' books. I would have had to come up with around five thousand dollars, then do all my own promotion and distribution. I certainly wasn't interested in that. Not when I got a reputable regional press interested in my book. They didn't pay a lot, but it didn't *cost* me money to get it published. And they do the publicity and distribution. I don't have to create my own press kit and ship my own books."

"Then I could write something—*The ABCs of Office Management*, maybe—and they'd publish it?"

"For a price. They'd print any number you wanted. Then they'd send all the books to you, and you'd sell them. Or store them in your garage."

"Which would be a likely fate for any book I'd write."

"When I heard they were publishing Maia's book, I didn't want to say too much about it," Dolly said. "Maia seemed so proud of her book. I figured she didn't know the difference between vanity publishing and regular publishing. I have no reason to embarrass her."

Dolly left, and I sat at my desk mulling over what Dolly had told me. It made Maia's behavior look really peculiar. There's absolutely nothing wrong with paying to publish a book, I told myself. If you wanted to see your family history or all your grandmother's recipes in print, fine. If Maia's life wasn't going to be complete until *Love Leads the Way* was in print, paying to publish it was worth the money. But why was she acting as if the book's publication were the literary event of the year?

I was aroused from my mulling when the telephone rang. It was Joe. "How about dinner?"

I looked at the work piled up on my desk and sighed. "I'd have to eat in a hurry. I was gone most of the afternoon."

"Taking care of Monte?"

"Among other things. I'm going to have to work at least a couple of hours. I guess I'd better grab a sandwich and stick to my desk."

"Maybe both of us could do that, then I'll come by your office about nine. If you're still hungry we'll get a bite. If not—well, I'd like to see you."

We left it at that. I hoped Joe wasn't planning some sort of serious discussion of our future. I hadn't had time to figure out where I stood on that.

So I planned to snag a snack from the break room and work on through. But again, someone else changed my plans. This time it was Aunt Nettie.

She came to my office with a large box in her hands. "Here are the crème de menthe bonbons."

I realized she was holding the five-pound box of crème de menthe bonbons Gray Gables had ordered. "Oh," I said, "I forgot those. I was planning to work late."

"I guess I can take them." Aunt Nettie looked really tired. She had taken the news about Aubrey without flinching, but she'd had a long day. I knew she was dying to get home and get her shoes off.

"Oh, no. I can take them," I said. "No problem."

I told her I was planning to grab a sandwich sometime, so I'd drop off the bonbons when I went out. Then I'd go back to work until Joe picked me up around nine o'clock. She approved and left for home. I closed out the computer, put on my lightweight khaki jacket, and picked up the box of bonbons.

Gray Gables is a historic estate. The High Victorian home on the property was built in the 1890s by a former ambassador and is still owned by his descendants. And like many modern-day people who inherited these snazzy estates, the current owners were having trouble financing the place. Between the taxes for waterfront property in Warner Pier and the staff required to keep up the house and the grounds, the current owners had found themselves in a tight place financially.

So that summer they'd turned the property into a conference center. They took groups of at least twelve and charged a stiff rate. The food, or so I'd heard, was superb. And every night the beds were turned down and a TenHuis crème de menthe bonbon was placed on each pillow.

Usually the owner-operator picked up the bonbons, but today she'd requested that we bring them to her. Five pounds of bonbons was an order well worth driving two miles to deliver. I might even have told myself that a short drive would clear my head, except that I'd already driven all over western Michigan that afternoon, and I had grown more confused than ever.

But the weather had changed a little during the hour and a half I'd been indoors. The wind had switched to the west and had grown stronger. The fall leaves were flying down the street as the wind whipped them off the trees. It wasn't much colder yet, but the change in wind direction meant the temperature was likely to drop into the thirties that night.

Anyway, I put the bonbons on the floor of the van's front seat—I didn't want to take a chance of them sliding off the seat if I should come to a sudden stop—then I drove across the Orchard Street Bridge. The river approaches the lake from the southeast, then makes a sharp right just as it comes to Warner Pier. From there it flows due west into Lake Michigan. Once the road crosses the Orchard Street Bridge, a right-hand turn puts you on Lake Shore Drive, curving around along the lake and leading to houses, including the one Aunt Nettie and I shared. To reach Gray Gables I turned left onto Inland Road, which roughly follows the river. I mention all this because it turned out to be important.

The late afternoon sunlight was slanting through the trees, turning the woods to red, gold, orange, rust, purple, and all the glorious colors of fall. October is beautiful everywhere in the northern hemisphere, I guess, but sometimes it seemed as if western Michigan got more than its share of the goodies. I was quite annoyed to see the wind whipping the leaves around, tearing them off prematurely. I want the leaves to stay colorful as long as possible.

For the most part, however, the woods were still thick. That gave me a few qualms, but I reminded myself to look at the beautiful color, not think about how the trees blocked the view of the horizon.

My feelings about trees are typical of people born and raised on the plains, I guess. On the one hand we value trees highly. In my hometown, for example, a building lot with trees costs more than one without, and in plains cities architects design buildings with an eye to saving mature trees. But for us true plains natives, thick woods are scary, just as open plains are scary to people raised in the woods. Aunt Nettie says she felt "exposed" when she visited my North Texas hometown. There was nothing to hide behind. But I feel spooked when I'm in thick woods; something could be hiding behind those trees.

I felt safe in the van, however, and I poked along, enjoying the lovely colors.

There are lots of houses along Inland Road, but they are farther apart as you get near to Gray Gables. In fact, there were no houses for about a half mile before the road came to the estate, and Inland Road dead-ends at its gate. I felt sure the gate would be open, since the conference center was expecting guests, as well as me.

So I was surprised when I saw the wrought iron gate was closed. I stopped, ready to honk for admittance.

As I did, two things happened, suddenly and almost simultaneously.

First, the van grew hard to steer and pulled to the right.

Before I could say, "Rats! I've got a flat," the second thing happened.

The entire windshield became checked, turning magically into opaque glass.

The sound of the shot didn't register in my tiny brain until a moment later.

# Chapter 13

In real time it may have been only a split second until I reacted, but at the moment it seemed as if I spent an hour sitting there, staring stupidly at that checkered windshield, not moving, just trying to figure out what had made the appearance of the glass change so magically.

That shattered windshield probably saved my life. I would have been a perfect target if the rifleman could have seen me clearly. The checkered windshield must have made me hard to hit.

Anyway, I heard the second shot as I was diving for the floor. Since the van has captain's chairs, the quickest way to get to the floor was to drop between the seats. I somehow wound up in an L shape, with my head and torso on the floor of the backseat and my legs and feet between the front seats.

At first, driving off didn't seem like a viable option. The van's motor was still running, true, but I couldn't see out the front window at all, and I had a flat. I wouldn't be able to drive off very fast.

When the third shot hit, however, driving off began to seem like the smartest way to go.

I pulled my legs into the backseat—not the most graceful trick I've ever performed. I wiggled around on the floor until I faced the front of the van. I reached forward to the gearshift. Yes, I could pull it into reverse. Since I have long arms, I might even manage to push the accelerator with my hand and back up the van. There was no way of telling what I'd back into, but I didn't see how I'd be any worse off.

I did it. I moved the gearshift into reverse, then leaned forward and pushed the accelerator with my hand. The van seemed to shoot backward. I could feel the flat going bump, bump, bump, and another shot clunked into the van. At least I was able to get a fix on this one. It was coming from the left of the van, and it hit the motor or the fender—something in front of me, anyway.

I kept pushing the accelerator, figuring that anyplace else was better than the place I was in. More shots came, some in the roof, some in the hood. And they definitely came from the left and in front. The shooter obviously couldn't see me. He was just firing at the van. Which still left me in a very sticky spot.

I was beginning to wonder if I could drive clear back to town without looking behind me, when the van jolted to a stop and threw me backward. I looked out the rear window and saw trees. The van had angled into the bushes and trees at the side of the road.

Now what? I didn't have time to think about it. I reached for the dash and hit the button that pops the rear deck. Then I scrambled over the seats to get to the rear of the van. The deck's door had opened, but it hadn't popped up very far, since the trees and bushes had stopped it. I was able to push it up until there was a space at the bottom of a foot or eighteen inches.

All I could see outside was bushes, but that looked better than what was inside. I crawled out headfirst, wriggling through the crack and slithering into the bushes like a snake.

I pulled myself along with my elbows, trying to get deeper into the trees and brush and farther away from the road. Behind me I heard a couple more shots hit metal, and I allowed myself to hope that the rifleman thought I was still inside the van.

I soon felt as if I'd crawled a mile, but when I looked back the van was just about fifteen feet away. I crawled harder.

For the first time in my life, I wished the woods were thicker. I didn't dare stand up for fear I'd be clearly visible. Since I had only a general idea of where the gunman was, I didn't know when he might get a glimpse of my khaki jacket and blond hair moving along. He wasn't likely to mistake me for a woodchuck, though I could hope that my jacket looked like fallen leaves. Or maybe it didn't. I rolled over on my back and wriggled out of the jacket. My green, long-sleeved polo shirt would offer better camouflage, at least for the top half of me. I couldn't do anything about my jeans. I pulled a small branch off a bush and stuck it in the clip that held my hair in a clump at the back of my neck, with the leaves over the back of my head. The branch poked my spine, and I must have looked like a fool, but that didn't seem important.

I left the jacket behind and kept crawling. I wouldn't allow myself to look back for what I thought was a long time. I began to wonder if I could stand up and run for it without getting shot. The wind was whipping the tops of the trees around, but they weren't moving so much down on the ground. When I finally peeked over my shoulder, the van was just a white blob through the trees. I'd crawled fifty or sixty feet.

Then I saw movement near the van. I froze, lying motionless with my nose to the ground.

But what if the rifleman was coming into the woods after me? I couldn't stand not to look. I lifted my head and peered toward the van. All I could see was a dark figure moving beside the van. Then I heard a door open.

The rifleman was looking inside the van. This was my chance. I jumped to my feet, losing the branch I'd used to hide my hair. I ran behind a big tree, an evergreen of some kind. Then I stood still, not daring to breathe, hoping that the wind would make all the trees move enough to hide the way my tree was quaking.

I heard a bang, but it wasn't a shot. The van's door had slammed. Apparently the guy with the rifle hadn't seen my dash.

I moved the branches of the evergreen aside, very gently, willing the dark figure not to see the motion. I could make out the van and the figure, but I couldn't see any detail. It was just a blob moving around. But it could easily move toward me, into the woods.

I didn't dare stay where I was.

I looked for another likely hiding place, one farther from the van. Trees and bushes were all I could see in any direction. I picked a likely tree—another nice, thick evergreen—selected a path to it, and skedaddled. I reached it without any shots being fired. I stood still a minute, then picked another tree that looked as if it could hide a six-foot blond. This one was a maple with lots of bushes around its trunk. I ran for that one. I picked another tree. I ran for it. I kept this up for a long time.

For the first time in my life I subscribed to Aunt Nettie's view that trees were for hiding behind. Unfortunately, I was also highly aware of my own view of trees as hiding places for potential enemies.

But I slogged on, seeking out the thickest bushes and trees I could find for what seemed like hours. Finally I decided I needed to assess my situation. I looked at my watch, then crawled under the low branches of an evergreen. I was determined to lie still for five whole minutes and try to see if the rifleman was following me.

I couldn't hear anything except my own panting and the wind high in the trees. Had I escaped? I was shivering; I hoped my shaking wouldn't rustle the dry leaves that covered the forest floor. A picture of a forest popped into my mind—a still forest with one tree shaking like mad. The one I was under.

I was so giddy the picture almost made me laugh. I tried to force myself to lie still. This wasn't hide and seek. It wasn't even paintball. It was life or death. My life. My death.

Still I heard nothing. My panting gradually turned into longer breaths. I lay quietly. I counted to two hundred. It had been long enough for me to check my watch, I decided. Surely the five minutes I'd allotted were up. I lifted my head and looked at my wrist.

That's when I realized the next danger I faced. Because now, under the branches of the evergreen, I couldn't read my watch. It was too dark to make out the time. I wouldn't be able to read it until I'd punched the little button that lit up the face. But I knew what time it was.

It was time to panic.

It was nearly dark. I had no idea which way I had run since I fled from the rifleman. The temperature was dropping. And I'd left my jacket under some bush.

I was beginning to believe I'd gotten away from the rifleman, but I might be in as much danger here as I had been in the van. I was lost in the woods with no flashlight and no jacket. And it was getting dark fast.

I crawled out from under the evergreen and stood up. That was one of the worst moments in my life. Five generations of North Texas ancestors hovered over me, murmuring, "Trees, trees, trees, trees! Trees in every direction. You can't *see* where you're going! You can't *see* the horizon! Nobody's even going to start looking for you until you don't show up for your date with Joe at nine o'clock! You'll be dead by then! They won't find your body until the spring thaw! Animals will gnaw your bones!"

It was all I could do to keep from running off in all directions.

Then a different group of North Texas ancestors began to murmur. "Wait a minute, gal. There may be trees, but east is still east, west is still west, and north and south haven't budged. Dangerous wild animals are scarce in this part of Michigan; this ain't the Upper Peninsula. You might stumble over a skunk or a deer, but they won't eat'cha. You kin git outta this, baby doll."

I took three deep breaths and resolved to start getting out of it while there was at least a glimmer of light coming from the overcast sky.

Speaking of light, that wasn't going to be any help in deciding which way to go. The blankety-blank trees were hiding the sky. I couldn't tell which quadrant was lighter, which way the sun had set.

So I listened. On my left I heard highway noise. That would be the trucks on Interstate 196. On my right I heard Lake Michigan. That cool west wind was whipping the normally placid water into surf. It might not be booming like the Pacific, but it was loud enough to hear.

If the Interstate was on my left, and the lake was on my right, I was facing south. The highway and the lake were usually from a mile to three miles apart. I turned right, toward the lake. If I kept the sound of the highway behind me and walked toward the sound of the surf, I'd be headed due west. I'd eventually hit Lake Shore Drive. The route I'd picked meant I was going to head directly into the wind, but I couldn't help that.

It was getting colder, and the wind cut right through my T-shirt. But I'd be warmer if I kept moving.

I did it. I will say it wasn't easy. Walking through the woods as it gets darker and darker is not fun. But I kept moving toward the sound of the surf.

The terrain in west Michigan isn't hilly. Of course, there were gullies and rises and trees and vines and other stuff I don't want to think about. But I kept moving, with the wind in my face and headed toward the sound of the surf.

Once I fell, slid down a slope, and wound up with my feet in a creek. But it was a sneaker day, so I didn't lose my shoes. I squished up the other side of the creek bank. And when I got to the top, I could hear the lake again. The blessed, beautiful lake. I walked on toward it, placing each foot down carefully to be sure I had a firm place to step before I put any weight on it. A twisted ankle could be fatal.

My teeth were chattering, even before I fell in the creek, and I got colder and colder as I walked. The temptation to step behind a tree and huddle down out of the wind was great. I sure wished I had that khaki jacket I'd abandoned. But that couldn't be helped. I gritted my teeth and kept on walking west. Toward the lake.

The Texas ancestors kept at me. "Come on, baby girl. We fought drought and Comanches and built that little town on the prairie. We didn't do it by giving in. Keep on. One foot in front of the other. Head west. You come from tough stock."

The Dutch side of the family began to lecture me, too. "If you come from tough Texas stock, Susanna Lee, you come from tough Dutch stock, too. Do you think we had it easy? Leaving a civilized country to settle in the wilds? To be drafted into service in the Civil War when we didn't even speak English? To try to be a skilled woodworker in a place where people built their furniture from logs with the bark still on? To face winters as cold as Holland's without a warm house, without a tile stove? We didn't fear the cold. We kept going. Of course you're cold, but you're a healthy young woman. You'll get to Lake Shore Drive before you get pneumonia."

My first ray of hope arrived when I came to a house. I could see its roof—a straight line where everything else was curved. I burst out of the woods and into a yard.

But there were no lights on and when I walked up to it, I saw— actually felt—that the windows were covered with shutters. It was a summer cottage and was closed for the winter.

At least it would have a drive, a driveway or lane I could follow to Lake Shore Drive. But I circled the house, and I couldn't find the drive. It was too dark to see it.

I almost decided to break into the cottage and wait for morning. But the shutters were nailed on tight, and I didn't have as much as a stick to pry them off.

I listened for the surf, faced west, and slogged on. I climbed up rises and slid down the other side. My wet socks squished inside my wet shoes. I kept the wind in my face and listened for the surf.

And finally, I saw a light.

It was off to my left. As quickly as it appeared, it disappeared. Then it reappeared. I realized it was a stationary light; the blowing branches were making it appear and disappear. I turned toward the light.

I took one more fall, stumbling over a fallen branch and landing on my knees. Then the brush thinned out. I stepped onto sand, then onto asphalt. I had reached Lake Shore Drive.

I threw my head back and yelled. Or I tried to yell. The "Yeehaw!" I had thought would be a victory cry came out as a meek little croak. But I was standing on a paved road. If my feet hadn't been so cold, I would have danced.

I stood there, looking across the road and down about fifty yards to a row of Asian-looking lanterns on top of a wall. I had not only reached Lake Shore Drive, I knew where I was. I was about two miles south of Aunt Nettie's house, across from the Hart compound. I even knew who lived there. Timothy Hart. I felt sure he'd let me use his phone.

For the first time, I began to cry. Rescue was within sight.

I limped toward Timothy Hart's house, breathing a prayer. "Please, God, don't let Timothy be drunk."

I didn't think Timothy would be dangerous, drunk or sober, but approaching the house of a drunk in the dark just didn't seem like a good idea. He might have passed out, for one thing.

But I climbed through the gate, and when I looked at Timothy's little farmhouse, I saw a light in the living room and Timothy walked in front of the window. I couldn't run, but I still made pretty good time getting up those front steps and pounding on the door. And Timothy Hart answered the door, white mustache neat as ever, every beautiful white hair in place. He looked every inch the distinguished older gent. And he was sober.

"Lee! What's happened?"

I fell on his neck. "Oh, Timothy, someone tried to kill me and I had to run through the woods! I'm freezing to death! Can I come in and take off my shoes and call for help?"

After Timothy finished gaping, he took care of me like a baby. When my fingers were too stiff to untie my wet shoelaces, he took my shoes off for me. He brought me a blanket and wrapped me up. He gave me hot coffee. I accepted all that, but I drew the line at a hot bath.

"I'll wait until I get home," I said. "Can I use your phone?"

"Of course. You should call the police."

"First I'll call Joe."

Timothy patted my shoulder and handed me the telephone. Joe answered his cell phone on the second ring. I began to pour out the whole story. I was sobbing, but I didn't even know it until Timothy handed me a box of tissues.

Then I realized Joe had been trying to say something. I stopped and let him speak. "Where are you?"

"At Timothy Hart's."

"But you said the rifle shots were fired over by Gray Gables."

"Yes. I ran through the woods."

"Through the woods? That's at least two miles."

"Well, I took my time!" I looked at a grandfather clock in the corner of Timothy's living room. It was nearly seven o'clock. "I was running through the woods for two hours!"

"My god, woman!" Joe took a deep breath. "Have you called the cops?"

"Not yet." I sobbed. "I just wanted to talk to you!"

"Listen, don't move. Don't call anybody. Don't do anything. Stay there. I'll call the chief. Then I'll be there."

I barely had time to use Timothy's bathroom before Joe's truck pulled up outside. I hadn't washed my face; I wanted to look as if I'd had a bad experience. Right that moment I wanted sympathy more than I wanted admiration, and I'm delighted to say that Joe provided it. He had called Aunt Nettie, so she arrived as well, and both of them petted me and gave me all the sympathy I could wish for. I was hugged so hard my ribs were sore for a week. However, neither Chief Hogan Jones nor any of his minions came.

"I thought you were going to call the chief," I said.

"I did," Joe said. "He was in Holland having dinner with Van-Dam. They'll be here in a minute."

I was almost sorry when they did show up, because I had to tell the whole story in an orderly fashion. It took a while to get my thoughts together.

VanDam and Hogan Jones both pressed me on the dark figure I had seen near the van.

"I wish I could tell you something," I said. "It was just a dark figure. Somebody in a hooded jacket or maybe just a sweatshirt. It might not have even been the guy with the rifle. It might have been one of the neighbors over there trying to find out what was going on."

Hogan shook his head. "I don't think so. At least nobody has reported a wrecked or abandoned van over there. It wasn't found until I sent a car over to check."

"I guess my van's a total loss."

Hogan patted my hand. "It may be, Lee. But you're not."

He meant the remark to be comforting, but it sent me into another fit of shivering. I pulled Timothy's blanket tight and turned to Joe for a hug. But the chief motioned, and Joe got up. He, Hogan, and Van-Dam retired to Timothy's kitchen for a conference.

In a moment they came back. Hogan pulled a kitchen chair up close to me, so he could look straight into my face. Joe sat down beside me, and VanDam loomed behind Hogan. I expected Hogan to say, "Here's the plan."

But he didn't. He said, "Okay, Lee. We don't know who fired those shots at you, but it's very likely it was the same person who tried to shoot Aubrey Andrews Armstrong."

"That makes sense. How many mad riflemen can we have in a town the size of Warner Pier?"

"But we know a little more about him now. He's a local."

"A local?"

"At least he has enough local knowledge to know that TenHuis Chocolade furnishes chocolates to Gray Gables. He knew that if he called in an order you'd run right out there."

"He must have even known that I'm usually the one who makes deliveries."

Hogan nodded. "And he knows you got out of that van alive and crawled off into the bushes."

"Right. So?"

"So let's be cagey here. Let's let the bastard think he killed you."

# CHOCOLATE CHAT
## PET PROTECTION

Chocolate can be very dangerous to our household pets.

The culprit is theobromine, one of the chemicals found in chocolate. In small amounts, it can cause vomiting and restlessness in pets. Other symptoms of chocolate poisoning are increased respiration, muscle spasms and seizures. Larger amounts can be fatal.

Pure chocolate—baking chocolate, for example—is the most dangerous. Half an ounce of this might kill a small dog, such as a Chihuahua or a toy poodle, while it might take four ounces to be fatal to a large dog, such as an adult Labrador or a collie.

Cats typically have a lower body weight than dogs, and are consequently at even greater risk of theobromine poisoning.

One unexpected source of theobromine? A type of garden mulch, sold commercially by a number of chains, is made from cocoa bean shells. It's good for plants, but could harm pets, so check the ingredients carefully before you buy.

And remember: chocolate people-treats should *always* be kept away from pets.

# Chapter 14

"Yeah, Lee," Joe said. "Maybe you could just disappear for a few days."

I barely had to think a minute. "That sounds heavenly," I said.

Yes, at first disappearing sounded like a wonderful idea. But I quickly realized it isn't the easiest thing to do.

Sure, we'd all like simply to retire from the world on occasion. No phone calls, no letters, no e-mail. In fact, people have been known to do that. But those people probably weren't planning to come back. My disappearance had to be short-term, and that's a problem. I mean, when you go on vacation, you stop the newspaper, right? If you just disappear, you can't do that. Newspapers and the other routine matters of life pile up.

My very first comment showed I had the wrong idea. "I guess I could work at home for a few days."

The chief shook his head. "Nope. No work."

"No work? But this is our busy season!"

"Yeah, but nobody's going to believe you're dead if you're still turning out work."

Aunt Nettie spoke. "We could manage, Lee. I could tell you what comes up, you could tell me what to do, and I could do it."

This time the chief smiled as he shook his head. "No, Nettie. You'd have to be away from the office as well. You'd be involved in the search for Lee."

"Oh!" Aunt Nettie gave a little gasp. "I guess you're right. It wouldn't be very realistic for me to keep on making chocolates if Lee were missing."

"That's right," VanDam said. "It will have to be a complete masquerade or there's no point."

We worked on the details. Aunt Nettie and I would stay home twenty-four hours a day. She would answer the phone. If people came to the house—"And they will," Chief Jones warned. "The ghouls will gather."—Aunt Nettie couldn't let them in. If she couldn't avoid letting them in, I'd have to hide out. We'd have to leave most of the shades drawn. Aunt Nettie would have to stay away from the shop.

The worst part was I'd have to let my friends believe something terrible had happened to me.

"How about Lindy? I'd have to tell Lindy," I said.

"Nope." The chief's voice was firm. "And the same with the people at the shop. If they know you're all right, someone is sure to let it slip. The only way is just to disappear, Lee. If you can't do that . . . well, we'll have to think of a different plan."

I was confused. "But what's the point of all this? Why do you want the rifleman to think I'm dead?"

Joe answered. "First off, Lee, it's the best way to keep you safe."

"I appreciate that. But couldn't I just go to a motel in Holland or something? Then I could at least do some work."

"That's an alternative we could consider," Chief Jones said. "But I'd like to try the disappearing act for a few days. It will give us an excuse to search the woods around here thoroughly, for example. We can look in people's outbuildings. And you never know when somebody will say the wrong thing, let something slip."

"What about Timothy?" I said.

We all turned to look at him. Timothy Hart was the weak link in all this, of course. Tim is a sweetheart in a lot of ways, but he had spent years in an alcoholic fog. He's not the person I'd pick to share an important secret.

Timothy drew himself up proudly, then assured us he had been dry for nine months.

"I will not say a word to a soul," he said. "I'll stay home from AA."

"We don't want you to do that," Chief Jones said. "Just remember, Tim, that one dropped hint at the Superette could be fatal for Lee."

Timothy promised silence with great solemnity. But the chief's warning left me more scared than I had been since I fell out of the woods onto Lake Shore Drive. Somehow the chief's comment made the whole thing seem real. Until then it had had a dreamlike quality.

When we got back to Aunt Nettie's house, I did insist that I be allowed to phone my parents in Texas, so I could tell them I was really all right before news of my disappearance hit the news media. It turned out that my mother, who's a travel agent, was in Mongolia, so I called my dad in Prairie Creek, Texas.

As soon as he figured out I was alive and not in need of medical attention, he wanted to know about my van. My dad owns a small garage, and he'd found that van and fixed it up for me.

"I haven't seen it," I said. "It's still sitting over there where the guy with the rifle was. But I'm afraid it's in pretty bad shape, judging from the number of shots it took. I know the windshield's gone, and maybe the tires."

"That's easy to fix," he said.

"I'm sure you and a good body man could get it back in tiptop condition, Dad. But I don't think I'll ask you to try. I never want to see that van again."

I teared up and had to hand the phone to Chief Jones then. The chief warned my dad not to speak to any reporters. "A hint that Lee is alive could mean she's not," he said.

By then I was able to talk again, and I took the phone to say good-bye. "Bye-bye, Daddy. Don't worry about me."

"Take care, honey. I'll do my best to act real natural."

There was no reason to believe the rifleman was watching any of us, but the chief and Lieutenant VanDam were determined to make my disappearance look real. For example, the chief, who must have thought of this plan the minute Joe called him in Holland, had first sent a patrolman in an unmarked car to check out my van. Joe got the job of making the official "discovery" that I was missing.

Joe had said good-bye at Timothy Hart's. Later he told me he stopped and picked up a sandwich, trying to act as if that was the reason he'd been roaming around, then went back to his apartment and cleaned up his painting supplies. At nine p.m. he walked across the street and banged on the door of TenHuis Chocolade, giving an imitation of a guy trying to keep a date.

Meanwhile, I got in and out of the shower. That turned out to be a painful process, since my elbows were skinned worse than when I learned to ride a bike the Christmas I was seven. Aunt Nettie smeared them with antibiotic ointment and covered them with gauze. By the time Joe called the house to complain that I had stood him up, I was tucked into bed in a flannel nightie. I listened on the upstairs extension while Aunt Nettie assured him I hadn't come home.

"Oh, dear, Joe. Where can she be? It's not like her to—well, just disappear."

Joe didn't laugh. "She said something about making a delivery after work."

"That wouldn't have taken her long. She was taking some mints out to Gray Gables."

Joe pretended to think that over. "That end of Inland Road can be pretty lonely this time of year with all the summer cottages closed. I'll drive out there and make sure she didn't have car trouble."

Aunt Nettie made me comfort food—a grilled cheese sandwich, a cup of hot chocolate, and two Mexican vanilla truffles ("Light vanilla interior in milk chocolate")—and brought it upstairs on a tray. I turned on my dim bedside lamp and ate it. After I finished, I lay down knowing it would be a half hour or more before anything else happened. Joe had to "discover" my van, call the police, and wait for them to arrive before he could call Aunt Nettie again. I guess I fell asleep. I found out later Aunt Nettie had unplugged the upstairs telephone. I slept through most of the night's excitement. I've always suspected Aunt Nettie of dissolving an antihistamine in my hot chocolate.

Aunt Nettie had the hard role, of course. She had to be up all night, taking calls from the police and acting worried.

The next day was more of the same. I mainly stayed upstairs. Of course, I did have to sneak downstairs to the bathroom now and then, since we only have one. This meant Aunt Nettie had to keep all the downstairs shades pulled. Chief Jones stationed a patrol car in her driveway, ostensibly to keep reporters away, actually to give the two of us warning of visitors.

But the main problem with being a missing person was boredom. By that afternoon I was out of my skull, ready to throw a shoe at the television and all set to trash every book in the house.

I wanted to read the files of the Warner Pier *Gazette*, and I couldn't do that.

I told Joe as much when he came by under the guise of consoling Aunt Nettie.

"I never realized that solitary confinement is cruel and unusual punishment," I said.

"What bothers you the most?"

"I'm *missing* everything! I don't know what's going on."

"The cops are mainly tramping around in the woods," Joe said. "I thought you got enough of that last night."

"I did. But I still want to know what's happening. I had big plans for today."

"Lee, have you been detecting again? Chief Jones said—"

"I wasn't doing anything that any citizen couldn't do. All I'd planned for today was a trip to the *Gazette* office. I was going to look at their files."

"What files?"

"Files on everybody who seemed to be mixed up with Aubrey Andrews Armstrong."

"You mean Maia and Vernon?"

"And Maggie McNutt. And maybe Ken."

"What did they have to do with Armstrong?"

I bit my tongue. I couldn't tell Joe all the details. "Maggie was afraid of him," I said. "She thought he was a crook." I didn't mention seeing the red Volkswagen near the fruit stand just after I found Silas Snow's body.

Joe looked at me and shook his head. "I'll try to find you some new reading material," he said.

But it was Chief Jones who showed up at five p.m. with a large, flat bundle.

Aunt Nettie let him in while I stayed away from the door. He plunked the bundle on the dining room table. "Here, Lee. Joe says you need something to keep you busy."

"What's that?"

"It's five years' worth of bound Warner Pier *Gazette* copies. It wasn't the easiest thing I ever accomplished, but I pulled rank and got them from the library."

I eyed them suspiciously. "You had to pull rank?"

"They're normally not checked out."

"I know. But what do you want me to do with them?"

"Look through them. See what you find out. About Maia. About Vernon." He waved his hand. "Joe said you'd planned to look the *Gazette* files over."

"Yeah, but Chuck was going to let me see his personal files. I figured they'd be clippings, not whole newspapers."

"I'll go by there tomorrow and photocopy everything in Chuck's files. And I'll let you see it. But they're probably not too complete. It would help me if you'd look through these papers."

I gave the chief a short list of people who had been involved with Aubrey Andrews Armstrong or who had showed any interest in him: Maia, Vernon, Maggie and Ken, Silas Snow himself, maybe Chuck O'Riley—it was hard to go much further than that.

"I guess Silas had a hired man," Aunt Nettie said.

The chief nodded. "Yes, his name is Tomas Gonzales."

I wrote that down, but I didn't expect to stumble over it in the Warner Pier *Gazette*. Except for Mayor Mike Herrera and schoolkids, the Hispanic citizens of Warner Pier tend to be invisible.

The whole thing had the air of a make-work project designed to keep Lee busy and out of the hair of law enforcement. I didn't like it. But I'd agreed to the disappearance, so I could hardly say I was too busy to look at five years of old *Gazettes*.

"I'll start after dinner," I said.

"Oh, my!" Aunt Nettie said. "I forgot to tell you, Lee. Hazel and Dolly insisted on cooking dinner for me. Dolly's supposed to bring it out just after five."

"We'll have to hide these *Gazettes*, then," the chief said.

We barely had time to stow the heavy bound volumes upstairs when our police companion in the driveway beeped his horn to warn us someone was coming. I sat in a comfortable chair in the corner of my room, ready to stay quiet. There are no secrets in Aunt Nettie's house; the smallest whisper or the tiniest creak of a bedspring is heard throughout the house.

Of course, that meant I could also hear every word spoken in the living room. I sat down, picked up my book, and cocked an ear for Dolly Jolly's booming tones.

But the voice of the visitor didn't boom. It tinkled. The visitor and

Aunt Nettie had to come right into the living room before I realized who it was. Lindy Herrera.

"This is just unbelievable!" she said. "Who? Who could try to do any harm to Lee?"

She was crying. I felt like such a louse. I nearly got up and went downstairs. But I'd promised the chief that my "disappearance" would last at least two days. I reached for a Kleenex.

Aunt Nettie was sniffling, too. "Lindy, we're not going to lose hope yet. I'm sure this will have a happy ending."

That made Lindy cry harder, of course. I sat there, listening to her grieve and feeling lower than a snake's belly. How did Chief Jones talk me into this? Why did he want me to hide out, anyway? I didn't really have a clear idea.

Lindy only stayed about ten minutes. When she left, Aunt Nettie, still making soothing noises, walked out with her.

I didn't dare peek out the window, but I heard Lindy's car leave, and I heard Aunt Nettie come back in.

She was talking as she came in. I stayed put, afraid that some new visitor had showed up to grieve. But Aunt Nettie wasn't comforting the new visitor. In fact, she was talking rather oddly.

"We'll just put your things in the corner of the dining room," she said. "I'll get you some dinner. Then we'll settle down for a quiet evening."

I heard some shuffling around, but nobody replied. Then Aunt Nettie spoke again. "Oh, all right. If you want me to, I'll scratch your tummy."

# Chapter 15

It was Monte. Lindy had brought the chocolate Labrador puppy back.

Was she insane? How could Aunt Nettie and I take care of a dog? Had Lindy left? Was it safe for me to go down and ask just what was going on?

Aunt Nettie called up the stairs, answering my question. "Lee, you can come down now."

I thudded down to the living room, and Monte greeted me joyfully, running in circles, snuffling at my feet, and barking a welcome. "Monte! I thought you were safe at the vet's!"

"Lindy's vet doesn't board dogs," Aunt Nettie said. "He called her today and said someone would have to pick up Monte. So she did. She was going to keep him at her house, but after the poisoning episode she was afraid to do that. Besides, she and Tony are at work and the kids are at school all day, so there was nobody to look after Monte. She was going to put him in a boarding kennel, but I thought it would be better to have him here."

"Why?"

Aunt Nettie's face screwed up. "Oh, he's such a nice little dog! He needs more attention. Being in a kennel—Lee, you were complaining about being in solitary confinement. Why would we wish that on Monte? After all, we're both here."

"But I can't go outside to walk him."

"It won't hurt me to walk him. Or we'll get the patrolman to help us."

The patrolman's warning horn beeped. Another car was coming. "That must be Dolly with dinner," Aunt Nettie said.

I ran for the stairs. Monte barked and followed me, scrambling up the stairs. I settled myself in my little room with Monte in my lap. If I made a noise, at least Aunt Nettie would have the dog to blame.

A few moments later Dolly's voice boomed beneath me. "No word yet?"

"Not yet, Dolly. I'm considering that good news. How did the day go at the shop?"

"Fine! Fine! We got the Whole Foods order off! Have the police given you any hint of what could have happened to Lee?"

"Not really, Dolly. They say there was no blood in her car. That's a good sign."

I heard a loud creak, and I recognized it as the noise an old wicker rocking chair makes when someone heavy sits in it. I gathered Dolly had sat down. When she spoke again her voice barely boomed. She sounded extremely depressed.

"Nettie, I'm so afraid I could be partly responsible for—for whatever has happened to Lee."

"Whatever do you mean?"

"If I could just be *sure!*"

"Sure of what? Dolly, if you know anything about this attack on Lee, you've got to tell Chief Jones or the state policeman."

"I don't know anything, really! I just suspect!" Listening to Dolly's voice, I could picture the misery on her broad, freckled face. "It seems like the act of a madman. And there's a person around here I feel sure is crazy!"

Aunt Nettie gave an impatient snort. "I could name more than one, Dolly. But whoever lured Lee out to Gray Gables was smart, you know. It wasn't just a random act of violence. He went to a lot of trouble to get her out there—faking a phone call. Putting nails in the road so she'd have a flat. It doesn't seem crazy."

"Crazy like a fox!"

"Maybe so. If you have any specific suspicions we'll call that patrolman who's outside in the driveway. He'll get Chief Jones on the radio and call him back here so you can tell him."

"It's too humiliating!"

"Humiliating!" I could hear the anger in Aunt Nettie's voice. She rarely gets angry, but when she does, look out. She might be half Dolly's size and her voice might be a third the decibel level, but when she's stirred up I'll put my money on Aunt Nettie against a horde of cannibals brandishing spears.

And at that moment Aunt Nettie was definitely stirred up. "Dolly, if you're keeping some knowledge away from the police because you're afraid it will *embarrass* you—well, you're not the woman I thought you were! I won't stand by and let you get away with that! You won't have to wait on the police to get the third degree! I'll give it to you myself!"

"Oh, Nettie, I don't know a thing about Lee!"

"Then what do you know?"

"All I know is what became of Dennis Grundy!"

Dennis Grundy? I couldn't believe I'd heard right. What on earth could Dennis Grundy have to do with some guy shooting at me with a rifle?

I guess Aunt Nettie felt the same way, because she yelled out words that echoed what I was thinking.

"Dennis Grundy! Dennis Grundy? Who cares about Dennis Grundy?"

"Dennis Grundy was murdered!"

"I don't care! He has nothing to do with Lee."

"That's what I'm afraid the police will say!"

Aunt Nettie was silent a moment. She wasn't yelling when she went on. "Dolly, just what do you know about Dennis Grundy? And why do you think it matters?"

There was more sniffling from Dolly. Then she spoke loudly.

"The Snows killed him!"

"What? I thought he ran off with the daughter—Julia."

"No! That's what they let everybody think. But they really killed him."

"Why?"

"Oh, it was like a shotgun wedding that didn't come off, I guess. Julia was pregnant. He wasn't ready to marry her. Somehow he wound up dead."

"What became of Julia?"

"She went to a home for unwed mothers. She was angry with her family! She hated her father! She never went home!"

Finally Aunt Nettie got around to the question I'd been dying to ask. "How do you know all this?"

"Julia Snow was my grandmother!"

Dolly Jolly must have been completely deaf if she didn't hear the gasp I gave. It must have reverberated right through the floor of my bedroom and on through the ceiling of the living room. Dolly was the granddaughter of the heroine of Maia's cornball novel? Dolly was a relative of Silas Snow and of Maia Michaelson? It was hard to believe.

"That's the real reason I came to Warner Pier. I wanted to know more about the Snow family." Dolly gave a gasp louder than mine. "Oh, Nettie! You won't tell Maia!"

"I won't tell anybody, Dolly. But why do you think it has any connection to our current problems?"

"Because there must be a streak of insanity in the Snow family! Maia must be the one who killed Silas. Her own uncle! And now she's attacked Lee. She must be crazy! Maybe I'm crazy, too!"

Aunt Nettie immediately began to concentrate on calming Dolly, assuring the red-haired giantess that she seemed to be perfectly sane.

Dolly gave a brief outline of what had become of Julia Snow. Julia had gone to a home for unwed mothers and had given Dennis Grundy's baby up for adoption. She had moved to Detroit, where she found a job in a bakery. She married a fellow baker and they had a successful business. She had only one other child, Dolly's mother.

Julia had kept quiet about her youthful indiscretions until her last illness five years earlier, during which Dolly had helped nurse her. Then she had rambled on to her granddaughter, giving Dolly a confused account of her early life.

"Gramma was really confused at the end, but she always claimed her family killed Dennis Grundy," Dolly said. "She wasn't always clear about which one had done it. Her father seemed most likely. I always thought she didn't really know. But after she died—well, I thought I'd come over here and find out what kind of people the Snows were. And I think they're all crazy!"

Aunt Nettie continued to assure Dolly that the Snows might be crazy, but Dolly didn't seem to have taken after them. She left after about fifteen minutes, promising that she'd contact Chief Jones.

That fifteen minutes gave me time to think over Dolly's story, and after that brief reflection I didn't think much of it. It was startling to learn that Dolly was a descendant of Julia Snow, who had been a central character in a Warner Pier legend. And even more startling to learn that Julia had claimed that her family killed her lover, Dennis Grundy.

But what could that possibly have to do with the things that had happened that week? Silas Snow had been beaten to death with a shovel behind his own fruit stand. Aubrey Andrews Armstrong had been the target of a rifleman, then had disappeared leaving all his belongings including his cherished pet behind, and becoming himself a suspect in the death of Silas Snow. And then the rifleman had apparently tried to kill me.

I couldn't see any connection between those events and the seduction of a country girl by a small-time gangster seventy-five years earlier.

Dolly's theory seemed to be that Maia was some kind of homicidal maniac. I didn't believe it.

Of course, I couldn't believe Maggie or Ken McNutt or anybody else I knew—including Aubrey Andrews Armstrong—could be guilty, either. The whole situation was unbelievable.

I heard Dolly's Volkswagen bus drive down the lane, and I slowly came downstairs. I found Aunt Nettie in the kitchen, frowning.

"What did you make of all that stuff Dolly was handing out?" I asked.

"You heard?"

"Yes, but I don't really understand."

"I didn't either. I just hope that Dolly goes straight to Chief Jones and doesn't go around town dropping hints. She could put herself in danger."

"True. But I heard her promise to go to the chief. What about Maia—do you think she's a mad killer?"

Aunt Nettie poured a plastic dish of green beans into a saucepan and put it on the stove. "It seems like a silly idea. Of course, I keep thinking of the old Maia, before she was an author." She gestured at the saucepan. "Hazel and Dolly sent green beans, mashed potatoes, and a small pork loin. Everything is in the oven but the green beans. There's certainly plenty for both of us."

"I'll set the table. And after dinner I'll get started on the old *Gazettes.*"

The bound *Gazettes* turned out to be something of a physical challenge. They were hard to read. A bound newspaper, even a tabloid-sized one like the *Gazette,* comes in a big, awkward book filled with smudged type. The best light in Aunt Nettie's house is in the dining room, and I needed to read upstairs, so that I wouldn't have to hastily hide the big books and myself if someone came to the door. But we were trying to keep the upstairs dark, so it would look as if no one was up there. We couldn't set up a bright light there. We finally improvised some window coverings with old army blankets and put up a card table with a good reading lamp in the room across the hall from mine.

Aunt Nettie gave the blankets a final twitch. "There! Good luck."

"I still feel as if I've been given a make-work project to keep me out of trouble."

"I hope it works. You've already been in enough trouble to last a lifetime."

I'd barely opened the first book, however, when Joe showed up. He brought along a long tube. "A gift from the chief," he said.

"And what is it?"

He popped the end off the tube and pulled out a cylinder of paper. "It's a map."

"More research?"

"To help with the newspapers. He's interested in all the neighbors around here. Anybody who could have fired that shot at Armstrong, then escaped on foot."

"But, Joe, even if the rifleman escaped on foot, he could have had a car stashed in any driveway along Lake Shore Drive. There's so much traffic along there no one would have noticed."

"True. But the neighbors have to be investigated."

Joe and I spread the map out on the card table and looked at it. "The chief has marked Dennis Grundy's cottage with an X," Joe said.

"I see it. Where is that in relation to Aunt Nettie's house?"

Joe pointed to it. "Yikes!" I said. "I thought the Grundy cottage was at least a mile south of Aunt Nettie's. But it's lots closer than that."

"More like a half mile," Joe said. "If you go by the back road."

"That means we're a lot closer to Maia and Vernon, too. And to Silas Snow's fruit stand. Since the Grundy cottage is on the Snow place."

"Of course, that's a big farm."

"Yes, but it's near the Haven Road exit, and Aunt Nettie's way north of that. I thought since it was a mile on the Interstate, it must be a mile on Lake Shore Drive."

"Actually, the Interstate curves, so it's all in a sort of horseshoe. The two properties are lots closer by way of Lake Shore Drive. And even closer than that if you cut down this road." He peered closely at the map. "It's named Mary Street. I didn't know it existed."

"I didn't, either," I said. "It's those trees. They get me all confused. I can't tell directions."

Then I remembered how I'd told directions the night before. By ear. Traffic behind me, surf in front. I shuddered. Joe put his arms around me. We stood there awhile, and I had a good cry on Joe's shoulder. He didn't say anything.

Then Aunt Nettie called up the stairs. "I walked the dog, and put him in his crate. Now I'm going to bed! Good night, you two."

I lifted my head. "Good night, Aunt Nettie!"

Joe called out, too. "Good night!" Then he kissed my forehead. "I guess I'd better go."

I put my arms around him. "I don't want you to," I said.

He gave a rueful laugh, but he kept holding me. "With a cop outside in the drive and Aunt Nettie downstairs?"

"I don't care. I want you to stay."

I talked him into it. At least he stayed a long time. When I woke up at four a.m. he was there, but at six he'd gone. He left a note. All it said was, "I love you." That's all it needed to say.

Aunt Nettie and I both got up at our usual times, but we had a leisurely breakfast. She'd just made a second pot of coffee at nine o'clock when our cop companion beeped his horn and Chief Jones's car pulled into the drive. He stopped and talked to the patrol officer who had wasted his time in our driveway. I figured the officer was telling him Joe had stayed nearly all night. I still didn't care.

The chief looked solemn as he came in. "Morning, Nettie. Lee."

Aunt Nettie smiled. "Good morning, Hogan. Do you want a cup of coffee?"

"Maybe. I've just got a minute. But I have to tell you two one bit of news."

The chief was so serious that his comment made my stomach go into a spasm of fear.

Aunt Nettie looked stricken. "What's happened?"

"Nothing, maybe. But we found Aubrey Andrews Armstrong's SUV this morning."

# Chapter 16

"Oh, Hogan! Is he dead?"

"He's still missing, Nettie. He wasn't in the SUV."

I jumped into the conversation. "Where was the SUV?"

"In a creek bed off the road to the winery."

"Then it wasn't in our neighborhood."

The chief screwed up his face. "Depends on how you look at it. Where's that map I sent out?"

Aunt Nettie and I led the chief up to the spare bedroom, where the map was laid out on the bed. We all gathered around it, and the chief pointed with a ballpoint pen. "Here's the Grundy cottage. Here's Silas Snow's fruit stand." The pen swooped. "Here's the Interstate." The pen moved east of the Interstate, then tapped. "And here's where the SUV was found."

"Gee," I said. "When you look at from a bird's angle, the winery road is real close. But if we want to buy a bottle of Lake Michigan Red, we have to go way around because we can't cross the Interstate."

"That's true if you drive. But Jerry Cherry tells me that when he was a kid he used to cross the Interstate through culverts and under bridges."

"Then you think someone who lives here on Lake Shore Drive could have ditched the SUV, then walked home?"

"Sure. Or they could have ditched it and someone picked them up."

I left it to Aunt Nettie to make the next comment.

"You mean Aubrey, don't you? Aubrey could have ditched his own SUV and had some confederate pick him up."

"Anything's possible, Nettie." The chief gestured at me. "Lee's escape through the woods night before last proves that people can roam around this area at will without being seen. If you look at this map, you can see how many houses there are. You'd think Lee wouldn't have been able to walk even a quarter of a mile without falling into somebody's backyard." He tapped the map again. "But here's Gray Gables, and here's the Hart compound. It's more than a mile, and Lee walked it without stumbling into an occupied house."

"I wanted to find one, too," I said.

"You made that expedition through a heavily wooded area, Lee. We retraced your steps with dogs, and you went over some pretty rough terrain. But my point is that people can move around out here without being seen. So finding Armstrong's SUV in a certain spot doesn't incriminate—or clear—anybody. Including Armstrong himself."

Aunt Nettie pressed coffee on the chief, and he took a cup with him as he left. His last instructions were to me. "Good luck with those old *Gazettes*," he said. "Joe said you thought it was make-work. But it needs to be done, and we don't have anybody available to do it. You might find out something that is key to this whole deal." He walked on toward his car, then turned back. "Don't forget to check the land transfers."

So I got dressed and started in on the *Gazettes*, working backward from the most recent issues and referring to the list of names the chief had brought. By lunchtime I knew a lot about our neighbors.

I knew that the Baileys, who lived closest to Aunt Nettie, had gone to the Bahamas last winter and that their son had been promoted to first sergeant in the U.S. Army. I knew about the Bahamas, of course, since I'd picked up their mail. But neither of them had mentioned the son's promotion, and I hadn't read about it earlier. I found out that Silas Snow had sold thirty acres of orchard land to a developer from Grand Rapids. By cross-checking with the map, I figured out that this plot was farther down Lake Shore Drive, nowhere near the Grundy cottage or the fruit stand. I discovered that Chuck O'Riley had come to Warner Pier because he had relatives in the area; he was the nephew of a Mrs. Vanlandingham who owned an antiques shop in Warner Pier.

These discoveries showed the difference between the Warner Pier *Gazette* and a city paper. None of these items would have appeared in the *Dallas Morning News,* or even in the *Grand Rapids Press* or the *Holland Sentinel.* But the *Gazette* would print nearly any news release sent to it, and it loved any type of personal news: college students who made the dean's list, church suppers, club fund-raisers, land transfers. The only two newspapers I ever saw report land sales were the *Gazette* and the *Prairie Creek Press,* back in my Texas hometown, which is about the size of Warner Pier.

I kept on skimming through the *Gazettes.* Ken McNutt, I learned, had taken first prize at an antique car competition, being recognized for the excellent mechanical condition of his red 1959 Volkswagen. The son of the Wilsons, another set of Aunt Nettie's neighbors, had won a scholarship to Perdue. Sally Holton, who lived in a spectacular house right on the lake, had been a hostess for the garden tour of the Warner County League of Garden Clubs. Vernon Ensminger had written an angry letter to the editor, complaining about our state representative's stands on wildlife conservation. "An intelligent policy does not pit hunters against 'tree-huggers,' " he wrote. "No one loves the outdoors and the beauties of nature like hunters. We're the ones who get out to enjoy them and who encourage our families to learn about birds and animals." I knew my dad, also a deer hunter, would endorse his position.

The *Gazette* is just a weekly, of course, and I was able to read at a pretty good rate, once I'd figured out how to recognize a piece contributed by the State Department of Agriculture or by General Motors. Those weren't going to have any local names. And a lot of the articles were already familiar, since I do read the rag, known informally as the "Warner Pier Gaggette," every week.

I got back to early summer when I hit a really interesting article— Chuck's interview with Maia Michaelson, published when her book came out. In it she described her early writing as "a secret vice." She had deliberately kept her ambition to be an author a secret, she had told Chuck. "No one knew of my hidden life but my dear husband, Vernon," she said. "He has been a wonderful help and encouragement to me."

How had she learned to write? "If I have a talent, it's simply a God-given gift," Maia said. "I simply tune in to the eternal. My characters speak to me. Sometimes I feel that I am simply channeling their words, their hopes, and their longings."

Chuck pressed her on how her skills were developed, asking if she had taken writing classes. "Oh, no!" Maia said. "Inspiration can not be regimented! Writing to please a professor would smother the creative impulse."

It made me glad I'm an accountant. We learn our professional skills from people who have already figured out standard ways to perform our required chores. We don't have to start from scratch and teach ourselves—with or without "creative impulse."

But the interview also made me doubt the news Dolly had given me about Maia's publisher. Dolly had been sure that the publishing house did nothing but vanity publications. Maia, however, gave Chuck a whole paragraph about how she had submitted her manuscript to the editor, how she had waited with bated breath, praying that it would be accepted, and how she had greeted the news with ecstasy.

"When I heard from them, I didn't know whether I should laugh or cry," she said. "I danced all around the house!"

That didn't sound as if the editor's acceptance had included a bill for several thousand dollars. Maybe Dolly was wrong.

Maybe that should be checked out. I had Aunt Nettie call the chief. Luckily she had the number of his cell phone. After she handed the phone to me, I quickly sketched Dolly's belief that the publisher of Maia's book did only vanity publishing, contrasting this with Maia's account of selling her book.

"It may not have anything to do with anything," I said, "but it's a little discrepancy, and that's what you said you were interested in."

"Joe's working for me full time," Hogan said. "I'll get him to check it out."

Aunt Nettie again spent the morning answering phone calls from concerned friends. The chief still had a Warner Pier patrolman stationed in the driveway to keep people from approaching the house, but the phone rang and rang. Aunt Nettie brought me a sandwich at noon, and I kept reading. By then I was back more than a year—like I said, once I learned which articles to check, I could go through a *Gazette* pretty fast.

I made sure I looked through the obituaries and checked the names of survivors. The Snows and Ensmingers had faced another family funeral, I learned, when a cousin had died a little more than a year ago. She'd lived at South Haven, but the *Gazette* ran the obituary because she was originally from Warner Pier. Or I guess that was the reason. Tracy Roderick had lost a relative, too—her grandfather. Her mother was listed among the survivors of a "leading Warner County fruit farmer" six months earlier. Tracy herself had been in the paper a lot, because of her class activities. Most students at WPHS were.

Another source of local names, I discovered, was activities of the various planning commissions in the county. I remembered that the Baileys had tried to build a rental unit on their property. The commission said no.

Actually, the two square miles I was studying had come before the township or village planning and zoning bodies fairly often. Property values in the area had skyrocketed in recent years, and developers were trying to buy up property and put in whole additions. Mostly the commissions hadn't agreed to this, though one new addition with about twenty-five lots had been approved. I already knew this; when the wind was from the east, I could hear the dirt-moving equipment from my bedroom.

By then I was two years back, to a time before I moved to Warner Pier. Another developer, I learned from the *Gazettes*, had applied for permission to develop forty acres closer to Aunt Nettie's house. I checked the location, and it was right next to the Grundy cottage. Hmmm, I thought, Silas could have sold another piece of property—just the way he'd sold the one farther south—and made a bundle.

I was surprised when I read that he had opposed the addition. In fact, he'd not only come before the township commission to speak against it, he'd stated that he was refusing an offer from the developer.

"That land's been in my family for more than a hundred years," Silas told the commission. "It's good orchard land. It would be an out-and-out crime to cut down those trees and wreck that farmland. I won't go along with it."

Silas's refusal to sell forced the developer to limit the size of the project, and the commission turned the deal down, saying they didn't want the area developed piecemeal.

This episode seemed weird. Silas hadn't objected to development a mile south. Why had he sabotaged it there? I turned to the map again.

The plot the developer had tried to subdivide was just south of the Grundy cottage. He must have wanted to buy the cottage and the orchard behind it, where the rifleman had hidden and shot at Aubrey.

I gnawed a knuckle and thought about the Grundy cottage. Why wouldn't Silas sell it? He didn't rent it out. He could have torn it down and added the lot to his orchards, but he hadn't done that, either. He just let it sit. That didn't seem like wise use of his resources, but he had the reputation of being a sharp businessman. I wondered idly just what Vernon and Maia would do with it.

Aunt Nettie had been not only answering the phone but also entertaining Monte. Now he came lumbering into the room on his big puppy feet, looking for a little attention from me. I got up, found an old sock, and played tug of war with him for a little bit. When he tired I gave him the sock to chew on, sat down, and ate my leftover from lunch—a mocha pyramid bonbon ("Milky coffee interior in a dark chocolate pyramid").

That chocolate, I remembered, was Maggie McNutt's favorite. I decided to skip ahead in the *Gazettes*, back to the September she and Ken were hired. In a town the size of Warner Pier, new teachers are always profiled. It took me only a few minutes to find the headline: FIVE NEW TEACHERS JOIN WP FACULTY RANKS.

Chuck hadn't been editor in those days, but the story was strictly routine, obviously taken from the résumés of all the new teachers.

Ken, I learned, had received a bachelor's in math from Kalamazoo College, then had gotten a master's in education at the University of Michigan. He'd been a member of the mathematics honorary society and the Young Conservatives. Throughout the first paragraph, his background seemed as nerdy as Ken looked and acted.

Then I came to the second paragraph. "Before attending college," the article said, "McNutt served four years in the U.S. Marine Corps."

The marine corps? I was stunned. Ken looked as if a twenty-mile hike would do him in. How had he managed the marine corps?

The article concluded with a list of Ken's marine corps experiences. He'd served in the artillery section of the marines, and he'd been stationed in the Mideast, as well as several places in the United States. He'd even earned medals.

And one of them was for marksmanship.

Wow. Not only was Ken a much tougher guy than he looked, he was certified as a rifle shot.

Of the people I'd been looking over, two took part in activities involving rifles. Vernon was an avid deer hunter—even writing letters to the editor about the sport—and Ken a former marine who had earned medals for marksmanship.

And Ken had been near the Grundy cottage the afternoon when someone shot at Aubrey.

But my stomach went into two knots. I liked Ken. I didn't want him to be involved in all this mess—Silas's death, Aubrey's disappearance, the attack on me.

I got so excited that I jumped to my feet and paced up and down. This convinced Monte that I was ready to play again. Maybe I was. A little exercise with a rolled-up sock got me calmed down, but it made Monte whimper and head for the back door. Aunt Nettie took him for a walk around the yard, and I went back to my reading. Having learned the scoop on Ken, I was eager to find out about Maggie.

But I didn't learn much more than I already knew. She and I were pretty good friends. In fact, I would have sworn that Maggie's life was an open book. She was ready to talk about anything—her family, her college years, her time in California. I would have thought I knew all there was to know about her.

Then she'd told me about that threat from Aubrey, his warning that he could blackmail her if she told anybody about him. I still hadn't figured that one out.

But the story in the *Gazette* simply recapped things I already knew. Maggie had studied drama at Northwestern. She had worked in California for seven years. She had returned to the University of Michigan to earn her master's degree. Her hobbies were birding, decorating, and baking bread.

While in California, Maggie had worked at the Pasadena Playhouse and had roles in several films. A list of the films followed.

And one of them was a western. I'd seen it. It was about a wagon train of women, left alone by the men of their party, who withstood an Indian attack. It had been a real shoot-'em-up.

Did that mean Maggie had learned to shoot a rifle?

Well, so what? I had fired a twenty-two myself. My Texas cousin, thrilled with the rifle he'd gotten for his sixteenth birthday, had taken me out to show me his prowess at knocking cans off fence posts. He condescendingly gave me a turn. He wasn't a bit pleased when I could destroy tin cans as well as he could.

I paced the bedroom floor again. I liked Ken. I liked Maggie. I considered them close friends. I did not want close friends involved. I wanted the villain to be Aubrey or some unknown cohort he had brought to Warner Pier. I wanted this crime wave to be the fault of outsiders, not hometown folks.

But just after I had found Silas Snow's body, I had almost run into the red Volkswagen with a WPHS sticker in the back window. There was a ninety percent chance that that car had been driven by either Ken or Maggie.

I just had to ask Maggie if she had been out there or not.

I walked into the next room, checked my purse for Maggie's cell phone number, then punched it in. I was so intent on reaching Maggie that someone answered the phone before I remembered I was supposed to be dead.

# Chapter 17

To make things worse, the person who answered the phone was Tracy Roderick.

I made some sound—half snort and half gasp—and hung up.

Whew. That was a narrow escape. Tracy would have recognized my voice after one syllable.

But I did want to talk to Maggie. Did I have to run it through Chief Jones? Or could I simply get Aunt Nettie to summon Maggie and Ken to the house and question them for me? Besides, wasn't it time I was found, safe? Being a missing person was beginning to give me a severe case of cabin fever.

I was still standing there with my hand on the telephone when it rang again. I jumped a mile. After climbing down from the ceiling, I realized I had picked up the receiver, since I had it my hand when I jumped and it was still there when I came down. Luckily, I hadn't made a noise, and I had the presence of mind to keep quiet while Aunt Nettie answered the kitchen phone.

Her voice was cautious. "Hello."

"Oh, Mrs. TenHuis! Have they found Lee?" The voice was Tracy's.

"I don't know anything new, Tracy. I'm sorry."

"I just had the weirdest experience, Mrs. TenHuis. I'm at play rehearsal—"

"At the high school?"

"Yes. I'm at play rehearsal, and I was sitting beside Mrs. McNutt's cell phone, and it just rang. And whoever it was didn't say anything. They just hung up. But it was so weird!"

"Why? It must have been a wrong number."

"I know it's crazy, but . . . you know that little noise Lee makes sometimes? Like when her computer acts up? A kind of a disgusted sniffle?"

"I think I know what you mean, Tracy."

"Whoever called made exactly that noise! Mrs. TenHuis, I just know it *meant* something! You know! I just feel sure it meant Lee's all right!"

I stood there holding the telephone, and I didn't know whether to laugh or cry. I felt awful because I was fooling Tracy, making her worry because she thought I was missing in very suspicious circumstances. At the same time, her gushing conclusions about the "message" my snort had given were hilarious. I covered the receiver and shook all over, trying to stifle my laughter.

Tracy was talking again. "Mrs. TenHuis, I said a prayer for Lee. I just know the Lord will help you find her."

Aunt Nettie's voice was kind. "Tracy, I really appreciate that. You're a lovely young woman, and your prayers are really important."

"Well, Lee really makes working at TenHuis Chocolade fun. And I appreciated her helping me with my hair. But it's just so weird. First Mr. Armstrong disappears. Then Lee. It's as if there's some mal . . . mal . . . mal-violent force at work."

Tracy's spin on "malevolent" made me feel better about my own twisted tongue.

After a few more soothing words from Aunt Nettie, Tracy hung up. I was still standing there with the receiver in my hand when Aunt Nettie also hung up. But I had stopped laughing. I was crying. I just had to be found alive—quick. From the chief's standpoint, my disappearance might be helping solve the case. But it was making all my friends dreadfully unhappy.

And I was just beginning to realize how many friends I had.

I sat down on my unmade bed, found a tissue in the box on the bedside table, wiped my eyes, and blew my nose. I heard Aunt Nettie coming up the stairs, and I didn't even jump up and make the bed. I just left it unmade, the tumbled sheets and blankets clearly showing it had been occupied by two people.

Aunt Nettie poked her head into the room. "Did you hear Tracy?"

"Yes. I feel terrible. We've got to tell Hogan that this disappearance isn't working. It's just too hard on people."

"He's supposed to come by later. We can carry on until then, I guess. Did you call Maggie?"

"Yes. Like an idiot."

"It's lucky you didn't say something, instead of just sniffing."

"I know! Poor Tracy would have known my voice in a minute. She would have thought I was a voice from the beyond and planned a seance."

"Why did you call?"

"I thought of something I wanted to ask Maggie, and I just automatically picked up the phone. I completely forgot I was on the missing list."

"Why did you want to talk to Maggie?"

"About her alibi, I guess."

"Alibi? For what?"

"It doesn't matter. I'll figure another way to approach it. I guess I'd better get back to my *Gazettes*."

"And I'll get back to Monte. I think he wants to go out and play. Again."

Aunt Nettie went back downstairs. For a moment I envied her. It was a beautiful day, though the wind seemed to be turning to the north. At least she got to go outside. I was cooped up in a room with heavy blankets on the windows. And I was itching to talk to Maggie.

I began to make the bed, and I found dark hair on one of the pillows. Which naturally brought me a few fond memories of Joe.

"Joe!" I said aloud. "Joe could call Maggie for me."

There was one catch in that. I couldn't ask Joe to question Maggie without telling him why I thought it would be important to find out if Maggie had been near Silas's fruit stand at the time the old man was killed. I couldn't ask him to question her without revealing that Maggie had a link with Aubrey. And I'd promised Maggie I wouldn't tell anybody—*anybody*—that he was threatening to blackmail her.

The whole thing was a mess, and I'd walked right into it on my own two feet by trying to protect Maggie and Ken.

When Ken had driven by in the red Volkswagen, I could have immediately said, "Gee, I think that's the car I nearly ran into near Silas's fruit stand right after I found his body." If I had, then Hogan Jones could have called Maggie and Ken as a matter of routine and asked if they'd been out near the fruit stand. But if I brought it up now, the chief was going to want to know why I hadn't mentioned it earlier. I didn't want to tell him I hadn't wanted to link Maggie to Aubrey in even a remote way.

"Why?" he'd ask. "Why didn't you tell me you saw that Volkswagen near Silas's fruit stand?"

I'd answer, "Until I saw Ken out at the Grundy cottage in the red VW, I didn't realize that's who I'd seen."

"Why didn't you tell me after you saw Ken in the red Volkswagen?"

"Because right after I saw him, before I had a chance to tell anybody anything, someone took a shot at Aubrey."

"So?"

"Well." I pictured myself fumbling around for an answer. "Because I didn't want you to know there was any link between Maggie and Aubrey."

"And why shouldn't I know that?"

And the only good answer I could have would be, "Because Aubrey was blackmailing her, and that makes it look as if she had a motive for doing him harm."

Maggie did have a motive to wishing Aubrey harm, and therefore Ken did, too. Maybe it was time I let Maggie answer for herself. And let Ken answer for himself. I couldn't imagine what either of them could have had to do with Silas Snow.

In fact, I couldn't picture Maggie doing anything to hurt anyone. But I wasn't so sure about Ken, at least since I discovered he had been a marine. Ken had enough training to know how to kill someone. And I was beginning to suspect Ken might have a lot of hidden depths.

I had boxed myself in. I couldn't avoid telling the chief about Maggie's link to Aubrey, though I didn't have the faintest idea of how that could link to Silas, and a link to Silas seemed to be part of the mix.

I gave up. This was too confusing for me. I was simply going to have to turn it over to Chief Jones. I went downstairs and asked Aunt Nettie to call him.

Her eyes got wide. "What's wrong?"

"I just thought of something I need to tell him." I went back upstairs to my *Gazette*s, feeling glum. I ground my teeth as I heard Aunt Nettie on the telephone, and my heart sank a few minutes later, when I heard a car door slam outside. I heard a low male voice downstairs and I listened for footsteps on the stairs, dreading to see the chief walk through the door of Aunt Nettie's extra bedroom.

But the chief didn't come to the door. Joe did.

I jumped up. "I am really glad to see you!"

He gave me a long kiss before he spoke. "I'm glad to see you, too." He nuzzled my ear. "I sure hated to leave this morning."

"I was sorry you did. I don't think Aunt Nettie would have minded if you'd stayed for breakfast. But that's not why I'm glad to see you. I mean, it's not the only reason."

"That's not very complimentary."

"Sorry. But I've got to talk to Chief Jones, and I guess I need moral support."

"He couldn't come right away, so I told him I'd fill in. What's up."

I sighed and outlined the whole situation. I tried holding back Maggie's admission that Aubrey had some hold over her, but Joe went into his attorney mode and began to cross-examine me.

I tried not to answer. "I don't want to break Maggie's configuration!"

That stopped Joe for a couple of beats, but he figured it out. "Confidence? You don't want to break Maggie's confidence?"

I nodded miserably.

We were sitting face-to-face in the only two chairs in the room. He took me by the upper arms and pretended to shake me. "Don't you realize somebody tried to kill you?"

"Believe me, I realize it! I've got the scratches and bruises to remind me."

"And you're still trying to protect people?"

"Joe, I feel sure Maggie didn't have anything to do with this."

"She probably didn't. But the chief still has to talk to her. If she was out there by Silas Snow's fruit stand—"

"*If* that was her car I nearly ran into."

"What if she saw somebody else's car out there, Lee? We've got to ask her. She might not know a thing. But any little crumb of information could help matters."

"Maybe I could just tell her the whole thing's going to come out, give her a chance to come forward and tell the chief on her own."

Joe thought. I could tell that's what he was doing, because he took the opportunity to gnaw on his thumbnail. He has hands like a boat repairman—all banged up—and he bites his nails. Other than that, he's perfect. Or he would be if he didn't want to get married.

Resisting the temptation to get a nail file and start giving him a manicure, I sat quietly until he spoke again. "Maybe we could talk to Maggie. Or I could, I guess. I could tell her to go see the chief."

"I'd feel so much better about doing it that way, Joe."

We went into my room, and Joe called Maggie's cell phone number. We both put an ear to the phone. This time Maggie answered her own phone. First Joe had to answer questions Maggie had about my disappearance. There was nothing new, he told her.

"Listen, Maggie," Joe said. "There's one other thing. Lee told me that the night she found Silas Snow's body, she saw your car out there by his fruit stand."

"Oh!" Maggie sounded startled. "I didn't know anybody saw me."

"She wasn't sure it was you."

"There's no secret about it now, I guess. I was so worried about Maia getting taken by that fake movie producer. Anyway, I tried to talk to her when we ran into each other in the chocolate shop, but Aubrey Andrews Armstrong"—she spit the words out—"turned up, and I couldn't. So I went out to her house that evening."

She sighed. "I guess Lee told you I had run into him in California."

"She tried not to break any confidences," Joe said.

"Well, I guess my career, and maybe my marriage, are just about shot anyway. But, back to Tuesday. After I left the chocolate shop, I went back to the park to make sure the kids did the cleanup. It took more than an hour to pick up all the dirty paper napkins. But I was still worrying about Maia. So after I left the park, I went to her house to try to warn her about Armstrong."

"How did she take the news?"

"I didn't get to give it to her. Nobody answered the door."

"Oh. But Maia and Vernon's house is east of the Interstate. Why did you go over to the fruit stand?"

"What do you mean?"

"The fruit stand is on the west side of the Interstate. That's where Lee said she saw you."

"But I wasn't there."

"You just said you were at Maia and Vernon's."

"Yes, but I went back to the Interstate—from the east, just the way you'd expect—and I got on it headed north, and I went back to town."

"So you were never on the west side of the Interstate?"

"No." Maggie took a deep breath. "Does this mean that Lee *didn't* see me after all?"

"It might. She said that as she came out of the fruit stand she nearly ran into a red VW."

"A red one! I wasn't driving the red one! I had the new one. The acid green. Ken . . ."

She quit talking, but it was easy to finish her sentence.

It hadn't been Maggie I'd nearly run into as I drove out of the fruit stand. It had been Ken.

She promised to call the chief, and Joe hung up. We looked at each other.

"Why would either Maggie or Ken kill Silas Snow?" I said.

"Guessing by the weapon used—a shovel—it was a crime of passion. If one of them got really mad . . ."

"People don't get that mad at folks they don't know, Joe."

"True. We tend to murder those nearest and dearest to us."

"I hope that's not really true. But you've had a lot more experience with killers." In his previous life as an attorney, Joe had been a public defender. I knew he had defended accused killers.

"That was just a wisecrack, of course, Lee. Most people never have a reason to kill anybody. But anybody could be pushed over the edge, I guess."

"How?"

"It has to be something that they perceive as a real threat—either to their physical being, as killing in self-defense; to their property, like killing a burglar; or to their . . . I guess you could call it self-image. I guess killing your wife's lover would be a twisted form of that. Then there's revenge, getting even with somebody who harmed you or threatened your view of yourself."

"It's hard to fit any of those motives with either Maggie or Ken and Silas Snow. I don't think either of them had ever met Silas. They wouldn't have cared what he thought of them."

"Which probably means that they were out near the fruit stand for perfectly innocent reasons."

We were still mulling over the Ken, Maggie, and Silas relationship—or lack thereof—when the phone rang again. Aunt Nettie caught it downstairs, then called up to tell Joe it was for him.

"Probably Chief Jones," Joe said. He picked up the receiver.

I could hear the rush of profanity three feet away. "You *blankety-blank*! I'm going to come out there and mop the floor with you, you worthless piece of *excrement*! What do you mean? Telling my wife all that trash!"

# CHOCOLATE CHAT
## HALE AND HEART·Y

The good news about chocolate is—it's good for you.

Chocolate contains phenolic chemicals, the same chemicals behind red wine's well-documented ability to fight heart disease. Japanese research indicates that phenolics fight disases such as cancer and heart disease by increasing immune function and suppressing cell-damaging chemicals.

A 1.5-ounce chocolate bar contains as many phenolics as a five-ounce glass of cabernet. As might be expected, dark chocolate contains more phenolics than milk chocolate, and white chocolate contains very low levels.

But watch out! Chocolate may be healthful, but the fats and sugars mixed with it may counteract its value. For example, contrary to folklore, chocolate apparently does not promote tooth decay, higher cholesterol, acne, or hyperactivity. Alas, if you mix chocolate with *sugar*, all these things may result.

As for weighty matters: New products have been introduced over the past few years claiming to offer chocolate in low-sugar, low-fat, and low-carb versions. Just remember to read the labels carefully. "Low-sugar," "low-fat," and "low-carb" products are not always "low calorie."

# Chapter 18

It wasn't Chief Hogan Jones, but I recognized the voice booming out the receiver and bouncing a yard away into my ear. It was Ken Mc-Nutt.

Nothing he said was very original; it was simply so surprising to hear that language and fury coming from the usually mild-mannered Ken. For the first time I *believed* he'd been a marine. Heck, judging from the words he used, I'd have believed he'd sailed with Captain Kidd.

Joe's reaction also surprised me. He didn't say a word. He didn't even seem to resent being cussed out.

He just listened until Ken ran down. When silence finally fell, he said, "Are you mad because I advised Maggie to go to Chief Jones or Lieutenant VanDam and tell one of them she was out near Silas Snow's fruit stand the night he was killed?"

The cursing broke out again. Joe held the phone at arm's length and waggled his eyebrows at me. He still seemed more amused than angry. When Ken again seemed to have run out of things to say, Joe spoke again. "I advise you to go talk to Jones or VanDam, too, Ken."

More swearing. This time the tirade didn't last as long, but it was still loud. Ken ended it with one statement I heard as clear as the call of a wood thrush on a Michigan summer night.

"I'm not going to let anybody hurt Maggie! I'll kill 'em first!"

"Nobody wants to hurt Maggie, Ken. But if she was out near the fruit stand, she may have seen something important."

"She wasn't near the fruit stand! She went to the Ensmingers house. And she didn't even see anybody there!"

For the first time Joe reacted to Ken's tirade. He snapped out an answer. "What did you say?"

"I said Maggie knows nothing about Silas Snow's death."

"No! No, you said—" Joe broke off. "Listen, Ken, this is vitally important. The fact that Maggie *didn't* see anybody. Has she told anybody else that?"

For the first time Ken spoke in an ordinary tone of voice. "What do you mean? She told you a few minutes ago."

"Yeah, and I didn't catch the importance of it until you repeated it. Maggie may be in danger because of what she *didn't* see. You've got to get her to a safe place."

"A safe place?" Ken sounded dazed.

"Yes. Are you at the school?"

"No. I'm at home. Maggie's at the school. She told me the number you called from."

"Call her and tell her to stay there. Go get her. Put Maggie on the floor of the backseat. Take her straight to the police station, around at the back. Make her run from the car to the station. Ask for VanDam. And stay there until you see him. Don't let her sit near a window."

There was a long silence. "Joe, I know I lost my temper. But you don't need to get even with me with some elaborate leg pull."

"Ken, this is no joke! Maggie could be in real danger. If you don't want to drive her to the station, I'll call VanDam and ask him to pick her up. Call her and tell her to stay away from windows until he gets there."

"No! No, I'll take her. But, Joe, if you're kidding . . ."

"I am not kidding, Ken. This is exactly the piece of evidence Van-Dam and Hogan Jones have been looking for."

I was full of questions, of course, but Joe shook his head. He waved his hand at me, then punched numbers into the phone.

"Hogan," he said. "I just found out something." He quickly told the chief what Maggie had said. "I told Ken to get her to the station as fast as he can," he said. "You may be able to get enough for a warrant."

He gave a few more grunts of the "uh-huh" and "uh-uh" variety, then he hung up.

"I'd better get down to the station, meet Ken and Maggie," he said.

"Joe! What's going on?"

"I gotta go. You know enough to figure it out."

I followed him downstairs, still asking questions. Joe wasn't talking. He charged the back door, but Aunt Nettie and I wouldn't let him open it until we told him we couldn't take much more of my "disappearance."

"It's just too hard on people," I said. "My friends call up crying, and I feel like a louse."

Joe smiled. "I'll tell the chief. I think Maggie's evidence will allow him to bring in the killer. Maybe you can be found alive this evening."

He moved toward the door, then turned back. "I forgot to tell you one thing. I called the publisher of Maia's book."

"Oh? Did he pay her for it?"

"Yes and no. It seems that Vernon came to him and told him his wife's big ambition was to see the book in print. Vernon paid to have it published and even threw in an extra thousand so the publishers could offer her a small payment they called an 'advance.' Vernon even offered to pay more to ensure their silence, but the guy claims he didn't take the money."

I discovered I was furious. "That's the meanest thing I ever heard of."

"Meanest?"

"Yes. For Vernon to fool her that way, to let her think a publisher really wanted that awful book. It's a terrible thing to do."

"But if she really wanted to see it in print . . ."

I shook my head, but Aunt Nettie was the one who answered. "No, Joe. Vernon's motive might be good, but he fooled her. He wasn't honest. This has got to be kept secret. Not one of us can tell a soul. Not a soul. If the word gets out, Maia will be humiliated."

"I promise I won't tell anybody but Hogan. And I promise I'll never lie to either of you. Though I'm not smart enough to make either of you look foolish."

"I do a pretty good job of that for myself," I said.

Joe laughed, then gave me a kiss on the mouth and Aunt Nettie one on the cheek. He went out the kitchen door. Monte tried to go with him, but I caught him and kept him inside. Monte stood on his hind legs, scratching at the screen and whining as Joe drove away, traveling much faster than he usually did. He really seemed eager to meet Ken and Maggie. I still didn't understand why.

I looked after his truck. "I heard Maggie's story, too," I said. "I don't see anything to base an arrest on."

"What did she say?"

I repeated the story to Aunt Nettie.

"I don't see any special significance in it, either." Aunt Nettie sighed and gestured toward Monte, who was still scratching at the screen. "Monte's going to tear that screen up. I guess I'd better take him out again."

"I'll take a turn."

"No, Lee! You can't be seen."

"I won't be seen. I've been studying that map Hogan brought out. I can find a deserted road to walk on."

"You could skulk in the bushes, I guess, but somebody might come along."

"According to the map, I can go along the Baileys' drive and cut across to the Sheridans' cottage. Behind them I hit Mary Street, and that parallels Lake Shore Drive and goes clear down to One Hundred Eightieth Street. Every house on it is marked 'summer cottage.' There won't be a soul there."

"And that policeman sitting in our drive? What's he going to do when you stroll past him?"

"He's just here to keep reporters from coming in and asking rude questions. We're not prisoners."

She frowned, but I carried the day. After all, I wasn't confined to the house because I was safer there. As long as the rifleman thought I was dead in the woods, I was safe wherever I was. No, I had hidden out for nearly forty-eight hours so that Hogan Jones and VanDam could trick the killer of Silas Snow.

The wind was still blowing and the temperature was in the fifties, so I got a jacket. By then Monte was jumping around madly, realizing he was going out.

"He does need a longer walk," Aunt Nettie said. "I just took him around in the yard, since I had to stay within earshot of the telephone." She frowned. "Do you want me to come along? I don't want you to be nervous."

"Nervous about being in the woods? I may be, but I think it's better if I go out there and face the trees. It's a case of getting back on the horse that threw you."

"Be sure to come home before dark."

"It won't be dark for a couple of hours. I'm not going that far."

Monte and I started off. I didn't deliberately elude the cop in the driveway; I just happened to go out the back way, along the path to the Baileys' house, and he just happened not to see me.

Monte was a happy puppy. I tried telling him, "Walk," in a firm voice, but he knew I was no authority figure. He ran this way and that, yanking at his collar when he came to the end of the leash. I was glad I had the leash; he would have disappeared in a minute without it.

We walked alongside the Baileys' house—they were out of town—then went through their backyard and into the trees behind the house. A little path there led to the cottage of the Sheridans, their neighbors on the other side. That cottage was shuttered securely; the Sheridans wouldn't be back in Warner Pier until after Memorial Day.

Monte and I passed the Sheridans' cottage, then turned down their drive. It curved and exited on a sandy lane, which according to the map was named Mary Street. I had thought that road was just an extension of their drive.

Monte was doing fine, yipping at the occasional bird and sniffing at mysterious aromas he found in the bushes and trees that lined the lane. I acted much the same way, I guess. After the hours I'd spent closed up in an upstairs bedroom with blankets on the windows, it was good to be outside, breathing fresh air and feeling the exhilaration of brisk temperatures. I did my share of frisking around.

I was managing my phobia all right. The woods were threatening, true, but I didn't feel panicky. I felt liberated. Monte and I didn't hurry, we just strolled down that sand lane. Our easy pace allowed me to mull over Maggie's story as I went.

Gradually our surroundings changed. The woods on the left-hand side of the road cleared out. I could see a little sky on that side. We walked on, and the trees cleared more. We passed one final elm, and Monte and I found ourselves in an apple orchard—lots of short trees, but with plenty of space between them. I could see the sky.

I stopped and looked around. The elm I'd just passed, the apples— I was sure they were McIntosh. The scene was definitely familiar.

I spoke out loud. "Monte, this is Silas Snow's orchard. That elm is the one where the fruit ladder was propped. These are the apple trees Joe and I walked around to look at." I turned toward the west. "The Grundy cottage is beyond those bushes."

Monte cocked an ear at me, then scuttled ahead, trying to turn down the lane toward Lake Shore Drive, the lane Ken had come down in the red Volkswagen. I followed his tugging, and in a minute I saw the weather-beaten white siding of the cottage. We circled the little house as Monte snuffled around in the high weeds. When we got to the front porch, I sat down on the step, allowing Monte to scamper around at the end of his leash.

It was quiet, except for the wind in the trees. I could hear the lake surf, though it was much fainter than it had been the day I ran through the woods. Occasionally a bird called. Monte even sat still for a few minutes. It was the perfect place to continue mulling over Maggie's story. After all, Joe has said I could figure out what she *hadn't* seen that was so significant.

So I mulled. I began with the uncharacteristic reaction Ken had displayed when Joe urged Maggie to go to the police and tell them she had been near the fruit stand the night Silas Snow had been killed. Even though I had heard Ken's fury broadcasting through my very own telephone, it was hard to believe. What had caused him to go . . . well, berserk? And what had he said? "If anybody tries to hurt Maggie, I'll kill 'em."

Of course, Ken didn't mean it, I assured myself. When Joe had listed off common motives for homicides, he hadn't listed that: protecting a loved one. Or would it be classified as part of a motive Joe had listed: protecting one's property?

But whatever his motivation, Ken had declared that he would kill to protect Maggie. How did that make her feel? Treasured? Or threatened?

Would Joe kill to protect me? Did I want him to? On the other hand, would I kill to protect Joe? I'd once tried to hit someone I thought was threatening him. Did that count?

Did all devoted married couples feel that way? Would Uncle Phil have killed to protect Aunt Nettie? Would Vernon kill to protect Maia?

I reminded myself that Vernon had spent several thousand dollars to make Maia's dearest wish come true, getting her novel into print. I might feel he'd been misguided, but he'd wanted to please her. Would he do more? Would he actually harm someone to protect her? I had no idea. In fact, my speculations were a silly way for me to spend my time.

Time. I held the leash in my hand and leaned back against the porch railing, almost dozing. Time.

The word reverberated out of my subconscious, and suddenly I was wide awake, with my adrenaline surging.

"Time! That's what Maggie's story does." I was so excited I spoke aloud. "She says she went by to try to see Maia after the drama club finished the cleanup at the park. And when she got to Maia and Vernon's, nobody was there!"

Maggie had left TenHuis Chocolade just after three o'clock. She said it took the kids more than an hour to clean up the park. So it would have been after four, but probably before five, when she started for the Ensmingers'. Nobody had answered her knock. But according to Maia and Vernon, they'd both been home at that time, taking showers and resting. They alibied each other.

"Monte," I said. "They lied. They're the two people with the strongest motives to kill Silas Snow, and they both lied about where they were when he was killed."

In my excitement, I had stood up. Monte was still snuffling along the cottage's foundation, checking out the weeds and saplings in case critters had left interesting smells along there. He was nearly to the corner of the cottage, close to the bathroom.

"Come on, Monte. We need to get back to Aunt Nettie's."

I guess I was still thinking about Maggie's destruction of Maia's and Vernon's alibis, because I forgot that Monte was fascinated with the bathroom. On our previous visit he'd tried to crawl under it.

The room sat on cement blocks and was barely attached to the main cottage. The dirt under it looked dark and crumbly. I could understand why Monte wanted to try get under there and practice his digging skills. But I didn't want Monte to carry that dirt back to Aunt Nettie's.

"No, Monte," I said. "Don't go under there!" I moved toward him, ready to pick him up.

But I had allowed the leash to develop some slack, and Monte took advantage of it. Like a flash he was under the bathroom, and a shower of soil came flying out as he began to dig.

"Monte! Stop that!" I tugged at his leash, but Monte wasn't budging. In fact, the dirt stopped flying out, and Monte's tail disappeared. I pulled at the leash again. I didn't want to yank too hard at his collar, but he wasn't taking a hint. I jerked. Still no result. In fact, there was no give to the leash at all. For a horrible moment I thought Monte had slipped his collar.

"Monte!" I dropped to my stomach in the weeds and looked under the bathroom.

To my annoyance I saw that the leash was looped around a cement block that was a central support for the bathroom. To my relief I saw that the other end was still attached to the puppy's collar.

"Monte! You naughty boy! Come out of there."

I was ignored, of course. In fact, unless Monte was a lot smarter than an ordinary dog, he wouldn't be able to figure out how to unwind his leash from the cement block.

I was going to have to crawl under there after him.

"Yuk!" I said. "Monte, I have a notion to leave you there."

That wasn't really an option. So I began to inch my way under, crawling through that nasty-looking dirt I hadn't wanted Monte to track into Aunt Nettie's house.

The bathroom sat between eighteen inches and two feet above the ground, so the crawl wasn't too tight. I had to keep my head down—not hard to remember when I pictured how many spiders were probably spinning webs on the bottom of the bathroom floor. I edged in. My sore elbows reminded me that I'd been doing this same sort of thing forty-eight hours earlier as I crawled through the bushes to get away from the rifleman. Luckily, I was wearing a jacket and some big Band-Aids to protect the scabs.

The bathroom wasn't large. My feet were still sticking out when I reached the cement block Monte had encircled with his leash. I tried to untangle the leash carefully. I didn't want to pull the cement block out of position. Doing that might mean a cast-iron, claw-foot bathtub or something just as heavy would come crashing through the floor and land on my head. So I reached around the block and took hold the leather strap close to Monte, then I tossed my end as far as I could and pulled gently.

In a minute I had all of the leash on one side of the cement block, and I was reeling Monte in, hand over hand, as if he were a fish. I wasn't too careful about not yanking on his collar. I wanted to get hold of him and get out of there.

Monte objected to being hauled out, naturally. He began to yip and pull away, but I said, "Come," firmly—as if that was going to make a difference. But like it or not, he did come. In a moment I was gripping his collar, and he was licking my face.

"Quit, Monte! If I get the giggles we'll never get out of here."

Miraculously, Monte did quit. He quit yapping, and he quit licking. His ears pricked up, and he twisted around, looking at something closer to the foundation of the house.

"What's the matter with you? Is something there?"

If there was something under that bathroom with Monte and me, I didn't want to know what it was. The most likely thing was a skunk. Even a woodchuck or a chipmunk could be bad. I began to scoot backward.

Then I heard the noise that Monte must have heard first.

It was a rapping noise. Regular. Rhythmic. It was not a wild animal noise. It was a human noise.

And six or eight feet away, in the foundation of the Grundy cottage, I saw a thin sliver of light.

# Chapter 19

The next thing I saw, of course, was stars, because I jumped so high that I banged the back of my head on the underside of the bathroom floor.

Meanwhile I was wrestling Monte, who was sure there was something under that bathroom that he should be chewing on. He was alternately yapping and whining, and he definitely did not like being hauled up close to me and gripped. His clumsy puppy feet were still scrabbling madly, and he ignored my repeated shushes.

I could barely hear the tapping.

It was fairly loud. *Tap, tap, tap.* Then, slower. *Tap. Tap. Tap.* Then fast again. *Tap, tap, tap.* At the same time, the sliver of light grew brighter, then dimmer, then brighter again.

I couldn't pretend it was a skunk. There was a cellar of some sort under the Grundy cottage, and somebody was in there.

I tried to muzzle Monte with my hand. "Who's there?" My voice croaked.

"Help!" The answering voice was much louder than I expected. I realized there was an opening in the cellar wall. Probably where there had once been a window. It had been blocked, but there was apparently nothing but a board between me and the person in the cellar. And there was a crack around the outside of the board.

"Who is it?" I repeated the words.

"Help! I've been kidnapped! Get me out!"

At that point Monte went absolutely wild. I don't know if he smelled a familiar smell or recognized a familiar voice. But I'll swear he knew who was in that cellar.

I called out again. "I'll get help! But who are you?"

"It's Aubrey! Aubrey Andrews Armstrong!"

I guess I'd already figured that out. Who else was missing around Warner Pier?

I began to scoot backward, coming out from under the bathroom and taking the protesting Monte with me. Aubrey began to bang on the board again.

"I'll try to get you out!" I yelled. The banging stopped.

I kept scooting until I was out from under the bathroom. My hair was full of spider webs and my clothes were covered with dirt, but I could stand up. I gave a shudder and hoped I wouldn't have to go under anything like that bathroom ever again. Then I began to try to figure out how to get into the cellar.

I made a quick circuit of the house, but couldn't find an entrance. I didn't find another cellar window, or even a former window. If such an opening existed, it was under the little front sleeping porch. That was even closer to the ground than the bathroom, and I definitely wasn't interested in crawling under there.

No, the cellar must be entered only from inside the cottage. I'd have to break into the house.

There was a back door, but no back step or porch; the solid wooden door opened directly onto the grass. And when I examined it, the grass was crushed. Someone had been walking on that grass. Apparently that was the way Aubrey's kidnapper had gone in and out of the cottage.

I tried the door. It was locked, of course. I looked around for a rock or a stick I could use to smash it open.

Monte was driving me crazy, tugging at his leash and barking. I looped his leash around one of the saplings growing in the yard, one far enough from the bathroom that he couldn't crawl under again. I tied the leash securely. Then I felt in my pocket and found a handful of doggy treats I'd brought along. One of them kept him quiet for a moment.

I picked up a dead limb at the back of the yard. I used it to whack at the door a couple of times, but all it did was chip the paint. That wasn't going to work. I'd have to get in through a window. I carried the dead limb around the house, looking for a window that would be easy to climb through, once I either got it open or smashed through the glass.

And as I walked my brain belatedly began to work.

It occurred to me that the guy in the cellar wasn't just any guy. He was Aubrey Andrews Armstrong. Despite his charming personality, Aubrey was a bad guy. He was a crook who had, or so I was convinced, tried to con my Aunt Nettie. He had tried to blackmail Maggie, one of my best friends. He had conned Maia—who might be a foolish woman, but who didn't deserve to be tricked—by telling her he was going to make a movie of her book. He had enticed high school kids like Tracy with visions of movie stardom.

I wasn't afraid of Aubrey, but maybe I should be. After all, he had barely appeared on the scene when Silas Snow was killed. Maybe he *was* involved in that, in spite of his alibi.

True, if Vernon and Maia had lied about being home at the time Silas was killed, it looked as if the two of them were the most likely culprits. But Maia was closely hooked up with Aubrey; he might be her accomplice.

Letting Aubrey out of that cellar might be the dumbest thing I ever did in my life. It might even be the last thing I ever did in my life.

I decided Aubrey could stay in his cellar a little longer. I tossed my dead branch aside. Then I went back to the bathroom, lay down on my stomach, and called out. "Aubrey!"

"Get me out of here!"

"I can't get into the house! I'll have to go for help!"

"No! No! It's nearly five o'clock! He'll be back!"

"Who?"

"Vernon! He locked me down here."

Vernon? I didn't have time to analyze the situation thoroughly, but Vernon was definitely on the list of possibles for Silas's killer.

But why had he kidnapped Aubrey?

I had no idea. Not that Vernon wouldn't make an ideal kidnapper. He was so dependable. Aubrey would trust him, just as I would have. If Vernon came by my house at three a.m. and said, "Let's go for a ride," I'd get right in his pickup. And if Vernon were going to kidnap somebody, the Grundy cottage would be a logical place for him to keep his captive imprisoned. Vernon was in charge of the Snow property, at least for the moment, and he could well be familiar with the cottage and its facilities—such as a cellar none of the rest of us had realized was there. And the Grundy cottage was remote from year-round houses. Unless some of the high school kids decided to go treasure hunting, no one was likely to come by.

Yes, I could picture Vernon as a kidnapper.

Aubrey started banging on the board again.

I yelled. "I'll hurry!"

Then I jumped to my feet, moved to the sapling where I'd tied Monte, and began to loosen his leash.

I was still on my knees when I heard a motor.

It sounded powerful. Could it be a truck? I couldn't see it, but it seemed to be pulling into the Grundy cottage. I froze as the sound stopped. Then I heard a door open. It was right on the other side of the cottage.

It had to be Vernon. He was there to check on Aubrey. And he'd been entering the cottage by its back door, a door that wasn't ten feet from me.

The leash came loose, and I grabbed it. Then I scooped up Monte and ran for the nearest hiding place—under that darn bathroom. I dropped to my stomach and, moving sideways, I scrunched back in among the spiders and dirt.

My life depended on Monte. If he made a noise, Vernon might haul me out, and if Vernon was really a killer, he might then beat my head in.

I pulled the little dog close to me. Then I took another doggy treat from my jacket pocket and gave it to him. I understood the danger, but Monte was only a baby animal. If he barked, yipped, or whined, I'd be killed.

I cuddled him and stroked his chocolate fur, each motion a prayer. Beyond him I saw heavy farmer's boots come around the corner of the cottage. A picnic cooler, the kind with a top that swings open, was placed on the grass. I heard sounds of metal on metal, then the back door of the cottage swung in. A large, strong hand reached down and picked up the cooler. Vernon—I couldn't see his face, but I didn't doubt it was him—went inside.

I gave him a moment, listening to the noises from inside the cottage; then I gave Monte another doggy treat to keep him quiet, and I crawled out from under the bathroom. I got to my feet, scooped the dog up, and tiptoed across the yard, headed for home, telephone, and police.

That was my intention, anyway. But the back door to the cottage was standing open. I hoped that Vernon was down in the cellar with Aubrey, but I didn't dare pass that open door. I stopped and looked through the crack between the door and the jamb.

The door opened into the little kitchen area of the cottage. I could see glimpses of the apartment-sized range, the tiny refrigerator, and the back of the small counter that separated kitchen area from living room. Right in the middle of the kitchen floor was a trapdoor, fastened down with a padlock.

And kneeling on the floor beside it was Vernon.

I nearly died. We weren't three feet apart.

Luckily, Vernon was looking down, fooling with the padlock. I jumped back and stood beside the door, with my back against the wall. If Vernon turned around or put his head out the door . . . well, I might be able to outrun him.

Unless he had his rifle handy.

I decided passing the open door was too risky. I'd have to circle around the house.

I edged to my right, giving Monte another dog yummy, passed the bathroom, and went along the south side of the cottage, keeping as quiet as possible. I reached the corner by the disheveled porch and started to cross in front of the cottage.

Then I saw movement through the trees.

Immediately I jumped back, behind the solid wall of the south side of the cottage. I knelt and peeked around the corner. In that position my head was behind the old rusty cot frame in the corner of the sleeping porch. I hoped I'd be able to see if someone was coming. I squinted my eyes, trying to locate the movement I'd seen.

It wasn't hard. I'd barely poked my head around the corner when the bushes between the cottage and Lake Shore Drive parted.

Maia stepped out.

My first thought was that she must have come to rescue Aubrey. She was such a fan of his. Maybe she had figured out that Vernon was holding him prisoner and had come to let him out.

Then I noticed Maia was holding a rifle across her chest. Maybe she hadn't come to let Aubrey out. Maybe she'd come to kill him.

I'm no expert on firearms, but my father is a deer hunter, and he tried to get me interested in the sport. The rifle Maia was carrying would have been right at home in a Texas deer camp. It had a long barrel. It had a scope. I could see the bolt used to cock it.

Maia was marching along, holding the rifle with its barrel pointed upward, as if she were making a training video on hunting safety. She was smiling a little. Her eyes were fixed. She walked between the cottage and Vernon's truck, which he'd parked in the drive, and disappeared from sight.

Now how was I going to get home? If I went around the back, past the back door, Vernon might look out and see me. If I went around the front, I might run into Maia. If I went through the bushes to get to Lake Shore Drive, I'd be crashing around, and one of them would hear me.

I decided I had to cross in front of the house and peek around the corner. Maybe Maia had followed Vernon to the back door. She'd been marching forward so purposefully that I doubted she'd notice me unless I punched her between the shoulder blades.

So, feeding Monte another treat, I crossed in front of the cottage and peeked around the corner. No Maia. She'd apparently gone around the corner and was behind the house. I started to slip around on the other side of Vernon's truck. I could hide behind it and get to Mary Street.

This would have been a good plan, if there hadn't been a window in the cottage. Somehow I'd forgotten that, and I crossed right in front of it.

It was a miracle that neither of them saw me. But I saw what was going on inside, and I was so startled I stopped in my tracks and looked into the cottage.

I didn't see Maia. What I saw was Vernon. He was kneeling on the kitchen floor, right where he'd been when I saw him a few seconds earlier, but he'd turned to face the door. He was holding his arms up as high as his head. He had his back to me, because he was looking out the back door.

Then I saw the rifle barrel.

It was pointed through the back door. Right at Vernon. Maia was holding her husband at gunpoint.

I couldn't see her, but the cottage was small. I could hear Maia's voice. She was speaking calmly and rationally.

"Don't you see, Vernon? I had to kill Uncle Silas. He was going to lie, to tell everyone that my grandmother—my very own grandmother!—killed Dennis Grundy. I'm so sorry you interfered. Now I'm going to have to kill you."

Maia was going to kill Vernon. And maybe Aubrey.

What could I do?

Before I could figure out the answer to that one, it was too late to think about it. I guess I got so scared I lost muscle control. I didn't faint, scream, or wet my pants. I did something worse.

I dropped Monte.

Barking joyously, he ran for the corner of the cottage, eager to get back under that darn bathroom, where he could dig and yap at his master.

I jumped for the trailing leash, then realized I'd better let the dog go. I needed to get out of there. I probably should have run for Lake Shore Drive, but I was facing toward Mary Street, so I ran that way. As I passed the corner of the cottage, I heard a man's voice, roaring. And I heard a scream.

I looked right, ready to duck a rifle shot—as if I could—and I saw Vernon sprawled on top of Maia. They were struggling for the rifle. Maia still had it, but Vernon was trying to take it away from her. And somehow Monte and his leash were part of the mix.

I didn't consciously change my route, but the next thing I knew I'd joined the fray. I was kicking at Maia's hand. Then I grabbed the butt of the rifle and yanked.

Maia was screaming, Vernon was growling, Monte was barking madly, and, from inside the cellar, Aubrey was yelling for help.

Suddenly the rifle went off. The kick made Maia lose her grip, but I still had hold of the butt. I flew backward and landed on my rear end. But I had the rifle.

Vernon was still trying to pin down Maia. Neither of them seemed to be bleeding, and I didn't think I'd been shot, either.

I scrambled to my feet and looked at the rifle. I fought the impulse to throw it into the bushes.

Instead I yelled. "Stop fighting!" Then I threw back the bolt and cocked the rifle.

That noise got their attention. Both Maia and Vernon stopped moving, though Maia had begun to sob.

"Maia's not the only person with deer hunters in her family," I said. "I know how to use this thing."

Maia sobbed. "But you're dead!" she said. "I tried so hard to kill you. The police said you had disappeared."

"I'm back," I said. "And you'd better not move a muscle."

It took me a few seconds to figure out what I wanted them to do. After all, we were in a deserted spot. Even firing off a rifle was not guaranteed to bring the cops running. I had two prisoners—three if you counted Aubrey. What was I going to do with them? March down the road to Aunt Nettie's? That didn't seem like a sensible idea. Finally I figured out a simple plan.

"Vernon," I said. "Dump Maia down in that cellar with Aubrey."

Both of them were tangled in Monte's leash, so it wasn't easy. Maia fought and screamed, but Vernon finally managed to get her into the cellar. He'd removed any stairs or ladder that had once been there, so he just dropped her over the edge. Then he turned to me. He looked relieved. "That'll keep her safe for the moment."

I still had the rifle pointed at him. "Now you. Into the cellar."

"But, Lee, I didn't kill anybody! I just penned Aubrey up to keep Maia from killing him!"

"I don't care why you did it. Get down there."

He still hesitated, and I spoke again. "If you leave them down there alone, they'll kill each other."

He grimaced, knelt and slid into the cellar feet first. Just before his head disappeared, I spoke again. "Wait! Where's the padlock? And the key?"

"They're on the counter."

Monte had been whining, wanting to go down in the cellar and join his master. Luckily, he was afraid to jump that far. I was able to scoop him up, swing the trapdoor shut, and lock it. I hid the rifle under the porch.

Then I ran for Aunt Nettie's, still holding Monte in my arms.

I pounded along, down the overgrown road that led to Silas's apple orchard. Then I turned onto Mary Street and began to run down the sandy lane. I felt as if I was home free.

Until I rounded a curve, and I collided with a tree trunk.

At least that's what it seemed like at the moment. I ran right into a tall, thin, hard thing that loomed up right in the middle of the road.

The tall thing and I were lying in a heap before I realized I had run headlong into Joe.

I dropped the dog and threw my arms around Joe's neck. "Everyone's gone besieged! I mean, berserk! I locked them up!"

But Joe wasn't listening to me. He was talking. "Lee! Lee! If anyone's done anything to hurt you, I'll kill 'em! I couldn't go on living without you!"

# Chapter 20

Then we spoke—or maybe we yelled incoherently—at the same time. I said, "Where did you come from?" Joe said, "Did you tangle with Maia?"

"I tangled with Maia! With Vernon! And with Aubrey! With every nut on the lakeshore!"

"You found Aubrey? Hogan was sure he was dead."

"He wasn't a minute ago, but he may be now. He's locked in the cellar of the Grundy cottage with Maia and Vernon."

"You're kidding! How did that happen?"

"It was the only way I could think of to make the three of them stay put. What are you doing here?"

"Looking for you. We heard the shot. Nettie's calling the cops."

Then he kissed me. Not passionately. Tenderly. He pulled me really close, which is an awkward thing to do when you're both sitting in the middle of a sandy road and there's a big puppy involved. But he managed it. And when he spoke again, he'd stopped yelling. He whispered. "Lee. If anything happened to you—I just couldn't go on. When I heard that rifle shot, I thought my heart had stopped beating. I didn't see how you could escape that crazy woman with a rifle twice. If you don't marry me, I may . . . I don't know what I'll do."

It was the most romantic thing anybody ever said to me. Joe didn't want to get married. He wanted to marry me.

We might have sat in the dirt, snuggling, for a long time, but Monte decided he needed attention. He wiggled in between us, put his front paws on Joe's shoulders, and began to lick his face. We both laughed, and we were getting to our feet when I heard footsteps, coming fast. It was, of course, Aunt Nettie. She hugged my neck. The tears in her eyes told me how relieved she was to see me alive and unhurt.

"I'll go to the Grundy cottage and wait for the chief," Joe said. "You two go back to the house."

"The rifle's under the bathroom," I said.

"How did it get *there*?"

"I wanted to hide it after I locked everybody in the cellar."

Joe closed his eyes and shook his head. "Let's not go into it. You'll have to make a statement later." Then he kissed me on the cheek. "I'll just have to remember that Texas gals can be pretty fierce. They can face down three villains armed with rifles and come out on top."

He trotted off down the road toward the Grundy cottage. Aunt Nettie and I went back to her house, and I took a shower and washed my hair. It took two washes and three rinses before I felt spider-free.

Aunt Nettie kept stalling about dinner. It was eight o'clock, and I was getting pretty hungry when Joe and Chief Jones showed up, and I realized why she'd been waiting.

The chief came in the dining room, put his hands on his hips, stared at me, and shook his head slowly. "Lee, what are you? Some kind of vigilante? Vernon says you grabbed that rifle away from Maia and threw the two of them down in that cellar without even letting go of the pup."

"Actually, the puppy accomplished it all. He distracted Maia. That let Vernon jump her. Then Monte wound both of them up in his leash. I didn't try to grab the rifle until he had them subdued."

"That's not the way Vernon tells it."

"Maybe Monte and I worked as a team. But is what Maia said true? Did she kill her uncle?"

"She's saying she did," Hogan said.

Aunt Nettie interrupted to insist that Joe and Hogan join us for dinner. It wasn't too hard for her to persuade them; especially when she said she'd hoped they'd come by, so she'd cooked enough for four. "And don't explain anything until I come," she said. "Just make small talk."

Ten minutes later she had a platter of bratwurst and sauerkraut on the table, along with carrot and raisin salad and two kinds of bread from the good bakery. "You'll have to talk and eat at the same time," Aunt Nettie said. "Lee and I have a lot of questions."

I asked the first one. "Hogan, is Maia explaining why she killed Silas Snow?"

"Not very clearly. Something about her grandmother. Since her grandmother's been dead since the 1930s, that's hard to understand."

"Was her grandmother the mother of Julia Snow? Or the wicked stepmother, the one in the book?"

Aunt Nettie answered. "I've been asking the ladies in the shop," she said. "She was the stepmother. Julia's father—I think his name was William Snow—had been left a widower with the one daughter, Julia. I guess he sort of let her grow up on her own. Finally, when Julia was fourteen, he married again. The second wife, Ellen, was only eighteen. Naturally, she and Julia didn't get along. She had a new baby the first year she and William were married. That was Maia's mother. Ellen had another baby the year after Julia ran off. Silas. But her health wasn't good. She went over to Jackson and stayed with relatives while she was pregnant. And she died, or so they said, when Silas was born. Silas and Maia's mother were raised by William's sister."

The chief stopped with his fork in the air. "Did you say, 'Or so they said?' Didn't the ladies in the shop think this second Mrs. Snow really died?"

Aunt Nettie sighed. "Hazel asked her mother, who's way over ninety but sharp as a tack. And she said that the stepmother was sort of nutty. She hadn't mentioned being pregnant again to anybody in the neighborhood. And she left the first baby behind; William's sister came to take care of her. At the time, there was some gossip about the new baby, Silas. Some people thought he looked a lot more like Julia than like the stepmother."

I gasped. "That fits right in with what Dolly told us. Julia told Dolly that 'her family' killed her lover. She blamed her father, I'm sure. But if it had really been her stepmother . . . Well, there's a situation."

Joe shook his head. "If the two women—both of them just teenagers—had been rivals not only in the household, but also for the affections of this gangster-type, they certainly had the makings of a hot situation."

"Darn," I said. "Maybe it *would* make a good movie."

We all thought that over, then Aunt Nettie went on. "Dolly's grandmother, Julia Snow, told Dolly her baby by Dennis Grundy had been adopted. But her father could have arranged to take the baby himself."

Hogan shook his head. "That would make Silas the son of Julia Snow and Dennis Grundy. Hard to believe."

"And who knows what happened to the stepmother, Ellen," I said. "Even if William wasn't willing to turn her in for murder, he may have thrown her out. If he didn't kill Dennis Grundy himself."

"We'll never figure all that out," Hogan said. "It's been too long. But I can see that, if Silas told Maia a story so different from what she'd written—well, she was none too stable to begin with. She might have thought it would ruin the chances that her book would be the basis of a movie. It could well have pushed her over the edge. And she picked up the shovel."

I shuddered. "But how did Vernon get involved?"

"His story is that he found Maia standing over her uncle's body. He got her home, then made her take a long shower. He told her to say that they'd been together at the house from four o'clock until Aubrey and Nettie came to pick them up at seven."

"But Maggie had come by their house."

"Right. Actually, they could have claimed they didn't hear the doorbell for the shower. Or some other reason. We wouldn't have been able to disprove it. But Maia's too nutty to cover up anymore, and Vernon's—well, resigned is the best word, I guess. He did all he could to protect her."

Joe spoke then. "Actually, Vernon claims he was simply trying to keep her from killing anybody else until he could get her committed."

The chief made a growling noise. "Not that that would have kept us from charging her. But he thought it would."

I remembered how Vernon had sobbed after I told him Aubrey was probably a con man. To realize that Maia had killed her uncle because she had a false idea her book was going to be made into a movie would have been hard to take. That raised another question, and I asked it. "Why did Maia try to kill Aubrey?"

"Because Vernon told her it looked like he was a crook. Then he mentioned he'd told Armstrong he could go over to the Grundy cottage. Next thing he knew, or so he claims, Maia had slipped out of the house and her deer rifle was gone. When he heard that somebody had taken a shot at Aubrey, he didn't know just what to do."

"He tried to drug her," I said. Joe and Hogan both stared at me, openmouthed, but Aunt Nettie nodded.

We told them about going out to Ensminger house on a condolence call and finding that Maia was out and Vernon wanted to know why she hadn't taken her medicine. Then, when I went back a day later, Maia was none too coherent. "I guess when Vernon couldn't keep Maia at home, he kidnapped Aubrey to keep him out of her way," I said.

"That's his story, anyway." Hogan shrugged. "I'll leave the charges up to the prosecutors."

Hogan took a big bite of bratwurst, and Aunt Nettie spoke. "But why did Maia try to kill Lee?"

Hogan nodded toward Joe, and Joe took up the tale. "That first time we went to the Grundy cottage, Lee and I walked back into the orchard. We noticed a fruit ladder by a big maple tree. But right about then, you and Aubrey called out that you were ready to go, so we turned around and went back. What Lee and I didn't notice was that Maia was up in that tree."

"What!" I gasped. "And we didn't see her?"

"No, the leaves were thick. But as near as the lab guys can tell from the angle of the shot that hit Aubrey's van, the rifle was fired from up in that tree." Joe gestured with his fork. "Lee, when you went out to the Ensminger place and saw Maia, did you mention that tree?"

"Not that I can remember. I asked Vernon some questions about orchards. Maybe I mentioned ladders. Or something."

"Whatever you said, Maia interpreted it as a threat. She decided to lure you out to the lonely end of Inland Road and take care of the situation."

Aunt Nettie suddenly dabbed at her eyes with her napkin, then left the table. I started to go after her, but Hogan waved me back into my chair.

"Let me," he said. "I've had a lot of experience with tearful ladies."

Joe and I stared at our plates. Then he reached over and squeezed my hand.

"Don't say anything," I said. "You don't want two weeping women on your hands."

He grinned. "Maybe you'd like to know what Ken was doing hanging around Snow's place."

"What?"

"Looking for property. He thought Silas might sell him an acre or so, maybe even the Grundy cottage. He and Maggie had talked about building a house."

"I thought they were interested in buying Lindy and Tony's house and remodeling."

"They were. They are still, I guess."

"But Maggie called Lindy and told her they might be leaving Warner Pier."

"That was when Maggie thought Aubrey was going to tell whatever it is she doesn't want told. She thought she was going to lose her job over it. But she and Ken weren't communicating very well. He got the idea she wanted to build a house from scratch, maybe in a more rural area. So he tried to approach Silas about buying a lot."

"What a mix-up."

Aunt Nettie and Hogan came back to the table then. Apparently Hogan had had the right formula for cheering her up; Aunt Nettie looked pink and smiley.

"Okay," I said. "When is Aubrey going to come and get his dog?"

Joe and Hogan cleared their throats and looked all around the room. Even Aunt Nettie changed her expression from happy to slightly guilty. "Oh, dear," she said. "Hogan, you simply have to tell Lee what's going on."

"Don't tell me," I said. "We're stuck with Monte."

Hogan laughed. "You are for a few days at least. I'm holding Aubrey for Wisconsin authorities."

"What! What did he do?"

"They allege he ran a con in a small town, claiming he was

going to make a movie there and looking for local investors. I got a notice about it a couple of weeks ago on a little e-mail news list I follow."

"So you knew he as a crook the minute he showed up! And you let Aunt Nettie get involved with him!"

Aunt Nettie giggled. "Actually, I was encouraged to get involved with him."

"Hogan!" I was scandalized.

"Lee, I couldn't hold him without a warrant. And if he left Warner Pier the Wisconsin police would have to wait until he showed up someplace else. I thought if we made it look as if there was a strong possibility that a well-to-do businesswoman such as your aunt was interested in his project, he'd hang around. I didn't think it would take more than forty-eight hours to settle the whole thing."

He reached over and squeezed Aunt Nettie's hand. "I will admit I didn't anticipate his actually taking her out. But he didn't have any history of violence, and Nettie had the sense never to be alone with him for more than a few minutes."

Aunt Nettie laughed. "Just call me Undercover Auntie!"

"Why didn't you tell me?" I said.

"Well," Hogan said, "you were so scandalized at the thought of your aunt going out on a date . . ."

"Not on a date! On a date with a strange man I found very suspicious!"

Hogan nodded. "And you were right to be suspicious, Lee. You rumbled Aubrey Andrews Armstrong right away. And so did Joe. He barely met the guy, and he came running to me about him."

Joe nodded. "Hogan recognized the description, including the dog, right away, and we decided to keep quiet until he could find out where Armstrong was wanted."

"But what about the other people in Warner Pier he cheated? Like Sarajane, at the B and B?"

"I think there's enough money in the Victim's Compensation Fund to satisfy Armstrong's local debts."

"Good. But that leaves my first question unanswered. What about Monte? Do Aunt Nettie and I have to build a fence and enroll in obedience classes?"

"That I can't answer," Hogan said. "Monte still belongs to Armstrong. He'll have to decide what to do about him. Since a purebred dog is worth quite a bit of money, Monte may be for sale."

I found out a few more things over the next few days.

The antique money, Hogan learned, had been planted by Maia, as Aubrey and Joe had suspected. She apparently thought this would make her novel seem more authentic and attractive to a movie-maker.

Aubrey Andrews Armstrong's business card—the one I'd been looking for when I discovered the body of Silas Snow—had turned up in the trash can at the fruit stand. I'd never thought to ask Hogan if it had been found.

The director of the Michigan Film Office e-mailed on the next Monday, telling me and Chuck O'Riley that a fake movie producer had been making the rounds of the upper Midwest and that we should contact law enforcement officials.

Maggie never offered to tell any of us what threat Aubrey had used to blackmail her. I think, however, that she did tell Ken. He's just as protective of her as ever. And they did buy Lindy and Tony's house.

Little Tony Herrera, ten-year-old son of my pal Lindy, listened to his parents talking about the case and got the idea that Monte was going to have to go to jail with his master. He cried all night. When his grandfather, Warner Pier mayor Mike Herrera, heard about this, he drove to the Warner County Jail and made Aubrey Andrews Armstrong a cash offer for the dog. Aubrey, who definitely needed money at that moment, agreed to sell. He did make Mike promise that Tony and Monte would enroll in obedience training. So Monte now lives with Tony, Lindy, Little Tony, Marcia, Alicia, and Pinto in the Vander-meer house—with a bedroom for each kid and a big backyard. Pinto still rules that backyard.

The most surprising outcome was revealed after Joe and Hogan left on the night the arrests were made. Aunt Nettie and I stood on the front porch to wave both of them off. Then she turned and gave me a big hug.

"I'm all right now," I said. "You don't need to worry."

"I'm not worried! I'm excited!"

"What about?"

"Lee! Hogan asked me to go out to dinner with him!"

I squealed. Aunt Nettie squealed. We hopped around like sixteen-year-olds planning for the junior prom.

"That's wonderful!" I said. "He's the catch of Warner Pier. You'll be the envy of all your friends."

"Yes." Aunt Nettie smiled her sweetest smile. "But that's not why I want to go."

As for Joe and me—well, I advised him to go with the white tile for the bathroom in his new apartment. Then he could put up a patterned wallpaper. And, yes, I went along to help pick out the wallpaper.

The wedding's set for May.

# The Chocolate
# Mouse Trap

*To Dave,*
*still my special guy*

# Chapter 1

"I'm sick and tired of killing this stupid inspirational junk," I said. "If Julie Singletree doesn't stop sending it, I'm going to kill her, as well as her messages."

I'd been talking to myself, but when I raised my eyes from the computer screen, I realized I was also snarling at Aunt Nettie. She had nothing to do with the e-mail that had been driving me crazy, but she had innocently walked into my office, making herself a handy target for a glare.

Aunt Nettie smiled placidly; she'd understood that I was mad at my e-mail, not her. "Are you talking about that silly girl who's trying to be a party planner?"

"Yes. I know she got us that big order for the chocolate mice, but I'm beginning to think the business she could throw our way can't be worth the nausea brought on by these daily doses of Victorian sentiment."

Aunt Nettie settled her solid Dutch figure into a chair and adjusted the white food-service hairnet that covered her hair—blond, streaked with gray. I don't know how she works with chocolate all day long and keeps her white tunic and pants so sparkling clean.

"Victorian sentiment isn't your style, Lee," she said.

"Julie is sending six of us half a dozen messages every day, and I am not interested in her childish view of life. She alternates between ain't-life-grand and ain't-life-a-bitch, but both versions are coated with silly sugar. She never has anything clever or witty. Just dumb."

"Why haven't you asked to be taken off her list?"

I sighed and reached into my top desk drawer to raid my stash for a Bailey's Irish Cream bonbon ("Classic cream liqueur interior in dark chocolate"). I'd worked for TenHuis Chocolade for more than two years, but I wasn't at all tired of our products, described on our stationery as "Handmade chocolates in the Dutch tradition." When you're hassled by minor annoyances, such as e-mail, nothing soothes the troubled mind like a dose of chocolate.

Aunt Nettie was waiting for an answer, and I was hard put to find one. "I suppose I kept thinking that if I didn't respond she'd simply drop me from her jokes and junk list," I said.

"You didn't even want to tell her you don't want to receive any more spam?"

"Oh, it's not spam. She's made up a little list of us—it's all west Michigan people connected with the fine foods and parties trade. Lindy's on it, thanks to her new job in catering. There's Jason Foster—you know, he's got the contract for the new restaurant at Warner Point. There's Carolyn Rose, at House of Roses—she carries a line of gourmet items. Margaret Van Meter from Holland—the cake-decorating gal. And the Denhams, at Hideaway Inn. We're all on the list. And since we all deal in fancy foods, Julie has named us the 'Seventh Major Food Group.' You know—grains, dairy, vegetables, fruit, meat, fats, and party food."

"It *is* a funny name."

"It's the only witty idea Julie ever had." I gestured toward the screen. "This message is typical. 'A Prayer for the Working Woman.' I haven't read it, but I already know what it says."

"What?" Aunt Nettie smiled. "Since I've worked all my life, I might benefit from a little prayer."

"I can make you a printout, if you can stand the grossly lush roses Julie uses as a border." I punched the appropriate keys as I talked. "I predict it will be about how downtrodden women are today because most of us work."

"Since I own my own business, I guess I'm one of the downtrodders, not the downtrodden."

"Exactly!" I spoke before I thought, but luckily my reaction amused

Aunt Nettie. We both laughed. Then I began to backpedal. "You're a dream to work for, Aunt Nettie. You're definitely not a downtrodder. And you're not downtrodden, because you enjoy your job. But Julie can't seem to make up her mind. If she isn't sending stuff claiming today's women are put-upon because we have to work, she's sending stuff saying we don't get a chance at the good jobs. I can understand both views, but she wraps them up in enough syrup to make a hundred maple cream truffles."

"You'll have to assert yourself, Lee. Tell her you don't like her e-mails."

I sighed. "About the time I tell her that, she'll actually land a big wedding, and the bride will want enough bonbons and truffles for four hundred people, and we'll lose out on a couple of thousand dollars in business. Or Schrader Laboratories will plan another banquet and want an additional three hundred souvenir boxes of mice."

I gestured toward the decorated gift box on the corner of my desk. Aunt Nettie had shipped off the order two weeks before, but I'd saved one as a sample. The box contained a dozen one-inch chocolate mice—six replicas of laboratory mice in white chocolate and six tiny versions of a computer mouse, half in milk chocolate and half in dark.

Schrader Laboratories is a Grand Rapids firm that does product testing—sometimes using laboratory mice and sometimes computers. A special item such as the souvenir made for their annual dinner means risk-free profit for TenHuis Chocolade; we know they're sold before we order the boxes they'll be packed in.

"That was a nice bit of business Julie threw our way, even if she did get the order from a relative," I said. "I can put up with a certain amount of gooey sentiment for that amount of money."

"It might be cheaper to give it up than to hire a psychiatrist. You've got plenty to do. Tell Julie your mean old boss has cracked down on nonbusiness e-mail."

Aunt Nettie smiled her usual sweet smile. "And I really am going to add to your chores. We need Amaretto."

"I'll get some on my way home."

Amaretto is used to flavor a truffle that is extremely popular with TenHuis Chocolade customers. Our product list describes it as "Milk chocolate interior flavored with almond liqueur and coated in white chocolate." The truffle is decorated with three milk chocolate stripes, but its mainly white color makes it an ideal accent for boxes of Valentine candy and at that moment we were just four weeks away from Valentine's Day. I knew Aunt Nettie and the twenty-five ladies who actually make TenHuis chocolates had been using a lot of Amaretto as they got ready for the major chocolate holiday. But liqueurs go a long way when used only for flavoring; one bottle would probably see us through the rush.

I handed Aunt Nettie the printout of Julie's dumb e-mail—all ten pages of it. Julie never cleans the previous messages off the bottom of e-mails she forwards or replies to. Then Aunt Nettie went back to her antiseptically clean workroom.

I wrote "Amaretto" on a Post-it and stuck the note to the side of my handbag before I turned back to my computer. I manipulated my mouse until the arrow was on REPLY ALL and clicked it. Then I stared at the screen, trying to figure out how to be tactful and still stop Julie's daily drivel.

"Dear Seventh Major Food Group," I typed. Maybe Julie wouldn't feel that I'd singled her out. "This is one of the busiest seasons for the chocolate business, and my aunt and I have decided we simply have to crack down on nonbusiness e-mail. At least half our orders come in by e-mail, so I spend a lot of time clearing it. As great as the jokes and inspirational material that we exchange on this list can be," I lied, "I just can't justify the time I spend reading them. So please drop me from the joke/inspiration list. But please continue to include me in the business tips!"

I sent the message to the whole list, feeling smug. I was genuinely hopeful that I'd managed to drop the cornball philosophy without dropping some valuable business associates along with it.

I wasn't prepared the next day when I got a call from Lindy Herrera, my best friend and a manager for Herrera Catering.

"Lee!" Lindy sounded frantic. "Have you had the television on?"

"No. Why?"

"I was watching the news on the Grand Rapids station. Oh, Lee, it's awful!"

"What's happened?"

"It's Julie Singletree! She's been murdered!"

# Chapter 2

I hadn't known Julie well.

Lindy and I had met her two months earlier at the West Michigan Bridal Fair, a big-time event held in Grand Rapids. I'd gone to the fair for both professional and personal reasons.

On the professional side, as business manager of TenHuis Chocolade, located in the Lake Michigan resort town of Warner Pier, I'm responsible for marketing. I also keep the books, write the salary checks, send out the statements, and pay the taxes. As one part of its business, TenHuis Chocolade provides arrays of truffles, bonbons, and molded chocolates for special occasions—occasions that have been known to include wedding receptions. We also make specialty items—tiny chocolate champagne bottles, chocolate roses, molded chocolate gift boxes with names on top, and dozens of other chocolate objects—that would be suitable for weddings. Visiting a bridal fair would be a good way to make some contacts that could possibly lead to sales.

On the personal side, I was planning my own wedding, and it wasn't proving to be an easy job.

For nearly two years I'd been dating Joe Woodyard, a Warner Pier native who earns his living by an unlikely combination of careers. He's an expert in restoring antique wooden boats and is also city attorney for the town of Warner Pier, Michigan (pop. 2,503). We'd both had unhappy first marriages, so it had taken us—or at least me— quite a while to decide to head for the altar a second time.

This time, we both vowed, we were going to do it "right." As if there's a foolproof way to get married. The problem was that Joe's version of "right" didn't mesh with mine.

Early on Joe and I had discovered that we'd both flown to Las Vegas to get married the first time around. That more or less ruled out a romantic elopement. Been there, done that.

So Joe asked if I wanted to go back to my Texas hometown for the ceremony.

I laughed harshly. "Then I'd have to invite my parents."

"You don't want to invite your parents?"

"Not both of them. But it's fine if your mom wants to be there."

"Now wait a moment, Lee. You don't want either of your parents to come to our wedding?"

"My dad would be okay. He's helped me out a lot. But he'd have to bring my stepmother. And if she's there, my mom would go bananas. So it's just better not to get into it. Can't we just have Aunt Nettie? And Lindy and Tony and your mom—and Mike, if you want to. And maybe Hogan Jones."

Mike Herrera is my friend Lindy's father-in-law and boss—and he dates Joe's mother. And Hogan Jones is Warner Pier police chief, and he's been taking my Aunt Nettie out. Small towns are like that: interconnected.

Joe was frowning. "Don't you think your mom will be upset if you don't ask her to the wedding and do ask your aunt?"

I thought about it a moment. "Frankly, Joe, I don't care if my mother is upset, as long as she's upset in Dallas, not in Warner Pier. She hasn't exactly been supportive of me and my needs and desires. If she had her way, I'd still be married to Rich. I'm sorry, but I'm not on good terms with my mother or my stepmother. It would really complicate matters if I tried to have them at the wedding."

Joe's frown deepened. "Then the wedding will have to be really small."

"Does that bother you?"

"I admit I'd put the money from selling the Chris-Craft Utility aside to pay for a big blowout. I thought you might want to get married in Texas, then have a reception up here."

That pretty much stopped the discussion. Obviously Joe did want to have a biggish wedding. I didn't. Right at the moment I didn't see any chance of compromise. A big wedding would involve my parents, and no miracle was likely to make me friends with both of them at this late date.

But when I went up to DeVos Place, the Grand Rapids convention center, for the West Michigan Bridal Fair, maybe I was looking for some solution to our problem, some way to have a big wedding for Joe and a little one for me. Some way to involve my parents in the whole event and not cause an open split.

The convention center was a madhouse, of course. The brides and the bridegrooms looked either frantic or confused, and the mothers were terrifying. And that was just the parking lot. I paid my admission, but I was almost afraid to go in the door. The inside was likely to be even worse.

And it was. It was a hubbub of music, talking, arguing. ("I'm *not* wearing Aunt Emma's stupid mantilla, Mother! It makes me look like a Spanish tart.") Lace, satin, sequins, embossed napkins, multitiered cakes, crystal punch bowls, silver candelabra, wrought-iron arches, exotic flowers—for a moment I was definitely sorry I'd come. But I took a deep breath, shouldered my tote bag, and started working the crowd. Up one aisle and down the next, picking out the caterers and wedding planners, asking to speak to the person in charge of the booth, giving a brief pitch on chocolate, and thrusting a brochure at them. In there somewhere I usually managed to mention my own wedding; that got their attention faster than the TenHuis brochure.

By the end of the second aisle I was glad I'd had the sense to wear flat heels. That's when I heard someone call my name. "Lee! Lee McKinney! Over here!"

I turned around and saw a booth with an arch that read, HERRERA CATERING—THE COMPLETE PARTY PROVIDER. And under the arch was a friendly face. "Lindy!"

Lindy and I have been friends since we worked at TenHuis Chocolade together the year we were both sixteen. She still has the same dimpled smile that made her the prettiest girl on Warner Pier Beach. She's a little plumper now, after having three kids, and she's recently had her brown hair cut into a sophisticated bob.

"Come over here and sit down," Lindy said. "You look as confused as the rest of these brides."

"I guess TenHuis should have taken a booth. But that's expensive."

"It would be a waste of money, since weddings aren't your main business. I can hand out some of your brochures."

"Thanks. Are you going to be able to get away for lunch?"

"Sure. I brought Delia—Mike's secretary. She's at lunch now. I never come to these without a partner to act as backup for when I need to hit the ladies' room."

"Smart idea."

"I told Jason Foster we'd go to lunch with him. Do you remember Jason? He was a bartender for Mike for five years."

Mike, Lindy's father-in-law, is officially Miguel Herrera. He owns three restaurants in Warner Pier, plus the catering service. He employs a lot of people, both full and part-time, but Jason stood out.

"I'll never forget Jason," I said. "He and I were tending bar the night . . ." My voice failed me, but Lindy nodded. She had also been working the big party when Clementine Ripley bit into an Amaretto truffle and dropped dead. A lot of people remembered that night.

"Does Jason still wear his hair in a queue like George Washington?" I asked.

"Yep. And his forehead is higher than ever, so it still looks as if all his hair slid backward. And you know what Jason is up to now."

I grinned. "Well, I did hear that he had the contract to operate the new restaurant at Warner Point."

"Right. Mike was dying to take it on, but, of course he can't do that and be mayor, too. Just a little conflict of interest. I guess Joe told you all about it."

"All Joe told me is that he was signing the property over and leaving its operation up to the city."

Warner Point is a Warner Pier landmark, of sorts. The property formerly belonged to Joe's first—and ex—wife, Clementine Ripley. Ms. Ripley, who had a national reputation as a defense attorney, had died there two years earlier, leaving her legal affairs in a mess after eating the previously mentioned Amaretto truffle. Not only was the property heavily mortgaged, but she had also failed to make a new will after she and Joe were divorced. Under the old one, he inherited. This had been a personal problem for me, because the guy I was falling in love with had had to spend more than a year concentrating on the business affairs of his ex-wife. Neither of us found this romantic.

To add to the confusion, Joe had been determined not to benefit financially from the situation, beyond being reimbursed for his personal expenses. It had taken him a long time, but he had recently managed to turn the property—including its showpiece mansion—over to the City of Warner Pier. Mike Herrera and the city council wanted to develop it as a conference center, and Jason Foster had signed a contract to operate the restaurant and catering facility.

Lindy nodded. "Jason's trying to drum up some wedding receptions for the new restaurant."

"A competitor for Herrera Catering?"

"Not really. We cooperate, share employees and equipment. He's going to introduce me to a wedding planner at lunch. I thought you might like to meet her, too."

So that's how I met Julie Singletree. Jason, Lindy, and I walked over to the luxury hotel adjoining the Convention Center and went into the restaurant that overlooks the river. Julie impressed me immediately. Not only had she snagged a large table with a prize view; she was the cutest little thing in the place.

Julie's short black hair was perfect, her black eyes snapped, and her black suit fit like a million dollars, which was probably what she paid for it. She was the very picture of an up-and-coming professional woman. A miniature professional woman. That suit couldn't have been any bigger than size 3, and even in three-inch heels, Julie barely reached my shoulder.

I am, after all, close to six feet tall—nearly a foot taller than Julie. It also occurred to me that I was older than Julie. I was about to turn thirty, and Julie looked as if she were barely old enough to sign the tab for enough champagne for a wedding reception. And I was also dowdier than Julie, even in my good navy blazer. Before she could make me feel inferior, I straightened my shoulders and reminded myself that I'm a natural blond. That's not unusual in western Michigan, but it counts for something.

Her business, Julie told us, was just getting started. "My grandmother gave me an *advance* on my inheritance. She's a *sweetheart*! I'd just feel *awful* if I wasted her money!"

Then she waved her hand casually. "I ran into some more *Warner*

*Pier* people over at the show. So I invited them to *join* us. I hope you don't *mind*. My grandmother has a *cottage* down there, and I always spent the summer there when I was a kid. I simply *adore* Warner Pier, so I hope I can *capture* all the business down that way."

"Who is your grandmother?" Lindy asked the question faster than I could. Somehow I wasn't surprised when Julie blushed slightly and said her grandmother was Rachel Schrader. The name made it plain that Julie's grandmother could afford to give her granddaughter an advance on her inheritance.

Mrs. Schrader was well known as a west Michigan philanthropist, and her Warner Pier "cottage" was no little weekend cabin. It was a mansion sitting on more than a hundred acres of lakeshore property. Lindy, Jason, and I were careful not to meet each other's eyes.

Julie went on talking, verbally italicizing at least one word in every sentence. And in a few minutes, Warner Pier people wandered in and began to join us. Of course, Lindy and I already knew all of them. Warner Pier merchants can hardly avoid getting acquainted with each other. There aren't that many of us.

Ronnie and Diane Denham came next. They own the Hideaway Inn. Ronnie's a retired engineer, so he handles the maintenance for their bed-and-breakfast. Diane had been a teacher, but her avocation is cooking. She specializes in fancy breakfasts. They told us they'd decided to advertise the Hideaway as a honeymoon destination.

Both Ronnie and Diane have wavy white hair, the kind with great body. Both have bright blue eyes, and both are on the plump side. They've always reminded me of Mr. and Mrs. Santa Claus.

As Julie greeted them, I remember wondering if Joe and I would look that much alike after thirty years of marriage. Joe and I are both tall, bony people, and if his dark hair turned gray and my blond hair did, too . . . It was a frightening idea. But I thought his eyes would stay blue and mine hazel.

Carolyn Rose came clomping in. Her high-heeled boots were audible clear across the restaurant, and almost immediately I heard her low, throaty voice. "I hope this place has decent coffee." She didn't greet anybody; just yanked out a chair and threw herself into it, tossing her fake fur jacket over the back and running her fingers through her unnaturally bright red hair. "I had to get the flowers to the Huizenga funeral before I could leave Warner Pier. Somehow my usual dose of caffeine got lost in transit."

Like many Warner Pier retailers, Carolyn kept her shop open only a few hours a week in the winter—our off-season. She had no winter employees; so I knew she'd had to make up the sprays and wreaths, then take them to the funeral home herself, unload them, and help the funeral home people arrange them for the service.

Jason stood up to look for a waitress. His appearance seemed to draw the attention of a woman who had been hesitating at the door. She waved at our table enthusiastically, then walked over to us, smiling broadly. "Hello, Julie! Greetings all! I'm Margaret Van Meter."

She plunked herself down in the last chair at our table as if her name were so famous we'd all know who she was. When I glanced at Lindy, however, she looked as blank as I felt.

Julie gestured. "Margaret's a *baker*," she said. "She makes the most *fabulous* wedding cakes."

Margaret produced a handful of photographs of cakes and began handing them around. Or maybe "photographs" was too fancy a name for what Margaret had. "Snapshots" would have been more accurate. They were out of focus, with busy backgrounds. Some of the wedding cakes seemed to be tilting as if the bride and groom were planning to honeymoon in Italy and had been trying to get in the mood for a weekend in Pisa.

Margaret herself matched the photos: her mousy hair was straggly; her makeup was nonexistent; she was wearing jeans and a sweatshirt. She looked as if she'd gotten ready in the dark.

But the cakes in the photos—once you allowed for the amateur photography—were gorgeous.

Margaret began talking as emphatically as Julie had been. "No, I never use mixes," she told Diane Denham. "And I offer twenty flavors of fillings. Ooops!" She reached over and retrieved one of the photos. "How did that one get in there?"

"It looks interesting," Lindy said. "Is that your family?"

"The whole crew."

Margaret let Lindy have the photo, and I looked over her shoulder to see it. Margaret wasn't in it, but everybody else seemed to be. There were kids of every age up to eight or so—I counted six of them, including a small baby. They were grouped around a husky blond guy.

"You see why I can't get out to take a job," Margaret said. "I'm hoping I can earn some money at home."

Lindy produced a snapshot of the three Herrera kids, and we all seemed to forget we didn't know each other very well. It turned out to be a highly successful lunch, if you judge by the amount of laughing and funny stories. Jason's tale about the political candidate who was falling down drunk at a campaign banquet—well, I'd better not name names, but it was hilarious.

Of course, the Warner Pier crowd brought up my engagement.

"Oh!" Julie gave a squeal. "I *hope* you need a wedding planner."

"I'm sorry, Julie. I don't think we could justify a wedding planner. We're still discussing, but right now we're not planning for anything major. Lindy and her husband are going to be the only attendants."

"No *reception*?"

"We don't know yet."

"No cake?" Margaret sounded plaintive.

"Maybe. We haven't decided." Actually, I had been thinking one of Margaret's cakes might be just right, even if it had to be the smallest size.

"But you'll definitely need a romantic place to spend the wedding night." Ronnie Denham waggled his white eyebrows and grinned.

"This is the sexy go-round for both of us," I said. "So maybe we do need to emphasize romaine."

*That* stopped the conversation. I'd gotten my tongue completely twisted—a situation I'm sorry to say isn't all that uncommon.

I would have corrected my idiotic remark—"This is the second go-round for both of us. So maybe we do need to emphasize romance." But Lindy began to laugh.

Everyone joined in, even me. I've had to learn to laugh at my malapropisms. Or else I'd cry.

Lindy spoke again. "Sometimes Lee hides the fact that she's one of the smartest people in Warner Pier. And now maybe I'd better get back to the show."

"No, *no!*" Julie wasn't having it. "Not until we exchange cards!"

So we all brought out business cards—Margaret didn't have cards, so Lindy lent her some and she wrote her name, address, phone, and e-mail on the backs. The next day we all had an e-mail from Julie, telling us how *fantastically superwonderful* the luncheon had been and urging us all to stay in touch. That was when she declared us the "Seventh Major Food Group."

"Party food needs to be recognized," she wrote. "Maybe we'll start a movement. Grains, veggies, fruit, meats, dairy, fats/sugars are joined by PARTY!"

Her idea had seemed harmless enough, even though Julie had later turned out to be an annoying correspondent. I'd only seen her a few other times. She'd show up in Warner Pier without warning and ask if Lindy and I could go to lunch. The table talk was always about Lindy, me, or some of the other Seventh Food Group members. Julie never talked about herself, but she was always urging others to bare their souls. I didn't know her well enough to bare mine, so she and I hadn't become close friends.

Still, I wasn't prepared for the news that Julie had been murdered. It made me feel bad about sending her that e-mail asking her to drop the cornball sentiment. But I didn't feel guilty.

After all, there wasn't any connection between Julie's death and her e-mail.

# Chapter 3

The e-mails flew furiously over the next few days, as the Seventh Major Food Group exchanged information, shocked reactions, and gossip about Julie's death.

From the television and newspaper reports we learned that the circumstances were mysterious, or at least that the police weren't revealing much. Julie's body had been discovered by an uncle, Martin Schrader, who had gone by her apartment to take her to lunch. The lunch date had been planned the day before, but when Uncle Martin knocked, Julie didn't answer her door. Her SUV was in the parking lot. Uncle Martin got nervous and contacted the apartment manager. Reading between the lines of the news reports, I deduced that Uncle Martin had had to do some arm twisting before the manager would let him in. When the door was finally opened, Julie's body had been in plain sight, lying in the living room. The police said she had apparently died sometime the previous evening.

The police were cagey about the cause of death, saying they'd wait for the results of the autopsy. But I quizzed the Warner Pier police chief, Hogan Jones—who just happens to be a special friend of Aunt Nettie's. Hogan in turn quizzed some buddy he had on the Holland police force, and I learned that Julie's neck had been broken. There was no sign that she'd been sexually assaulted, or so Hogan's pal said.

Julie had lived in what we Texans call a "garden apartment," with a set of sliding doors that led to a private patio and deck. The deck door, Hogan found out, had been jimmied, and the police believed the killer got in that way.

Julie's apartment was in a complex just off U.S. Highway 31, one of Holland's major arteries. She had run her party and wedding planning business out of her apartment. The complex was fairly large, so there was lots of coming and going in its parking lot. That, added to the noise from the heavy traffic on the highway, meant that no one had noticed any strange activity around Julie's apartment. There was snow on the ground, but if any helpful footprints or tire tracks had been found, the police weren't saying anything about them, and Hogan's informant didn't volunteer any information Hogan wanted to share with me.

The Food Group members were all aghast, but each was aghast in a different way. "Oh, these girls today!" Diane Denham wrote. "They are so trusting. They meet people and invite them home when they know nothing about them, or about their families. They're so foolish." She was ignoring the evidence of the break-in, apparently. Ronnie usually left all the e-mail to her, so we didn't know what he thought.

Carolyn Rose represented the florists of the world. "I see the family is planning to designate memorial contributions to the Lake Michigan Conservation Society," she wrote. "Well, whatever floats their boat. Julie may have been Little Miss Knows-All, but she loved flowers. I'm planting a bed in the Dock Street Park in her memory. When I get time."

Having delivered the florist's credo, she had a few words to say about Julie. "Poor kid. It seems like a girl could have a little fun without getting murdered."

Jason singled out the killer for his remarks. "It must have been a madman," he wrote. "Julie could be thoughtless, but only a crazy person would have wanted to hurt her."

Margaret really seemed the most saddened. "I just loved Julie," she said. "She actually used to come by my house and bring lunch for me and the kids. She loved playing with them. She brought them wonderful presents. She was lonely. Now she'll never find the one person God meant for her."

Lindy's comments also reflected her own concerns. "Did Julie have an alarm system? Did she have Mace on her key chain? It can be scary, coming home late at night. I call Tony from my cell phone, and he looks out the back door, makes sure I get from the car to the house without any problem. Poor Julie."

I found myself annoyed by the general attitude that Julie could have done something—anything—to prevent being murdered. "Life is an uncertain business," I wrote. "I'm devastated by what has happened to Julie. But thinking that it wouldn't have happened if she'd had different friends, or if she'd had a burglar alarm, or if she hadn't crossed paths with a maniac—well, that's all just speculation. We'll have to wait and see what the police find out. We don't have enough facts to know why Julie was killed."

Despite the prevalence of murder in books and television, it's pretty unusual in real life. Most people are never touched by violent death, so the Food Group was upset. Each of us was hitting REPLY ALL two or three times a day.

The final round of e-mails set up plans for the group to attend Julie's funeral. It was to be "private," according to the *Grand Rapids Press*, but Jason called the funeral home and checked. We'd be welcome, he reported. It was to be at the home of Julie's grandmother in Grand Rapids. That caused a flurry of comment, but Jason told us the fabled Rachel Schrader was in poor health. "I guess it's hard for her to get out, especially in the winter," he wrote.

Lindy and I offered to pick up Margaret Van Meter as we drove through Holland, and the Denhams asked Carolyn Rose to go up with them. Jason said he had some errands to do before the service, so he went on his own.

As Lindy and I left for the funeral, the weather was as glum as our mood. January isn't the best month western Michigan has to offer, unless you're a cross-country skier, and that day seemed particularly dismal. It wasn't snowing, but the clouds looked cold enough to let loose a couple of inches any minute, and the temperature was around twenty degrees. Aunt Nettie had insisted we take her light blue Buick; I suppose it did look more suitable for a funeral than Lindy's bright green compact or my red minivan, the vehicle my dad had found to replace one that had been—well, shot to pieces—the previous fall.

In Holland, we almost got lost finding Margaret's house—an old two-story frame that looked as if it would be extremely drafty. Margaret opened the door and waved when we pulled into the drive. A moment later she climbed awkwardly into the backseat of the car. She had pulled a red stocking cap over her mousy brown hair, and she wore a bright red ski jacket that wasn't quite the same color as the hat. Her long corduroy skirt was purple, the worst possible color to wear with the red jacket. Obviously the red jacket was her only winter coat.

Suddenly I felt overdressed in my good leather boots and the belted camel hair coat Aunt Nettie had given me for Christmas. Lindy, in a long navy blue flannel coat, looked neat and professional. Margaret looked like a hard-up mother of six small children. Then Margaret smiled her wonderful smile, and I thought how lucky those six kids were to have her home with them.

"Thanks for picking me up," Margaret said. "Jim really needed the van today."

"Who's keeping the kids?"

"My mother-in-law. She's really good about helping me out. She's highly upset over this murder. She acts like it's unpatriotic or something."

I didn't understand. "Unpatriotic?"

"Because it happened in good old reliable Holland. We never have murders here, according to her. She still thinks this is a Dutch farming community."

"Times do change," Lindy said. "And Holland has certainly changed since my grandparents lived here."

"Sure it has. But Gramma still thinks it's strange to see an aisle of Hispanic food in Meijer's. She's buying the rumor that some dark, swarthy guy was seen walking down the alley behind Julie's apartment."

Lindy's laugh didn't sound amused. "Well, Tony Herrera was home all night," she said.

The chill in her voice made me turn the heater up another notch and try to change the subject. "I know how to get to Grand Rapids, but do either of you know how to get to the Schrader house once we're there?"

"I printed out the directions Jason sent," Margaret said. "I never heard of having a funeral in a home before."

"I expect the Schrader house has plenty of room for a private funeral," Lindy said. "Jason says he tended bar at some benefit in that house once. He says there's a reception room the size of a ballroom."

The Schrader house also had a porte cochere, we learned when we pulled into the drive. The house was a classic Prairie style, and I wondered if it was an early Frank Lloyd Wright. Valet parking had been arranged, and inside the entrance hall uniformed maids were taking coats.

Lindy muttered in my ear as our coats disappeared, "If they hire this much help for a small private funeral, I want to cater somebody's birthday party."

We waited in the hall until Jason, Ronnie and Diane Denham, and Carolyn Rose appeared. Then we were escorted through a pair of double doors and into the big reception room Jason had described. It was nearly time for the service to start, and we were seated near the back, on folding chairs draped with white slipcovers.

The room was a good place for a small funeral service. No standard funeral sprays or wreaths were visible. The small platform that could have held musicians on another occasion was packed with greenery, and enormous baskets of white roses stood on either side of it. About seventy-five people were present. A musician at a grand piano in one corner played unobtrusively, and the minister sitting in a thronelike chair on the platform was tall and handsome enough to complete the picture. We already knew that Julie was to be cremated; we were to be spared the ghastly march past the coffin.

Everything was in perfect taste. I couldn't help thinking that Julie couldn't have planned it better herself. Julie might have been young, but she had been a traditionalist. She expected hostesses to get out the good silver and candles.

I'd seen no sign of the Schrader family's entrance, so I was surprised when the minister rose and called on us to pray. Where were they? There was no alcove that could have hidden them. I wondered if they were sitting at the back. Irreligiously, I sneaked a peek over my shoulder, and I found myself looking directly into a remarkable face.

It was the face of an old woman, and it looked as if that woman had suffered. She had beautiful white hair, and her face was heavily lined. She looked like the personification of grief. But Julie's snapping black eyes looked out from under her brows and met mine.

I should have looked away, but I was mesmerized. *That's what Julie would have looked like in fifty years*, I thought.

It was obviously Julie's grandmother.

I forced my head to twist around and face the right direction—I have a few manners—but I don't remember another thing about that service, except that it was brief. Twenty minutes was all it took to say good-bye to Julie Singletree.

Mrs. Schrader and the other family members must have slipped out during the final prayer, because the back row was empty when the minister dismissed us and I was able to look around again. As we left the room, a handsome and distinguished man I thought must be the funeral director greeted the mourners. He invited us across the hall, into a dining room where coffee, cookies, and finger sandwiches were offered. No elaborate wake was planned, I gathered.

The Food Group didn't know any of the other guests, of course, so we stood around talking to each other in subdued voices. In a few minutes we were approached by a young guy—he had dark hair and eyes like Julie's, but he was of normal height, not tiny as she had been. He wasn't bad looking, but his dark suit looked as if he'd slept in it, and he had a hangdog expression.

"We're glad you came," he said. His voice was high and almost squeaked. "I'm Julie's cousin, Brad Schrader."

Jason, who seemed to be taking leadership for the occasion, introduced each of us. "We were in an informal networking group with Julie," he said. "All of us are in the food and party business."

Brad Schrader nodded. "Seventh Major Food Group? Julie told me about you guys."

"None of us knew her too well," Jason said.

"Julie and I were the only two kids in our generation, the last of the Schrader clan," Brad said. "We tried to keep in touch. But Julie was closer to your group than she was to me. She enjoyed your e-mails."

"Julie was the one who kept the group alive," Jason said. He didn't explain that Julie had more time to fool with e-mail than the rest of us did. Her business was just getting started; the rest of us were busy.

"Julie loved Warner Pier," Brad said. "Just the way I do. We both spent summers at Grandma's place down there when we were growing up. It's our real hometown."

"You grew up in Holland, too?" Carolyn Rose asked the question.

"Not me. Can't you tell by my accent? My dad was the Schrader kid who didn't go into the family firm. He moved to New York and worked in publishing, which made us the poor relations. I grew up in the Bronx. Julie's dad commuted to Grand Rapids and worked at Schrader Labs' main installation." He turned to me abruptly. "Ms. McKinney? You're with TenHuis Chocolade?"

"Yes." I was surprised at being singled out.

"My grandmother wanted to meet you."

Brad Schrader made an awkward motion, pointing me toward the door into the next room, without so much as an "excuse me." He had apparently made his token gesture of hospitality to the group. He certainly lacked Julie's social skills. I felt rather sorry for him.

Brad pushed me through the next room—a living room where about thirty mourners were standing around—then into a smaller sitting room. And all the way across the living room and into the smaller room I wondered why on earth Mrs. Schrader had singled me out. Was she a chocoholic hoping I had a few truffles in my pocket? Had she noticed me because I towered over all the other mourners? Was I going to be scolded for turning around during the opening prayer?

The small room was decorated in classic Craftsman style. Mrs. Schrader sat in a wheelchair beside a fire, which burned in a fireplace embellished with beautiful ceramic tiles I was willing to bet were original to the house. She gave me her hand graciously and signaled that I was to sit in a small chair pulled up beside her. Brad faded into the crowd.

When she spoke, her remark surprised me. "Are you Henry Ten-Huis's granddaughter?"

"Yes, I am." The light dawned. Mrs. Schrader owned property at Warner Pier, where my grandfather had operated a gas station. She must have been a customer. "He had the Lakeshore Service Station and Garage for thirty years."

"Yes, and I bought a lot of gasoline from him. But I knew him before that. We went to high school together."

"Oh! Yes, he did go to high school in Grand Rapids."

"He was two years ahead of me. I'll never forget how handsome he was in his Marine uniform. That would have been about 1944."

"I knew he served in the Pacific."

"I'm glad you know about him. He died young. Before you were born, I'm sure. But you have a certain look that reminds me of him."

I touched my hair. "I guess he passed on the blond gene. In all his pictures he looks very fair. I'm sorry I never knew him."

Just then the distinguished-looking man from the hall, the one I'd mentally pigeonholed as the funeral director, loomed over her. "Mother, the Johnsons are waiting to talk to you."

I managed not to gasp. This was no funeral director. He must be Martin Schrader, the uncle who discovered Julie's body.

"Mr. Johnson can't stay," he said. "You know his health . . ."

"I know." Mrs. Schrader sounded angry. "All my old friends are either dead or dying. Martin, this is Ms. McKinney. You should remember her grandfather, Henry TenHuis."

Martin blinked. He was obviously trying to think who the hell Henry TenHuis was, and his mother was letting him squirm.

I took pity on him. "My grandfather had a garage and service station in Warner Pier back when gasoline cost considerably less than it does now. And I just learned that he went to high school with Mrs. Schrader."

Martin Schrader made a quick recovery. "Of course! I used to fill my bicycle tires at his station. Do you live in Warner Pier?"

His mother didn't give me time to answer the question. "I've been in the TenHuis Chocolade shop many times," she said. "Back before arthritis and heart trouble took all the pleasure out of my life. Philip TenHuis must be your uncle."

"Yes. But Uncle Phil is gone now, too. My aunt runs the shop."

Mrs. Schrader threw her head back defiantly. "And you have enough family feeling to go into the business. I suppose you are your aunt's heir."

I couldn't believe she'd asked such a rude question. I'm sure there was a long silence while I decided how to answer it. "The question doesn't arise," I said. "Aunt Nettie is the corpse—I mean, the core! She's the core of the business! Without her skill as a chocolatier we have no product to sell."

I stood up. "It was extremely kind of you to talk with me, Mrs. Schrader. Julie loved and admired you greatly."

Her face crumpled. She took my hand, but this time it wasn't a gracious handclasp. It was a clutch. She grabbed the hand as if it were a lifeline. She tugged at it, and I found myself kneeling beside her chair while she whispered in my ear.

"I loved Julie," she said. "I loved her! She was darling! Why? Why? Why can't we keep the ones we love? Who can have wanted to take Julie away from me?"

I didn't have any answers, of course. All I could do was hold her hand in both of mine. "I don't know," I said. "I don't understand how this can have happened. We're all going to miss Julie terribly. I'm so sorry."

She nodded and turned away, producing a handkerchief from somewhere. I was dismissed. I rose as gracefully as I could, trying to remember how to get up from the Texas curtsy I had learned for beauty pageant competition. I moved away and an elderly couple took my place.

I started back into the big reception room, but someone touched my arm. It was Martin Schrader. I took a good look at him. He had a very high forehead, but once his hair began it was thick and silvery gray. He was—well, a handsome man. And he looked reliable. He'd be a perfect mouthpiece for a major company like Schrader Laboratories.

He spoke gravely. "Ms. McKinney, I'd like to ask a favor. If I came down to Warner Pier, could we have dinner or lunch?"

I must have looked startled, because he went on hastily. "I need to talk to some of Julie's friends. Someone her own age."

"Actually, Mr. Schrader, I only met Julie a few times. Our friendship was mainly by e-mail."

"That's what I'm interested in." He leaned close. "The police think someone broke in to rob Julie. But I don't understand why the main thing he took was her computer."

# Chapter 4

I guess I stared at him a minute. A computer didn't seem to me to be that odd a thing to steal, but this wasn't the place to discuss it. I moved back to his original question.

"I'll be happy to talk to you about Julie anytime, Mr. Schrader. It isn't necessary to take me out to lunch."

"Oh, but I'd like to." Was his smile wolfish? I decided it wasn't; it looked pleasant, just slightly harassed.

I smiled back insincerely. "I promised my finesse—I mean, my fiancé! I promised my fiancé that I'd cook dinner for him tonight. But any other time would be fine. Let me give you a card."

The mention of a fiancé didn't seem to disturb Martin Schrader. I gave him a TenHuis Chocolade card. By then some other guest was hovering, wanting his attention. I turned away and rejoined the Food Group. They all looked curious, so I explained that Mrs. Schrader had known my grandfather.

I didn't mention her son's invitation. In fact, as I thought his remarks over, I became determined to make sure any meeting with Martin Schrader occurred in my office. Not that he had indicated any interest in a social relationship. He'd given the impression of an uncle who was worried about his niece's death. But why had he singled me out to talk to? I didn't know Julie any better than any of the other members of the Food Group did. In fact, I thought Margaret had known her better than the rest of us. They had lived in the same town, and Julie had apparently dropped in on her often.

But Martin Schrader's request probably didn't mean anything. He was upset over Julie's murder and casting around for any scrap of information. At least, I had convinced myself of that by the time we had collected our coats and were standing under the porte cochere waiting for the cars to be brought around.

"Ms. McKinney?" The voice came from behind me. It was barely audible, but I heard its distinctive squeak. I turned to find Brad Schrader standing there.

"I'm sorry to bother you," he said. "I wanted to apologize for my uncle."

"Apologize?" Had Martin Schrader decided he didn't want to talk to me after all and sent Brad with his excuses?

Brad went on. "I saw him taking you aside. I hope he wasn't . . . objectionable."

"He was very polite, Brad. Why did you think he'd been objectionable?"

Brad looked down and shuffled his feet. "Well, sometimes he . . ." Then he looked up, took a deep breath, and spoke in a rush. "He's the family lech, see. More or less a dirty old man. I wouldn't want him to annoy you."

I had an impulse to laugh, but I managed to contain it. "Don't worry, Brad. I can handle middle-aged leches." I shook hands with him and told him again how sorry I was about Julie.

"I'll miss her e-mails," I said. "She was always sending something interesting."

Brad nodded. "She was on several lists," he said. "I guess that's where she got all that joke stuff."

"I didn't always have time to read the things she sent," I said. "But we probably all have a big file of her past messages. I can always go back and read them again."

That idea seemed to make Brad more morose than ever; he didn't reply, and I was out of small talk, too. Luckily, Aunt Nettie's blue Buick showed up then, and Lindy, Margaret, and I got into the car.

I waited until we were out of the driveway before I began to giggle. The thought of inept Brad trying to warn me off his poised and worldly uncle was simply laughable.

Of course, I had to explain my amusement to Lindy and Margaret.

"Huh," Lindy said. "Julie's relatives might be rich, but they're just as odd as mine."

"Mine are odd, too," Margaret said. "I asked my mom once if our family was crazier than anybody else's, and she said no. She said we just knew them better."

"Same here," I said. "If we're picking the oddest, I'd put my mom up against Uncle Martin and Cousin Brad combined. But one thing Martin Schrader said was really interesting. That part about talking to some of Julie's friends, to 'someone her own age.' "

"Why do you say that?" Lindy said.

"Think about that gathering we just left. Was there anybody there Julie's age?"

We all were silent for a few seconds. I was reviewing the crowd, and I guess Lindy and Margaret were, too, because they spoke at the same time.

"Not really," Lindy said.

"Just a few," Margaret said. "There was that group that clustered around the couches in the big room. They looked younger than most. But I eavesdropped on them, and I think they all worked for Schrader Labs. One of them was Martin Schrader's secretary."

"Maybe Julie's friends are having a separate service—more of a wake or a party," Lindy said. "That's what Warner Pier's artsy crowd does sometimes."

"Maybe so," I said. "If Julie went to high school in Holland, you'd think some of her friends would still be around."

"There aren't too many of us," Margaret said.

I swiveled my head toward her. "Did you go to high school with Julie?"

"Yes. Didn't either of us ever mention it?"

"No. I thought you met through some party or wedding."

"Julie and I graduated from Holland Christian the same year. But we didn't run in the same crowd. I really got to be friends with her during the past year."

"Maybe her friends are not high-toned enough for the Schraders," Lindy said. "Maybe they deliberately didn't invite them to the funeral."

We all thought it over again, but it was Margaret who finally said what we were all thinking—right out loud. "Julie was so cute. You'd think she would have had a boyfriend."

But none of us could think of any boyfriend-type person at the service.

"You know," I said, "thinking back to the Food Group e-mails, Julie never mentioned a boyfriend, did she? In fact, we never learned much about her personal life."

"You're right," Lindy said. "She never had much to say about herself. When Diane and Ronnie became grandparents again, they put a message out right away. When Tony Junior made the honor roll for the first time, I told everybody I saw, and I put a message on the Food Group list. Even you, Lee. You've mentioned working on the new apartment several times."

"And I let everybody know when I was so worried because Jim's hours got cut back," Margaret said. "And Jason—he told about the horrible weekend he spent painting his living room, when it rained and the paint wouldn't dry. But Julie—she never said a word about herself. Just weddings and parties she was planning and all that philosophical stuff."

"Strange," I said.

"Odd," Lindy said.

"Weird," Margaret said. "But I can understand Julie not wanting to talk about her relatives. If the uncle is a lech, the cousin is a nerd, and the grandmother is bossy as all get out . . . well, if you can't say anything good, shut up."

We shut up. Or at least we changed the subject. Lindy and Margaret traded stories about their kids, and I kept my mouth shut and concentrated on the road. That was because it began to snow just as we reached the southern edge of Grand Rapids.

Since I was raised in Texas, I didn't get a lot of experience driving in snow when I was growing up. Now ice, yes, Texas usually has a couple of dandy ice storms every winter. I've seen some horrible sleet and freezing rain around both my hometowns, Dallas and Prairie Creek. But thick, heavy snow is strange to me. It makes me nervous.

I reminded myself that Michigan highways are well maintained— we saw several snowplows during the trip—that Aunt Nettie's Buick was a good, heavy car with the proper tires for driving in snow, and that I was smart enough not to hit the brakes suddenly or spin my tires trying to start up. But I was still nervous, maybe because I was afraid I'd do something stupid rather than because I was afraid I'd have a wreck. Though having a wreck in somebody else's car is not high on the list of the things I want to do.

But we didn't have a wreck. The only bad moments were three or four times when semis passed us going a million miles an hour and threw sheets of snow onto our windshield. The road didn't get too bad, though it snowed harder—naturally—the farther south and west we went. It's called "lake-effect snow." Tradition has it that the closer you get to Lake Michigan, the heavier the snowfall gets, and it's true. I've read a scientific explanation for this, but don't ask me to repeat it.

We dropped Margaret off in Holland, then drove on to Warner Pier. I took Lindy to the big old house she and Tony had moved into right before Christmas. Tony Junior and his chocolate lab, Monte, came out on the porch to greet us. Lindy invited me in, but I declined, and she put her hand on the door handle.

"Gosh!" she said. "I'll always wonder if the killer was in Julie's apartment when I went by there that night."

"What! You were at Julie's apartment the night she was killed? Have you told the police?"

"I told Chief Jones. He said he'd pass it along to the Holland detectives, and they might want to talk to me. He said I shouldn't mention it, so don't tell anybody else."

"What were you doing there?"

"I went up to visit Maria Nunez at Holland Hospital. You know, the gray-haired waitress at the Sidewalk Café. She had pneumonia, but she's better now. Anyway, I was coming back by Food Fare, and I realized I was near Julie's. So I stopped."

"When was this?"

"About nine o'clock. It was kind of late to drop in on somebody, so I just knocked once. She didn't come to the door, and I went away."

"So you didn't see anything suspicious?"

"It was dead silent, Lee. Oh! That's not a good choice of words, is it? But I couldn't see into the apartment at all. It's not as if the window blinds were open or anything. All I saw was the parking lot."

"And there was no car in it that bristled with axes and guns, huh?"

"Nope. I slipped and fell into a really weird, bug-eyed car that was parked backward, but it probably belonged to one of the other tenants. And you know me, it could have been a Rolls-Royce, and I wouldn't have known the difference."

I laughed. Lindy's indifference to cars is legendary among her friends. Her husband swears he puts an Indiana University pennant on her antenna, even though she's not a Hoosier fan, because Lindy would never find her car in a parking lot if it didn't have a red-and-white flag on it.

I promised Lindy I wouldn't say anything about her visit to Julie's apartment; then I left, saying I wanted to check on TenHuis Chocolade before it closed up.

Which was a fib. Actually, I wanted to call Joe Woodyard. I was supposed to see him shortly, but I wanted to talk to him right that minute. I wanted to tell him about the strange funeral for a nice girl who apparently had several peculiar relatives, but no friends. I wanted to tell him Uncle Martin wanted me to go out to dinner with him, and I felt uneasy about going, but I couldn't say exactly why, and, no, it wasn't because nerdy Cousin Brad told me Martin was a lech. The whole day had been strange, and I wanted to talk about it with someone who cared.

So I drove carefully to TenHuis Chocolade, parked in front of the shop and went in. I waved to Aunt Nettie, inhaled six deep breaths of chocolate aroma, helped myself to a Dutch caramel bonbon ("Soft, creamy, European-style caramel in dark chocolate"), then went to the telephone.

Naturally, I couldn't find Joe. He wasn't at his boat shop. He wasn't at his apartment. He didn't answer his cell phone.

We had a date for seven o'clock, when he was supposed to come out to the house I shared with Aunt Nettie. I really had promised I'd cook dinner for him. But we'd made that plan after Hogan Jones had asked Aunt Nettie to go out to dinner with him that evening. Would the snow change their plans? Would it change ours? Aunt Nettie and I saw enough of each other without double dating.

I was still wondering when Aunt Nettie came into the office. She looked serious. "How were the roads?"

"Not too bad."

"It's supposed to stop pretty soon. Hogan and I still plan on going into Holland for dinner."

That was one of my questions answered. But before I could react, Aunt Nettie pulled a bright pink envelope out of the pocket of her white, heavy duty food service apron. "I got an unexpected letter," she said. "I wanted to show it to you."

"Who's it from?"

"My sister-in-law. My brother's widow. Read it."

She shoved the envelope across the desk. It was not only bright pink, but the flap was scalloped and printed to look like lace. I opened it. The notepaper was scalloped to match, and it also had tiny hearts dancing across the top.

" 'Dear Nettie,' " I read. " 'I know we haven't been in touch much since Ed died, but you've always been good about remembering Bobby at Christmas and on his birthday. Plus when he graduated from high school. I have appreciated it.'

" 'Well, Bobby is now close to graduating from Eastern Michigan. He's majored in marketing, and he's done pretty good. He has worked part-time as a waiter, and I'm proud of him. Since he's my only chick, I guess I ought to be!'

" 'Anyway, you said in your Christmas letter that the business is back on track and you and Phil's niece were thinking of expanding. Will you need to hire someone around June? It would be such a good opportunity for Bobby!'

" 'I'm sorry to be so pushy, but I'd never forgive myself if Bobby missed such a good chance to be involved in a successful family business.'

" 'I'm doing fine. The plant has had some layoffs, but so far my job seems safe.'

" 'Love, Corrine.' "

So help me, as I read those final words, I could hear Mrs. Schrader's voice echoing in my ear. "I suppose you are your aunt's heir."

It took me a minute to form a reply. And then I blew it.

"It would have made a better imposition if Bobby had sent a recipe himself," I said.

Usually Aunt Nettie can figure out what I was trying to say, but that one confused her completely. She looked at me with an expression of openmouthed incomprehension.

In fact, my statement had thrown me completely. For a moment I didn't have the slightest idea myself what I'd been trying to say. Then I began to scramble. "I mean—I mean—Bobby would have made a better impression if he had written and sent his résumé himself."

Aunt Nettie's face smoothed into its usual placid contours. "I agree," she said. "I haven't seen Bobby in years. I have no idea whether or not he'd be a good worker."

"I wonder if Bobby knows his mom wrote you. He might not even be interested in a clerical job. And that's what we need. Or what I need. I could use somebody to help with the orders and shipments and to handle the front counter. Or did you have something else in mind?"

"I didn't really have anything specific in mind, Lee. Corinne has always acted like I was completely helpless without Phil. When I wrote her at Christmas—well, I guess I was trying to brag a little. After all, we were finally able to begin paying ourselves full salaries! I must have overdone it."

"We're entitled to brag a little," I said. "Last year was the best Ten-Huis Chocolade ever had."

"What do you think we should do?"

"*You* should do? About Bobby? Talk to him, I guess. The problem with family members is that they're easy to hire, but hard to fire. I marvel that you had the nerve to hire me."

"That was an easy decision. You'd worked here earlier. I knew you were a hard worker and had a head for figures."

"And I needed a job."

"Well, if you'd been chief accountant for IBM, I wouldn't have had the courage to offer you this little job." She looked at me seriously. "Lee, I know you are capable of much more important things than shipping TenHuis chocolates around the country. When that big opportunity comes, I want you to take it."

"Are you trying to get rid of me?"

"No! No! But I know things can't go on forever. Your life will change. My life will, too."

After that unsettling remark, she left the office.

Getting married was all the change I could contemplate right at that moment. But Aunt Nettie had confused me. Somehow, I felt that conversation wasn't only about her nephew Bobby and the possibility that he might want a job.

I picked up the phone and punched the speed dial for Joe's boat shop again. Now I desperately wanted to talk to him. More than my day was messed up; my whole life seemed to be.

But Joe was still not at home, not at work, not answering his cell phone. I angrily went through the mail and the phone messages. I was concentrating so hard on my disappointment over not reaching him that I jumped about a foot when the phone rang.

"Hi," Joe said.

"Where are you?"

"City hall."

"City hall? You never go to city hall on Mondays."

"I had a little emergency and needed to use the city phone. When did you get back?"

"About an hour ago. Are we still having dinner?"

"I was counting on it."

"Good. I need to talk to somebody."

"Now?"

I checked the time. Five o'clock. "I guess I can wait until I see you. I just need a sympathetic ear."

"So do I. This afternoon has been nutso."

"What's wrong?"

"Just a little e-mail problem."

"E-mail!"

"I'll tell you about it when I see you, if six isn't too early."

I said six was fine, and Joe hung up.

E-mail? Joe was having a problem with e-mail?

I thought e-mail was supposed to enhance communications. But it had indirectly linked me with some very unusual people. And now it was a problem for Joe.

Huh.

## CHOCOLATE CHAT
## LITERARY CHOCOLATE

"Venice is like eating an entire box of chocolate liqueurs in one go."                                                —Truman Capote

"My momma always said life was like a box of chocolates. You never know what you're gonna get."                —Forrest Gump

"What use are cartridges in battle? I always carry chocolate instead."                              —George Bernard Shaw

"Chocolate is a perfect food, as wholesome as it is delicious, a beneficent restorer of exhausted power. It is the best friend of those engaged in literary pursuits."—Baron Justus von Liebig

# Chapter 5

Aunt Nettie was still dressing when I heard Chief Hogan Jones pull into the drive. I guess she heard the car, too, because she stuck her head out her bedroom door. "Lee! Can you talk to Hogan a minute?"

"Sure. Keep on primping."

Aunt Nettie giggled. Since she had started dating after three years of widowhood, she really had become like a girl again. And she was dating Hogan Jones—the catch of the Warner Pier older crowd.

Aunt Nettie hires a man with a snowplow to keep her drive cleared. Since everybody uses our back porch as an entry, especially during the winter, the man also keeps the short flagstone walk cleared. Luckily, he'd come that afternoon. I met Hogan at the kitchen door. It had occurred to me that he might know something I wanted to know, and I was pleased to have the opportunity to ask him.

When I opened the door, Hogan was stamping his boots on the sidewalk.

"Come on in," I said. "Aunt Nettie's almost ready, but you and I get to talk for a minute."

"I need some calm conversation to settle my nerves after the drive out here. That new drop-off on Lake Shore Drive is a doozy."

Lake Shore Drive, of course, gets its name because it runs right along the shore of Lake Michigan. This is nice, in general, but if we have a winter with lots of west wind, there's a drawback. Big chunks of ice—six or eight feet thick—form along the shore. They break off and float out into the water. Then a west wind comes and drives them right back to the lake's edge, where they grind away at the beach and bank like bulldozers. That winter the ice had eaten the bank away at one spot until it was right up to the pavement. Get an inch too close to the edge, and the car would go tumbling down. The street department had put up a barricade, of course, but it didn't look very substantial.

"You're chief of police," I said. "Call the street department and tell 'em it's a safety hazard."

"I already told them, and they already knew. But they're trying to get some more concrete barriers. Until they can get hold of some, they're stuck with that orange tape and a few wooden barriers with big spaces between."

"Well, since you made it safely, I wanted to ask you a question."

"I hope it's not about Julie Singletree." Hogan stepped inside the kitchen and wiped his boots on the throw rug. Hogan is in his mid-sixties, and he's not handsome, but he has an appeal I can appreciate. It's something about his close resemblance to Abraham Lincoln in both height and rugged features. He looks reliable, intelligent, humorous, and macho.

"Why don't you want me to ask about Julie's death?" I said. "After all, Julie was a friend, or at least an acquaintance, of mine."

I gestured toward the living room, and Hogan followed me, frowning. "I don't have any excuse for getting interested in a crime that happened in another city," he said.

"I did appreciate your getting some details for me the day after she was killed. But I'm not asking you to do that again. This time I just wanted an opinion."

"I got lots of those. And they're worth every cent you pay for 'em."

"I went to Julie's funeral today—the whole Food Group did—and Julie's uncle told me her computer was stolen from her apartment."

"So?"

"So, he said he found this very strange. But why? Isn't a computer a common thing to steal? Like TV sets or CD players? Anything easy to hock?"

Hogan frowned. "I don't know that there's a general rule about burglars, but yeah, they've been known to take computers."

"Then why was Martin Schrader surprised?"

"Maybe he's just dumb about how burglars operate." The chief's eyes shifted as he spoke, and I looked at him closely.

"Do you know what else was taken?"

"Not everything. Like I said, I don't really have any excuse to ask about it."

"Aw, c'mon, Hogan. Don't try to tell me cops don't gossip just like the rest of us."

He grinned. "You know better than that, Lee." Then he sighed. "I guess it won't hurt to tell you what I heard on the grapevine. The word is that the burglar or killer or whoever it was didn't take much. Just a few things. And he messed the apartment up some."

"Like he'd been searching for something?"

"No, like he didn't care if he left a mess behind him. Some drawers were pulled out. A couple of things were turned over." Hogan cleared his throat. "The Holland detectives think he probably came on foot."

"Did they find tracks?"

"Sure. Thousands. Julie lived in an apartment complex, remember? Nobody left the track of a size fifteen extra wide Nike on her carpet, if that's what you mean."

"In other words, the tracks aren't any help. I suppose there aren't any fingerprints either."

"Fingerprints are never any help unless you find somebody to match them with. And then you have to prove that somebody was never in the apartment at any other time, for any other reason."

By now Hogan and I were sitting in chairs in front of the brick fireplace in the living room. He pointed to the wood stacked inside. "Do you want me to start you a fire?"

"No, thanks. Joe's coming over. He likes to do it. All you guys are fire builders."

Hogan smiled. "I hope he can cheer you up, Lee. I know that having a friend killed is a real jolt. All I can tell you is that it does look as if somebody broke in, probably some kind of burglar. My guess is that Julie surprised him, he panicked and hit her."

"She was a little thing, Hogan. A foot shorter than I am. It wouldn't have been hard to kill her."

He nodded. "Yeah. My Holland buddy told me that. Anyway, the burglar must have decided to get out of there in a hurry."

"Where did the tale about the dark guy walking down the alley come from?" Hogan looked surprised, and I repeated the gossip Lindy and I had gotten from Margaret Van Meter.

Hogan shrugged. "I hadn't heard that one. But I doubt a witness would have seen if a guy walking down the alley was dark or fair or in between. The temperature was close to zero that night. If the guy wasn't wearing a heavy jacket and hat, his hair and skin would have been the color of ice. Anyway, the Holland detectives think the killer just took the few things he could carry in one trip, which makes them think he was on foot."

"He wouldn't have wanted to look like Santa with his pack."

"Right. He couldn't have carried anything too bulky. Which might be why he took the computer, but not the monitor or the keyboard—"

"Monitor or keyboard? But Julie had a laptop! She had it along the day she came down to see the mouse samples she ordered for the Schrader banquet."

"There were two computers. She had that flashy new Gateway she carried around to plan parties with. It's still there. And she had an old Macintosh that she used for correspondence and e-mail."

"That's a weird way to manage your computer life."

"Maybe not. She kept the Macintosh connected to the phone line. The laptop was in a briefcase."

"And it wasn't stolen?"

"The laptop was inside the case and stashed in a closet. The burglar probably didn't realize what it was."

"You say the killer didn't take the Macintosh keyboard? What else did he take?"

"I didn't hear the whole list. Her jewelry box was gone. The descriptions are circulating. Her grandmother and uncle say she just had a few family pieces."

"Their idea of a 'few family pieces' might include the Kohinoor. So nothing else is missing?"

Hogan laughed. "No, there's more. But I haven't seen a list. All I know about specifically is her mouse."

"You mean the killer took her computer and mouse, but not the keyboard?"

"Not a computer mouse. A real mouse."

"Julie had a mouse?"

"Apparently it's a Schrader family tradition. My buddy was laughing about it. The Schrader lab originally did a lot of testing involving mice, and the family members all think they're wonderful pets. So Julie had a pet mouse, a white one. She kept it in a fish tank in the living room. The tank got knocked over, and the mouse escaped. It hasn't been found."

"Oh, my gosh! That'll come as a surprise to the next tenants."

"Her uncle set a trap—you know, one of these live traps—and left it there. I assure you that the Holland PD doesn't want the mouse as evidence. As soon as it turns up, they'll call the uncle."

"One of the Holland cops will probably open a drawer, and it'll pop out and scare him to death."

Hogan and I chuckled over the fate of the Holland detectives who had to search Julie's apartment, knowing that a mouse might scurry out at any moment. Even a small, tame, white mouse could be pretty surprising if you looked under the couch and found it looking back at you.

We were still chuckling when Aunt Nettie came out. Hogan complimented her appearance—she did look rosy and pretty—and they left. I put a card table up in the living room and set it for dinner in front of the fireplace. I was sure Joe would want to have a fire, and we might as well enjoy it.

I couldn't help thinking about Julie. Poor little Julie, so small and easy to kill. A tear welled up, and I had to get a tissue. I moved to the sink, scrubbed the baking potatoes seriously, then stabbed them vigorously with a paring knife. Pretending I was giving Julie's killer a few whacks made me feel a little better. The tears had stopped by the time I had the potatoes and meatloaf in the 400-degree oven.

Meatloaf and baked potatoes—not exciting, but one of Joe's favorite meals. He tells me anybody can tell he and I were both raised in moderate circumstances. We both like meatloaf, hot dogs and sauerkraut, porcupine meatballs, and even tuna casserole. As a Texan, I've introduced him to taco salad and chicken-fried steak with cream gravy, and he seems to like those, too. He'd better.

The house smelled pretty good by the time Joe slammed the door of his pickup and came up the back walk, stamping his feet the way Hogan had. He was clutching what was obviously a bottle in a paper sack in his left hand. We greeted each other affectionately, though Joe used only one arm.

"You didn't have a great day, I guess," Joe said after I'd been kissed thoroughly.

"Not until now. But it doesn't sound as if you did either. How come you had to spend time at city hall? You usually limit your city attorney business to Tuesdays."

"Actually, I usually work on it some every day, but I work at home. A little reading and some e-mail. But today a minor flap blew up, and I had to do some telephoning. It involved a conference call, and that's easier to do with the city hall phones."

"What happened?"

Joe plucked a bottle of Michigan red out of his paper sack. "How about a glass of wine before I tell you?"

"Sure. I set the table up in the living room, in case you want to have a fire."

"You open the wine; I'll light the fire."

Joe's work life might be described as bipolar. He finished Warner Pier High as "most likely to succeed"—class president, plus state honors in debate and wrestling. He kept up his scholastic and leadership record at the University of Michigan, and sailed into law school. His mother—who owns a Warner Pier insurance agency—thought he was headed for a career in corporate law. But after he graduated, Joe amazed and annoyed her by going to work for a legal aid nonprofit. Then he married a woman who was one of the nation's most famous—or maybe infamous—defense attorneys, a confidante to the rich and famous. Joe doesn't talk about her unless I ask, but she must have nearly wrecked his life. At least she wrecked his love for the practice of law. After two years of marriage he quit law, got a divorce, and opened a boat shop, specializing in the restoration of antique wooden speedboats.

"Honest craftsmanship," he had told me. "The best way to keep your self-respect."

But a few months earlier he'd edged back into law when he took a part-time job as city attorney for Warner Pier. He supposedly gave them the equivalent of one day of work a week. He had taken the job because of me, and I wasn't sure I liked that. He had been making so little money in the boat business that he hadn't felt he could ask me to marry him. The part-time job paid for an apartment in downtown Warner Pier, an apartment we'd be sharing in three more months.

But I didn't want Joe to feel that he had to compromise on how he wanted to run his life because of me. The idealism that had driven him out of the practice of law was one of the things I liked about him. My father was an auto mechanic; I would be perfectly content with a craftsman as a husband. Besides, I'd tried the upscale life during my first marriage, and I didn't like it.

But I tried to put all this aside when I carried a tray with crackers and cheese and two glasses of wine into the living room. The couch had a good view of the fire, and we settled down on it.

"What's this e-mail problem you had?" I said.

Joe laughed. "It's not really an 'e-mail' problem. It's an 'e-go' problem."

"Ego? Yours?"

"Not this time. Have I told you about Ellison Peters?"

"Is he on that e-mail list of small town city attorneys?"

"Oh, yeah. But he's a cut above the rest of us. The 'small town' he represents is St. Anthony. You know, 'Tony City.' "

"Over by Detroit?"

"It's the place people move to when they want to go upscale from Grosse Pointe. We may think we have lots of millionaires around here, but Tony City makes Warner Pier look like the low-rent district."

"And Ellison thinks his city's economic status gives him clout?"

"Definitely. Not that he has the money to live there himself. But he's one of these with a slick suit, a slick haircut, and a slick car."

"But is he a slick lawyer?"

"He's a pretty good lawyer. Just a shade too dignified for me to invite him out to the boat shop. Anyway, he has appointed himself chairman of the small town city attorneys e-mail list."

"What did he do to cause a problem?"

"He's decided we should present a case at a moot court competition. He committed us without consulting the rest of the list." Joe laughed. "Some of the other guys aren't very excited about it."

"If he can't get enough people to take part, he can't pull it off. Why is this a problem?"

"There was a lot of e-mailing back and forth when it came up." Joe laughed again. "And some of the people failed to remove all the old messages before they sent new ones."

I began to see. "Oh, no!"

"Oh, yes. The word 'idiot' was used."

We both laughed. "Then you," I said, "had to spend the afternoon on the phone calming this guy down."

"Right. It took a conference call between four of us. But we got Ellison to climb off his high horse. It's all going to work out."

Then Joe got up and poked at his fire. He was looking in the fireplace, not at me, when he spoke again. "All the guys on the list want invitations to the wedding."

There went the evening, right down the drain.

# Chapter 6

Darn. Joe had obviously come with a new array of arguments designed to get me to agree to a big wedding.

"I'd better check on the meatloaf," I said. I got up and went to the kitchen.

I fled the living room because I didn't want to argue about it. Again. Oh, I knew we had to settle the issue sometime, but not that night. I got angry at the thought.

Besides, a tricky little voice told me, if I waited long enough we wouldn't have time to plan a big wedding before April, and Joe would have to give up the idea.

I had looked at the meatloaf and turned the fire on low under the green beans when I heard Joe coming.

Joe spoke slowly. "Did I say something wrong?"

"Oh, no. I'm just upset tonight. The funeral and everything."

"Are you sure?"

"Positive. I've put the fire under the green beans—Texas style, with bacon bits. We can have another glass of wine."

Joe looked concerned, but again I told myself I didn't want to discuss the wedding plans that night. I led the way to the living room and tried to change the subject.

"Julie's family is a bit strange," I said.

"How so?"

I described the funeral and the reception afterward, including my tête-à-tête with Rachel Schrader, and ending with Uncle Martin's declaration that he wanted to discuss Julie with "someone her own age."

"Actually," I said, "I'm not Julie's age. I'm at least five years older. Or at least I thought I was. Julie's age wasn't in her obituary. But I found out today she went to high school with Margaret. Margaret knows her a lot better than I do, actually."

Joe laughed. "Margaret's the one with six kids, right? She might not be nearly as interesting to Martin Schrader as a gorgeous six-foot beauty queen."

Suddenly I was as angry as ever, and all my intentions of not discussing how angry I had been flew away. "Gorgeous six-foot beauty queen! You sound just like my mother."

Joe looked taken aback. "Your mother? Why?"

"The only reason I got into the beauty pageant business was my mother. She pushed and pushed. She kept telling me it would help my self-esteem, give me confidence."

"You seem to have plenty of both. Maybe it worked."

"No! It destroyed both. How would you like having a pageant director tell you to work on your inner thighs? Having the musical director tell you not to worry about your tiny, weak little voice because he can beef it up with the sound system? I may have learned how to fake confidence, but if I have any self-esteem, it's because I learned to stand up for myself and tell the beauty business—and my mother—to go jump."

Joe sipped his wine, then put the glass down on the coffee table. Then he turned toward me, but leaned back in the corner of the couch. "Did I ever tell you that you have a beautiful"—he paused and cleared his throat—"mind?"

I looked at him narrowly. "Just don't forget that," I said.

Then we were both laughing, and I had laid my head on his shoulder, and he had put his arms around me.

"Am I wrong in thinking I brought this on by talking about our wedding plans?" Joe said.

"You made me think of my mom, I guess, and she's a major reason that I don't want a big wedding. Besides, Joe, I'm almost thirty years old. I'm too old to be a blushing bride."

He pulled me closer. "I don't expect you to blush for anybody but me. But that's beside the point. Your problem with the wedding isn't really about your parents."

"I thought it was."

"No, it's about something more important. It's about you spending fifteen years of your life avoiding confrontation with your parents."

"That's silly! My mother and I argue all the time."

"No, you don't. You get mad at your mother all the time, but you never tell her what you think. You haven't really told her to 'go jump.' You've just started avoiding sensitive topics."

"I don't think I do that."

"Remember Christmas? We wanted to spend Christmas Day with her, then go to Prairie Creek to see your dad the day after. But she said we'd have to do it the other way around so she could stay over a day in Hong Kong. All you said was, 'Yes, Mother.' "

"Why fight about it? She's entitled to her plans."

"Yes, but those plans forced us into spending Christmas Day with your stepmother's family. We didn't have a chance to really talk to your dad until late that night, and only for a short time. And having us show up a day early annoyed Annie and her daughter."

"They're always annoyed with me over something."

"I don't think Annie was annoyed with you. She was mad at your mom."

"Why?"

"Because your mom forced us to change our plans and our new plans interfered with Annie's family reunion. Now, Brenda's another case. Brenda's just flat jealous of you."

"Jealous! Why?"

Joe hugged me tighter. "Because your dad loves you best."

I stared. "But he's my dad! He's just her stepdad."

"Does Brenda have a father?"

"Well, he's never around."

"I noticed she didn't get a Christmas present from him."

I sighed. "I guess it is pretty hard on her."

"Besides, you're the beauty queen. You're the one who graduated from college with really good grades. You're the one who can wrap your dad around your finger with the flicker of an eyelash."

"You make me sound awful!"

"From Brenda's viewpoint, you are. She can't possibly compete for your dad's attention when you're around. And all it takes is a phone call from you and he drops everything and buys you a car."

"I paid for it! He just found it for me."

"And drove it to St. Louis for you to pick up."

"Well, I notice he found a good car for Brenda's high school graduation present. And I bet she didn't have to pay for it."

"We've gotten way off the subject I thought we ought to talk about."

"Oh? I thought we were analyzing my relations with my family."

"Oh, it's a much broader subject than that. We're analyzing your relations with me and my relations with you."

"That's a more interesting subject, I guess."

"I hope so." Joe stopped talking and gave me a kiss. "But our interpersonal relations worry me sometimes."

"Why?"

"Because sometimes you treat me like you treat your mother."

"My mother!"

"Yes. You avoid confrontation. You let me have my way— sometimes—because you don't want to argue about it."

"If it's something I don't care about . . ."

"Then say, 'I don't care.' And say it as if you mean it. Don't refuse to discuss something because you're afraid we'll argue over it. And don't stonewall me just as a way to win an argument."

He'd seen right through me, right through to that tricky little voice that told me if I stalled long enough the wedding issue would decide itself. I didn't know what to say.

But I didn't have to say anything, because Joe gave me a kiss that I'll remember a long time. Then he patted my fanny gently. "Think about it, okay? But we don't have to talk about it anymore tonight. Nothing should interfere with meatloaf."

"First things first, huh?"

"I've got *my* priorities straight."

It's easy to see why I fell for this guy. A little later I got up and went to the kitchen to finish up the dinner. Joe followed me. He stood in the doorway and watched me slice the meatloaf and get the baked potatoes out of the oven.

"What did you tell Martin Schrader?" he said.

"When he wanted to talk to me about Julie? What could I say? I told him I would." Then I finished up the story, telling Joe about Brad Schrader's warning.

"Are you uneasy about meeting Martin Schrader?" Joe asked.

"Not really. I'm certainly not going to meet him at a lonely cabin in the woods, like the naive heroine of a romantic novel. But I wouldn't be afraid to talk to him in my office or in a restaurant. Of course, I might want to drive my own car to the restaurant."

"And you'll wear a business suit." Joe grinned.

"My black pants suit and the heavy boots with the chunky heels. The modern suit of armor. Ready for battle." I picked up the dinner plates, already served, and gestured at the salad with my elbow. Joe obediently lifted it and followed me into the living room.

"Joe," I said. "You've lived around Warner Pier most of your life, and Martin Schrader has been around here all of his—at least in the summers. Is he notorious as a skirt chaser?"

"I never heard of it. But I was gone nearly ten years. Besides, I definitely don't move in the same circles he does. I'll ask Mom. She sells the summer people a lot of insurance, and she doesn't do it by ignoring who lives next door to whom and who's seen having dinner with whom."

The rest of the evening was ordinary. Joe and I talked about the wedding, decided to send his mother flowers on her birthday, argued about what the city council should do to try to solve the Warner Pier parking problem, then touched on the old house Lindy and Tony had bought. We were doing the dishes when Aunt Nettie and Hogan came home. We lingered in the kitchen, so they could have the living room, and Joe went home before eleven.

I stay over with Joe sometimes, but he rarely stays with me. The house Aunt Nettie and I share simply doesn't have any privacy. The walls are so thin that a conversation anyplace upstairs is plainly audible downstairs. And there's not a lot of space. Aunt Nettie had talked about putting in a second bathroom, upstairs, but since I was planning to move out, she dropped the idea.

I'd just gotten into my pajamas when the phone rang. I answered the upstairs extension.

"Lee?" It was Joe. "When I drove by Mom's house she was still up, so I stopped and asked her about Martin Schrader. She told me something interesting."

"*Is* Martin a notorious skirt chaser?"

"Not really. She knew of only one person he'd dated locally. Carolyn Rose."

I nearly dropped the phone. Carolyn Rose? The florist member of the Seventh Major Food Group.

"Ye gods!" I said. "At the funeral this afternoon, he didn't speak to her at all. They acted like complete strangers."

"All Mom knew is that when Carolyn first opened her shop—that's more than five years ago—she came to Mom for insurance. And she told Mom she was moving to Warner Pier because it was close to her 'boyfriend.' Mom said she almost bragged about who he was—Martin Schrader."

"I guess he didn't turn out to be the marrying kind."

"Not if that's what she wanted . . ."

Joe and I said good night, and I climbed into my bed, stared at the ceiling, and thought about Carolyn Rose. It was more fun than thinking about the issues Joe had raised about my personality.

Carolyn had an interesting personality, too. Outwardly, she was a tough businesswoman. Maybe her name should be "Thorne," rather than "Rose." I wondered if she had really cared about Martin Schrader, or if she was attracted by his financial attributes.

Martin would be considered quite a catch, of course, if you were looking for a successful man from a prominent family. And he was certainly attractive. But he had to be at least in his fifties and apparently he'd never married; he was definitely in the confirmed bachelor category. And the way his mother sat on him would give any girlfriend pause for thought.

One thing was for certain, I concluded before I picked up my bedtime book. I would never mention Martin Schrader to Carolyn Rose.

I was barely out of bed the next morning when the phone rang again. It was Joe. He'd forgotten he had to make a quick trip to Lansing on city business that day. Could I order the flowers for his mother's birthday?

"Tell Carolyn to send me the bill," he said.

"Sure," I said. And as I said it, I'll swear, the thing that popped into my mind was, "That'll be a good excuse to talk to Carolyn Rose about Martin Schrader." When I realized what I'd been thinking, I shuddered. I definitely did not want to talk to Carolyn Rose about Martin Schrader. Or that's what I told myself.

I went by House of Roses on my way to work. Of course, I could have taken care of the whole thing on the phone, but somehow— despite my resolution of the night before—I decided it would be friendlier if I went by personally. I took the precaution of rehearsing what I wanted to say beforehand. I didn't want my tangled tongue tripping me up, producing "Martin," as in Schrader, when I'd meant to say "marguerite," as in daisy.

House of Roses is located in a late-Victorian cottage on the state highway that skirts Warner Pier. Carolyn had battled the planning commission until she got permission to give it a trendy, "painted lady" look, with the siding a brilliant yellow and the trim orange, green, and pink. I knew that Carolyn kept very few flowers in stock during the winter months; she wasn't going to get much drop-in business in a town of just 2,500.

I was almost surprised to see an SUV that wasn't Carolyn's parked in her graveled—and snow-covered—parking area. Carolyn's only vehicle was the panel truck with "House of Roses" on the side. I parked beside the SUV and waded to the porch, where I stamped the snow off my boots.

Inside, the shop was chopped up into a lot of small rooms. It smelled like flowers, even though most of the arrangements in sight were artificial. There was a Valentine's Day display, of course, which featured some fresh red and white carnations and a few silk roses. The specialty foods area, with fancy nuts and crackers, looked tired. Winter is definitely an off time for retailers in a beach resort town.

I didn't see either Carolyn or the driver of the SUV when I came in. I called out, and Carolyn's head of fake red hair poked out of a back room. "Hi, Lee," she said. "Come to rehash the funeral?"

"Actually, I'm detailed to order flowers for Joe's mom's birthday."

"Good. You're my first customer. And my computer's on the fritz. Jack Ingersoll is here working on it." That explained the SUV. Jack ran a computer service from his home in Warner Pier, though most of his clients were from elsewhere.

Carolyn was coming out from the back. "Let me give you a cup of coffee while we talk about Mercy's flowers. I need to think about something besides this damn computer."

"What's it doing?"

"Nothing! It's eaten all my files. No correspondence, no bookkeeping, no e-mail. All gone. But I'm sure Jack can find everything. How do you take your coffee?"

"Black. Did you and the Denhams have any problem getting home yesterday?"

"No. We probably beat you, since you had to swing through Holland with Margaret Van Meter. Did you know she went to high school with Julie?"

"I learned it yesterday. I was surprised that Julie wasn't sent away to some fancy boarding school."

"That's what I would have expected, too. But Margaret told me they both went to Holland Christian. Conservatives."

Actually, I don't know if Holland Christian High is conservative or not, but it has that reputation. Certainly Holland is a conservative community, and Holland Christian high school is associated with the Reformed Church, in the minds of the community, if not legally. Carolyn and I both nodded.

I expected Carolyn to ask about Mercy's flowers next, and I started to trot out the request I'd thought out, the one that I was sure I could say without getting my tongue tangled. But she fooled me. She handed me my coffee, leaned casually on the counter, and said, "Actually, knowing Martin Schrader as intimately as I once did, I find it hard to believe Julie was sent to a religious high school."

As I say, she caught me completely off guard. My tongue took off of its own volition. At least, I'm sure my brain didn't tell it to say what came out.

"Martini Schizo seemed to be garnishing his mother," I said.

Carolyn and I stared at each other—she looked amazed, and I probably looked completely gaga. Then she laughed.

So I laughed, too. "I'm sorry, Carolyn," I said. "I washed my tongue, and I can't do a thing with it. I meant, after the funeral, Martin Schrader seemed to be intent on guarding his mother."

Carolyn was still laughing. "Lee, forgive me," she said. "I got all set to be totally cool about Martin Schrader, and you . . ." She quit talking and began laughing again.

I couldn't be offended. "As you can guess from my twisted tongue, I had a minor run-in with Martin Schrader and with his nephew. It's on my mind. And, yes, I had heard that you formerly dated Martin, and I was determined not to mention him to you."

Carolyn took a tissue from her pocket and blotted her eyes. "Actually, I think that's the first time I ever laughed about Martin. I feel much better for it. What happened to you?"

I quickly outlined Martin's request and the warning from Brad that followed it.

Carolyn went right to the heart of the problem. "You can hardly refuse to talk to a grieving uncle—if that's what Martin is—about his murdered niece," she said.

"I know. Of course, I'm not worried about meeting Martin, since I wouldn't meet anyone I don't know very well anyplace except my office. Or maybe a restaurant. I was more interested in Brad's comment. Is it true? Is Martin a 'dirty old man'? Or is that Brad's idea?"

"I think Brad's a callow youth," Carolyn said. "He's still young enough to be shocked by the thought of anyone over forty having sex. Martin is a chaser—as I found out the hard way—but 'dirty old man' is going too far. I don't think you need to take too many precautions if he wants to talk."

Still giggling now and then, Carolyn and I agreed on some flowers for Mercy Woodyard's birthday, and she called her supplier to make sure our selection—bronze roses—would be available. While she was on the phone there at the sales desk, I could hear a voice muttering swear words in her office, where Jack Ingersoll was still working. Carolyn had just confirmed my order and offered me a bill to deliver to Joe when Jack opened the office door and looked out.

"Carolyn! Have you checked all your windows?"

"That's what I've got you here to do, Jack. My Windows could be completely missing and I wouldn't know it."

Jack shook his head vigorously. "No, not Windows! Windows! Lowercase 'w,' not capital. The windows to your shop!"

"What do you mean?"

"As near as I can tell, there's nothing wrong with your computer or any of its programs."

"Then where did all my records go?"

"All I can figure is that someone got in, opened your computer, and erased everything in it."

# Chapter 7

Jack came out of the office, all hair and snow boots, looking more like a mountain man than a computer nerd. "I'll swear there's not a thing wrong with your computer, Carolyn. I think somebody erased everything. Who's been fooling with it?"

"Nobody! Nobody's touched it but me."

"That's hard to believe. Could anybody have accessed your files without your knowing?"

"I don't see how."

"Was anybody suspicious in the shop late yesterday?"

"In January? In Warner Pier? I didn't even open up yesterday. And Lee's my first real, live customer today. Nobody could have gone into the office without my noticing."

Jack scratched his head. "Back to my first idea. You could have had a burglar."

Carolyn and I both laughed. "Why?" she said. "What would a burglar want here? I don't keep money here overnight, and I haven't begun to restock for the summer season. There's nothing here a burglar would want. Unless it was that computer. And it's still here."

"You better check your windows. Somebody's been messing with that computer, and if they didn't get at it while you were here, they must have done it while you weren't."

Carolyn was still scoffing, but she began to go from room to room, checking inside, and Jack took a look outside. In less than a minute, he put his head in through the back door and called out. "Look at the corner window!"

My curiosity was thoroughly aroused, so I followed Carolyn into a workroom. The window Jack wanted checked was over a large stainless steel sink. Anybody coming in or going out that window would have had to step into the sink.

"Don't touch anything," I said. "If somebody did get in, there might be fingerprints."

"I can't believe anybody burglarized the place," Carolyn said. "But I will say I don't usually leave the sink quite that dirty."

I peeked over her shoulder and looked into the bottom of the sink. There was dirt there, but—heck, this was a florist's shop. Flowers have roots, and roots are often buried in dirt.

"It doesn't look like footprints," I said.

Carolyn picked up a white ballpoint pen from the counter and used it to point to the window's standard, thumb-operated latch. "It's unlocked," she said. "But—hells bells! I'm not careful about keeping things locked. Not in the winter!"

I understood what she meant. It's a folk belief around Warner Pier. We're all convinced the summer people and tourists take all the crime home with them on Columbus Day. We seem to feel that Warner Pier is a Michigan version of Brigadoon; after the outsiders leave we lapse into a state of small town innocence until outsiders reappear the next June.

Jack was back inside by then. "Somebody's been stomping around in the snow under that window," he said. "I couldn't see any recognizable tracks, but maybe you'd better call the police."

Then he looked at his watch. "Your computer is up and running. I'll have to get into the hard drive to try to find out if anything can be salvaged. And I'll be glad to talk to the chief—or whoever he sends—about the break-in, but right now I'm going to run out to Hideaway Inn. Diane and Ronnie Denham have some kind of problem, too."

The Denhams had computer problems, too? That news gave me a severe case of jumping stomach—that queasy, upset feeling when my innards bounce around, up in the throat one minute and down in the toes the next.

What if Jack was wrong? What if Carolyn hadn't had a break-in? What if she had some sort of computer virus that destroyed all her files?

She and I exchanged e-mail daily. If she had a virus, I could, too.

Carolyn was calling 9-1-1, but I decided the Warner Pier police could investigate a possible burglary without me. I drove back to TenHuis Chocolade as quickly as possible. I almost skidded into the curb when I pulled up in front of the shop, and I did skid on the sidewalk as I ran toward the door. I opened my computer before I took my coat off, and as soon as it loaded I began opening files. I felt a surge of relief when I saw everything was there. Correspondence. Orders. Accounts receivable. E-mail. All the files I ordinarily use. Safe.

"Whew." My tummy settled into its normal place behind my navel. Then I got out a disk and backed up everything in all my business files right that minute.

While the computer was humming and clicking over that job, the door to the shop opened, and Jason came in.

He came directly into my office, and he didn't mess around with small talk. "Listen, Lee, you've got a dial-up Internet connection with WarCo, don't you?"

"Yes. Why?"

"Don't connect, whatever you do. I got a virus that ate my whole system. I talked to WarCo, and they said it seemed to have come in by e-mail. Don't connect until you check with them, okay?"

I may have gasped. "Oh, no! The Denhams have computer problems, too, Jason, and so has Carolyn Rose."

"Do they have direct lines?"

"I don't know about the Denhams, but I don't think Carolyn does. She said that when she opened her computer this morning everything was gone. But Jack Ingersoll doesn't think it was a virus. He thinks somebody actually broke into her shop and erased everything in her computer."

"Weird!"

"It certainly is. I just backed up all my business files, but I haven't connected to WarCo yet. Thanks for the tip-off."

I agreed to call Margaret, and Jason said he'd talk to Lindy and Mike Herrera. Then Jason left.

Margaret answered on the first ring, and I was greatly relieved to hear that she hadn't had any computer troubles.

Margaret said her husband, Jim, was taking computer classes at the vo-tech school. "He knows what a dunce I am," she said, "so he set me up with a program that lets me keep my e-mail online. I never download anything. If I need a record, I just print it out. So if I have a virus, it's the server's problem, not mine. I don't use this computer for anything but e-mail and a record of orders and payments. And to print up bills. It does help at tax time. But mostly the kids use it to play games."

I called Lindy to make sure Jason had caught her. She had her laptop with her. Its files were fine, she said.

"I took the day off, because I've got to work tonight," she said. "Mike has a city council meeting, of course, and he wants me to be at Herrera's to close tonight." Herrera's is Mike's upscale restaurant. He keeps it and the Sidewalk Café open most of the winter. In addition to her catering job, Lindy fills in whenever he needs her at one of the restaurants.

Lindy promised to back up her files, and I hung up, relieved to find that not everyone in the Seventh Major Food Group seemed to have been hit by either a burglary or a computer virus.

By then the computer had finished copying the files I was most concerned about, and I took the disk out, marked it with "backup" and the date, then put it in my desk drawer. I resolved to think about something else. I hung my jacket on the coat tree in the corner, traded my snow boots for a pair of loafers, and wandered back into the shop, taking deep, soothing breaths laden with chocolate aroma. Aunt Nettie wasn't in sight, but the place was bustling, just the way a chocolate business should be four weeks before Valentine's Day.

I stopped beside Dolly Jolly, one of our newer employees. Dolly had popped up in our lives the previous summer, when she rented a remote cottage near Warner Pier to use as a retreat while she wrote a cookbook. When fall came, she decided she wanted to stay in Warner Pier. She rented the apartment over TenHuis Chocolade, and she asked for a chance to learn the chocolate business.

Dolly is unforgettable. She's taller than I am, built like a University of Michigan linebacker, and has brilliant red hair and a matching freckled face. And she can only speak at one decibel level—the top of her voice.

"Hi, Lee!" she shouted. At the same time she flipped a five-inch mold over and gently tapped until what looked like a bowl of dark chocolate—actually a puffed, hollow heart—fell gently onto a metal tray, where it lay beside identical hearts.

"Hi, Dolly. How's the stock holding out?"

"Fine! But you might want to ask Nettie! She said something about needing raspberries!" Frozen raspberries are used to make the filling for a popular TenHuis bonbon.

I nodded. "We don't want to run out of raspberry creams." Because of their lovely pink insides and their yummy flavor, raspberry creams ("Red raspberry puree blended into a white chocolate cream interior, covered in dark chocolate") are highly popular at Valentine's. "Where's Aunt Nettie?"

Dolly pulled over a second tray, loaded with small solid chocolate hearts, cupids, and arrows. She began to fill the bigger hearts with an assortment of the small items. "She's in the break room working on something! Did you see the messages I left for you?"

"I guess not."

Dolly shrugged. "There were only a couple of calls! They said they'd call back! But this one guy came by!"

"Did he leave a name?"

"I left it on the desk! Martin? Martin something!"

I thought a moment. "Martin Schrader?"

"Older guy? Kinda short?"

Of course, to Dolly anybody who isn't playing in the NBA is "kinda short." But at not quite six feet, I'd looked down slightly when I talked to Martin Schrader face-to-face.

"Beautiful head of white hair?" I said.

Dolly nodded. I stood by and watched as she took a second five-inch dark chocolate heart, spread melted dark chocolate around its edge, then "glued" the two hollow hearts together. The most obvious result was a puffed, dark chocolate heart filled with special little Valentine symbols in dark, milk, and white chocolate. The second result would be a profit for TenHuis Chocolade; these were popular with our customers. Dolly used a spatula expertly, trimming away any chocolate that oozed out from the seam.

"Beautiful job," I said. "Aunt Nettie's sure happy that you wanted to come to work here." Dolly's face turned a shade brighter than usual, and I went on back to the break room. I found Aunt Nettie sitting at a table, hunched over a yellow legal pad.

She looked up and frowned. "I wish you could write this letter for me, Lee."

"You usually make me write all your letters. Why can't I write this one?"

"It's to Corrine."

I sat down across from Aunt Nettie. "Yes, you need to answer her yourself."

"If only I knew what to tell her about Bobby."

"You could just treat it like any other application, I guess. Tell Corrine all we have open is a routine clerical job or something like you've got Dolly doing—a sort of apprenticeship in how to make chocolate."

"Yes, I could do that. Then I'd ask for a résumé."

"If Bobby's interested."

"If he's interested."

I took a minute to tell Aunt Nettie about the computer problems that had hit Jason, House of Roses, and Hideaway Inn. Then I went back to my desk, feeling a little bit angry, a little bit fearful, and a little bit jealous. After all, Bobby was a blood relative to Aunt Nettie. I wasn't. As a matter of fact, he was probably her closest relation. If she were to fall into a vat of chocolate and drown that afternoon, Bobby could well get everything. I didn't even know if Aunt Nettie had a will or not. I could be working for Bobby and living in Bobby's house, the one *my* great-grandfather had built with his own hands.

Again Rachel Schrader's voice echoed in my subconscious. "I suppose you are your aunt's heir."

I sat down in my chair and slammed a desk drawer. Stupid! I was acting stupid! I'd only worked for TenHuis Chocolade a year and a half. Aunt Nettie had made chocolates for thirty-five years. The business belonged to her. She could do anything she pleased with it.

I stared at my computer screen and tried to think about something else. Anything else. E-mail. I called WarCo—our local server here in Warner County. They said they had identified the virus that hit Jason, and sure enough, a copy had also gone to me.

"What!" Fear gripped me.

"We got it stopped. It came from a fake address."

"How can you tell?"

"Easy. This one is pretty notorious. It was originally used by a guy who was a regular ecoterrorist."

"A what?"

"He claimed to be a supporter of ecology, only he did it by sending viruses to companies he thought didn't use ecological principles he approved of. They caught him finally."

"I hope they sent him up for life."

"No such luck. Anyway, the scuttlebutt is that he managed to convince the authorities he was only a tool of the organization he worked for. It may have been true. He got off with a big fine and a severe warning, but no jail time."

"Why would he want to attack the Seventh Food Group?"

"Oh, I don't think it's the same guy. I think someone has appropriated one of their addresses. Everybody in the trade knew the addresses."

Assured that my e-mail was safe, I opened it up. There were a dozen orders and queries. For the next forty-five minutes I concentrated on clearing them out. I replied to the queries, attaching my stored price list to several of them. I acknowledged the orders and moved them out of the e-mail file and into a special file I keep for those. I printed out a note from my mother, detailing her itinerary for a trip to Brazil, then hit REPLY and sent a message urging her to have fun. I didn't go into my personal problems with her.

I had no other personal e-mail besides that one message from my mom. For a moment I missed Julie's annoying jokes and inspirational items.

By the time I had finished handling e-mail, I was in a much better frame of mind. I might still be jealous and suspicious of Bobby, but I felt calmer and more confident in Aunt Nettie's ability to handle her own affairs.

And I was thinking about computers, so the problems that had hit the Seventh Major Food Group came back to mind. I gave in to curiosity and called Diane Denham to find out about the electronic woes at the Hideaway Inn.

Diane sounded dispirited. "I'm really upset over this virus," she said.

"Then you got hit by the same virus that hit Jason?"

"That's what Jack Ingersoll thinks. Our files are gone, Lee! Kaput! Zip! All our reservations for next summer. All our accounts. All our correspondence. Gone! Why would anyone do this?"

I didn't have an answer, so I listened sympathetically until Diane was ready to hang up. Then I tried vainly to work on my own business. But it was no go. I simply couldn't concentrate. Finally, I went back to the shop and found Aunt Nettie.

"I give up," I said. "I'll have to work late tonight."

"Why? What's wrong?"

"Nothing's wrong with the business. I just can't get these computer problems out of my mind. It's nearly time for Tracy to come in for her after-school gig on the counter. I'm going back to House of Roses and see if the police found out anything."

Aunt Nettie smiled. "If you're not going home for dinner, maybe you and I could snatch a pizza. Whenever you're ready."

"That'll be fun. You and I don't eat dinner together—just the two of us—very often these days. Since your social life is so active."

I left Aunt Nettie smiling, put on all my winter regalia, and went back to House of Roses. When I went in the shop's front door, Carolyn looked out of her office.

"I don't see any crime scene tape," I said. "Have the police been here?"

"Chief Jones came himself."

"I think he does all the detective work." Warner Pier has only four guys on the force, after all.

"He certainly acts as if he knows what's what when it comes to a crime scene. And he thought Jack was right. He found scratches on that window. Plus, he thought somebody had deliberately messed up the tracks outside the window—you know, so they couldn't be identified. But he said it would be hard to catch the burglar."

I followed Carolyn into her office. "When does Jack think he can work on your hard drive?"

"Not for a week or more. He's got to do a job in Holland. Some insurance office. He said he could come in the evening, but I don't want to hang around here all day waiting for customers and all night keeping Jack company."

Carolyn reached for her telephone pad. "By the way, I got confirmation on the roses for Joe's mother. The bronze variety is available."

"Good. The rust and cream colors ought to look good in her office. Did they confirm the price? I'd better write it down."

Carolyn looked through some papers on her desk. "The price is right here. Someplace."

I picked up a notepad Carolyn had placed at a spot that would be handy for customers, then reached for a ballpoint pen. On the corner of the desk was a brass jug full of the rainbow-hued ones she passed out to customers. And right in the middle of twenty-five rainbow-hued pens was one white one.

Carolyn picked up a slip of paper and turned back toward me. "Help yourself to a pen," she said. "I'm trying to get rid of those."

"Are you changing your logo?" I said. "That white pen is really different."

"White pen?" Carolyn frowned, then focused her eyes on the brass vase and its contents. "Where did that come from?"

She picked it up and turned it over, looking at it closely.

I could see the light dawn. She might as well have yelled, "Eureka!"

"What is it?" I asked.

Carolyn gave a sly smile, then chuckled. "It's nothing. I just remembered where this pen came from." She stuck the pen in her center desk drawer, then smiled at me. Her whole mood seemed to have changed. She'd been depressed. Now she was elated.

"I'll have Mercy's roses out by noon tomorrow," she said. And she actually hummed a little tune.

I was going to ask just what had changed her outlook, but her phone rang. Carolyn answered it. "Sure, Lee's here," she said. Then she handed me the receiver.

It was Tracy, the high school girl who was helping us with retail sales every afternoon during the Valentine rush.

"Lee?" Her voice was low. "There's a guy here to see you. A Mr. Schrader. He says it's important."

Rats. As soon as I'd left the office, Martin Schrader had come back. I sighed and decided I might as well get the meeting with him over.

"Okay," I said. "Tell him to wait in my office. I'll be right there."

I told Carolyn I had a minor emergency at the office and drove back to TenHuis Chocolade. As I entered the shop, Tracy beckoned to me. "I almost never got that guy to sit down in your office," she said. "He kept roaming around the shop."

"He's probably just nervous, Tracy. He's the uncle of that girl who was murdered in Holland. I'm sure the whole family is upset."

"He's her uncle? He doesn't look old enough to be anybody's uncle."

I turned and looked through the glass wall that surrounded my little cubbyhole of an office. I expected to see the distinguished and handsome gray-haired Martin Schrader.

But instead I saw a skinny, dark-haired guy with a hangdog expression.

My caller was not Martin Schrader. It was his nephew, Brad.

# Chapter 8

My first reaction was annoyance. I'd cut short my questions for Carolyn because I felt obligated to talk to Martin Schrader. And my visitor turned out to be his nerdy nephew. I wouldn't have hesitated to let Brad sit an hour. After all, he hadn't even hinted that he was going to drop by.

My second reaction was a major itch on my curiosity bump. Why had Brad come?

Common politeness required that I find out; so did extreme nosiness. I went into the office, shook hands with Brad, and sat down at my desk.

"I didn't expect to see you again so soon," I said. "What brings you by?"

Brad's voice squeaked as much today as it had the day before. "I guess I wanted to ask your advice." Brad dropped his head and stared at the floor. "I was wondering what was the best way to get acquainted in Warner Pier. You know, meet people."

I was astonished. "Let's back up here, Brad. I didn't even know you lived in Warner Pier."

"I don't exactly. I live a mile north, in a little house on my grandmother's property. It's always been called 'the cabin.' I drive to Grand Rapids to work."

"You work for Schrader Laboratories?"

"Yeah. Uncle Marty thought I should try to learn something about the family firm." Brad's voice held an undertone of sarcasm on the two final words, but his eyes didn't match it. They took on a whipped-puppy look. Then he spoke again. "Julie told me you'd only been here a few years, but you seemed to know everybody in Warner Pier. I guess I thought you might have a magic method of getting to know people."

All of a sudden my heart went out to Brad. He was such a nerd, with an annoying voice and an insecure manner. Which didn't mean he wasn't a nice guy. But he must have always had trouble making friends because of his unfortunate mannerisms.

"I don't know that there's any magic trick you can use to get acquainted in a new community, Brad. If I managed it in Warner Pier, it's because I work for my aunt, and everybody in town knows her. So they all have to be nice to me. Plus, I'd worked here summers when I was in high school, and I got to be friends with Lindy Herrera back then. She's introduced me around, too. And after I started dating Joe Woodyard, the guy I'm planning to marry, he introduced me to his friends. So I may have been a stranger in Warner Pier, but I had a lot of local connections."

Brad was looking even more downhearted. Obviously, he didn't have local connections.

I tried to think of something encouraging to suggest. "I did do a couple of things on my own, though. I made an effort to meet people I thought I'd have something in common with. My banker, for example. We're both interested in getting ahead in business. I went down to her office the first time we needed to talk, and I enjoyed meeting her. So, the next week, I called and asked her to go to lunch. We've become really good friends. She suggested that I sign up for a chamber of commerce committee, and I jumped at it." I laughed. "I think any community will warm up to a willing horse."

"A willing horse?"

"You know the old saying, 'Work a willing horse to death.' Find some activity you're interested in. And volunteer."

"I support the Lake Michigan Conservation Society."

"Great! They should have a lot of things going on—cleaning beaches? You'll have to get out and do the grunt work, of course. Sweep floors. Wash dishes."

"They don't seem to have projects like that. It's mainly lobbying."

"Then find some organization that does need manual labor. If you're interested in ecology—"

"I am! Sort of."

"There are other groups around that need workers. Pretty soon you'll discover you know people. You'll be running into them at the Superette. If I did anything active to get acquainted in Warner Pier, that was it."

Brad still looked doubtful. "But you've got an edge. You're really pretty."

"There's nothing wrong with your looks, Brad." That was true, I realized. Brad didn't *look* odd; he *acted* odd.

"Appearance may attract people on a superficial level," I said, "but real, true friends aren't concerned about your looks. Being friendly and cheerful is a lot more attractive than physical beauty."

Brad gave me a sly look out of the corner of his eye, but he didn't say anything. If he had, I knew what it would have been—"Easy for you to say." I decided there was no point in telling Brad I'd ruined years of my life worrying about my looks because my mother thought they were important.

"But you've got that cute Texas accent," he said.

"Don't tell me that! I worked with a speech coach three years trying to get rid of that cute Texas accent."

"It's better than my New York one."

I gave my widest grin. "You can always offer people a cuppa 'kwaffee.' That sounds pretty cute."

Brad finally smiled back. "How about the other people Julie knew here in Warner Pier? Are all of them natives?"

"Lindy is. But Carolyn Rose just came here a few years ago. I think the Denhams bought Hideaway Inn after Diane took early retirement. They haven't been here long."

"What about the others on the list?"

"I don't know if Jason's a native, but he's lived here a long time. And Margaret grew up in Holland. In fact, she went to Holland Christian with Julie."

"Yeah, Julie told me they knew each other in high school."

I was getting tired of being quizzed by Brad. Maybe I could find out a few things about Julie if I turned the tables and began questioning him.

"Didn't Julie ever introduce you to any of her friends in Holland?"

"Oh, she wanted to, but it never worked out. Tell me about Mrs. Herrera. She's with Herrera Catering? Where is that?"

"Their offices are right down the street, over the Sidewalk Café. But Lindy's not there much."

"Does she work from home?"

"Sometimes. Her job is special assistant for her father-in-law, Mike Herrera. She fills in wherever he needs her. Like tonight, she's in charge of Herrera's, their upscale restaurant."

I tried to turn the conversation back to Julie. "You know, Brad, all of us in the Food Group thought that Julie must have a boyfriend. She was a darling girl. But she never mentioned anybody special in her e-mail, and we didn't spot anybody at the memorial service who seemed to be a likely candidate."

"She hadn't been dating anybody seriously that I knew about."

"I can't believe Julie didn't have an active social life. Would your uncle know anything about it?"

Brad shrugged. "I think Uncle Martin kept trying to introduce her to guys in Grand Rapids. You know, doctors and lawyers and executives." Again I caught that slight sarcasm when Brad referred to his uncle. Or was it the reference to business, as in "executives"?

"I guess I can ask your uncle," I said.

"Ask him? About Julie?"

"Yes. He's supposedly coming by here this afternoon."

I glanced at my watch, and as I did I caught a swift movement out of the corner of my eye. When I looked back at Brad, he was standing up. The movement had been Brad. He had leaped to his feet like a jackrabbit with a coyote after him.

"I've bothered you long enough," he said. "Please don't tell Uncle Martin I came by." He was moving out of the office.

I stood up, too. "You can't leave without a sample of TenHuis chocolate."

"Oh, you don't need to give me candy." By now he was out of the office and in the middle of our little retail shop.

I followed him. "It's not 'candy,' Brad. It's chocolate. Quite a different thing. Come on now. You'll hurt my feelings if you don't have a sample. What do you like? Dark chocolate or milk chocolate?"

Brad kept edging toward the door. "Dark, I guess."

"Okay, how about Jamaican rum? Our sales material calls it 'the ultimate dark chocolate truffle.' Or a double fudge bonbon? 'Layers of milk and dark chocolate fudge, enrobed in dark chocolate.' "

"Either one!" Tracy, who had been listening to all this, opened the glass showcase, took out a Jamaican rum truffle in a pleated paper cup, and held it out to Brad. He pulled a stocking cap down over his ears, took the truffle, and stood there looking at it.

Then he turned back to me. "About Julie and her love life—actually, I think she'd been afraid to date since her marriage broke up."

"Her marriage? Julie had been married?"

Brad nodded and waved his Jamaican rum truffle at me. "Thanks," he said. Then he scampered out the door before I could say anything more than, "Brad!"

He went off up the street, almost running, though he did pop his truffle into his mouth while I could still see him through our big window.

"What a weird guy!" Tracy said.

I guess I answered her, but I was thinking about the stunning announcement Brad had made as he left. Julie had been married? She'd never mentioned it. But Julie had never mentioned anything about herself. She had concentrated on learning all about other people, but her own ideas, needs, desires, and history had been a deep secret.

Who had Julie married? What had happened to the marriage? "Her marriage broke up," Brad had said. Had she been divorced? Separated? Was she still married? Was her husband her heir? Did the Holland cops know that he existed?

Tracy spoke again. "Actually, if you got that Brad Schrader guy on one of these redo shows—you know, got him a new wardrobe, a new haircut, and taught him how to talk . . ."

"Then he wouldn't be the same person," I said. My voice was sharp. Where did Tracy get off criticizing Brad? She was no glamour girl herself, though she had smartened up a bit in the past few months. I reminded myself that she was just a high school kid, and I forced my voice to be softer. "Brad's a nerd, but that doesn't mean he isn't a nice guy, Tracy."

I went back to my office feeling more sorry for Brad than ever. He had run away because he didn't want to meet his uncle and had asked me not to tell his uncle he'd come by. Every time there had been the slightest reference to Martin Schrader, Brad had displayed an uneasy attitude. Was Martin Schrader trying to be a mentor to Brad? Did Brad resent it? Or were they battling over something? What about Brad's father and mother?

Brad had given me a lot to think about, and the most important thing was the news he had dropped about Julie. She'd been married. I eyed my computer and thought about going on the Internet to check out the wedding stories in the *Grand Rapids Press* back issues. But I didn't even know if Julie had been married in Grand Rapids. Or in Holland. Or in Michigan. Though I'd expect a Schrader wedding anywhere would be news for the *Grand Rapids Press*.

I was dying to talk to somebody about this. To Lindy. The very person. I reached for the phone, then looked at my watch. It was nearly five o'clock. Lindy would be busy at Herrera's, getting ready to open. I couldn't bother her with a tidbit of gossip, no matter how fascinating.

I decided I'd better simply get back to work. Maybe Martin Schrader would show up yet that afternoon, and I'd ask him about Julie's marriage. I turned to my computer and thought chocolate.

I checked my e-mail again, sorted a couple of new messages into the right electronic files, then began handling orders. At five thirty Aunt Nettie came in and said she had to run a few errands in Holland. "Do you mind putting our dinner excursion off until I get back?" she said.

"Not a bit." I opened my desk drawer. "I have my trusty stash of Amaretto and Dutch caramel."

She laughed and left. Each TenHuis employee is allowed two chocolates each day—truffles, bonbons, or molded solids. We're supposed to stay out of the fancy molded items, such as the puffed heart filled with tiny chocolates that Dolly Jolly had been working on earlier. Amaretto truffles, Irish Cream bonbons, and Dutch caramel bonbons are my favorites. I snag a couple from the counter every morning, and if I don't eat both during the day, I leave the uneaten ones in my drawer. Lots of days I can't find time to relish prime chocolates, so I often save up a stash of a half dozen or so.

I ate a Dutch caramel—these have soft and creamy insides, nothing like the stuff used to make caramel apples—and went back to work. But in the back of my mind I was still thinking about Julie, about the startling news Brad had given me, and about how much I wanted to talk to Lindy about it. I guess that was the reason, after Aunt Nettie got back from Holland, that I suggested we skip the pizza and go to Herrera's for dinner.

"Herrera's?" Aunt Nettie looked down at her white pants and tunic, topped by a blue sweater. "I'm not very dressed up."

"This is Warner Pier. Nobody dresses up."

"But there's a difference between designer sportswear and a food service uniform."

"I thought a nice dinner would be a little treat for us. I've got room on my MasterCard."

"You've convinced me."

So, at seven forty-five p.m. Aunt Nettie and I parked in front of Herrera's, went in and were warmly greeted by Lindy, who was acting as hostess.

Herrera's is down on the water; a great location in the summertime, when the tourists and summer people fill every table and form a line outside. The main room is large and paneled in limed oak, with large-scale landscapes by local artists. In the summer these emphasize pastel colors.

In the winter, when the view of the frozen river turns off any desire for iced tea or jellied consommé, the room's fancy plantation shutters are firmly closed. Mike makes a few other changes to make the place feel warmer—red velvet draperies replace the white linen ones he uses in spring and summer, the candles on each table are larger than the votives used in warmer weather, and the pale landscapes are replaced by equally large-scale ones in darker tones.

But it's still an impressive ambience. The service is impressive, too. Lindy sent over a bottle of wine, and the wine steward popped the cork and filled our glasses before we could do more than glance at the menu. He draped the bottle with a napkin and put it on the corner of the table.

Aunt Nettie ordered chicken Cordon Bleu—Herrera's version is not prepackaged—and I went for the pork loin with tart cherry sauce. We both ordered soup and skipped salad.

I'd told Lindy I had a piece of hot gossip for her, so she joined us just as the soup was served. She was as astonished as I was to learn that Julie had been married.

"It must not have been while she was living in Holland," she said. "She sure never gave a hint."

"Margaret will know."

"Probably. But she's never given a hint either."

"How about Jason?"

Lindy stood up. "I'll check on the kitchen. Then I'll call him."

"Honestly," Aunt Nettie said. She smiled, but she was scolding me, too. "Poor Julie is dead. Does it matter if she had been married or not?"

I ate soup and thought about it. Was I simply being nosy? I ate three spoonfuls of soup while I came up with the answer.

"I don't think our interest in Julie's marriage is merely nosiness," I said. "Not in the gossipy sense, anyway. I think it's guilt. Julie was the focal point of our little e-mail group, the one who kept it going. She did all of us some favors on the business front, and she made an effort to be friendly to all of us. She dropped in on Margaret, who's pretty housebound with those six kids. She came down to Warner Pier and took Lindy and Carolyn and me to lunch. She sent the Denhams some business, I know.

"But when she died, I realized that none of us knew anything about her. We hadn't even known she'd been married! I know Julie and I weren't close friends, but it makes me feel bad because I took her for granted while she was alive."

Aunt Nettie's smile was good-humored. "As long as you don't think you have to get involved in the investigation of her death, Lee."

"Oh, no! I've been down that road before, and I had to buy a new van to prove it! Any more murders, and they're gonna cancel my insurance."

We both laughed and settled back to enjoy our dinner. But way in the back of my mind, a few thoughts did bubble up. The Holland police thought Julie had been killed by a burglar. That burglar had stolen—among other things—her computer. Jack Ingersoll thought House of Roses had had a burglar. A burglar who did nothing but destroy Carolyn's computer records. Jason and the Hideaway Inn had been hit by a vicious computer virus. Could these things be connected?

If anything happened to my computer, I might get pulled into the investigation of Julie's death whether I wanted to be or not.

When Aunt Nettie and I had finished dinner, Lindy came over to say she had talked to Jason, and he hadn't known anything about Julie's marriage. But he was going to call someone who might know, then call her back. Aunt Nettie went on home, but Lindy brought a pot of coffee, and I lingered while the Herrera's crew cleaned up. She finally got around to telling me that her e-mail had been attacked by the same virus that hit mine, but our local computer server, WarCo, had been able to stop it before she connected. Another narrow escape.

Ten o'clock came, the last customer had gone, the kitchen was cleaned, and Lindy had packed up her laptop. Still no word from Jason.

"I don't think he'll call this late," Lindy said. "I've let everybody out the back."

"I'm parked out front," I said. "If you'll let me out that way, I'll be gone."

"It's been nice to have company."

The stars were bright as I crossed the sidewalk. I could see the lights of the town glinting off the ice in the river. I paused to look at the view, then realized Lindy was standing at the door, waiting for me to get into my van safely. I did so, checking behind the seats and in the rear deck. Okay, I admit it; Julie's death had made me jumpy.

Well, I thought, if Lindy can watch and make sure I'm safe, I'd better do the same for her. I knew she was parked in the alley, so I warmed up the van for a minute, backed it out, then drove down the street and turned the corner. Halfway down the block I swung into the alley. My lights hit Lindy's compact car.

It took me a moment to register the two figures beside the car.

One figure was on the ground, lying terribly still, and the second held something that looked like a club.

## CHOCOLATE CHAT
## CHOCOLATE THROUGH THE AGES

(Describing the first view of cocoa beans by Europeans) "They seemed to hold these almonds at a great price; for when they were brought on board ship together with their goods, I observed that when any of these almonds fell, they all stooped to pick it up, as if an eye had fallen."

—Fernand Columbus, recorded in 1502, during the fourth voyage of his father, Christopher Columbus

"If you are not feeling well, if you have not slept, chocolate will revive you. But you have no chocolate pot! I think of that again and again! My dear, how will you ever manage?"

—Marquise de Sévigné, 1677, quoted by Sophie D. Coe and Michael D. Coe in *The True History of Chocolate*

"The superiority of chocolate, both for health and nourishment, will soon give it the same preference over tea and coffee in America which it has in Spain." —Thomas Jefferson

# Chapter 9

I hit the horn and held it down. I guess I was yelling, too. And I slipped the van into neutral and gunned it. Don't ask me why. I guess I just wanted to make a lot of noise.

All this commotion got results. The guy dropped the club and clutched something to his chest, then jumped up and ran.

I stopped with my fist still on the horn. Now I could see that the figure on the ground was Lindy. Or at least it had a red cap like Lindy's and was wearing Lindy's blue down coat. This did not surprise me, since I'd been expecting to see Lindy in that alley.

I had finally acquired a cell phone, and luckily, it was in my purse. I punched in 9-1-1 as I hopped out of the van, then knelt beside Lindy in the headlights. She was breathing, thank God.

It seemed like hours before the Warner Pier patrol car got there. I stood over Lindy, clutching the cell phone and talking to the dispatcher, terrified that her attacker would come back. I was afraid to move her, but I pulled off my wool scarf and slid it under her cheek, which had been resting on the icy ground.

The Warner Pier EMTs, who are volunteers, were only a minute behind the cops. By the time they pulled into the alley, Lindy was groaning and stirring.

The next hour was confusing. Hogan Jones and Joe showed up just after the EMTs, both of them on foot. They'd still been at the city council meeting, and both had run the four blocks from City Hall since it was faster than getting into their cars.

Joe showed a satisfying relief that I wasn't hurt—the dispatcher had paged the chief and told him only that I'd called in a 9-1-1 report on an attack behind Herrera's. The chief had nudged Joe and told him I was in danger, and they had arrived with no more information than that. I guess it was lucky neither of them had a heart attack. Mike Herrera was close behind them, so I gathered that the city council meeting had adjourned abruptly.

Joe and Mike left almost immediately to tell Tony what had happened. Joe stayed at Tony and Lindy's to babysit the three Herrera kids so Tony could follow Lindy to the nearest hospital, thirty miles away in Holland. Mike came back to the alley to let the police into the restaurant and be available with other information they might need.

The chief asked me a lot of questions, but I didn't have many answers. I hadn't seen much.

The guy—or gal—who'd been standing over Lindy had worn standard west Michigan winter gear: a dark parka or ski jacket with a hood. The hood had been over the attacker's head. I hadn't been able to tell if the person was dark, light, fat, thin, or in between. He—or she—had run off at a crouch, so I couldn't even tell if the attacker was tall or short. The face had been a dark blob, which might have meant it was covered by a stocking mask or a ski mask. Or it might have simply meant the attacker kept his face out of my headlights. His jacket had had no distinctive features—no stripes, checks, or readable brand names.

A short piece of scrap wood was lying beside Lindy, and apparently this was the club I had seen the attacker raising. It was the kind of thing that might be found in any Dumpster in the alley. The chief and the patrolman looked for footprints, but the alley had been plowed, so the snow wasn't deep, and in the middle of a January night it was mostly ice anyway.

"I guess the guy is agile," I said. "I would have fallen down and broken my neck if I'd run off the way he did."

"We'll check in the daylight," Chief Jones said. "But I doubt we'll find anything."

Joe came back about then. Tony had alerted Lindy's mom and dad, and they'd arrived to watch over the sleeping kids. Tony had already called from the hospital with a preliminary report that Lindy was demanding to go home, so we were deducing that she was not seriously hurt.

"It must have been a thief," I said. "The guy ran off carrying something, and I don't see her purse anyplace."

"We'll have to ask Lindy just what she had on her," the chief said. "Joe, you follow Lee home."

He'd alerted Aunt Nettie, of course, so she insisted that Joe come in so she could comfort us with coffee and bonbons—crème de menthe ("The formal after-dinner mint") and Italian cherry ("Amarena cherry in syrup and white chocolate cream"). We sat around the dining room table, and I had to tell the whole story.

After I finished, Aunt Nettie shook her head in disbelief. "It's hard to imagine that a thief would attack Lindy," she said. "It's not likely she would be carrying the night's take from Herrera's."

"I'll bet that ninety percent of Herrera's customers use credit cards," Joe said. "If you took the night's take from Herrera's, it probably would be less than fifty dollars in cash money and a whole lot of receipts. You're right. It doesn't sound like a thief."

"Then who was it?" I said. "A sex maniac? When the temperature is down in the teens? He *would* be a maniac. But it did appear that Lindy's purse was missing. At least, it wasn't in the car."

"Did she even have a purse?" Aunt Nettie said. "I've seen Lindy stuff her car keys in her pocket."

"I saw her pack her belongings up before I left," I said. I closed my eyes and tried to remember. "I didn't pay much attention. But you're right. She did stick her keys in her coat pocket. She had a little, flat envelope purse. And she put it in the zipper pocket on the side of her laptop case."

I gasped. "Golly! That's what was taken. Not her purse! Her laptop!"

Joe called the chief and told him to look for the laptop in the car and inside the restaurant.

After he hung up, he nodded at me. "I think you're right. Lindy never goes anyplace without that laptop."

"She wouldn't have left it at Herrera's," I said, "because she didn't work there every day. She would have taken it home."

I was sure that was right. Lindy's laptop—the computer she used to plan events for Herrera's Catering, the machine that handled her schedule, the gadget she used for her e-mail—it had gone down the alley with the formless figure who had attacked her.

And the computers of Jason, Carolyn Rose, and the Denhams had also been involved in weird events that day.

"This is the fourth time." I whispered the words.

"The fourth time for what?" Joe asked.

"It's the Seventh Major Food Group," I said. "Odd things are happening to all our computers."

He looked incredulous, and I realized I hadn't seen Joe all day. I hadn't had an opportunity to tell him about the damage to Jason's computer, to the Denhams' computer, to Carolyn Rose's. So I told him.

"But that's crazy," Joe said. "Everybody knows an expert can get that stuff back. All those political and Wall Street scandals have showed that to the public. Even if you try to erase everything on a computer, it's still on the hard drive someplace."

But I was convinced. "Maybe we're being attacked by a computer illiterate," I said. "I'm going to talk to the chief about it."

Aunt Nettie gave a big yawn at that point—it was after midnight—and we adjourned our meeting.

Joe kissed me good night, then headed for his truck. He called out one last bit of advice. "Keep your cell phone by your bed!"

"We won't have any problem," I said. "I don't have a computer here. I just hope nobody breaks into the shop."

I put on a flannel nightgown and piled all my extra blankets on top of my quilt. I was shaking, and it was probably nerves, not cold. I burrowed under all this weight of wool, acrylic, and cotton batting. I'd begun to feel warmer and was drifting off to sleep. A year from now, I thought, I'll be sleeping with Joe every night, and I'll stick these icy feet right on his back. After all, what are husbands for?

"Husbands." The word jolted me awake.

For a minute I didn't know why. Then I remembered the question that had occupied Lindy and me most of the evening.

Julie's husband? Who had he been? When and where had they gotten married? The attack on Lindy had completely distracted me from that question.

Chief Hogan Jones was a friend. I could ask him if the Holland police knew Julie had been married. I dropped off to sleep thinking that I had quite a lot to talk to him about.

I called his office first thing in the morning, but he wasn't there. Instead, he dropped by TenHuis Chocolade about ten a.m. It wasn't a very satisfactory visit. I might have had plenty to talk to Hogan about, but it turned out that he had even more to talk to me about.

He was mad when he walked in, and we got even further at odds when he seemed to interpret my information about Julie's marriage as an insult to law enforcement. He blew his stack.

"Of course the Holland police know Julie Singletree had been married!" It was the first time I'd ever heard Hogan yell. "That's the first question they ask!"

"Who did she marry?"

"I'm not telling you, Lee!"

"Why not?"

"Because you don't need to know."

"But Julie was a frog—I mean a friend! Julie was a friend of mine."

"If she was such a friend, why didn't she tell you about her marriage herself?"

He had me there. Recklessly disregarding the mood he was in, I tried another tack. "Are they looking at everyone's computers?"

"The Holland police are handling their own investigation. They haven't asked my advice. And they don't need yours!"

"But the Seventh Major Food Group—"

"Lee! Stay out of it!"

"Look, Hogan, two friends of mine have been attacked, and one of them was killed. Three others have had weird things happen to commuters. I mean computers! Am I supposed to ignore this?"

"You're supposed to be reasonable and leave it to the police! I'm not talking to you about this any more!"

We might have left it at that and parted without any more yelling if Aunt Nettie hadn't joined in. She'd heard us, I guess, and she showed up at the office door. "Now just what are you two arguing about?"

Neither of us answered, so she smiled her sunny smile and spoke again. "Come now, surely you can both discuss your differences without yelling."

That was not the right thing to say to Hogan Jones right at that moment. He pointed a finger at me, but he spoke to Aunt Nettie. "You talk to her! She's going to get in trouble, nosing around where she has no business!"

I yelled back. "I'm just worried about my fiends! My friends!"

Aunt Nettie drew herself up with great dignity. "Hogan, if Lee is concerned about her friends, I hardly think that's a quality worthy of criticism."

"These are not close friends."

Aunt Nettie's voice was icy. "Lindy is."

"We're keeping an eye on Lindy. We're keeping an eye on everybody. But we may not be able to if Lee keeps stirring things up!"

"I don't believe Lee has 'stirred things up,' Hogan. She has merely had concerns for her fellow human beings, and she's acted on them. She hasn't interfered with law enforcement in any way. She's just trying to help her friends."

"These are not her friends!"

I got back into the fray at that point. "You keep telling me these people are not friends. But that's stupid, Hogan! We may not be buffet—I mean bosom! We may not be bosom buddies, but so what? I'm still convinced that strange things are happening to all of us. They may be in danger! I've got to do what I can to head that danger off."

"But you don't really know these people!"

"What does that matter? Even if they're complete strangers, I can't let something happen to them without trying to stop it!"

"You don't get it!"

"No, I don't! I don't understand why you don't want me to try to help them!" I stood up then and leaned across my desk. "Whether I know them well or not, they're my friends!"

Hogan leaned across the desk, too, and we stood there, practically nose to nose. And when he spoke again, his voice had become quiet. Too quiet.

"These are not friends," he said. "These are suspects."

Then he zipped up his jacket and left.

# Chapter 10

Neither Aunt Nettie nor I spoke until Hogan was out the door.
"Oh, my," Aunt Nettie said. "I hadn't thought of it that way."
"Neither had I," I said.

I was relieved when she went back to the workroom, leaving me to think over Hogan's parting comment and to feel stupid on my own.

Well, naturally. From the viewpoint of law enforcement, if something was happening to the people in the Seventh Major Food Group and to their computers, the members of the group themselves would be the obvious suspects. After all, if there was something strange going on, who was most closely involved?

But could a member of the Seventh Major Food Group have actually killed Julie? The idea seemed ludicrous. None of us knew her well enough, for one thing. What possible motive could any of us have had for killing her? We all liked her. Or I thought we did. Of course, Carolyn had once called her "Little Miss Knows-All." But she hadn't dropped out of the newslist over it.

I tried to put the whole matter aside. And maybe I did, for an hour. But as lunchtime neared, I began to wonder how Lindy was doing. Finally, at eleven forty-five, I called. I told myself that if Lindy was in bed, her mother would be there to answer the phone. But Lindy answered on the first ring.

"Hi, Lindy. I hope I didn't get you up."

"No. The doctor said I should take it easy today, and Tony's enforcing his prescription. I'm going nuts sitting around here. I need someone to talk to."

"Do you want me to bring you some lunch?"

"Bring me a strawberry truffle, and I'll make grilled cheese sandwiches."

"Deal."

I loaded up a half-pound box of TenHuis's best—four of Lindy's favorite strawberry truffles ("White chocolate and strawberry interior coated with dark chocolate"), plus some solid hearts for the kids and four mocha pyramids ("Milky coffee interior shaped into a pyramid and enrobed with dark chocolate"). I knew Tony liked those.

I parked in Lindy's drive a few minutes after twelve. It was a bright, glary day. The sun glinted off the snow-covered yard and off the roofs of the houses in Lindy's neighborhood, making me grateful for my sunglasses. Lindy's sidewalk had been cleared, and she opened the front door as I stepped onto the porch. I didn't comment on the big bruise on her left temple.

"Sure is good to see a human face," Lindy said.

"I'm almost surprised that the chief is letting you stay alone. After all, somebody actually hit you in the head last night."

"It must have been a thief, Lee. Somebody too dumb to realize I wouldn't have any money on me."

Joe, Aunt Nettie, and I had demolished that theory the night before, but I didn't argue. I noticed that Lindy carefully locked the door behind me and that she was wearing her cell phone on the belt of her jeans. She was obviously being cautious, and there was no point in my making her more nervous than she was.

We talked about home decor while Lindy grilled our sandwiches. She and Tony had bought the 100-year-old frame house a few months earlier, and they had a long list of do-it-yourself projects waiting for them. At the moment all the living room furniture was piled in the dining room because Tony had promised to paint that weekend, but there was plenty of room for their family to eat in what Aunt Nettie called the "breakfast nook." Some previous owner had added the built-in table and benches to the kitchen, maybe sometime in the 1940s.

We'd eaten our sandwiches and carrot sticks, and Lindy had opened the box of candy before either of us mentioned Julie.

"The chief came over and grilled me for half an hour this morning," she said. "He's afraid this business last night is connected to Julie's death."

"He came by the shop and lectured me. Told me to stop being so nosy."

"That's like telling your aunt to stop cooking, isn't it?"

"I'm afraid you're right. Nosiness is a basic part of my personality. But I'm trying to follow his recommendation. So you'll have to tell me what he wanted to know without my asking about it."

Lindy grinned. "The first part of it wasn't too surprising. He wanted to know if I remembered anything about last night. I don't. I remember closing the back door. Then I woke up in the ambulance."

"I think that's fairly typical, from what I've read about head injuries."

"I was lucky not to be hurt worse. The chief told me the reason I was lucky was that you decided to drive around to the alley."

"No biggie. You'd waited at the front door of Herrera's to make sure I was in the van safely. It seemed as if I should return the favor."

Lindy gave a slight shudder, and I scrambled through my brain for a new topic to introduce. But Lindy spoke again before I could. "The main thing the chief was interested in, Lee, was the Seventh Major Food Group. He wanted to know all about the people in it. How well I knew them. What I thought of them. Of course, you're the only one I know very well."

"How about Jason?"

"We knew each other off and on the whole time he worked for Mike, but he tended bar, and I usually worked in the restaurants, so it wasn't a regular thing. Mike thinks a lot of him. But I will say that Jason is the only person I ever heard complain about Julie before she died."

"Did he hate her dumb jokes as much as I did?"

Lindy laughed. "You're the only one I heard complain about those—though I agreed with you! No, Jason had some other problem with her. He griped about her talking too much. He said her mouth was the size of a CNN satellite and broadcast just as widely."

"Oh, gee! She must have really blabbed something he didn't want mentioned."

"She did tend to do that. She told a couple of things I didn't really want mentioned. You remember that day all of us had lunch? Julie, Carolyn, you, and me?"

I nodded.

"She picked me up, and between here and the Sidewalk Café I made some remark about how Tony and his dad didn't always get along. I shouldn't have said anything, but they'd been snarling at each other the night before, and I had it on my mind. Anyway, she brought it up for general lunchtime conversation."

"I remember. You cut her off very well."

"Lee, you know all about the situation between Mike and Tony. Tony just doesn't want to work in a restaurant, and Mike doesn't understand his attitude! But I didn't really want to go into it with Carolyn. I don't know yet how I managed to mention it to Julie."

Lindy was looking tired, so I did the dishes while she took the medicine the doctor had given her for headaches. She promised to lie down as soon as she locked the door after me. I headed back to the shop, but after I'd parked on Peach Street I walked across to Mercy Woodyard's insurance office, instead of going directly to my desk. I wanted to check on the bronze roses I'd ordered for her birthday.

I expected Joe's mother to mention the roses as soon as I walked in the door. After all, I'd signed the card "Joe and Lee."

But she didn't say a word. She accepted my birthday greetings in a friendly way, but she didn't mention the roses. And they weren't in sight in the office. When Mercy got a phone call, I even peeked into the inner office to see if she'd put them there, but there was no sign of any cut flowers.

We discussed the plans for her birthday celebrations—Mike Herrera was taking her out to dinner that evening, and Joe and I were taking both of them out the next week.

"I'll gain one year and ten pounds," Mercy said, smiling. "I don't deserve all this attention."

I went back to TenHuis Chocolade puzzled. Carolyn had promised to have the roses to Mercy before noon. Carolyn had an excellent professional reputation. If there was a problem with the flowers we'd ordered, I'd have expected her to call and explain. Maybe, I thought, she'd called Joe. I'd better check with him.

I went into the shop and took my usual six deep breaths of chocolate aroma. I waved to Aunt Nettie, took off my coat, and reached for the telephone. Before I could punch in Joe's number, the door swung open, and Diane Denham rushed in.

She came straight into my office. "What's this I hear about someone attacking Lindy?"

"It happened last night. I just had lunch with her. She doesn't seem to be hurt badly."

"Oh, my goodness! First Julie, then these computer disasters, and now this! I can't believe it."

"How'd you hear about Lindy?"

"From Chief Jones! He was out at the inn. He wanted to know all about the Seventh Major Food Group. Are we the object of a vendetta?"

"That doesn't seem likely, Diane. We don't have all that much in common."

"Really we have nothing in common but that snoopy Julie."

"Snoopy? You found Julie snoopy?"

"Didn't you? She was always asking personal questions."

"I guess she was. The main thing I noticed about her questions was that she wouldn't answer them."

"She sure *asked* them. She should have been a detective."

"What do you mean, Diane?"

There was a moment of silence. Diane touched her beautiful white hair before she spoke. "Oh, never mind! I guess all of us have things we'd rather not talk about. Somehow Julie wormed them out of you."

"Wormed them out?"

"You sound just like her! She just kept asking until you discovered you'd told her things you didn't mean to." Diane gave an exasperated snort. "I only came by because I wanted to find out if Lindy had been hurt. Tell her I asked about her, okay? Oh, and I need four dozen crème de menthe bonbons. We've got a business conference coming in next weekend."

I left Diane roaming the office and shop while I went back to get her a box of crème de menthe bonbons. Lots of the Warner Pier B and Bs put these on the guests' pillows at turn-down time.

Diane paid for her bonbons and left without saying anything more about Julie. I was really puzzled. What had Diane been talking about? What had Julie known that Diane hadn't wanted known?

I remembered that I'd been planning to call Joe to see if he knew why his mother's flowers hadn't been delivered. I shook my head, picked up the phone and called the boat shop.

I'd almost decided Joe wasn't there when he picked up the phone. "Vintage Boats."

"Hi. It's Lee. You haven't heard from Carolyn Rose, have you?"

"Nope. Should I have?"

I told him that his mother's flowers apparently hadn't been delivered. "I was going to call Carolyn and ask about it, but I thought I'd better check with you. I didn't want to nag if she'd called to tell you there was some problem."

"I'll call her. After all, I'm paying the bill."

I left it to him and went back to work. In a few minutes, however, Joe called back. "I got the answering machine," he said. "I left a message."

"I could try her home."

Joe thought my offer over. "I hate to call business people at home, but—you know her pretty well. If you wouldn't mind . . ."

But the only answer I got at Carolyn's home was electronic—another answering machine. My stomach began to knot up. I wasn't annoyed. After all, Carolyn didn't have to answer to me. Was I worried? That wasn't quite the right description, either. I finally settled on concerned. So many strange things had been happening to members of the Seventh Major Food Group, having one of them out of touch made me concerned.

I tried to put Mercy's roses and Carolyn's whereabouts out of my mind. I organized my work. I had plenty of that. There was my own regular work, plus, that close to Valentine's Day I had to wait on the counter, since we wouldn't have any sales help until Tracy got out of school. Between the constant interruptions from walk-in customers and my concern—yes, that was definitely the right word—about Carolyn, I found it impossible to concentrate on the chocolate business.

When Tracy arrived, I simply gave up. I was so up in the air about Carolyn that I decided to drive out to her shop, then maybe to her home. At least I could see if the House of Roses van was in sight at either location.

It was around the side of her cute painted-lady shop.

My first reaction to seeing it was relief. Carolyn must have come in. I got out of my van, picked my way through the slush in her parking lot, crossed the wide Victorian veranda, and confidently reached for the door handle. It wouldn't budge. The door to the shop was locked.

I peered through the windows that flanked the center front door, mentally cursing their lace curtains and the elaborate arrangements of dolls and doilies, flowers and froufrou that Carolyn had dressed them with. I couldn't see inside.

I walked around to the side of the building. The side door had a glass window that looked into the office. At least it didn't have a lace curtain. But when I looked inside, nothing out of the ordinary was visible.

This was not reassuring. With the van there, Carolyn should be there, too. Her winter hours were roughly ten a.m. to four p.m. It was now three fifteen. She should be there. At least she should have taken care of Mercy's bronze roses. Or called either Joe or me to explain why she hadn't done so.

I walked on around the house. There was the window over the work sink, the one Jack Ingersoll had suspected had allowed a burglar to get into the shop. Thanks to my extreme height, I was able to peek into that. All I saw was an empty workroom. Empty of people, that is. A large box was on the stainless steel worktable, and a tall glass vase stood beside it.

I went back to the van, climbed in, and called Carolyn's house on my cell phone. I talked to the answering machine again. Then I gnawed my nails.

But why was I so concerned? Because the shop ought to be open, and it wasn't? There was a ready explanation for that. Carolyn owned her own business. She could close up anytime she wanted to.

Was I concerned because the House of Roses van was there, and I knew it was Carolyn's only vehicle? There was a ready explanation for that, too. A friend could have come by to pick her up. They could be having a long lunch, visiting a museum, seeing a movie. Heck, Carolyn was a consenting adult. She could have gone off with a boyfriend and checked into a motel.

I just about convinced myself I was being silly. Then I thought about Mercy's roses, and I remembered something.

That box on the workroom table. It had printing on the side. And that tall glass vase beside it. It was exactly the kind of vase Carolyn and I had discussed using for Mercy's roses.

I jumped out of the van and plowed through the snow, back to the window that overlooked the workshop. Yes, my memory had been right. That box said "Grand Rapids Wholesale Flowers" on the side.

I was convinced that Carolyn had started to arrange Mercy's flowers, but something had interrupted her. She had left without even putting the flowers in her walk-in cooler. This was no casual lunch date. Something was wrong.

I started to call 9-1-1, but I chickened out. I was simply afraid to talk to Hogan Jones, to tell him I was being nosy again.

So I called Joe, told him the whole story, and asked him to call Hogan. After all, Hogan couldn't refuse a call from a fellow city official.

And he didn't. He agreed to come right out.

Joe came, too. He and I waited in the van while one of the patrolmen, Jerry Cherry, jimmied the back window and climbed inside.

Carolyn's body was under the worktable.

# Chapter 11

Carolyn was dead, but it was hours before I knew anything more than that.

As the investigators began to gather, and it became obvious that they didn't need me hanging around, I drove back to the shop. The chief told Joe to follow me. I had the feeling Hogan wanted him with me, not because he was worried about my emotional needs, but because he was concerned for my physical safety.

I made it to the shop safely. By then it was close to five o'clock and everyone was leaving. Aunt Nettie, Joe, and I huddled in the break room. Then I thought about Lindy—who'd barely escaped an attack the evening before—and I called her. She was fine, she said. The kids were home from school, her mother was there playing Monopoly with them, and a Warner Pier patrolman had just pulled into the drive.

That was reassuring, but I was still worried about the rest of the Seventh Major Food Group. Whether they were friends or suspects, I wanted to know if they were all right. I went to the office and called each of them. Jason didn't answer, but I left a message on his machine. Margaret answered on the first ring. Like Lindy, she also had a house full of kids, and she said a Holland policeman had been by to check all her doors and windows. Her husband was on the way home. Diane and Ronnie Denham also said they were all right, but Diane was too upset to tell me any more than that.

I was just breathing a sigh of relief when someone banged loudly on the door. I whirled to look. It was dark outside, but when I went close to the window in the shop's front door, I could see a face. It was Martin Schrader.

He didn't seem to be armed, and Joe and Aunt Nettie were there, so I let him in. At the moment Martin didn't look at all like the suave businessman I'd seen at Julie's memorial service. His distinguished gray hair was hidden by a warm hat, and instead of a tailor-made suit, he wore a navy blue down jacket. But the change in him was more than his wardrobe. His face didn't look suave either. It looked pinched and worried.

When he spoke, his voice was shrill. "What's happened out at House of Roses?"

I looked at Joe, wondering if I should talk about it. Joe shrugged. "It'll be all over town by now," he said.

I told Martin that Carolyn was dead. "We don't know any details," I said. "I got worried about her, and—with Joe to back me up—I more or less demanded that the shop be checked out. But the chief sent us home after they found her body."

Suddenly I remembered that Martin Schrader didn't know either Joe or Aunt Nettie, so I introduced them.

He acknowledged the introductions with an absentminded nod. "I can't believe this," he said. "Carolyn! Of all people. She was the original take-charge woman. The last person I'd expect to be the victim of a crime."

"Why?" I said.

My question seemed to surprise Martin. His eyes widened, then narrowed, and he walked up and down the shop a few steps. "I'm not sure why I said that. I guess I had the feeling that if someone tried to attack Carolyn, she'd tear them limb from limb."

"Carolyn did tend to be outspoken," I said, "but I wouldn't have expected her to have a lot of physical prowler. I mean, prowess! I don't think she was particularly strong."

"Her tongue could skin a man alive," Martin said.

"I'm glad to say she never spoke that harshly to me. But I can see her being aggressive."

"Aggressive! That's not a strong enough word." He stopped talking and looked at each of us. "I assume all of you know I dated Carolyn for a while—actually, several years back."

I nodded, and I guess Joe and Aunt Nettie did, too. "Warner Pier is a small town," Joe said.

"Yes. Well, one time my mother was down for the weekend, and she needed a prescription refilled. Carolyn and I went over to the Superette to pick it up. We took the bottle along, because naturally the pharmacist had to call her doctor in Grand Rapids and get an okay. And that druggist—the one who talks so much—"

"Greg Glossop." Joe, Aunt Nettie, and I spoke in unison.

"Anyway, he gave us the wrong medication. And Carolyn noticed right away."

"Good for her," Aunt Nettie said.

"Yes, that was fine. But what wasn't fine was the way Carolyn tore into him about it. I simply couldn't believe the way she talked to him. Then Carolyn acted—well, as if I ought to be *pleased* at the way she'd behaved." Martin frowned. "Believe me, if Mother had heard her—*she* definitely wouldn't have been pleased. After that I was always nervous about bringing Carolyn around Mother. Eventually we quit seeing each other."

And you felt that you'd had a narrow escape, I thought.

Joe and I exchanged quick glances, and I thought Joe's lips almost twitched into a grin before he spoke. "I'd heard Carolyn had a sharp temper. But I barely knew her. How well did she know Julie?"

"Julie!" Martin pulled his dark cap off with an exasperated gesture. "I don't know how Julie got mixed up with her. I nearly fell over when Carolyn showed up at the memorial service."

"Julie sought her out," I said. "Julie said she wanted all the party planning business from around Warner Pier. She was quite up front about wanting to make professional contacts down here. And Carolyn would have been a good contact for her. She had quite a successful business during the summer season, decorated for a lot of the big parties the summer people give. She and Julie could have referred business to each other. But I never got a hint that Julie knew that you and Carolyn had dated each other."

Martin shook his head. "Julie and Carolyn were exact opposites. Picturing them exchanging friendly e-mails boggles the mind."

"It's even stranger that they seem to have shared the same fate," Joe said.

Martin shuddered. "Murdered by intruders in their own spaces."

Joe spoke again. "How did you find out something had happened to Carolyn?"

"I drove by there and saw all the police cars."

"Okay, but why did you come here? I mean, to TenHuis Chocolade. How did you know Lee was involved?"

"As I drove by House of Roses, I saw Ms. McKinney pulling out of the parking lot. I guess you were behind her, in that pickup that's outside. When I saw all the law enforcement and an ambulance, I knew something bad had happened at Carolyn's shop."

Martin gave a guilty smile. "I guess I needed some Dutch courage. I went down to the Sidewalk Café and had a scotch—getting my nerve up to come and ask Ms. McKinney—Lee—what happened. I hadn't had the courage to pull in at Carolyn's, the way I had planned."

I felt surprised. "I thought you weren't seeing her anymore."

"I hadn't seen Carolyn for several years."

"Then why were you planning to go by the shop?"

Martin ran a hand through his hair. "Oh, didn't I tell you? Carolyn called my office yesterday. Left a message with my assistant. She asked me to come to see her. She said she had some information she thought I'd want."

I thought about that one for a minute. It was a surprise. Carolyn had discussed Martin with me the previous day, but she hadn't sounded as if she planned to be in contact with him.

What on earth could have inspired her call?

While I was thinking, Joe was doing his attorney act, quizzing Martin. All that Carolyn had told the assistant, Martin said, was that she had some information he might want. He'd had no idea what Carolyn's information had been. He'd been staying down at the Warner Pier house, but he'd gotten the message when he made a routine call to his office.

"You need to tell Chief Jones about that call," Joe said.

"Sure, if he has time to talk to me. There's no secret about the call, but I have no idea what Carolyn wanted to tell me, and I doubt it had anything to do with her death." Then Martin looked at his watch. "I'll call the chief in the morning. I told Brad I'd take him to dinner. We need to talk about Julie's estate."

"At one point you wanted to talk to me," I said. "Has that situation resolved itself?"

"Not really." Martin pulled a pocket date book out from inside his winter jacket and consulted it. "How about lunch tomorrow?" He turned toward Joe, including him in the invitation. "Sidewalk Café?"

Joe declined, but I accepted for one o'clock. Martin wrote the date in his book, then zipped his jacket. "I guess I'd better head back to the house to meet Brad."

"Are you and Brad both staying there?" Joe asked.

"Brad actually lives on the property and drives to Grand Rapids every day. I'm just down for a business meeting early tomorrow."

A business meeting? What business could Martin Schrader have that couldn't be done better in Grand Rapids? I almost asked, but decided that would be entirely too nosy, even for me. So Martin put his warm hat back on, and I unlocked and opened the shop's street door for him.

"I know Carolyn's death is a real shock to you," I said, "coming on top of losing Julie."

He looked at me with eyes that were as black as Julie's had been. And suddenly they looked really miserable. "Carolyn and I—well, I almost married her. Even though we had grown apart, yes, it's still a shock."

Married? The word jogged my memory. "Oh!" I yelped out the sound, then grabbed Martin's sleeve and tugged him back inside the shop. "I'd been wanting to ask you something!"

Martin looked wary, but he came back inside.

"Who was Julie married to?" I said.

He scowled. I had the feeling he didn't want to answer.

"I know I'm simply being nosy," I said. "But Julie—well, she had a way of getting people to tell her things. But she never told the rest of us anything about herself. Nobody on the Seventh Major Food Group newslist had any idea she'd been married."

"The marriage was over. It doesn't really matter who Julie married. He was just a whiner."

I persisted. "For one thing, Julie seemed so young. She didn't seem old enough to have been married."

"Julie was twenty-eight."

"Twenty-eight! She looked about twenty-one. Of course, I knew she went to high school with Margaret Van Meter, but I put Margaret at about twenty-five—in spite of all those kids."

Martin looked confused. "All those kids? Now who is this?"

"Never mind," I said. "I'm dithering. I'm just surprised. I'm surprised to learn Julie was as old as she was, and I was surprised to learn she'd been married and hadn't ever mentioned it."

"Nobody around Grand Rapids and Holland knew," Martin said. "Julie didn't want an official announcement made, so it never got in the paper. Their wedding was very small. They didn't even tell Mother until it was over. Then Julie said she didn't want a bunch of presents. Said it would make her new husband uncomfortable."

I'd learned a few things from watching Joe-the-lawyer ask questions. I kept quiet. Just looked expectant.

It worked, I guess. After a few seconds Martin went on. "Julie had gone back east to college. She got a degree in French, then started on her masters in art history. This fellow was a graduate assistant in the English Department." He gave an exasperated snort. "Like I say, he was a real whiner. Julie said he wouldn't come out to Michigan to meet the family, so Mother went to Boston to meet him. She wasn't impressed. She said he was an 'I'm gonna go eat worms' type. He seemed to be embarrassed because Julie's family had money. But it didn't keep him from marrying her!"

I nodded encouragingly, and Martin kept talking. "I had to take a trip to New York, so I went up to meet him. Julie's parents were dead. It seemed as if somebody should show an interest. I got the same impression Mother did. Julie had dropped out of graduate school, told her grandmother she couldn't accept an allowance any longer. She was working for a big country club, planning their special events. That didn't please her husband. It wasn't intellectual enough for him. But he didn't mind her paying the rent so he could play the part of misunderstood genius!"

"I can see how Julie might have gotten mixed up with a guy like that," I said. "She was always sympathetic to everyone."

"Yes! And when the whiner finally had some success," Martin said, "he walked out on her! If uncles were still allowed to go after young whippersnappers who did their nieces wrong—believe me, I'd have been there with my horsewhip!"

He turned back to the door. "So Julie never mentioned him to anyone, huh? I'm glad she had that much pride."

"I guess the police looked at him, made sure he wasn't around the night she was killed?"

"Oh, the creep had no motive for killing her. Besides, he was at a big dinner in New York that night. Now that he's famous."

"He's famous?"

"In some circles." Martin opened the door. Then he used his final comment as an exit line.

"Julie's ex-husband is Seth Blackman. He won some big literary prize last year. He was speaking to the assembled intelligentsia of New York City the night Julie was killed."

# Chapter 12

The minute the door was locked behind Martin I headed for my office. Joe was already there, leaning over to hit the button that turned the computer on.

He moved to let me sit in my chair. "Let's Google him," he said.

"It's nice to know you're as nosy as I am," I said.

Joe laughed, and Aunt Nettie, who never touches the computer, said plaintively, "What are you two up to?"

Joe explained how to use the search engine Google while I called up the screen and typed in "Seth Blackman."

"I hope I'm spelling it right," I said.

"If nothing likely comes up, we'll try Blackman with an 'o,'" Joe said. "Or 'ond.'"

But Blackman with an "a" seemed to be correct. We got a whole screenful of results. In the next twenty minutes we learned that Seth Blackman had been a graduate student at an elite New England college. His first novel had been published eighteen months ago, and the previous spring that novel had been named winner of the Bookman Prize. Whatever that was.

I might not know anything about the Bookman Prize, but winning it was earning Seth Blackman's novel a lot of attention. We found references to articles on him in the *New York Review of Books*, the *Atlantic Monthly*, and a number of other magazines a mere Michigan accountant had never heard of. Joe said he hadn't heard of most of them, either. "Literary," he said. "Which means circulation limited to English majors."

"Wait a minute," I said. "Here's a review with a description of the plot."

Joe leaned over my shoulder, and we read it together. "In this dark comedy, Adam Greening, a brilliant young writer, finds himself stifled artistically," the article said. "Pitied by his beautiful and wealthy, but immature, wife—whose maudlin and oversentimental mind cannot grasp his artistic ambitions—he struggles to achieve the worldly success she would be able to understand. His scholarly achievements fail to impress her or her family of Philistines, who condescendingly offer financial help. Finally, her shallow outlook on life leads him to take his own life."

I read it out loud, and Aunt Nettie looked puzzled. "How can the review call it a 'comedy,' if it ends in the main character's suicide?"

"It says it's a 'dark comedy,' " I said. "It goes on to say the wife is 'a hilarious picture of middle-class anti-intellectualism.' "

"Reading between the lines," Joe said, "I'd guess that Martin Schrader was exactly right about Seth Blackman. The guy is a whiner."

"It doesn't sound like a very good book," Aunt Nettie said. "But how does it reflect on Julie's ex-husband's character?"

Joe pointed to the screen. "I never met Julie, but the description of the book sounds as if he skewered her. He wrote a semiautobiographical novel—he gave us a broad hint about that, because his name is Seth Blackman and his hero's name is Adam Greening. Then he used the situation in which he found himself—a poor graduate student married to a girl who came from a wealthy family—as a plot device. This would appear to be deliberately designed to make the reader assume that Blackman used Julie as the model of the main character's wife, a 'maudlin and oversentimental' woman. Which, by the way, is a repetitious and redundant description by this high-falutin reviewer."

"He made fun of his own wife? But that's mean!" Aunt Nettie said.

"I agree," I said. "Martin Schrader was definitely right. The guy should be horsewhipped. On the other hand, I'm embarrassed. Apparently the things Julie's ex made fun of her about are exactly the things I found annoying. The overly sentimental poems and silly jokes. The gushing way of speaking."

"But, Lee," Joe said, "if you complained, you just did it to friends."

"I don't think I ever mentioned it to anybody but Aunt Nettie and Lindy. When I asked Julie to cut it out, I tried to be tactful."

"Right. You didn't publish a novel making fun of her. Besides, judging by what Martin said, Seth Blackman wrote the novel while she was supporting him, earning a good proportion of the living for the two of them. And she gave up her own graduate work to do it. Seth Blackman's assessment of Julie may have had some justice. She may well have been overly sentimental. But that's not the point. You don't hold people you care about—or once cared about—up for public ridicule."

Yeah, the way Joe had never made any public statement about the breakup of his marriage to Clementine Ripley, no matter how many tabloid reporters asked him about it. For a minute I remembered how much I appreciated him.

But I didn't say anything about that when I spoke again. "It sure explains why Julie never mentioned that she'd been married. This must have been a humiliating experience."

"It also explains why Martin didn't want anybody to know Julie had been mixed up with Seth Blackman. Judging from this plot synopsis, I'd guess that Blackman let the whole Schrader family have it. Embarrassed all of them."

Aunt Nettie shook her head. "It doesn't sound as if Julie and her ex-husband were very well-suited."

"To say the least," I said. "But this Internet stuff does make one thing certain. Unless he hired a hit man, Seth Blackman is not a suspect in Julie's death. As Martin said, he was giving a speech at a literary dinner in New York that night. The *New York Times* even had quotes. And a photo."

We all took a look at Julie's ex-husband. He was one of these soulful types—hair a little too long, eyes a little too sensitive.

"Too bad he was at that dinner," Aunt Nettie said. "It sounds as if he deserves to go to prison, just for general meanness, and now he won't. But I guess I'll go home. Do you two need to stay here until you talk to Hogan?"

"Probably not," I said. "He'll know where to find us."

Joe offered to bring a pizza out to the house, and Aunt Nettie said she had ingredients for a salad in the refrigerator. I followed her home, and Joe came a half hour later, bearing a large pepperoni with mushrooms. I hadn't expected to be hungry, but I discovered that I was.

Joe and I had just split the last slice of pizza when the phone rang. I jumped up. "Maybe that's Hogan."

But it wasn't Hogan's basso on the phone. It was a timid little voice. "Lee? It's Margaret. You weren't in bed, were you?"

I looked at my watch. "It's only eight thirty, Margaret. I don't usually go to bed this early. What are you up to?"

"I finally got all the kids settled, and I wanted to know more about Carolyn. I didn't like to ask when you called. I'm trying not to talk about all this in front of them."

"If you want details, Margaret—"

"Oh, no!"

"Good, because I don't have any."

"But do the police think that Carolyn's death had something to do with Julie's?"

"They haven't told me that, but it's hard not to see a connection."

"I hardly knew Carolyn. Was she anything like Julie?"

"I talked to Martin Schrader today, and he said she was the complete opposite of Julie in every way. I think that's right. Carolyn could talk really rough; Julie was sweet and gushy. Julie was always doing people favors; Carolyn was more competitive. Carolyn was cynical; Julie was sentimental."

Margaret's voice took on a sarcastic tone. "Oh, yes. Julie was sentimental."

It was the first comment I'd ever heard from Margaret that sounded critical of anybody. I was surprised it would be Julie.

"I found her a little too sentimental," I said. "But she had lots of good qualities. I guess you'd known her a lot longer than I had."

"Since high school. I'm ready to forget high school, if you want to know the truth. And Julie was trying to drag me into plans for our tenth reunion."

"Oh, gee! I guess somebody has to do it."

"Maybe so. But it doesn't have to be me. I've *atoned* for what happened in high school. I didn't want my nose rubbed in it. It's time to move on."

Margaret muttered a good-bye and hung up, leaving me with my mouth agape. Margaret had "atoned" for high school? What did that mean?

I thought over my own high school years. I'd done a lot of stupid things, things I regretted, and since graduation I'd learned to deal with the memory of being a dumb teenager. But I didn't think I'd use the word "atoned" when I talked about the process of growing up. The word had a sad sound. What had happened to make Margaret feel that she had to "atone" for her high school behavior? Most of us laughed at the silly things we'd done.

At least Margaret was all right. Nobody had broken into her house or shot out her windows or anything else dire. She was safe for the moment, as Lindy and the Denhams seemed to be.

But what about Jason? I'd never gotten hold of him. I looked up his home phone and called. It was a relief to hear his voice.

Jason had, of course, already heard about Carolyn. "Yeah," he said. "I thought I was getting arrested. I was down at the hardware store, and the cops drew up with sirens blaring."

"Why'd they do that?"

"Chief Jones said all the Seventh Food Group members might be in danger. They called the restaurant, and Ross told them where I'd gone. I wish they hadn't been so dramatic about it. I was perfectly all right."

"And how's your computer?"

"All reloaded and working. All I lost permanently was my e-mail." Jason gave another exasperated sigh. "I'm awfully sorry about Carolyn, but I didn't know her well. I'm shocked, but not saddened, if you know what I mean."

"I guess I feel the same way. She was prickly and hard to get to know. Not like Julie, who was maddening, but more loveable."

There was a moment of silence before Jason replied. "Right," he said. "Julie could be maddening, but she was basically a nice person."

His guarded answer had roused my curiosity. I decided to follow up. "Jason, you introduced the rest of us to Julie. How did you meet her?"

"Working a party last summer. I was tending bar—one of my moonlighting jobs—at a party in Holland. Some bigwig had taken over one of those restaurants right on the yacht harbor for a wedding reception. I guess Julie knew the couple. Anyway, she was running the show—over the objections of the restaurant catering staff. I'd been hired by the restaurant, but I didn't like the catering manager." Jason laughed. "I backed Julie, did some rearranging to get things the way she wanted them. The catering manager walked out in a huff, and Julie and I wound up in charge. I haven't been asked to tend bar there again."

"I can't imagine why not."

"I wouldn't go if they asked, unless they get a new catering manager. But after that Julie gave me a ring a couple of times, asked me to help with parties. I liked her ideas, and she wasn't hard to work with. With the new restaurant opening, we could have done some nice events. I can work with anybody—except that one catering manager."

I laughed. "I did notice a few qualifications in your opinion of Julie, however."

Jason's voice became wary. "Oh? What did I say?"

" 'Thoughtless' was one of the words used in some e-mail. And you didn't have any trouble agreeing to 'maddening.' "

"Nobody's perfect. You let her have it, too. Over those jokes and poems."

"Yeah, but that wasn't 'thoughtless,' Jason. Julie was almost too sweet and kind around me. What did she pull to change your opinion of her?"

Jason didn't answer, so I spoke in a moment. "Sorry. That was a nosy question."

"Oh, it's all right. All our friends know. She caused Ross some problems."

Ross. Jason's partner. "Oh," I said. "I've never met Ross."

"He's a good guy. We've been together for five years, you know, but Ross was married for fifteen. He has grown kids. Ross's dad is an old military type, a retired sergeant. He's in a nursing home in Holland, barely creeps around with a walker. He's never confronted Ross's lifestyle—and there's no reason he has to. When Ross and I moved in together, Ross's dad just acted as if we were saving money.

Oh, I'm sure he realized the situation wasn't just platonic, but nothing has ever been said.

"Then Julie showed up, one day when we were out at the nursing home. She needed to give me something, and it was a handy place to meet. She was damn sweet and gracious to Ross's dad. I was appreciating her nice attitude, when she makes some remark about her ambition to plan 'a lovely wedding for Ross and Jason.' "

"Oh, no!"

"Ross's dad—the poor old guy got tears in his eyes. He and Ross have had their problems over the years, but things are at least on an even keel between them now, and we don't want to have any kind of confrontation—with the sergeant's health being so bad. When I objected, she lectured me about confronting my problems, about being honest."

"That was rude!"

Jason took a deep breath. "I know this isn't a smart thing to say, considering recent events, but right at that moment I could have killed Julie. But I got over it."

Jason and I said a few more words, and I hung up. That Julie. Thoughtless. Yes, Jason had used the right word for her. And I thought I was nosy; I wasn't in the running compared to her. I went back to Joe and Aunt Nettie shaking my head.

I wondered what Martin Schrader would have to say about Julie when I met him for lunch the next day.

## CHOCOLATE CHAT
## HUMOROUS CHOCOLATE

"Strength is the capacity to break a chocolate bar into four pieces with your bare hands—and then eat just one of the pieces."
—Judith Viorst

"Research tells us fourteen out of any ten individuals like chocolate."
—Sandra Boynton

"There are two kinds of people in the world. Those who love chocolate and communists."
—Leslie Moak Murray in *Murray's Law* comic strip

"All I really need is love, but a little chocolate now and then doesn't hurt!"
—Lucy Van Pelt

"The 12-step chocoholic program: NEVER BE MORE THAN 12 STEPS AWAY FROM CHOCOLATE!"
—Terry Moore

"My therapist told me the way to achieve true inner peace is to finish what I start. So far today, I have finished two bags of M&M's and a chocolate cake. I feel better already."
—Dave Barry

# Chapter 13

Joe and I made our official statements on Carolyn's death the next morning. I think Hogan had been meeting with the Holland detectives until late the previous night. I know law enforcement had been busy.

Other than that, the morning was routine—or as routine as a chocolate business can be three weeks before Valentine's Day. I had nothing more to cope with than a dozen last-minute orders for multiple fancy holiday pieces—delivery ASAP—and walk-in customers. Dolly Jolly took care of a lot of the counter business for me. I could hear her voice boom. "A quarter-pound box of raspberry cream bonbons! And a half-pound of assorted truffles and bonbons! One minute!"

Only one e-mail showed up that was unrelated to the holiday, but that one seemed significant. The Seventh Major Food Group was revived.

A message came from Jason. "I had a call from Vince Veldkamp," Jason wrote. "He's run Veldkamp Used Food Equipment and Supply forever, but now he says he's selling out and retiring. All his inventory is going on the block. If anybody's interested, he says we can have a sneak preview Friday night at the Holland store. Lee, he says he's got a cooling tunnel and some other stuff left over from the closeout of Vanderkool's Chocolate. And Lindy, is Mike still looking for a freezer for Herrera's? Vince has one that sounds good."

I checked with Aunt Nettie and e-mailed back that we would definitely be interested in the cooling tunnel if the price was right. Aunt Nettie would also be interested in worktables and storage racks.

I found Jason's message comforting. It seemed to be a symbol that—someday—life would return to normal. The Seventh Food Group would go back to discussing professional concerns, instead of worrying about all of us getting killed. It made Dolly's calls to customers seem comforting as well. I reminded myself that TenHuis Chocolade was having a good Valentine season. Aunt Nettie and I had worked hard to get the business back on a firm financial footing, and it was comforting to know we'd made it, at least for the moment.

I needed that comfort when I thought about my planned lunch with Martin Schrader. I wasn't looking forward to it. I hadn't dressed in my black pants suit with the severe silk shirt and the heavy boots—I'd settled for brown flannel slacks and a sage green turtleneck—but I'd felt like wearing an intimidating outfit. Big business types like Uncle Martin can overawe me, and I didn't want to be trampled underfoot. I didn't understand why Martin wanted to talk to me; I only knew it was likely to be touchy, since it would concern his murdered niece.

The day was crisp and sunny, so at one o'clock the half-block walk down to the Sidewalk Café gave me a nice breath of fresh air. The Sidewalk Café's decor is a pun. Although it does have an outdoor dining area—closed in January, of course—that's not the reason for the restaurant's name. The café is designed to look like a sidewalk. Sidewalk toys—roller skates, tricycles, jump ropes, scooters—are hung on the walls. The floor is cement and is painted with designs that copy childish graffiti and hopscotch layouts. The restaurant is lighthearted, and the sandwiches, soups, and salads on the lunch menu are good.

When I came in, Mike Herrera greeted me. In his combined roles as my best friend's father-in-law, my boyfriend's mother's boyfriend, my boyfriend's boss, and the mayor of the town I live in, Mike has plenty of personal impact on my life. He's also the only other native of Texas I've identified as living in Warner Pier. He grew up in Denton, just north of Dallas.

Mike made himself a successful businessman the old-fashioned way; he worked day and night for years, and he's still not too good to bus tables or fry bacon if that's what needs doing in one of his three restaurants. He's an attractive man—a sort of heavyset Latin lover.

"Hi, Lee," Mike said. "You getting a sandwich to go or can I entice you into a real lunch?"

"I'm meeting Martin Schrader for lunch, Mike. Has he come in yet?"

Mike waggled an eyebrow to show he was about to make a joke. "Does Joe know about this?"

"Joe was invited along, but declined. Martin wants to talk to me about his niece."

"I'll give you the quiet corner." Mike grabbed a couple of menus and led me toward the back of the restaurant. "I want to talk to Martin Schrader myself, but maybe this isn't a good time."

"What do you want to talk to him about?"

"His mother's property. It's so close to Warner Pier that the city planning commission has begun to wonder what's going to happen to it after Mrs. Schrader passes on."

"You're on your own with that topic, Mike. I couldn't possibly bring it up."

"I can do my own political dirty work. How about a drink? Mimosa?"

"Have you got any real Texas iced tea?"

"I'll make you some."

There are wonderful cooks and restaurants in Michigan, but rarely do they understand iced tea. For one thing, they think it's only a hot weather drink. We Texans see it as standard fare year-round.

There are other differences. Iced tea cannot be made from mix as it almost always is in Michigan restaurants; it must be brewed from real tea. And it can't be served over a couple of anemic ice cubes. It has to be poured over a whole glass of ice cubes or cracked ice. The sugar and lemon are optional—at least in my part of Texas. This differs from the deep South. There, I understand, people want "sweet tea," which requires that the hot tea be poured over sugar, so that it dissolves thoroughly. Sweet tea is a fine drink, but I'm satisfied with the unsweetened version. If there is a lemon, however, it should be cut into a wedge, not a disk.

There are a lot of nuances to iced tea. Sometimes I think Mike and I are the only two people in Warner Pier who understand the drink.

Mike had just served me a tall, refreshing glass when I looked through the big front window of the Sidewalk Café and saw Martin Schrader get out of a large dark sedan. He stood bent over, looking back into the car for a few seconds, obviously saying good-bye. Then he slammed the door, and I caught a glimpse of a logo—black and white with a red wing-shaped thing sticking up—but I couldn't read the writing underneath. Martin swung around and came into the restaurant, unzipping his down jacket. He paused near the door, obviously trying to adjust his eyes to the change in light level, and Mike appeared from the kitchen and led him back to the corner table.

"I'm sorry to keep you waiting," Martin said. "My meeting ran a little longer than I expected."

"That's quite all right. It gave Mike time to make me some Texas tea."

Martin looked puzzled. "I thought Texas tea was slang for oil."

"It may be. But to Texans like Mike and me, it merely means well-brewed, properly iced tea."

Martin promptly proved himself a real Michiganian. He shivered. "Too cold for iced tea," he said. "Though I could use a Bloody Mary."

I refrained from remarking that a Bloody Mary was just as cold as a glass of iced tea. Martin ordered one; then he and I chitchatted idly while we selected and ordered our lunches. I went with the vegetable soup and cheese biscuits special, and Martin ordered a bleu cheese burger with a side of fries.

Then silence fell, and so did my stomach. We'd put off talking about Julie as long as possible.

We both spoke at once.

"About Julie—" I said.

"Thanks for agreeing to talk to me—" Martin said.

Then, of course, we had to stop and do the politeness thing—"You first." "No, you first."—before I prompted Martin. "You said you wanted to talk about Julie. Unfortunately, I don't really know a lot about her. As I told you, I didn't even know she'd been married."

"How did you find that out?"

"Oh, Brad mentioned it."

Martin's eyes opened wide. "Brad? At the funeral?"

Whoops. I'd forgotten Brad had asked me not to tell Martin that he'd been by my office. "Oh, I ran into Brad one day in Warner Pier."

I raced on, trying to change the subject. "Anyway, Brad didn't say much about Julie's marriage. But after you gave me his name, I looked Seth Blackman up on the Internet, and it sounds as if he's a real jerk. I can understand Julie not wanting to talk about him. But she didn't talk about anything else personal either—at least with the Seventh Major Food Group. Have you tried her other friends?"

Martin sipped his Bloody Mary before he answered. "That's one of the things that bothered me about Julie. She had practically become a recluse."

"She seemed to be getting some business."

"Yes, she made the rounds of restaurants and caterers. But she didn't get out socially. No dates. No movies with her friends."

"Did you try Margaret Van Meter? Apparently Julie used to go by and see her."

Martin pulled out his pocket calendar and wrote Margaret's name down, then promised to call her.

"I'm afraid I haven't been any help to you," I said. "What I know about Julie is not worth lunch."

"Oh, I haven't asked you the real question." He took another gulp of Bloody Mary. He was apparently having trouble asking that "real" question. I tried to put an expectant look on my face, and he finally spoke.

"Did Julie ever indicate that she was afraid of anything? Of anybody?"

I thought about it. Then I shook my head. "No, I don't recall her saying or doing anything that indicated she was afraid. Does that mean you're not buying the theory that Julie was killed by a burglar?"

"I'm not saying that idea is wrong. It just seems—well—dumb to assume that that's the case. I wouldn't want to see the police consider that as the only possibility."

"If they had that idea, it seems as if the killing of Carolyn would bring that theory into question."

Our food came then, and Martin didn't answer until he'd taken a bite of hamburger. "I talked to the Holland detectives this morning.

They're not sharing their ideas with me. But if I could have something specific to tell them, some incident, some remark Julie had made—well, it might point them in a different direction."

"Brad and Julie seemed to be in contact fairly often. I assume you've asked him."

Martin's eyes flickered toward me; then he dropped them and concentrated on his French fries. "Brad didn't have anything to say about it."

"We could look Julie's e-mails over," I said.

"You still have them?"

"Oh, yes. I'm notorious for not cleaning out my delete file for months at a time. I'm sure everything I've ever had from Julie is still in there. You're welcome to look at it."

"I'd appreciate that."

I laughed. "You didn't need to give me lunch to get a look at my delete file. I assure you there are no secrets in it. Just a bunch of chocolate orders and the occasional note from my mother. A phone call would have done the trick."

Martin responded gallantly, lifting his Bloody Mary glass. "But this is extremely pleasant. I'm enjoying getting acquainted."

I smiled. "I do have one nosy question I'd like to ask, however. Did you ever find Julie's mouse?"

"No! It's never turned up. How did you know about the mouse?"

I sketched my conversation with Hogan Jones, explaining that he was a close friend of my aunt's. "I'm afraid he and I thought it was funny. We kept picturing the Holland crime scene crew searching, afraid to lift an afghan or open a drawer for fear the mouse would pop out at them."

Martin smiled. "That could happen, but if it did they didn't tell me. I set a live trap, but as far as I know Blondie has never turned up."

"Blondie? The mouse's name is Blondie?"

"Right. As in ash blond. Julie was always partial to white mice. Now Brad, he likes the brown ones."

"Somehow brown ones don't seem as petlike. Too much like what we set traps for in my aunt's Michigan basement."

I guess it had become obvious that we weren't having a serious conversation, because Mike appeared, bearing a tray of dessert selections. "Pick one," he said. "On the house."

"Looks great," Martin said. "But I shouldn't eat too much. I've got to drive to Grand Rapids this afternoon. I don't want to fall asleep."

"I'll put it in a box, if you'd rather," Mike said. "Of course, I'm going to ask for some information in exchange."

Martin looked a little wary, but he nodded, and Mike pulled up a chair. "I'm putting on my Mayor of Warner Pier hat," he said. "I'm curious about the Schrader family property down here. Since it adjoins Warner Pier on the south and it's a big chunk of undeveloped land . . ."

Martin shook his head. "Mike, I can't tell you a thing."

"I noticed that, when your niece died, the family picked the Lake Michigan Conservation Society for memorial gifts."

"That was Brad's idea. My mother went along with it." Then Martin gave a deep sigh. "Look, there's a family trust, and Brad and I are both beneficiaries. But the Warner Pier property is not part of the trust. It belongs to my mother outright. She can do anything she wants with it—and I assure you she will! If you want to see it go to the Conservation Society—"

"No! No! The city doesn't have a policy that covers it. We're simply curious. We have to think about what might happen." Mike leaned closer to Martin and lowered his voice. "To tell the truth, I'd like to see all these big family properties remain with the families. But very few families can keep them these days."

Martin nodded. "Taxes."

"Taxes." Mike grinned. "And, of course, with the property outside our city limits, Warner Pier isn't getting a cut."

"Mike," Martin said, "if I get a hint of my mother's plans, I'll tip you off."

"That's all I'm asking. A tip would definitely be worth a piece of cheesecake."

We all laughed. Martin selected a piece of turtle cheesecake as his freebie, and I asked for bread pudding. Mike promised to send us coffee, then left.

"You were very gracious to Mike," I said. "He was being extremely nosy."

Martin shrugged. "My grandfather bought that property in 1935 for practically nothing. It wasn't good for orchards, so nobody wanted it. Now it's going to be one of the biggest items in my mother's estate."

"How is your mother? I mean, the word around west Michigan is that her health isn't good."

"She has good days and bad days. She's nearly ninety. She has arthritis and a pacemaker."

"Julie looked a lot like her."

Martin's eyes widened. "Yes, she did. Or she looked a lot like Mother looked when she was Julie's age. But how did you know?"

"The eyes. Black and snapping. They both could look right through you."

Martin blinked. Had I made him cry?

"Sorry," I said. "It just struck me when I met Mrs. Schrader. Now, gobble up your cheesecake, and we'll go look at the e-mail."

We made light conversation while we drank our coffee. Martin paid the bill and said good-bye to Mike. We both put on our hats and zipped up our jackets, then walked the half block to TenHuis Chocolade. I led the way into the office and plopped into my chair.

"Hang your jacket on the coat tree, if you like," I said. "This will take only a minute." I didn't bother to go online, but went straight to "deleted items."

When the folder opened, it took me a few minutes to realize that it held only a couple of dozen items.

The only Seventh Food Group message in it was the one I'd received from Jason that morning. Everything I'd received before Wednesday, a day earlier, had disappeared.

# Chapter 14

I did everything I could think of. I checked the computer's main recycle bin, looked in my other e-mail folders, racked my brain, used shocking language, and pulled out handfuls of hair. But my deleted and sent e-mail folders were empty, and my recycle bin was, too.

Martin Schrader reacted as if it were his fault, apologizing at length.

"Don't be silly," I said, when I was able to say anything that wasn't a swear word. "It has nothing to do with you. You just happened to be on the spot when I found out that the folders were gone. Actually, I can't believe I'm so lucky."

"Lucky?"

"Yes. Other members of the Seventh Food Group have had computer trouble, and they lost everything." I explained that Carolyn, Jason, and the Denhams all had their business records wiped out.

"Then Lindy Herrera was physically attacked, and her laptop was stolen," I said. "I seem to be getting off easy. Besides, I backed up my business records after all the others had trouble, and I've updated the disk every day since then."

"So you have a copy of your e-mail?"

I shook my head. "I'm afraid not." I reached into my drawer and pulled out my backup disk. "I didn't see any reason to back up my e-mail. I get a lot of orders in by e-mail, true, but I print them out or move them to different folders as I read them. Ordinarily I don't put anything in the delete file except things I'm through with, like messages from my mother or Seventh Food Group chitchat. When I backed up my files, I only backed up correspondence, accounting—things like that."

Martin looked extremely troubled. "Have you talked to the police about these computer problems?"

Martin seemed to think he was the first person who had thought of that. I tried to be polite when I told him I'd already been over it with Chief Jones, and that Hogan had passed that idea on to the Holland detectives.

"Of course, it wouldn't hurt if you talked to them as well," I said. I guess I thought an important businessman like Martin Schrader might have more clout with the police than a group of small business owners like the Seventh Food Group.

Martin left, and I called Jack Ingersoll. He wasn't answering his phone, as usual, but I left a message asking if there was any logical technical explanation for why two folders of my e-mail could be erased and the rest of the computer's workings left intact. I felt certain that the answer was no, but I thought I ought to ask before I called Hogan Jones to report the situation. It seemed pretty obvious to me that somebody had sat down at my desk, opened up my computer and killed those two files, plus my trash can.

But who? Who would have done that? Who could have done that?

Of course, anybody who worked at TenHuis Chocolade could have wandered into the office when I wasn't there, opened the e-mail program, and killed anything she wanted to kill. (All our employees are women.) But she couldn't have done it without being observed. My office was separated from the shop and from the workroom only by large panes of glass. It's a fishbowl. Nobody could go into the office during business hours without someone noticing.

But if people who worked there would have trouble getting into my computer, it would be even more difficult for an outsider. Nobody besides the staff would have any reason to be in my office—or at least no reason to fool with my computer. If they did, it would be sure to attract attention from Aunt Nettie or one of the other hairnet ladies.

The whole thing was nonsense. The missing folders were not important to me. It's not as if I checked them every morning to see if anything exciting had turned up. No, I just send stuff, and I don't look at the sent folder unless I have some question about it. I simply kill stuff from my incoming mail file, and it lingers in deleted until I get around to giving the final commands to kill it forever. I had no idea when I'd last looked in either file. It had been at least a month.

Of course, I could figure when the folders had been emptied. The dates on the handful of remaining items showed when it had happened.

The two folders had been emptied the day before. I looked at my calendar and thought back over the past few days, trying to remember who had been in my office, who had come into the shop.

I immediately realized that practically everybody I knew had been there either Tuesday or Wednesday, including some of the members of the Seventh Food Group. Jason had come by to tell me about his computer problems. Diane Denham had dropped by to ask about Lindy and had stayed to complain about how nosy Julie had been. Of course, Lindy hadn't been in, because she was home recuperating from being hit in the head by the thief who'd taken her laptop. Besides, Lindy was my best and oldest friend. If I had to suspect Lindy of fooling around with my computer, or worse, of murder—well, I just couldn't do it. Carolyn Rose hadn't been into TenHuis Chocolade, but death seemed to take her off the list of possible villains, too.

Margaret Van Meter had not been in my office that week either. Did that remove her from the suspect list? Or make her more likely? That idea seemed silly. With six kids, Margaret was so homebound she had trouble finding time to go to the grocery store. Getting out long enough to get into my computer or to commit murder would have been impossible for her.

Besides, these were all people I knew, people I considered friends. Then I remembered how Hogan Jones had described them. "These are not friends," he'd said. "These are suspects." At that thought I shivered harder than Martin Schrader had at the idea of drinking iced tea in January.

But all this had happened a few weeks before Valentine's Day, one of the busiest times of the year for the chocolate business. Dozens of people had come into TenHuis Chocolade during the past two days. Martin Schrader had been in three times, and his nephew, Brad, had been in once. But I didn't see how any of these people could have touched my computer unobserved.

Maybe Tracy had seen something. I glanced at the clock on the workroom wall. She would come to work in half an hour. I'd ask her.

I wound up spending most of that half hour standing at the counter in the shop. We had a rush of customers that didn't let up even after Tracy came in, and both of us had to work the counter until five thirty. Closing time had come before I had a chance to say anything more to Tracy than, "Please go to the back and bring up a tray of lemon canache bonbons." ("Tangy lemon interior with dark chocolate coating.")

My request for a short chat left Tracy looking as if she'd been called to the principal's office. She perched uneasily on my visitor's chair. "Did I shortchange someone?"

"If you did they haven't complained. No, something crazy happened to my computer, and I wondered if anybody had been fooling with it."

"Not me!"

"I'm sure it wasn't you, Tracy. I was wondering about visitors."

"Visitors? Like Brad Schrader?"

"Not him specifically. Anybody. Salesmen. Jason Foster was by yesterday, for example."

"Yes, but he went right in your office. And you were there."

It was hard going. Tracy's job was to mind the counter, not keep an eye on my office. She couldn't remember who had been in it, if I'd been there the whole time the visitors had been, if they'd looked at my computer, or if they'd taken a meat ax to it. Our whole conversation was a waste of time.

After Tracy left I sat and stared at the computer screen. How was I going to figure this out?

The key to the whole mystery was Julie Singletree. It was only after Julie was murdered that the Seventh Food Group began to have trouble with its computers. It was after Julie was murdered that Carolyn was killed, that Lindy was attacked. The whole problem had to hinge on Julie. Who would have wanted to harm her? And why?

I sat looking at that computer screen as if it were a crystal ball, and I were a fortune-teller. I needed to find out more about Julie. How could I do that?

Gradually, an idea formed. I picked up the phone and punched in a number. Joe answered on the second ring.

"Joe, how would you like to have dinner in Holland?"

"If you could wait until around seven, I could get another coat of varnish on this boat. Then you might talk me into it."

"Sounds fine. Then, afterward—I thought we might go by Margaret Van Meter's and look at wedding cakes."

He paused, obviously analyzing what I had said.

So I went on. "Whoever comes to our wedding, they're going to expect cake."

Joe chortled. "You're nosing around, aren't you?"

"It's a dirty job, but somebody's got to do it."

"Okay." Joe sounded resigned. "If I'm going to marry the nosiest woman in west Michigan, I'd better get used to it. I sure don't want you poking around by yourself."

"I'll call Margaret and see if she can talk to us."

Margaret said she should have the youngest kids in bed by eight thirty. "Jim will be home by eight, and he can supervise baths for the boys. So a half hour later should be a good time."

Joe and I barely had time to snag a burger at a popular Holland restaurant. Then he followed my vague directions, and we roamed around until we found Margaret's house.

"What does Jim do?" Joe said as we got out of his truck.

"He works for one of the office furniture suppliers. I think he delivers and assembles."

"He's lucky he's still got a job."

"Right." At one time, our part of Michigan was a center for manufacturing and sales of office furniture, but anybody who reads the newspapers knows that a lot of those companies are closing up operations in our area.

"I can see why Margaret wants to make some money," I said.

Margaret opened the door of the old frame house, smiling her sunny smile and holding a plump, blond baby who wore a blue blanket sleeper. Margaret's hair was pinned up into a knot and dribbles of something stained the front of her sweatshirt. "I kept Teddy up so you could see him," she said.

Joe and I admired the little guy, who Margaret said was ten months old. He grinned at us, showing off four teeth, then coyly buried his face in his mother's neck and peeked at us from under her chin. Two small girls ran to see who had come in and were introduced as Tessa and Marcy. They were two and three, Margaret said. Tessa sucked her thumb and grabbed Margaret's leg, but Marcy came right over to us and batted her eyelashes at Joe like a born flirt. Both wore footed blanket sleepers similar to their baby brother's.

Jim came in from the kitchen then. He was a husky blond guy, the kind who looks as if he could hoist a king-sized steel desk without batting an eye. The baby bottle he held seemed incongruous.

Jim and Joe shook hands; then Jim looked at little Teddy and grinned. "Come on, big guy," he said.

Teddy wriggled all over and made a flying leap out of his mother's arms. I gasped, but Jim caught him expertly and carried him up the stairs. Teddy grabbed the bottle and tipped it back as they went.

"I'll take you guys into the kitchen, if you don't mind," Margaret said. "I laid my sample book out on the table in there. You can look at it while I get the little girls in bed."

She led us through the living room, pausing to introduce us to three little blond boys who were still dressed—James, who was four; Davy, who was six; and Kenneth, who was seven. They were lined up on the couch, watching the Cartoon Network.

The kitchen was outdated in decor, but up-to-date in equipment. In the center was a big oak table. I expected to find that the kids had covered it with something sticky, but it had been scrubbed clean. In fact, Margaret's kitchen would have passed the health department's check with no problem. And the aroma was wonderful in there.

"I put a cake in the oven a few minutes ago," Margaret said. "It's almond flavor. I made a small sample one you can try, if you're interested in that flavor."

"Anything that smells that good, I'll be glad to taste," Joe said.

We sat down at the table and looked at snapshots of Margaret's cakes. I'd described them to Joe as works of art, but he was still surprised by their beauty. And their cost.

"It's the Australian method," I explained. "Or that's what I read in one of Aunt Nettie's magazines. They use a fondant icing, instead of the usual butter cream. And, yes, they're expensive. But they are gorgeous."

We looked at a list of Margaret's flavors for cakes—vanilla, almond, chocolate, strawberry—and the flavors for fillings. That list went on for a whole page. We'd just about settled on almond cake with peach-flavored filling when Margaret came back. She grabbed a small cake out of the oven and tested three larger layers with toothpicks. Then she slid the larger cakes back into the oven and set the timer.

"This little cake will give you an idea of the almond," she said.

"Do you have a wedding tomorrow?" I said.

"Oh, no. I won't use those layers for two weeks. I like to freeze them ahead. They'll keep up to three weeks, and they're a whole lot easier to frost if they're frozen when you do it."

"How about the fondant?"

"I make the flowers ahead. They keep real well, and I can make them at nap time or during the evening. Of course, I have to do the final icing and assembling on the day I deliver the cake."

Then we talked about our wedding cake, and Margaret approved our combination of flavors. "Though I expected you to order choco-late with chocolate frosting," she said. "Will you want a separate groom's cake?"

Joe and I looked at each other. "I think Aunt Nettie is going to do trays of truffles and bonbons instead," I said. "Margaret, this wed-ding isn't going to be one of your big jobs. It's not a formal do."

"A smaller cake can be beautiful. Do you want it decorated in all white? Or with color?"

"I was thinking of color, but I haven't found a dress yet, and nei-ther has Lindy. And I'll have to pick one before I can decide on a color for the flowers. So I'll have to tell you later."

"I don't have to know until that week." Margaret smiled happily. "I expect your mother will want to have some input, too."

"Joe's mom may," I said. "But I'm deliberately leaving my mom out of the plans. We have fewer arguments that way."

"Smart!"

I was surprised at Margaret's comment, and I must have looked it. So I tried to cover up. "I guess mothers want to have a lot of say."

"My mother did. Our wedding was miserable because of her nagging at us." Margaret smiled. "But we've had a wonderful marriage."

"I can see the two of you are really partners," Joe said. "You'd have to be, to handle these cute kids."

"Jim's just wonderful. He works so hard at the plant, and after work he goes to the vo-tech center. He's taking a computer repair class."

"You're lucky," I said. "I guess Jim's knowledge has kept you from having all the computer problems the rest of the Seventh Food Group have had."

Margaret began to praise Jim's virus protection programs. I turned my face toward Joe and mouthed a phrase at him. "Go talk to Jim." I only had to do it three times before he blinked, then stood up. "Hey, would Jim mind if I asked him about a computer problem I'm having?"

"Oh, no," Margaret said. "I think he's in the living room. He loves to talk about computers."

As soon as he disappeared through the door, I turned to Margaret. "Listen," I said, "I can't help but believe that all these computer problems, not to mention the killing of Carolyn and the attack on Lindy, are connected to Julie's death."

"All I know is that the police came out and really quizzed me about it all. They looked at our computer for a long time."

"Did they find the e-mails from Julie?"

"No, I don't save that sort of thing. And Jim has me set up so that I don't download from the Net to my computer. He says it's the safest way to stay away from viruses. So unless I do something special, after I've read it, it's gone. So I guess Julie's e-mail to us has just disappeared, unless you . . . ?"

I quickly explained my computer problems. "So I got off lightly, at least so far. I'm glad to hear that the Holland detectives looked into it. Julie herself simply has to be the key to this—well, I guess I'd call it a crime wave. And you were the only one of the Seventh Food Group who knew Julie very well."

Margaret's eyes slid away from mine. "We weren't really very close friends in high school. Then she was away from Holland a long time."

"I know. I talked to her uncle and found out all about the louse she married. But you said she used to come by and see you. What was she really like?"

Margaret shook her head, but she didn't reply.

I pressed on. "Come on, Margaret. Was she a gossip? Was she

snobbish? We all found that we'd told her things we didn't intend to tell. Was she genuinely interested in people? Or just even nosier than I am?"

That made Margaret smile a little. "I never knew why she used to come by and see me," she said. "I was glad to see her—sometimes I get so tired of the Disney Channel and three-year-old conversation. But, you're right—I did find that we were talking about things I really didn't want to discuss with her. See, some bad things happened to me in high school. Julie thought I wasn't 'dealing with them.' Whatever that means. She kept telling me I ought to see a counselor, for example. Like I was crazy!"

Margaret turned toward me, and her eyes were full of tears. "As if it were any business of hers how many kids I have!"

"Of course, it wasn't any of her business, Margaret. It sounds as if Julie had read too many self-help books." And Margaret hadn't read enough, I thought. But I kept that to myself.

"Julie definitely had problems of her own," Margaret said. "She was really lonely after she came back to Holland. I guess that's why she bugged me." She blinked hard. "Anyway, Jim says we're not having any more kids. He took steps. And my doctor says seven pregnancies is enough."

Before I could do more than feel slightly startled, Jim's head popped around the kitchen door. "Hey! Are you girls going to share that cake with Joe and me?"

Margaret cut the little almond-flavored cake and put the pieces on plates, then topped it with globs of white frosting she took from the refrigerator. We all went into the living room and ate cake. It was delicious.

Jim turned out to be a pleasant guy, though maybe not one to spend hours discussing philosophy or literature with. Luckily, Joe is willing to discuss mechanical and electronic things, so he kept the conversation rolling.

My brain was still bouncing around with the information Margaret had let slip. I nearly blew it as Joe and I went out the door. "The kids are absolutely darling," I said. "I'm so glad we got to see them all."

"All is right," Jim said. "Six is plenty!"

"I hope you two will want to have kids," Margaret said. "I couldn't live without mine."

I tried to be noncommittal. "We're pretty old to have a big family. Anyway, Margaret, thanks for putting us down for a cake. I'll let you know more details ASPG."

Three sets of eyes stared at me blankly. "ASPG?" Margaret said.

I'd done it again. "ASAP!" I said. "As soon as possible. As soon I find a dress and settle on flowers."

Joe rolled his eyes. "Come on, Lee," he said. "No more almond extract for you."

Everybody laughed—even me—and Joe and I climbed into his truck.

"Gosh, Joe," I said. "Margaret let something slip. First she said 'some bad things' happened to her in high school. Then she said she's had seven pregnancies. Six kids, but seven pregnancies. Do you think she had an abortion? Or gave a baby up for adoption?"

"That's a pretty broad speculation, Lee. She could have had a miscarriage since she and Jim were married."

"I don't know when she would have found time, with a kid every year. But it's possible, I guess. Oh, gee! An out-of-wedlock pregnancy would be about the worst thing that could happen to a girl who went to Holland Christian."

"I'm sure she wouldn't have been the first case they had, even at Holland Christian. But if you want to link her up with Julie and Carolyn's deaths—well, that's pretty far-fetched. With all these kids, and only two of them in school, I don't see how she could be racing down to Warner Pier to destroy computers and attack florists."

"You're right. I didn't consider her a possibility to begin with, and after seeing her kids and how busy they keep her—I think I can forget Margaret. Besides, she doesn't have the right skill set."

"On the other hand," Joe said, "Jim has exactly the right skill set. He could have done everything that's been done without breaking a sweat."

# Chapter 15

Joe was right, of course. In thinking of Margaret as Margaret—singular—I'd been ignoring the fact that she had a partner: Jim.

And Jim had all the skills the killer of Julie and Carolyn would have needed. He was strong enough to bash effectively. He undoubtedly knew Julie, so she would have let him into her apartment. He hadn't known Carolyn, or I didn't think he had, but if he'd identified himself as Margaret's husband, she wouldn't have hesitated to turn her back on him. As a delivery guy for an office furniture company, he probably had a company truck and unlimited opportunity to roam around west Michigan doing anything he wanted to. All he had to do was tell his boss that the day's delivery and assembly chores had taken longer than expected. He might have to disconnect the odometer on the delivery truck, but I had a feeling Jim could manage that with his eyes closed.

Plus, Jim apparently had specialized computer knowledge, gained as he tried to learn a skill that might lead to a higher-paying job. True, he was studying the electronic aspects of computers—the stuff that required a screwdriver—but I was willing to bet he could handle a little light hacking.

As for motive, Jim seemed to be devoted to Margaret. If he had felt that Julie threatened Margaret, he might have decided to take care of that threat permanently.

By the time I'd analyzed the situation, the cab of Joe's truck was warmed up, but I gave a violent shiver anyway. Joe reached over and took my hand. "Rabbit run over your grave?"

"It's awful, Joe. Awful to be suspicious of people you know, people you consider friends."

"I think that's one reason Hogan keeps trying to warn you not to be so curious, Lee. When either he or the Holland cops make an arrest, you're going to feel better if you can say, 'Oh, I never dreamed he was the one,' than if you had some part in piling up the evidence."

I considered that. Then I rejected it. "But I'm in regular contact with people who appear to be mixed up in these killings," I said. "I'm placed in a position where I can pick up things that Hogan and the Holland detectives can't. And because of that, things I may say innocently could be misconstrued. What if, for example, I said something like, 'Oh, Aunt Nettie got the biggest laugh out of that joke you sent on the Tuesday e-mail,' and what if I said it to the wrong person? It might accidentally put Aunt Nettie in danger."

"But nosing around may put *you* in danger, Lee. And that upsets me a lot."

I unhooked my seat belt, moved to the center of the pickup, and put my head on Joe's shoulder. "I try not to be completely stupid."

He kissed my forehead. "Then buckle up," he said.

"Darling! You really care about me!"

After we'd both chuckled—and I'd fastened the center seat belt—Joe spoke again. "So what's your next move?"

"My whole object is to get to know what Julie was really like. Her death started this whole chain of events, and it seems logical that her character inspired it in some way. The Seventh Food Group is involved—how I don't understand. So I want to talk to each member and find out what he or she thought about Julie."

"That makes sense."

"I thought Julie was pretty innocuous, myself. But I find that she had managed to alienate most of the other members of the group with her amateur psychologist act. She 'outed' Jason and his partner, Ross, to Ross's dad. She apparently knew about something unfortunate that had happened to Margaret in high school and kept trying to get her to 'deal with it.' This might have meant she threatened to tell someone else something that Margaret, or Margaret and Jim, didn't want them to know."

"So what's next?"

"So now I wonder what she did to the Denhams. They certainly weren't wholehearted fans of Julie Singletree."

Joe sighed. "When can we go see them?"

"You don't need to go."

"You're not going alone!"

"Actually, I was planning to see them in a group. The whole Seventh Food Group. We've all been invited to a preview of a closeout sale at Veldkamp Used Food Equipment and Supply tomorrow night. According to the e-mails, everybody's going. Maybe I can talk to Ronnie and Diane informally there. But I won't be alone. I'll stick close to either Lindy or Aunt Nettie."

The person I was to stick close to turned out to be Lindy, because Aunt Nettie decided not to go to the Veldkamp sale. I couldn't decide if she wanted an evening alone with Hogan—she did ask him over to dinner—or if she wanted me to make more decisions about TenHuis Chocolade on my own. It may have been both, but the evening with Hogan probably carried the most weight.

So Lindy and I went alone, and Lindy insisted on driving her bright green compact, despite her injury just two days earlier. "I feel fine," she said. "I guess it takes more than a whack upside the head to slow me down. The only thing that might make me nervous about picking you up is that place on Lake Shore Drive where the bank's caving in."

"The street department has a barricade up," I said. "Not that it would stop anything heavier than a bicycle."

"But at least I'll be able to tell the spot where I want to stay away from the edge. Now, Lee, you be sure to wear your warmest coat. I can guarantee that Veldkamp's warehouse is going to be as cold as a well-digger's fanny."

Lindy was right. We entered Veldkamp's through the heated showroom, but once we were escorted to the cavernous warehouse, we might as well have been in Santa's shipping department. I'd worn my wooly white hat and scarf, my red down jacket, my fur-lined boots, a pair of flannel-lined jeans, and long johns, and I had no impulse to unzip, unhat, or otherwise remove or loosen any garment I had on. Not only was it physically cold, the decor featured concrete floors, dim lights, huge cardboard cartons, gigantic black ranges, and stainless steel appliances in jumbo sizes. Not cozy. It would have felt cold in there on the hottest day of July.

The Seventh Food Group members were obviously not the only people who'd been invited to preview the closeout sale offerings. There were around fifty people roaming around, checking out plate warmers and kicking the tires of rolling tables. Lindy started looking for a freezer. I remembered that I'd promised Joe I'd stick close to her, but Veldkamp's warehouse didn't seem all that dangerous, despite the big equipment that could have hidden a regiment of mad bombers. I found a Veldkamp employee and asked directions to the cooling tunnel.

A cooling tunnel is a little air conditioner for chocolates. It's open at both ends and a conveyor belt runs through it, passing under a Plexiglas arch; cold air sprays into that miniature tunnel. Chocolate melts easily—that's why you can't hold it in your hand very long without having sticky fingers. So chocolatiers can mold it or dip it readily, but they then have to let it get cool before they can do a next step, such as adding another layer of chocolate. A cooling tunnel speeds this process up.

Aunt Nettie had explained what I should look for in a cooling tunnel and how much I should be willing to pay. The one Veldkamp's had looked pretty good—or it would once we'd cleaned it to Aunt Nettie standards—so I put in a written bid. Then I moved to the stainless steel section and began to look at worktables and rolling storage racks.

All the time I was keeping an eye out for Diane and Ronnie Denham, or I thought I was. So I don't know why I jumped about a foot when I rolled a six-foot-tall storage rack aside and came face-to-face with Diane.

"Oh!" I said. "You startled me."

Diane smiled her cheerful Mrs. Claus smile. She was bundled up in a long blue down coat and had a plaid wool scarf wrapped around her head. Just a few of her beautiful white curls peeked out over her forehead. "Hi, Lee. What are you looking for?"

"Storage racks and worktables for Aunt Nettie." I'd already decided to forget subtlety and simply ask for information from Diane, so I plunged right in. "I was also looking for a chance to talk to you."

"What about?"

"Julie."

Diane looked away from me. She put out a gloved hand and gently rolled a stainless steel rack back and forth. "Aren't the police looking into Julie's death?"

"Of course. I'm not interested in her death. I'm interested in her life. All sorts of bad things have happened to the Seventh Food Group since Julie was killed. I have a feeling that's because of things that happened while she was alive. I barely knew Julie, but I feel compelled to—well, get to know her posthaste. I mean, posthumously!"

Diane ignored my slip of the tongue. "I only met her a few times."

"That's what all of us say. But she managed to elevate—I mean, alienate!—at least half the members of the Seventh Food Group with her amateur psychology."

"I didn't know that."

"I just figured it out this week. Jason—this is just an example— she urged Jason and Ross to open up about their relationship with Ross's dad. Jason says the poor old guy is ninety years old and in a nursing home. Until Julie shot her mouth off, he considered Jason merely a friend of his son's. What good is it going to do for them to confront him with their relationship at this point in his life?"

Diane shook her head. "It wouldn't be kind at all, and it wouldn't affect Jason and Ross, either."

"Exactly! But I have a feeling that Julie was Little Miss Helpful to everybody she was around. I know she tried to talk to me about my divorce. I had a hard time dodging her. Did she give you and Ronnie the same treatment? What did you all think of her?"

Diane's face crumpled, and she turned away. "Julie was awfully nosy," she said. "She went way beyond asking personal questions. She had—well, she'd researched us on the Internet. I think she'd researched all of us."

"All of us?"

"Yes. But it was strange, Lee. She didn't offer to tell us anything about anyone else. About Jason, for example, or about you or any of the others. When you called her an 'amateur psychologist,' that described it. She thought everybody should put all their problems on display, should forget about keeping anything secret."

I shuddered. "I guess she simply hadn't gotten to me yet. I have as many secrets as anybody else. But she kept her own life completely secret."

Diane caught her breath sharply, and I realized she was looking at something behind me. I looked around and saw Ronnie coming toward us.

Diane leaned toward me. When she spoke again, she had dropped her voice almost to a whisper. "Lee, don't talk about Julie in front of Ronnie. In fact, there's no point in talking about this at all. We signed a confidentiality agreement. We cannot say a word. Under penalty of law."

I snapped my gaping mouth shut just as Ronnie joined us. "Hi, Lee," he said. "Diane, there's a set of big mixing bowls over there you might want to take a look at."

They went away, and I strolled aimlessly among the giant cartons and superduper mixers while I thought about what Diane had said. A confidentiality agreement? What was that exactly? Under what situation would an outwardly ordinary couple like the Denhams sign such a thing? The settlement of a lawsuit? Something to do with a juvenile offender?

It was a question for a lawyer. I resolved to ask Joe. Then I wandered back to the rolling racks and picked a couple out that I thought would suit Aunt Nettie. TenHuis Chocolade uses a lot of those racks—stainless steel gizmos on wheels, each around six feet tall and three feet square, with space for two dozen metal trays that slide in and out of metal supports. We could use a half dozen, Aunt Nettie had told me, but we had no place to put that many.

Was TenHuis going to have to expand? If we decided I needed an assistant, we'd need a place for him or her to work, and Aunt Nettie definitely could use more storage space. But where would we find the room? I tucked that idea away to think about after I'd figured out Julie.

Lindy and I left for Warner Pier about nine o'clock. She'd made arrangements for Mike to look over the freezer. I was mostly silent as she drove home; Lindy was mad at one of the teachers at Warner Pier Elementary, and I heard about her for the whole thirty miles, but I only listened to about half of it.

It wasn't until she had turned the green compact onto the Warner River Bridge that she said something that really caught my ear.

"You know, Lee, that car's been behind us all the way from Holland."

I twisted around to see the headlights of the car behind us. "Are you sure?"

"Not absolutely positive, of course, but I first noticed a set of head-lights that shape and size just as we stopped at the Twenty-fourth Street light."

"Why didn't you say something earlier?"

"I didn't think anything of it until the lights followed us through Warner Pier. And now he's closing up on us."

"Should you turn around and go back?"

"To the police station? There's nobody there this time of night. They close up and let the county dispatcher take calls."

"We could go to the Stop and Shop. It's open all night."

"Yeah, and some old guy's at the cash register. A lot of help he would be."

"He could call Tony or Joe. Heck, I've got my cell phone. I can call Tony or Joe. Or the cops." I reached for my purse.

"I've got another idea, Lee. Why don't I pull in a driveway and turn around. We can go back to town. If the car doesn't follow us—well, I'm going to feel pretty dumb if we call Tony or Joe, and it turns out to be somebody who lives farther on down Lake Shore Drive coming back from the Holland Multiplex."

The interstate coming down from Holland had been well plowed, of course, and thousands of cars had driven down it since the last snow, beating the pavement almost free of snow and ice. In contrast, Lake Shore Drive was barely two lanes wide, and it had only local traffic, so it had snow piled along the edges. But there were lots of driveways, roads, and lanes branching off it.

"Turn in at the Nolans' house," I said. "Where the big hedge is. If you cut the lights, it ought to hide us."

Lindy nodded. She sped up, wheeling around a curve in the road. I was looking back at the car behind us when she suddenly turned off the headlights, and I felt the compact swerve as she cut the wheels sharply right.

"Hang on," Lindy said.

Then she hit the brakes. My seat belt snapped, keeping me immobile. I kept looking out the back window. I could see a red reflection on the Nolans' hedge. "Foot off the brakes!" I said.

The red disappeared, as did a fainter white. Lindy had turned off the ignition.

For a moment I was scared that the car following us would come into the Nolans' drive right after us. Then where would we be? Caught between a hedge and a hard place.

But the lights went on by. The car behind us wasn't even driving very fast.

"Could you see what kind of car it was?" I said.

"I wouldn't recognize it if I saw it. The headlights just looked odd. But it sure didn't look like a madman trying to run us off the road, did it?"

"No. But let's drive back to town anyway."

Lindy started the car, backed out of the drive, and headed back the way we'd come. I kept a close watch, but no car was behind us. It was close to ten o'clock by then, and all the residents of Lake Shore Drive had apparently gone home. We saw lights through the bare branches of the trees, but we were the only car moving. We drove back across the Warner River Bridge and into town, and Lindy pulled into the parking lot that overlooked the bridge. Again she cut her lights.

"Unless our eyes are reflecting," I said, "we should be hard to see."

"We'll have to peek through our fingers if he comes back."

He didn't come back. We sat there looking at the bridge for ten minutes and not a single vehicle crossed it, either coming toward us or going away.

After a few minutes Lindy began to laugh. "I won't tell Joe about this, if you won't tell Tony."

"I do feel pretty stupid. But considering that you were actually attacked just a couple of days ago . . ."

"That was just a thief." Lindy's voice was firm. "I refuse to worry about this any more. I'm driving you home."

We laughed and giggled all the way across the bridge. The relief was great. But I couldn't help peeking out the back window now and then. So I saw the headlights first.

I gasped. A car had pulled out of a driveway and turned the same way we were traveling. It was moving fast; it fishtailed as it turned onto Lake Shore Drive.

"Not again!" Lindy said.

"Maybe it's not the same guy."

"They look like the same headlights to me," she said. "They reflect off that grill in the middle, and that grill looks like long teeth. Let's move!"

The little car took a leap forward. Lake Shore Drive follows the edge of Lake Michigan. It's a narrow blacktop road, and there was ice and snow along the edges. Not a good place for fast driving. But I didn't care, and Lindy apparently didn't either. She gunned the motor.

The car behind us was closing in. I didn't say anything, since Lindy could see it coming in the rearview mirror. I wanted her to concentrate on driving, not looking at the strange headlights behind us.

Lindy didn't panic. When she spoke, her voice was calm. "Where's that place where the bank's eaten away?"

"About a quarter of a mile farther on."

"I guess I could hit the brakes and try to make a U-turn."

"Then he could hit us broadside."

No, going on seemed to be our only choice. Lindy goosed the car, and it responded with more speed.

The car that was following us came closer. It came right up on the back bumper. Then it suddenly cut left, as if it were going to pass us. But instead it drove along beside us. But it wasn't moving parallel to us. It was edging closer to us, ready to sideswipe the car.

Then I saw orange in the headlights. "There's the barricade! He's going to try to push us over!"

Lindy's response probably saved our lives. She threw on her brakes.

Instantly the car beside us shot ahead.

Our tires hit a patch of ice, and the compact went into a spin, but we didn't hit the guy who had been chasing us. We had almost come to a stop when the car slid slowly into the wooden barricade. Moving almost in slow motion, we went over the bank backward, sliding down toward Lake Michigan.

# Chapter 16

I thought we were going to die. I knew how steep that drop was: straight down. And I knew how far it was: at least forty feet. And I knew what was at the bottom: the shallows of Lake Michigan, frozen solid. I expected us to plummet, hit hard, and be crushed to death as the car folded up like an accordion.

But it didn't happen that way. We didn't plummet; we slid gently. We didn't fall straight down; my feet were as high as my shoulders, true, but it was more like gradually tipping over backward in a kitchen chair than like a beach stone splashing into the water.

We hit the ice at the edge of Lake Michigan with a crash, but the car didn't fold up like an accordion. It bounced. It seemed to be all in one piece, and was even sitting fairly level. The motor was still purring, the lights were still on, and the heater fan was still blowing hot air.

And we had stopped moving.

"Lindy! Are you okay?"

"I think so! Are *you* okay?"

"I'm conscious, and nothing seems to be broken. Can you get out of the car?"

"Is that a good idea?"

"It might catch fire."

Lindy punched dashboard buttons. The headlights went out, and the heater fan fell silent. "That will make it harder for that guy to find us, if he comes back," she said.

"I wish we could get out of the car without turning on the interior lights, but we can't. So we'd better hurry."

Hurrying did not turn out to be an option. Lindy's door was jammed shut. Snow and ice were piled up outside my door as well, and it took me several hard shoves to get it open. Then Lindy couldn't find her hat. Refusing to leave the car without a hat didn't seem dumb right at that moment. The temperature was in the teens. I was sure grateful that we were both warmly dressed.

Once she found her hat, Lindy had to climb over the center console. She did a belly whopper onto the ice to get out my door. We were panting by the time we both were standing on the passenger's side of the car, hanging onto the door as if it were our last connection with solid ground. The footing was terrible, since the car was surrounded by clumps and clods and splinters of ice. The lake occasionally freezes smoothly, but crashing a car into it had thrown up all sorts of icy debris, regardless of how smooth the ice had been when we hit.

At least there was no open water. We didn't have to leap from floe to floe. Instead, we went toward the high bank we'd just slid down, stepping carefully and hanging onto each other as if we had Velcro on our gloves. We couldn't tell when we got onto the shore, actually. The chunks of ice seemed to go right up the bank, and I *knew* there had to be some beach someplace under the snow.

"Can we get up the bank?" Lindy asked.

"What if that guy is up there waiting?" I gestured to the right and toward the top of the bank. "There's a house up there with the lights still on. Maybe we can climb up."

We started walking. It's a miracle neither of us broke a leg. Of course, it wasn't too dark. Even when the moon is behind clouds, a layer of snow gives the terrain a sort of glow, so we could see a bit. Lindy began to mutter because she hadn't thought to grab her flashlight from the glove box. That reminded me that I had picked up my purse, and there was a penlight on my key chain. We used it occasionally, but mostly we walked over the chunky ice that covered the beach using the moonlight filtered through clouds and reflected from snow.

Then we heard a man's voice shouting, "Hello! Who's there?"

I put the penlight out, and Lindy and I stood still, clutching each other.

Lindy whispered. "Do you think it's the guy who ran us off the road?"

I whispered back. "He probably wouldn't yell. So it's likely to be whoever lives in that house. We'd better chance it."

I turned the penlight back on and waved it. Then I yelled, "Hello! We had a wreck! The car went over the edge!"

"Anybody hurt?"

"Not bad! How can we get up the bank?"

"My stairs are a little further along. I'll go get a ladder!"

Our rescuer turned out to be a retired gentleman named Oscar Patterson. I had never met him, but I'd noticed his mailbox, and I sure was glad to make his acquaintance. Like most of the houses on the Lake Michigan side of Lake Shore Drive, his home had a wooden stairway that led down to the beach. The bottom section had been taken down for the winter, so the ice wouldn't grind it into splinters, but he brought a ladder, and we were able to climb it to reach the first landing. After that, it was merely a matter of inching our way up, stair by snowy and icy stair, hanging onto the wooden handrail.

"I've been telling 'em someone was going to go over back there," our rescuer said. "I called the street department. They said nothing could be done until they could get hold of some more of those barricades. Now maybe they'll put up something stouter. Too late. As usual."

The next hour was full of events. Mr. Patterson and his wife clucked over us. We called people—Aunt Nettie and Hogan, Joe, and Tony. They all came rushing over, and our rescuers' driveway became packed with cars.

My biggest question was how we had avoided being killed. I was sure we'd gone over a real cliff, and by rights we should have been crushed to death.

But Hogan said we'd missed the steepest spot. "You went off about fifteen feet before the place where the road has been eaten away," he said. "It was a steep slope, but you slid down at a forty-five-degree angle, not a ninety. You were damn lucky."

"Thank God Lindy hit the brakes when she did," I said.

We had to tell Hogan the whole story. His biggest concern was that neither of us could describe the car that had pushed us off the road. Our vague description of its headlights was not a lot of help, though Lindy swore the car's grill had looked like monstrous teeth.

Other than scrapes and bruises, neither Lindy nor I seemed to be hurt, and the men in our respective lives took us home just as the wrecker arrived. I was sure glad to see my own bed, though I can't claim that I slept very well. One moment I was so grateful to be alive that I couldn't close an eye, and the next I was so puzzled as to who would have tried to push Lindy and me over that steep bank that I just lay in bed with my brain whizzing around.

Maybe the biggest puzzle was simply which of us he'd been out to get. I couldn't see any reason for either of us to attract the attention of a killer. Anyway, I mulled it over most of the night; I guess it was more comforting to do that than to remember what a close escape we'd had.

I finally fell asleep around five o'clock. Aunt Nettie must have tip-toed out, because I didn't wake up until ten a.m. Then I panicked. Even though it was Saturday, TenHuis Chocolade was keeping regular business hours, getting ready for the big holiday. I was late.

By the time I'd showered, dressed, and gone by the police station to sign a statement, it was noon. So I came in the door of TenHuis Chocolade in something of a tizzy. I couldn't afford to take a half day off, not even because I'd had a narrow escape followed by a sleepless night.

Dolly Jolly was working the front counter. "Hi, Lee!" she shouted. "Heard you had an exciting night! I'm assigned up here for the day! Nettie called Hazel in, asked her to fill the gap this week!"

I gave a sigh of relief. Hazel had formerly been Aunt Nettie's second-in-command. She'd retired two months earlier after her husband, Harry, suffered a stroke.

"If Harry can spare her, we can really use her help," I told Dolly. Then I went back to tell Hazel I was glad to see her.

Harry, she said, was doing better. Their son would be visiting for the next week. "It won't hurt him to take his dad to physical therapy," she said, "and it won't hurt Harry if he has to depend on somebody besides me for a few days." I thought her mouth looked a little grim, but I didn't ask for details.

I went to my desk, vowing to concentrate on the chocolate business all afternoon. At first I found this difficult, since the phone kept ringing. I knew it would mostly be friends calling to commiserate over the wreck, but it could be a customer, so I didn't dare not answer. The calls from friends made it hard to get anything done; they kept Julie's and Carolyn's deaths, the attack on Lindy, and the harrowing slide into Lake Michigan bouncing around in my brain. But about four o'clock something happened that focused my attention on TenHuis Chocolade in a big way.

The phone rang. Again. I tried not to sigh as I answered. "TenHuis Chocolade."

"Hello." It was a male voice, and it sounded young. And it didn't say anything more.

So I spoke again. "Can I help you?"

"Well . . . This is Bob Vanderheide. Is Aunt—Could I speak to Mrs. TenHuis, please?"

For a moment my mind was a complete blank. Bob Vanderheide? I should know that name. Then I remembered. It was Aunt Nettie's nephew. The one whose mother had written about his job prospects.

I decided to be friendly. "Bobby!" I said. "Hello! Aunt Nettie's in the black. I mean the back! In the workroom. I'll have to go get her. This is Lee McKinney."

"Oh, hi." Bobby didn't sound enthusiastic. "I guess we're cousins."

"Shirttail cousins. No blood relation. How are you?"

"Fine."

The conversation was not going anywhere. I told Bobby—or Bob—I'd find Aunt Nettie, put the phone down, and went back to the workroom. Aunt Nettie wasn't there. I checked the break room. Not there. The restroom door was open, so I peeked inside. No sign of her there either. Finally, I asked Hazel. Aunt Nettie, she said, had gone to the Superette for four quarts of whipping cream. So I'd have to handle Bobby—I mean, Bob—myself.

I headed back to the office. "Aunt Nettie stepped out for a few minutes. Give me your number, and I'll have her call you."

"No!" Bob paused again. "Listen, tell her that I need to be over on that side of Michigan on Monday, and I'll try to come by. Okay?"

"Sure. She'll want you to stay over, Bob."

"I better plan to drive back that night."

"I'll tell her. But we have plenty of room, and she'd love to have you stay."

"I just need to talk to her. I'll see her Monday afternoon." He hung up.

Oh, rats! Just what I needed. My rival heir was appearing.

I scolded myself for feeling that way about Bobby—I mean Bob. But I did. He was a blood relative to Aunt Nettie. I wasn't. He might end up owning TenHuis Chocolade.

Well, I wouldn't be working for *him*. No matter what happened. I could find another job. I could commute into Holland or Grand Rapids. I could scrub floors, wash dishes, or clean toilets.

My mental tirade was interrupted by Hazel, who put her head in my door and said Aunt Nettie was back. "Did you want something important?"

"Tell her that her nephew Bobby—I mean, Bob—called and said he'll be by to see her Monday afternoon."

"Oh, that's nice." Hazel smiled and went back to the workroom.

Nice. Hazel said Bobby's visit would be nice. I addressed myself to the computer screen and adjusted my attitude.

Hazel was right, of course. Aunt Nettie would be pleased to see Bob. I was acting like a jealous little girl, afraid my favorite aunt would ignore me for another child, one who was younger and possibly cuter. I'd better straighten up, or Aunt Nettie would be perfectly entitled to disinherit me.

I was able to laugh at the idea that I'd be cleaning toilets if Bobby took over TenHuis Chocolade. After all, I had a degree in accounting and a lot of job experience. I wasn't down to cleaning toilets yet. There was even the possibility that Bob would turn out to be a really smart guy who would be an asset to TenHuis Chocolade.

I was about to log on and check my e-mail when the next interruption came. My friend Barbara, the banker, came in. She had to hear all about the accident and the miraculous escape Lindy and I had had. I had to repeat the whole story. But it was only ten minutes before Barbara got up, ready to head back to the bank.

"I'm awfully glad you two made it out in one piece," she said. "Where had you been?"

I reported on our trip to Holland in an absentminded way, because Barbara's question had triggered a memory. One of my main purposes in going to the Veldkamp sales preview had been to quiz Diane and Ronnie Denham. I hadn't learned a lot from Diane, but she had said one provocative thing. Diane had told me she felt sure that Julie had looked all of the Seventh Food Group up on the Internet.

I doubted that there was anything about me on the Internet, but her comment had made me wonder if there wasn't something about the Denhams there. My old curiosity bump began itching madly. I connected to the Internet and looked up their names.

At first I didn't find a thing. There was only one mention of "Ronnie" or "Ronald" or "Diane" named Denham on the Internet. That mention listed them as proprietors of the Hideaway Inn. Then I checked the Warner Pier Chamber of Commerce membership list. Diane, I learned, had a middle initial. A minute later I struck pay dirt.

In another state, clear across the country, a guidance counselor named "D. B. Denham" had blown the whistle on a scheme her principal had worked out, a scheme which misappropriated a local foundation's scholarship funds. The local newspaper's stories on the scandal were indexed on the Internet, and so were the stories run by a major newspaper in the state.

I didn't have time to read all the stories, so I skipped to the end of the index. And I came up quite frustrated. The stories ended abruptly with an out-of-court settlement that was not revealed. Hmmm.

I looked back at a couple of the news items, and I began to read between the lines. The school board had been covering up like mad. The erring principal had been fired, true, but not before he had persecuted—that's not too strong a word—the whistleblower. The whistleblower, this D. B. Denham, had finally sued the principal and the school board because of the persecution and the board's failure to stop it. The school board, which had clearly been in the wrong, had been forced into an out-of-court settlement. D. B. Denham had accepted the settlement, signed an agreement not to reveal any more details about the case publicly, and taken early retirement.

"And bought a B and B in Warner Pier, Michigan," I said. "Hmmm."

No wonder Diane had resented Julie nosing into their affairs. If her connection with the case had made the papers, it would have endangered her settlement.

The phone had rung two more times while I was checking the Internet—one friend and one customer—and now it rang again. I didn't even bother to sigh before I picked up the receiver.

"TenHuis Chocolade."

"Is this Lee McKinney?" It was the voice of a woman. It didn't sound young, but it sounded firm.

"Yes. May I help you?"

"I hope so. This is Rachel Schrader. I'm going to be at the Warner Pier cottage tomorrow, and I'm hoping you can come to see me there."

## CHOCOLATE CHAT
## QUOTATIONS FROM BRILLAT-SAVARIN

Anthelme Brillat-Savarin was a French lawyer and gastronome who wrote extensively on food, drink, and gracious living in the early nineteenth century. Naturally, he had several things to say about chocolate. Chocolate was then almost exclusively a drink.

"If one swallows a cup of chocolate only three hours after a copious lunch, everything will be perfectly digested and there will still be room for dinner."

"It has been shown as proof positive that carefully prepared chocolate is as healthful a food as it is pleasant; that it is nourishing and easily digested . . . That it is above all helpful to people who must do a great deal of mental work."

"If any man has drunk a little too deeply from the cup of physical pleasure, if he has spent too much time at his desk that should have been spent asleep, if his fine spirits have become temporarily dulled; if he finds the air too damp, the minutes too slow, the atmosphere too heavy to withstand, if he is obsessed with a fixed idea which bars him from any freedom of thought, if he is any of these poor creatures, we say, let him be given a good pint of amber-flavored chocolate and marvels will be performed."

# Chapter 17

Stunned amazement swept over me. Rachel Schrader? The grande dame of western Michigan? She wanted me to come see her? I was dumbstruck, so when I was finally able to speak, naturally I said something dumb.

"Mrs. Shatter? I mean, Mrs. Schrader! Of course, I'll be happy to meet with you. What . . . ?"

I stopped in the middle of my question. I couldn't think just how to ask Rachel Schrader what the hell she wanted.

I might be confused, but Mrs. Schrader wasn't. "Naturally, Ms. McKinney, you're wondering what my business is, and how it concerns you. I'm calling because we are beginning to dispose of Julie's belongings, and I want to ask your help."

"My help? I mean, of course I'll be glad to help."

"I've always read the Warner Pier weekly newspaper, just because I own property near there. And last week I happened to note that the chamber of commerce is sponsoring a drive to collect clothing and household goods to benefit the women's shelter."

"Yes. It's one of our ongoing projects."

"Martin told me you were serving on the chamber board. I'd love for Julie's things to benefit abused women. If you wouldn't mind helping me by delivering them . . ."

"Of course, Mrs. Schrader. But—"

She didn't let me finish my sentence. "In addition, this will give me an opportunity to have a chat with the granddaughter of my old friend."

Her invitation was a royal command. I couldn't argue, though I did tell her TenHuis Chocolade would be open, even though the next day was a Sunday. Mrs. Schrader gave me two phone numbers—the Warner Pier house and her cell phone—in case I was going to run late. We agreed to meet at eleven o'clock.

I was still amazed as I hung up, and I headed straight back to the workroom. I felt sure Aunt Nettie would understand what was so peculiar about Rachel Schrader's request.

I tried to tell her about that request in simple terms, not imposing my own amazement. I wanted Aunt Nettie's honest reaction. And after I told her, I found it satisfying to see her eyes grow wide and even more satisfying to hear what she said.

"That's the oddest thing I ever heard of."

"That's what I thought," I said.

"Doesn't Mrs. Schrader realize that the women's shelter is *in* Holland? Why would she go to Holland, load Julie's things up, and bring them to Warner Pier to give them to the chamber drive? Some chamber person will have to load them up and carry them back to Holland."

"It would certainly be a lot easier to do it directly."

"Unless she thinks the chamber benefits in some way."

"Like winning a contest? She said she had seen the story about the drive in the *Warner Pier Gazette.* And that story made it quite clear that we were trying to benefit the shelter, not gain any benefit ourselves."

Aunt Nettie nodded. "So her request is obviously just an excuse. She wants to talk to you, Lee. Why?"

"That's the question. If she wants to talk to me, why take this indirect method? Why not just call me up and talk? I certainly would get together with Rachel Schrader any time of the day or night, on the phone or in person. Why does she feel she needs an excuse to ask me to come see her?"

Aunt Nettie and I shrugged and shook our heads in unison. Neither of us had an answer.

"Take her a pound of chocolates," Aunt Nettie said. "And at least you'll get a look at that house. It's supposed to be a real showplace."

I decided to keep seeing the house as my goal and to quit trying to anticipate what in the world Rachel Schrader wanted. Whatever it was, worrying wasn't going to help me figure it out. And it would be fun to see the Schrader house. Joe had pointed it out to me from the lakeside. From the water it looked like a flying saucer, if a flying saucer could be made of glass, floating in for a gentle landing on top of the dunes. Yes, it would be interesting to see the revolutionary structure up close.

So at ten forty-five the next day I headed for the south edge of Warner Pier and turned into the nondescript entrance to the Schrader property. I'd had to ask Aunt Nettie how to get there from Lake Shore Drive. There was certainly nothing of the showplace about the entrance.

Except the paving. Around Warner Pier, as in most rural neighborhoods, ordinary property owners have drives surfaced with sand or gravel. The Schrader driveway—naturally it had been cleared of snow—was asphalt. I will say that it was a one-way drive, quite narrow, but it was asphalt. The asphalt didn't cover a short drive, either. That drive stretched toward the lakeshore, disappearing into the woods as it curved to the right.

On the first curve was a small wooden house. It wasn't made of logs, but it had natural wood siding, and I was immediately sure it was the "cabin" that Brad Schrader had described. A Prius, a combination electric-gasoline car, had been backed into an open shed at the side. So I gathered that Brad was home, though I didn't see any sign of life as I drove by.

The road went on, passing through thick woods. Giant trees—some with bare branches and some evergreens—towered overhead. The snow on the ground was lumpy; young trees and other undergrowth would cover the ground in spring.

The woods were lovely. I could see why Mike Herrera was eager to find out what the family's plans for the site were. Judging by the length of the road into it, the property was several hundred acres in size—maybe more. And it ran along the lakeshore. With woods and beach, the property had everything to make it a fantastic nature preserve. On the other hand, it would also make a great site for a resort—if the right zoning could be arranged. I didn't know which Mike thought would benefit Warner Pier the most.

After driving what seemed like three miles, but which was probably under a tenth of that, I saw the glint of glass through the trees. I rounded a final curve and drew up before a dramatic house.

If the house looked like a flying saucer from the lake, from the land it looked like an egg—a brown egg. It was oval and apparently made of cast concrete painted a medium tan. But it was built in a strictly symmetrical design. A door—carved and painted black—was smack in the middle of the front façade. The door was flanked by broad floor-to-ceiling windows. Even broader expanses of concrete stretched out beyond the windows, forming an arc that reflected the shape of the six broad stone steps that led from the drive. Matching concrete planters curved around the steps. I suppose they held plants in warm weather, but now they were full of rounded humps. A closer look showed me that lake stones the size and shape of ostrich eggs were peeking through the snow here and there.

I parked and got out of the van, bringing the box of chocolates Aunt Nettie had sent. Apparently Rachel Schrader had told her staff I was coming, because the carved black door opened immediately, and an attractive gray-haired woman wearing a white pants suit came out.

The woman gave me a welcoming smile, which displayed deep dimples. She spoke in a strained, high-pitched voice. "Ms. McKinney? Please come in."

She ushered me into the house. "I'm Hilda VanTil," she said. "Mrs. Schrader's aide. She's out in the overlook."

Ms. VanTil took my coat and hat, and as she was hanging them up I got a glimpse of a control panel that must have powered a fancy security system. Then she led me through a foyer and a living room, both filled with the kind of completely unadorned furniture that costs the earth. The simple rooms could have seemed cold, but they didn't. The furniture, flooring, and walls were warm colors—corals, rusts, deep browns—and the textures were nubby and wooly and comforting. The few pieces of art—giant paintings and imposing sculpture—were strikingly displayed.

The room beyond was another story. Ms. VanTil had called it "the overlook," and that was a good name. It was obviously a space that had been designed to provide the best possible view of the dunes, the beach, and Lake Michigan. This was the part of the house Joe and I had seen from the lake, the part that had seemed to hover over the dunes like a spaceship just about to land.

The area was about thirty feet deep, with glass walls forming a sort of eight-sided drum that stuck out from the house like a pavilion. Mrs. Schrader sat next to the farthest window. She was in her wheelchair, and as Ms. VanTil and I entered the room she pivoted around to face us.

"Hello, Lee," she said. "Everyone always wants to see the overlook, so I thought I'd wait for you out here."

"It's spectacular," I said. "And you're right; I did want to get a look at it. I'd seen it from the lake, and I was curious about what all that glass enclosed."

Rachel Schrader turned her chair toward the lake again. "There's no point in a beach house, of course, unless you make the maximum use of the lake view. And I wanted to see the beach year-round, not just in the summer. I told the architect I didn't want one of those boxy enclosed decks that are the usual solution."

"He certainly took you at your word."

"Some people find the view of ice and snow and frigid water too chilling, but I enjoy it. Most of my family didn't agree with me. They like it in summer, when we open up the walls. Only Brad sees it the way I do. We think it's stimulating."

Before I could reply that it could definitely stimulate an armful of goose bumps, Mrs. Schrader wheeled around toward me again. "But sit down, Lee. Hilda is bringing us some coffee. Unless you'd rather move back into the living room?"

"No. You're right. The view is lovely. And it's perfectly warm out here."

The room held very little furniture, but I found a couch covered with brown sailcloth and sat on it. For twenty minutes Rachel Schrader and I chitchatted. We discussed the ecological problems of the Lake Michigan dunes, but only in a general way. Nothing was said about the fact that my hostess owned a substantial stretch of those fragile dunes. Then she told me stories about my grandfather. She asked about my background, and I gave a short account of how I'd come to be born in Texas and how I had wandered back to Michigan two years earlier.

"Then you and Nettie are the last of the TenHuis family," Mrs. Schrader said.

"The last of our branch, I guess. Of course, Aunt Nettie's only a TenHuis by marriage. And I've never really been a TenHuis at all—by name or by culture. I know very little about the Dutch settlers of west Michigan and a lot about the cowboy culture of Texas. Warner Pier people have been kind, but I know I'll always be a stranger here in a lot of ways."

"I'm afraid that will always be true of Brad, as well. He didn't have an easy childhood. But he says Warner Pier is as close to a hometown as anywhere else, and I'm hoping he'll put down some roots. Which reminds me—Martin said you had had some computer problems."

I didn't quite understand what had reminded her of computer problems, but I didn't ask. "All of the Seventh Food Group have had problems. I'm afraid one of us passed a virus along to the whole group. But at the moment, we're all back up and running."

Rachel Schrader leaned forward, and her black eyes snapped. "Do you have any idea what happened?"

I was surprised at her interest. I know from Martin that Mrs. Schrader was in her late eighties. Lots of older people are into computers, of course, but it's usually because they need to use the gadgets for business reasons or for a hobby. I couldn't imagine that this was the case with Mrs. Schrader. I paused before I replied, trying to anticipate just how much information she wanted.

"I'm just a user, not a computer expert," I said finally. "But Warner Pier does have a computer guru, and he's working on the problem."

"He hasn't indicated exactly what virus is involved?"

She really was interested. I felt faintly surprised. "He hasn't told me anything, but my computer wasn't one of the ones with the major problem. I could ask him."

"Oh, no! It's just idle curiosity on my part. Schrader Labs has done research along this line, so I was curious. But I have no reason to bother anybody about it. It doesn't matter at all. Not at all."

Mrs. Schrader was certainly being emphatic about something that didn't matter "at all . . . at all." I tried to think of a tactful way to follow up on the subject. But my thoughts were interrupted by the sound of a door opening. Then a high tenor echoed through the house. "Grandmother! Where are you?"

Rachel Schrader did her pivoting act, turning toward the living room. "Out here, Brad!" Then her head snapped toward me. "I asked Brad to help load the boxes into your van."

Brad slouched into sight, coming through the living room door. He looked as hangdog as ever, as if somebody had just kicked him. Even the red plaid lumberjack shirt he wore didn't make him look cheerful. He kissed his grandmother on the cheek, then shook hands with me.

"Nice to see you again, Brad," I said.

"Oh, yes," he said. "We talked at Julie's memorial service."

I blinked, but I don't think I blew Brad's secret. He apparently didn't want his grandmother to know he'd come by my office to ask for advice on getting acquainted in Warner Pier. Just like he didn't want his uncle to know.

"Where are the boxes?" Brad said.

"Hilda will show them to you." Mrs. Schrader shook a misshapen finger at Brad. "This is your last chance, Brad. Are you sure you don't want any of Julie's dishes? At least you should take that good set of cookware. I know she'd want you to have it."

A look of complete revulsion flashed over Brad's face. For a moment I thought he was going to throw up.

Then he regained control. "No, thanks, Grandmother. I'm saving my pennies so I can buy something fancy. Until then I'll get by with my Kmart set." He grinned stiffly. "I'll just find Hilda. She'll show me the boxes."

"Now, Brad, don't run off the way you did last time," Mrs. Schrader said. "I want to talk to you."

Brad nodded and left. I got up as well. "I'll open the van, then help Brad," I said. "This is a very generous gesture, Mrs. Schrader."

"When we get to Julie's furniture, I'll send it directly to the shelter. And one other thing." Mrs. Schrader produced a checkbook from a purse that hung from the arm of her wheelchair. She flipped it open, found a white ballpoint pen in the purse. Despite her warped fingers, she wrote rapidly.

After she'd ripped out the check, she folded it in half and held it out to me. "Here. This goes with the items." Then she smiled. "And take the pen, too. It's one of the new Schrader Labs promo pieces. They write quite well."

I wasn't so crass as to peek at the amount of the check, but I looked the pen over and gushed a bit. It was a nice one—the kind with gel ink—and had a tasteful design of a computer mouse chasing a lab mouse, spiraling around the body and down toward the writing end. Then I shook her hand—remembering to hold it gently—said good-bye, and went out the front door.

Brad was coming around the side of the house, carrying a large carton. Hilda VanTil was with him with another carton. I opened the van. There weren't a lot of belongings being donated. Hilda and Brad each brought out one more box, and I carried one out. That was it.

I expected Brad to go back inside in obedience to his grandmother's instructions, but he stood there on the porch, not saying anything. It was left to the sweet-faced Ms. VanTil to give me a warm good-bye in her squeaky voice. She added directions for how to get off the property. The drive was one-way, she said. I was to go forward. In my rearview mirror I saw her entering the front door, and Brad heading around the side of the house.

The outbound section of asphalt drive led through the same sort of woods that the inbound road followed. The whole thing was well-plowed, but I drove slowly, enjoying the snowy woods. Frankly, as a person born on the Texas plains, I find the thick woods of Michigan's summer a bit scary. I like them a little better when the leaves are off the trees.

I was so intent on the scenery that when a figure in a red plaid jacket bounded out in front of the car, I nearly ran him down.

I threw on the brakes and luckily didn't hit an ice patch. The van came to a stop safely, and I rolled my window down.

"Brad! You nearly scared me to death!"

"I'm sorry. I was trying to catch you before you got out the front gate."

"How'd you get here?"

Brad gestured behind himself. "There's a bunch of paths and roads through the middle. I use them all the time. Looking at birds and such. But I wanted to tell you something about Julie."

"What about her?"

"The person she was really scared of was that guy with the pony-tail. Jason."

# Chapter 18

"Why? Why do you think Julie was scared of Jason?" Brad shuffled his feet and looked more pitiful than usual. "It was all very nebulous."

"Come on, Brad! She must have said or done something to make you think she was afraid of him or you wouldn't say that she was."

"Well, once I was at her place, and the phone rang. She said, 'That might be Jason. I don't want to talk to him.' Then she let the answering machine pick up. And it *was* Jason. She made a face and turned down the volume so that she couldn't hear his voice. And I said, 'Who's Jason? A new boyfriend?' And she laughed, and she said, 'Not one of mine. He's a restaurant guy I know. He's pretty scary. He makes me feel creepy. I'm trying to avoid him.'"

"Did she say why she found Jason scary?"

Brad shook his head.

"That *is* pretty nebulous," I said. "Have you told the police this?"

Brad shook his head again. "They weren't very interested in talking to me."

"Why are you telling me?"

"You seem to know all those cops. Maybe you could drop a hint."

"I'd have to tell them it doesn't jibe with what I observed about Julie and Jason's relationship, Brad. They always acted like pals."

"I know it's screwy." Brad began to back away. "I've got to get back to Grandmother's house."

"Wait a minute, Brad. When did this episode happen?"

He was still edging away. "A couple of weeks before Julie . . ." His voice seemed to fail, and he turned. He called back over his shoulder as he ran back into the woods. "That's all she said!"

I watched him go. He slipped on the snow, but he didn't fall. He seemed to know just where to put his feet.

"That's the strangest thing Brad has done yet," I said aloud. "Running through the woods to tell me Julie said Jason made her feel creepy. That's impossible to believe."

I drove on, thinking furiously. Could Julie have been frightened of Jason? Saying he "made her feel creepy" didn't exactly prove that. Frankly, a lot of people are creeped out by openly gay guys with long gray ponytails, though I wouldn't have expected Julie to be one of them. Guys like that are very common in the Warner Pier area, since we're on the artsy side around here. Openly gay guys with long ponytails of any color fail to cause much excitement in our town, and Julie had always claimed that she especially loved Warner Pier.

Of course, Jason had admitted he was really angry with Julie after she "outed" him and Ross to Ross's elderly dad. Maybe that had happened about the time that Jason made the phone call Brad had overheard. But by the time Jason told me about the incident, he hadn't sounded as if he was furious with Julie. He sounded exasperated at her naivete, but not as if he'd been ready to sever all ties with her. He hadn't resigned from the Seventh Food Group over it.

So, should I do anything about Brad's report? I could tell Hogan Jones. But what would be the point?

I still hadn't decided whether I should repeat Brad's story to Hogan Jones when I reached Warner Pier. That's when I noticed something unexpected—a car pulling into the parking lot at the Warner Pier Chamber of Commerce office.

But it was Sunday. The office should be closed. Then I remembered. The chamber's executive committee was driving up to Grand Rapids as a group that afternoon to attend a reception for the congressional delegation. Apparently I'd driven by just as the group began to gather.

On an impulse, I wheeled into the parking lot. If the chamber manager was there, I could hand in Mrs. Schrader's check immediately. I also might be able to pick up the key to the storage unit where the items collected for the women's shelter were to be stashed.

The chamber office is near the Interstate in a building that, in one of those small-town coincidences, once held my grandfather's service station. It had been remodeled until its origins were completely disguised, of course, and now featured shingled sides and cobblestone panels that made it look more like a summer cottage than an office. The canopy that once sheltered the gas pumps was gone.

I parked the van beside a big black sedan, almost large enough to be classified as a limo. On its door was a very tasteful logo, white with a few accents of red, featuring an abstract wing. The words "Eagle Heights Real Estate Development" were painted below in letters so modern and so small they were almost unreadable.

Eagle Heights was owned and operated by the vice president of the chamber, Barry Eagleton. I knew him, of course, since we both served on the chamber board of directors. But I'd never noticed this car before. It must be new, I thought. Very classy. But why did it seem so familiar?

I had climbed out of the van and waded through the slush to reach the entry to the chamber office before I remembered. Then I whirled around for another look at that eagle logo.

The day Martin Schrader and I had lunch at the Sidewalk Café, Martin had been late. And when he arrived, he got out of a big black Lincoln sedan with a black-and-white logo on the front door. I hadn't seen who was driving, but the logo had included a red wing, over lettering too small to be deciphered from inside the restaurant. Now I decided the car must have belonged to Eagle Heights Development. And Martin Schrader had told me he was in Warner Pier that day "for a business meeting."

I stared at the black sedan and thought. The easiest conclusion I could jump to was that Martin Schrader had been meeting with Barry Eagleton. In other words, the potential heir to one of the biggest pieces of undeveloped property in the Warner Pier area had been meeting with the biggest developer of property in the area. Was Martin looking into a deal for developing the Schrader property?

I got quite excited. Then I told myself to calm down. There were a dozen other explanations.

Maybe Barry hadn't been driving the sedan with the logo that day.

Maybe it had been his sexy secretary. Of course, I didn't know that Barry had a sexy secretary, but if he did, Martin might have been riding around with her for reasons having nothing to do with real estate.

Or maybe Barry and Martin were looking into some sort of development deal that had nothing to do with the Schrader summer place. Martin or the Schrader family might well own other land in the Warner Pier area.

Or, maybe they were discussing some business deal that had nothing to do with development at all. Heck, maybe they were considering buying an aluminum storm door business. Or a health food shop. Or a car wash.

Maybe they'd known each other for years and had simply gone out for coffee. Or maybe Martin wanted to buy a house. Barry sold houses, as well as developing subdivisions.

But one thing was for certain. If Martin and Barry had been driving down Peach Street at noon, there was nothing secret about their meeting. Probably everybody else in town already knew about it.

So I could simply go inside the chamber office, talk to my fellow board member Barry Eagleton, and ask him what the heck he and Martin were up to.

I opened the door and went in. Several members of the executive committee were standing around and greeted me. I assured them I hadn't come to join the trip to Grand Rapids. Then I walked over to Zelda Gruppen, the chamber manager, who was sitting at her desk. Barry was standing near her.

Barry's a short guy—the top of his head is about even with my shoulder. He has slicked-down black hair, heavy eyebrows, a thick midsection, and a perpetual grin.

"Hey, Zelda. Hey, Barry." I remembered that Barry is one of the guys who kids me about my Texas accent, so I drawled the words out. Might as well let him have a laugh.

"Look what I've got." I waved Mrs. Schrader's check. "A donation to the drive to benefit the women's shelter. Isn't that as cute as a spotted pup under a red wagon?"

Then I told them where the check came from and gave a short version of how I happened to be the one Mrs. Schrader gave it to. Zelda—who's a typical west Michigan Dutch blond: sturdy and blue-eyed—took the check, and we all whistled at the amount.

"I've also got several boxes of clothes and household goods in the van," I said. "If you'll lend me the key to the storage shed, I'll take 'em over."

"Super," Zelda said. She took the key from the center drawer of her desk and handed it to me. "If we've left when you come back, just put the key in through the mail drop."

I turned to Barry. "Great car out there. Is it new?"

Barry's grin broadened. "Got it last week."

"It'll be awful nice for carryin' clichés—I mean, clients! Nice for taking folks around to look at property. A couple of hours in that dude, and they'll feel obligated to buy."

Barry chuckled. I wasn't sure if he was laughing at my twisted tongue or at the compliment to his car. "Keep 'em comfortable, I always say."

I leaned a little closer to him. "Say, did ah see you carryin' Martin Schrader down Peach Street a coupla days ago? What's he up to?"

Barry's grin became a bit forced-looking. "Oh, Martin's got lots of irons in the fire."

I smiled so widely I developed two new wrinkles at the corners of my eyes. "It's no secret that Mike Herrera is keeping a close eye on what the Schraders plan for their property south of town."

Barry looked away and rattled the keys in his pants pocket. "I guess the answer to that depends on just what happens when Rachel Schrader is gone."

"Martin didn't give you a hint?"

"Martin may not have much to say about the deal."

"Now, Brad, his nephew—he's such a tree hugger. I guess he'd want the property to go to that ecology group he works with. Maybe Martin would go for that, too."

Barry shook his head slowly. "The Lake Michigan Conservation Society hasn't got any money to buy property. They expect it to be donated. I don't think Martin can afford to go that route."

Zelda jumped in then. "How can that be? Schrader Labs simply can't be in trouble. They just got a new government contract. There was a big story on the business page of the Grand Rapids paper last week."

"Schrader Labs ought to be in tiptop condition," Barry said. "But

Martin doesn't own Schrader Labs. He's just a stockholder. His personal finances are another matter."

"Golly!" I said. "If he buys some chocolate, should I take a check?"

Barry laughed. "Oh, I'm sure his personal checks would be good. He's far from broke. You know how it is, Lee. Financial problems for the very rich are different from financial problems for people like you and me."

"I guess Martin's down to his last Mercedes," I said.

"Cadillac," Barry said. "He's a Michigan businessman, remember. We've all got to buy homegrown products."

We all laughed. I took the key to the storage shed and left.

So Martin might need money. Very interesting. Schrader Labs was in good shape, according to Barry, but Martin's personal finances needed a boost.

And the Schrader property at Warner Pier, or so Martin had said, was owned by his mother. There would be no financial benefit to Martin as long as she was living.

But so what? As Barry had said, financial problems for a person like Martin Schrader were different from the problems I might have. Where I might have to let my insurance drop if things got tight, a financial bind for Martin might mean he'd have to ski in Iron Mountain rather than Vail or cash in some stock he had intended to hold another year.

All this was interesting, but it didn't have any connection with my current problem. Should I believe Brad's tale about Julie being frightened of Jason? Should I report the yarn to Hogan? Should I call Brad and tell him I wasn't getting involved? Should I tell him to do his own dirty work?

I dropped the boxes for the women's shelter in their special storage unit, returned the key to the chamber office, and drove on to TenHuis Chocolade without reaching a conclusion. I went in, took my six breaths of chocolate aroma, and saw Dolly Jolly behind the counter. Seeing her there gave me an attack of conscience.

"Dolly, you're supposed to be learning how to handle chocolate, not working a cash register. I promise I'll stick around more."

"I don't mind, Lee!" Dolly's voice boomed as loudly as ever. "We've had hardly any customers! Guess they don't expect us to be open on Sunday. Nettie has me learning to tie those fancy bows! Packaging! That's part of the chocolate business, too!"

"Any messages?"

"Joe called!"

Joe answered at the first ring. The conversation didn't take long.

"Are you still planning to go to the preview of Jason's new place?" he said.

"I'd forgotten that was tonight. Do you want to go?"

"Since I'm almost the landlord, I guess it would be polite to show up."

"If you don't want to . . ." I knew going back to the house his ex-wife had built—where she and Joe had lived and where she had died—wasn't going to be easy for Joe.

"I can't let Warner Point become a hang-up. I want it to be a popular restaurant with loads of big dinners and receptions held there. So I'd better show. Lindy and Tony are going. And Mom and Mike will be there. Is seven o'clock okay?"

"Sounds great."

"Love you."

"Love you."

I hung up feeling a little warmer, despite the snow outside. It ought to be a pleasant evening. We don't see enough of Lindy and Tony. And I like Joe's mom. She doesn't hover, but she always seems concerned, unlike mine, who never seems to give a darn what I do. And Mike is good company, too, especially since he's almost quit trying to entice Tony into the restaurant business.

I really admire Mike, who worked himself up from a job as a dishwasher in Denton, Texas, to owning three restaurants and a catering service in a fancy Michigan resort. In fact, I often rely on Mike's advice, and now it occurred to me that he might help me solve the puzzle of what Brad had said about Julie being afraid of Jason. If anybody knew Jason, it was Mike. Jason had worked for him for years. Maybe Mike would know more about Jason and Julie's relationship than I did.

It was, I decided, worth a try. So I called Mike. I caught him at the Sidewalk Café. He agreed to drop by my office after his lunch rush was over.

He came in the door at two o'clock, looking a bit harassed, and plunked himself into the one chair in my little office. "What can I do for a fellow Texan?"

I'd decided to be deliberately vague. "I had it on good authority that a gal I know is afraid of Jason," I said. "But I've always thought he's a pussycat. Can you think of anything that might have caused that kind of a reaction to him?"

Mike rolled his eyes, and when he spoke his Tex-Mex accent suddenly appeared. "I thought that ol' affair had deesappeared. Won't people ever let nothin' be forgot?"

# Chapter 19

I'm sure my jaw dropped, but it didn't take me too long to recover. "Okay, Mike. Spill it," I said. "There's no way for me to learn the local gossip but to ask. What are you talking about?"

"Eet was jus' a misunderstanding."

"Who misunderstood?"

"One of the waitresses." He rolled his eyes again. "She was new, and she didn' get it. Jason, he's a good-looking guy, and he doesn't act like he's . . ."

Words failed him, so I completed his sentence. "Jason doesn't swish, and the waitress didn't realize he's gay."

"Yes. She made eyes at him. I don't think Jason caught on. But she thought . . ." Mike's vocabulary failed him again.

"She thought he understood her overtures?"

"Yes. So she waited for him in the parking lot after closing—one thirty in the morning. When he went to his car, she tiptoed up behind him, and she . . ." He ran out of words again.

"She put her arms around him, or something like that. How did Jason react?" I chuckled.

Mike looked pained. "Eet wasn't funny! He was startled, you see. So he threw his elbow . . . she got pushed to the ground. She broke her arm."

"That's awful! I can see it wasn't funny at all."

"Jason called an ambulance. He tried to apologize. But . . . she was embarrassed. She filed charges."

"What happened?"

"I talked her into dropping them. The chief understood it was jus' an accident. Jason paid her doctor bills. She moved to South Haven. I helped her get a job down there."

"But it caused a lot of gossip."

Mike looked miserable. "I hoped the gossip had gone away. Who's telling it now?"

"Nobody really, Mike." I sighed. "Brad Schrader—you know, the cousin of Julie Singletree . . ." Mike nodded, and I went on. "Brad told me Julie was afraid of Jason. He said he didn't know why. I suppose Julie could have heard something about that incident. But I think the idea of her being afraid of Jason is nonsense."

"Jason and Julie worked together a lot. I thought they were friends."

"So did I. Jason introduced me to Julie. But Julie did find things out. She had an uncanny knack for picking up gossip. I guess she could have heard this story, or a garbled version of it, someplace."

"It's been five years. I hoped it had gone away. But I guess it never will. After Julie was killed, the Holland detectives hauled Jason in and questioned him a long time. I thought that was the reason." Mike got up. "I know you won't say anything, Lee."

I put my fingers to my lips and pantomimed turning a key. Then I changed the subject. "I'm looking forward to tonight."

"Yes, Jason's new restaurant is going to be very fancy, and we'll be the first to eat there."

I knew that Jason wanted his new restaurant, Warner Point, to be an elegant dining experience, so as soon as I got home I examined my closet for something elegant to wear to the opening. I nearly came up empty. My wardrobe was long on casual—khakis, jeans, sweaters, and T-shirts. Elegant was in short supply.

Finally I discovered a white silk shirt and put it on over my good black wool slacks. Then I remembered the big, cold, black-and-white main room in the Warner Point house, and I took the shirt off and put on a black cashmere turtleneck. It had been my Christmas present from Joe and I didn't get too many chances to wear it. But the solid black outfit made me look as tall and bony as Abraham Lincoln. So I put the white shirt on over the sweater—buttoned, but not tucked in. I dug through my limited stock of scarves and found a long, thin one striped in jewel tones and accented with gold thread. I draped it under the shirt's collar and tied a knot in each end. I put on my good leather boots.

That was as elegant as I could manage. At least Joe gave a low whistle when I came down the stairs.

Then he grinned broadly. "Jason's going to want you as a permanent hostess. You're going to fit right in."

"What do you mean?"

Joe's only answer was to shake his head, but when we walked into the main room of Warner Point, I saw exactly what he had meant. I matched the decor so closely it was almost funny.

The Warner Point house, built by famed defense attorney Clementine Ripley in consultation with a famous architect, had not appealed to me on the few occasions I'd visited it. The walls of the main living area were heavily textured and painted a stark white. The finish of the woodwork and floors was dark, almost black. The furniture had been either upholstered in white or else dark and spindly. The artwork had been practically nonexistent. There had been no window treatments—just walls of unadorned French doors. I had thought the room felt like an icebox, even in July. The idea of it in winter, with all that stark white and black, plus views of snow and ice out those French doors, had been bone-chilling.

But Jason had warmed it up. And he'd done it by using jewel tones.

The fireplace, for example, was made of blocks of white stone that were reminiscent of chunks of ice. It had no mantel, and the stone was piled right up the wall, clear to the high ceiling. Now, in the center of that expanse of stone was a wool tapestry in an abstract design and executed in brilliant colors. It hung like a banner above a cheerful fire.

The French doors now were hidden by draperies of deep red velvet. The round tables that had replaced the spindly wooden furniture were covered with stark white linen, true, but each had a centerpiece of a glowing candle surrounded by a heap of shiny metallic starbursts. Colorful paintings and hangings and more candles in wall sconces formed cheerful vignettes for the smaller tables that lined the walls.

But Jason had left the stark white walls and dark, almost black, woodwork and floors. So Joe had been right. My outfit fit right in. My black slacks matched the floors and woodwork, my white shirt matched the walls, and the jewel-toned scarf matched the decorations. I looked as if I worked there.

I exchanged an understanding look with Joe, and we both laughed. Then we greeted Jason, made obligatory—and sincere—sounds of admiration, and accepted glasses of champagne. We circulated.

The room was rapidly filling up. The whole Seventh Major Food Group had apparently been invited. Diane and Ronnie Denham were circling the hors d'oeuvres, both looking rosy and Santa-ish. Margaret Van Meter rushed over to give me a hug. As usual, her hair was straggly, and she wore a dress that was too tight, but her smile was so sweet it didn't matter. Jim was one of the few guys there without a tie, and both of them were obviously excited to be having a night out. Jim's parents were babysitting, Margaret said. Lindy and Tony weren't there yet, but I knew they were coming.

Most Warner Pier city officials had come, too. Mayor Mike was there, of course, escorting Joe's mom, Mercy Woodyard. I spotted the city clerk and all but one of the city council members, and members of the chamber's board were coming in, too. I knew Chief Jones had been invited, but Aunt Nettie had told me he was at a meeting in Lansing. She had declined an invitation to come with Joe and me, saying she wouldn't mind an early night.

The only person whose presence surprised me was Martin Schrader. He came in with Barry Eagleton. Which was interesting. Neither of them seemed to be talking business that night.

I was thinking that it was nice to have a purely social evening for a change, but that changed when Lindy came in.

She rushed in the front door and dashed across the foyer. She paused and scanned the room, obviously so excited that the beautiful surroundings were making little impression on her. When she saw me, she practically ran in my direction.

"Lee! Lee! I've remembered something!"

"What?"

She answered in a whisper that carried through the room more loudly than a shout would have. "That car that nearly pushed us off the road! It was an old Jeep!"

I took her by the arm and led her into a corner. Then I tried to speak in a whisper that *was* a whisper. "How did you decide that?"

"Tony and I came in my rental car, the one the insurance company came up with, and I drove. A car came up behind us, and— Oh, Lee, those headlights looked exactly the same as the ones the other night. It had those up-and-down bars between them. Like long, horrible teeth. I nearly panicked."

"How did you find out it was an old Jeep?"

"It followed us into the parking lot here. It was Father Snyder."

"Father Snyder?" Father Snyder was the local Episcopal priest. "I can't imagine that he tried to push us off the road."

"Oh, I know that! I'm sure it wasn't him. But I do think it was somebody in an old Jeep like his. Come on! Father Snyder's waiting outside so you can take a look!"

Lindy dragged me outside without even letting me stop for my coat. Tony and Father Snyder were standing beside the priest's beat-up old Jeep. Both of them looked thoroughly ill at ease.

"Turn on the lights," Lindy said. "Let Lee see it."

Father Snyder, who's a round, cheerful young guy, spoke apologetically. "I like to drive this old rattle-trap in the snow. I let my wife have the good car—unless I need it for a funeral." He obediently climbed into his car and turned the headlights on.

"See!" Lindy was attracting a lot of attention from other people who were arriving. "See, Lee!"

I considered the front of the old Jeep. "Lindy. I didn't get as good a look as you did. I can't say one way or the other."

"Oh, Lee!"

"You were looking at the front of that car in your rearview mirror, Lindy. I looked back, but all I could see was bright lights and glare."

Lindy deflated like an inner tube at the end of a day at the beach. I patted her on the shoulder. "Listen, you need to tell Chief Jones about this. It might give him a valuable lead."

We settled for that. I led the way inside—I was freezing—and Lindy agreed to call the chief the next morning. Then I tried to remember how to have fun at a party.

It wasn't easy. Margaret and Jim didn't know many people, of course, so Lindy and I talked to them a lot, and we tried to introduce them around. Then Joe got cornered by one of the city councilmen, and I finally abandoned him and went looking for another glass of champagne. Jason was serving the sparkly, so he took the opportunity to introduce me to Ross, his partner. Ross seemed to be a nice guy, but as soon as Jason moved away, he began to quiz me about the current murder mystery. What had I thought of Julie? Why on earth would anyone have killed Carolyn? It's hard to be sociable when you're being cross-examined.

Finally, I simply muttered a lie—"I think my fiancé needs rescuing"—and went back to Joe. He did look happy to see me, and when I told him he needed to talk to his mother he seized the excuse and told the councilman he'd "research the question." We both fled toward Mercy.

Mercy was talking to someone who had his back to us. All I could see was a well-fitted, dark gray suit and a well-disciplined head of gray hair. Then he turned around, and I saw that it was Martin Schrader. Here I'd wanted to talk about something besides Julie's murder, and I had accidentally sought out the victim's uncle.

Mercy didn't seem sorry for us to interrupt her tête-à-tête with Martin. I was not surprised when she introduced him as a client of her insurance agency.

"Mercy saved our bacon two years ago, when the roof blew off the cabin," Martin said cheerfully. "She'd talked me into upping the coverage on contents, thank God. That stuff I thought was old furniture turned out to be antiques, and we got a nice settlement for water damage. We were able to refurnish the place."

"The cabin?" I said. "Is that the little house where Brad lives? Just as you enter the property?"

Martin looked at me sharply. "Yes, Brad lives in the cabin. He hasn't been bothering you, has he?"

"Oh, no." I belatedly remembered that I wasn't supposed to tattle on Brad and let his uncle know he had come by my office. "I like Brad. He helped me load up the things your mother gave to the chamber's campaign for the women's shelter."

Martin drained his glass, and I decided it hadn't been his first drink. Or his second or third. He turned his full attention on me. "Now what's the deal on this accident you and Mike Herrera's daughter-in-law had?"

I decided I didn't want to give Martin Schrader a full-scale description of the excitement. "Some guy tried to pass us there where the bank has fallen away on Lake Shore Drive," I said. "He got too close and shoved us over the side, but luckily we didn't go down where it's the stickiest. I mean, steepest! We missed the steepest part. Neither of us was hurt, but the driver left the scene."

"Where does Father Snyder's Jeep fit in?"

"I don't think it does." Martin frowned—maybe glared—and I felt that I had to go on. "Lindy saw Father Snyder's headlights in her rearview mirror tonight. She thinks the driver we tangoed with—I mean, tangled with! She thinks the driver who almost hit us may have driven an older Jeep like Father Snyder's."

"What do you think?"

"I didn't get that good a look at the car. Of course, Lindy's insurance company would like to find him. Her car was totaled."

I decided it was time to change the subject, even if it went back to Julie. "We—I'm speaking as a member of the Warner Pier chamber's board—appreciated the donation of Julie's household goods to our drive for the women's shelter."

"That was Mother's idea. She knew Julie loved Warner Pier."

"Were Julie and your mother close?"

"Mother was as close to Julie as anyone was, I guess. Julie had kept her distance from most people since . . ." He stopped talking, and I mentally finished his sentence with *since her husband turned out to be such a louse.* I cast around desperately for another subject for conversation.

"Your mother seems very—well, strong. At least mentally. I know she has trouble getting around."

"You're right; she's strong mentally. She's had several bad shocks in the past few years, and she rolled with 'em better than I have."

"At least she still has you and Brad."

Martin's face grew bleak. "Yes, she has Brad."

"He certainly seems to be fond of her. And at least he lives fairly near to her, though Warner Pier isn't that close to Grand Rapids. He drives there to work, right?"

"Yes." Martin gave me a sharp look, but he didn't say anything more. Obviously he didn't like to talk about Brad any more than Brad liked to talk about him. I paused and tried to think of a different topic to introduce. But Mercy jumped in before my tiny brain could improvise.

"Brad came to me for car insurance," she said. "I mentioned that so many people check out insurance online now. I was surprised when he said he never touches computers."

Martin looked at her sharply. "Why did that surprise you?"

Mercy smiled. "Because of his age, I guess. It seems as if everybody under thirty-five is a computer whiz these days."

"Oh, yes. Brad avoids computers. He's a regular computaphobe." Martin gave a barking laugh, then looked at his empty glass. "Guess I'd better get another drink," he said. He walked away, reeling only slightly.

I moved close to Mercy. "I hope Martin Schrader isn't driving," I said softly. "As his insurance agent . . ."

"I don't handle the Schrader cars," she said. "Just the Warner Pier property. It's a sort of a sop they throw to local business. But I'll put a bug in Barry's ear. Martin's definitely had enough."

She moved away, and Joe put his arm around my shoulder. "Let's go talk to somebody we really like to talk to," he said.

"How about Father Snyder? He's an awfully nice guy, and I don't want him to get the idea Lindy and I think he's the one who pushed us into the lake."

"Fine." Joe moved closer and spoke directly into my ear. "You sure are a knockout tonight. I could feel romantic, if I got a little encouragement."

I moved slightly closer to him. "Consider yourself encouraged."

He held my hand as we headed across the room, toward Father Snyder.

With the prospect of a romantic session with Joe to come, the rest of the evening went well. Joe and I helped each other dodge people— such as city council members—that one or the other of us didn't want to talk to. And if my spirits needed bucking up, I only had to catch Joe's eye. He'd always smile at me. He's a wonderful guy, I told myself. He loves me. A little thrill would travel up and down my innards. For the first time since Julie had been killed, I guess, I remembered how lucky I was.

The feeling didn't go away. It lasted through our good-byes to Jason, through a sort of preliminary courting session in Joe's truck, up the stairs to his apartment, and—well, clear through bacon, scrambled eggs, and coffee in his kitchen at four a.m. Joe didn't even bring up our wedding plans, bless his heart.

Crime only intruded again after I told Joe I had to go home.

He kissed me. "You're sure?"

"I've got to get some other clothes and my own car so I can go to work. Today's Monday."

"If you'd leave a few things over here . . ."

"It won't be long until I'll take over the closets and drawers, and you'll have to keep your stuff in a cardboard box."

He laughed. "I'll get some clothes on."

I began to gather up my belongings. My white silk shirt was draped over the back of the couch, but I had to look for a few minutes before I found the jewel-toned scarf. It was on top of my purse, heaped up in a chair—a regular nest of rich reds, blues, greens, and purples, shot with gold.

And in the middle of it was a white stick.

I stared at it a few seconds before I figured out what the white stick was. It was the white pen that Rachel Schrader had given me. It had fallen out of my purse and was lying among the folds of the colorful scarf.

It seemed familiar, somehow. But why?

I stared at it a long moment before I remembered.

The last time I'd seen Carolyn Rose, she'd had a bunch of colorful ballpoint pens fanned out in a brass jug on her desk. And in the middle of them had been one bright white pen.

Carolyn had picked it up and looked at it closely. Then a smile had spread over her face. A tricky smile, sort of sly-looking. She'd tucked the pen in her desk drawer.

The next day, Carolyn Rose had been dead.

# Chapter 20

I was still thinking about that white pen Carolyn had pulled out of
the jar of colored ones when I climbed into my own bed to catch a
couple of hours of sleep before I had to get up and go to work.

I stared at the dark ceiling. Had the white pen been one of the
Schrader ones? But Rachel Schrader had told me it was a new promo-
tional item. She'd said I was getting one of the first ones given away.
How would one have landed in Carolyn's pen jar?

Right after I'd left, Carolyn had apparently called Martin Schrader
and left a message, asking him to drop by and talk to her. Could that
have had anything to do with the pen? Could she have thought that
Martin had left the pen? So what if he had? Although it didn't sound
as if Martin had been around to see Carolyn for several years.

Unless . . . My half-waking mind went tripping back to the moment when Jack Ingersoll had urged Carolyn to look around for signs
of a break-in. I had followed her back to the workroom, and she'd
spotted the dirt in the sink. Had she picked up a pen from the counter then? I closed my eyes and concentrated. Yes, she had picked up a
pen from the counter, then used it to point at the window catch.

Had that pen been white? I thought it had.

Could that have been the pen she later pulled from the jar on her
desk? Could she have thought that pen had been dropped by the burglar? Could she have thought that burglar might have been Martin
Schrader? Carolyn wouldn't have suspected Martin of killing his

own niece, any more than I did. She might have called him to ask about the pen.

I turned over and whacked my pillow. It was too far-fetched. Impossible. The link between Martin Schrader and the white pen was simply too flimsy. Dozens of other companies distributed white pens as promotional items. Or you could buy a white pen that said something like "Bic" or "Rollerball" or "White Pen," for Pete's sake.

I guess I slept then, because the next thing I knew Aunt Nettie was moving around in the kitchen and it was seven a.m. But I was still thinking about that white pen after she'd left the house and I was eating my own breakfast. Finally, before I went to work, I called the Warner Pier police and got the department's secretary.

"Is Chief Jones still out of town?" I said.

"Until late tonight. Can I help you?"

"I suppose the chief did a complete listing of everything found out at House of Roses after Carolyn was killed."

"Complete? I'm sure he itemized everything connected with the crime."

"But not everything in the shop?"

"In a florist and gift shop? Like every rose, every vase, every piece of gift wrap, every little doodad House of Roses had for sale? We don't have that much paper in our budget, Lee. What did you have in mind?"

"It was a ballpoint pen." I could hear the indecision in my own voice. "I wondered, you know, if it might be a queue. I mean, a clue! It might be a clue."

There was a long silence before the dispatcher spoke again. "I don't know anything about a ballpoint pen. Jerry Cherry helped with the crime scene investigation. Do you want me to ask him to call you?"

"I guess so. It's obviously not an emergency."

It was nearly noon when Jerry called. I described the pen Carolyn had had and told him where I'd seen it.

"It wouldn't be on any kind of a list we'd keep," Jerry said, "an ordinary object like that. Unless it was found under the body or it was used as a weapon or something."

"Oh."

"But I've got the key. I could go out there and look for it. You say it was in a jug on Carolyn's desk, along with a bunch of those multicolored pens she handed out?"

"Right. But I think she put it in her center desk drawer."

I hadn't told him about my vague recollection that Carolyn had picked up a pen near the window the burglar had used. It simply seemed too silly. And I wasn't sure she'd done that.

Forty-five minutes later, Jerry called back. "No sign of the pen," he said. "It's not in that jug or in the center desk drawer. And I looked in the other desk drawers and by the cash register and other places where you might expect to find a pen. I didn't find it."

"That doesn't mean anything, does it? Some customer could have carried it away. Or Carolyn could have thrown it out."

"We did check the trash. It wasn't there. Listen, Lee, I'll tell the chief about this when he gets back. And Lindy called in this morning about the Jeep. I'll tell him about that, too."

Jerry and I chatted about Lindy's Jeep idea for a few minutes, and I was careful to tell him that I couldn't identify the make of car.

"But Lindy feels certain that's what it was," I said.

Jerry Cherry wasn't the only person who heard about Lindy's identification of the Jeep as the car that had chased us. The Warner Pier grapevine had been busy. I had been getting phone calls from the minute I walked into my office. Barbara, my banker friend; some angry Episcopalian I had to assure that Father Snyder was above suspicion, even if he doesn't drive on snow very well; Diane Denham, who quizzed me about the Jeep, then mentioned that Jack Ingersoll had done a terrific job getting their computer back up. And on and on. I must have had a dozen calls about that darn Jeep that might not even exist.

It was around two when Brad Schrader wandered in. He looked unusually down in the mouth, and with Brad that meant he stumbled over his lower lip as he came in the door.

"You're probably busy," he said. "I can wait until you have time to talk to me."

I fought down the impulse to say I'd never have time to talk to him and motioned him toward a chair. "Come on in, Brad. What's up?"

He sat down. "What did you say to Uncle Martin last night? He put me through a big inquisition this morning."

Probably Martin's hangover talking, I thought. But it wouldn't be tactful to bring that up, so I made a noncommittal answer. "Your uncle quizzed *me* last night, actually," I said. "Whatever I said to him was in reply to a direct question."

"What was the deal about an old Jeep?"

"Probably nothing. Lindy thought the car that pushed us off Lake Shore Drive the other night might have been an older Jeep."

Brad looked at his shoes. "I guess that's why he wanted to know if I'd been fooling around with the one in the storage shed."

I'm sure my jaw dropped. "There's a Jeep out at your grandmother's place?"

"It doesn't run. It's been on blocks since I was a kid."

"Where did it come from?"

"I think it was my grandfather's. He liked cars. He only used it to get around the property down here. Maybe he took it on camping trips with his buddies sometimes."

"So your uncle doesn't use it?"

Brad laughed scornfully. "Does Uncle Martin strike you as the type to go camping? He has nothing but contempt for nature!"

"Strictly a city boy, huh?"

"He can't tell a downy woodpecker from a hairy! Or a chickadee from a nuthatch! He thought phlox was a wildflower! The only stone he can spot is a Petoskey! The beach could wash out into Lake Michigan or be littered with medical waste, and he wouldn't even notice!"

Brad stopped talking and looked at me with an anguished face. "I'm sorry," he said. "I shouldn't have lost my temper. But Uncle Martin doesn't even care."

Wow. That had been quite an indictment. Somehow it made me like Brad better. When he had come out with that little tirade, he hadn't been self-conscious and only worried about himself. He really cared about the environment.

But his outburst explained one thing I hadn't understood. "I can tell you love living there in the woods," I said. "Even though it means you have to drive so far to work."

"What do you mean?"

"Don't you work in Grand Rapids? I guess I'm a Texas chicken about the weather. I wouldn't want to drive ninety miles every day in the winter, though I know half the people in Warner Pier do. Of course, you have an ecologically friendly car."

"How did you know that?"

"A Prius was parked beside your house when I came out to see your grandmother. I assumed it was yours."

Brad nodded and stood up. "I've got to make that drive to Grand Rapids this afternoon," he said. "I'd better get on my way. I just wanted to warn you that Uncle Martin is on the warpath."

"I don't think he'll bother me, Brad. Don't leave without a sample chocolate."

Brad shook his head.

"Come on," I said. "Didn't you like the Jamaican rum truffle?"

Brad kept walking. "I'm sorry," he said. "I'm sorry." Then he was out the door.

I stared after him, mystified. "That whole family is nuts," I said aloud.

Why had Brad come in? To complain about Martin? I had nothing to do with Martin. Brad couldn't expect me to intercede between him and his uncle, could he? Intercede in what? I didn't understand why they didn't like each other, unless it was their differing ideas on the environment. If they had a quarrel, it had nothing to do with me.

But Brad's feelings about nature and the environment were rather touching. I made a mental note to check Aunt Nettie's bird book. I'd hate for Brad to find out I couldn't tell a downy wood-pecker from a hairy, if that was his standard for judging environmental responsibility. And it wouldn't hurt to double-check which little black-headed bird was a chickadee and which a nuthatch. I knew both came to Aunt Nettie's feeder. I thought the chickadee was smaller and rounder.

Several customers came in during the next half hour, so I spent quite a lot of time behind the counter. In fact, when the phone rang, I answered it out there.

"TenHuis Chocolade."

"Lee! Lee!" It was Lindy, and she was excited. "Have you looked at your e-mail?"

"No. I hope it's not gone again."

"Mine isn't, but, Lee, I can't believe it!"

"What? Calm down and make sense."

Her voice dropped to a dramatic whisper.

"Lee, I got an e-mail from Julie Singletree."

I nearly dropped the receiver. The shop whirled for a minute. Then I regained control of my voice. "If I ever got a message from the Great Beyond," I said, "I wouldn't expect it to come by e-mail."

"Well, you've got one. At least my message says it went to both of us."

"But it can't be from Julie."

"Oh, it's not! That's just the address it came from. It's from her grandmother. Go look at it! Quick!"

I called to Dolly Jolly, asking her to watch the counter. Then I picked up Lindy's call on my desk phone and commanded my computer to download the latest e-mail on TenHuis's second phone line. Sure enough, there was a message with the "partygirl" address that Julie had used.

"It does give me a funny feeling to see that," I told Lindy. "I wonder how Rachel Schrader got into Julie's e-mail."

"Read it!"

I opened the message. "Dear Ms. McKinney and Mrs. Herrera," it said. "I know you'll be startled to receive this message from me through Julie's e-mail. The truth is, something very surprising has come up, and I feel that the two of you can help me. I'm e-mailing because I don't want to take the chance of being overheard talking on the phone.

"I found Julie's Macintosh computer hidden here in my house. Only Martin would have had the opportunity to put it there. I simply do not understand what is going on, but perhaps the two of you could help me.

"Could you come out to the Warner Pier house for a short conference? I should arrive there by four thirty this afternoon.

"Needless to say, I would prefer that neither of you mentioned this matter to anyone else. I am determined to accomplish two things. First, to see justice done in Julie's death. There will be no cover-up. Second, I want to spare my family any unnecessary pain and notoriety. I'm sure you can understand my feelings.

"Martin has been called to a meeting in Detroit, and Brad will be working until late tonight. Only my faithful Hilda will be present. After we discuss the matter, perhaps the two of you will go to the police with me. It won't be easy for me to turn my son in to the police."

It was signed like an old-fashioned business letter. "Most sincerely, Rachel Schrader."

I read the letter twice. "That's crazy," I said.

"Lee, we can't refuse to go. Not when it's Rachel Schrader."

"Lindy, we don't know that this is from Rachel Schrader. It could be from the murderer. The police are assuming that he stole Julie's Macintosh."

"But if it *is* from her, Lee, it would be really rotten not to go and talk to her."

"I'm not going without checking it out."

"How are you going to do that?"

"I'll phone her."

"Where?"

"She gave me the numbers for both the Warner Pier house and her cell phone that time I had to go out and pick up Julie's stuff."

I spent ten minutes looking for the phone numbers. This involved dumping out the gigantic tote bag I use as a purse and going through every scrap of paper and business card—and that was a lot of paper and cardboard. I finally found the numbers not in my purse, but scrawled on my calendar. I called the Warner Pier house, but there was no answer. Which was not surprising. Mrs. Schrader and Hilda VanTil were probably on their way down from Grand Rapids. So I tried the cell phone number.

"Hello!" Hilda VanTil answered with that distinctive high-pitched, nasal voice.

"Ms. VanTil? This is Lee McKinney."

"Oh, yes, Ms. McKinney. Mrs. Schrader said she had contacted you." Her voice faded as the cell phone displayed that common problem of cell phones along the lake shore. Then Ms. VanTil's voice came in strongly again. "You got her e-mail, eh?"

"Yes. I wondered . . ." I couldn't tell her I had wondered if the e-mail was really from Rachel Schrader. I improvised. "I was curlicue—I mean I was curious! Have you all left Grand Rapids?"

"Oh, yes! We just arrived at the Warner Pier house," she squeaked. "Mrs. Schrader is—well, indisposed. Can I have her call you back?"

"No. She wanted us to come out there. If she's arrived, Mrs. Herrera and I will be there shortly."

"Hokay! I'll tell her." Ms. VanTil's funny voice piped a good-bye.

This was beginning to sound as if it might be the real deal, though I still didn't understand just why Rachel Schrader would want to talk to Lindy and me before she went to the police. I called Lindy and told her as much.

"I don't see how we can refuse to go, Lee," she said. "It would mean denying a request from a grieving grandmother. And when that grieving grandmother is one of the wealthiest women in Michigan—well, just from a business standpoint, I feel we should go."

"Maybe so. But I'm getting legal advice first. I'm going to call Joe."

"But she said not to tell anybody."

"That's one of the things I think is the screwiest. Why doesn't she want us to tell anybody where we're going?"

Lindy said she'd come by to pick me up in her rental car. While I was waiting I called Joe. I got his answering machine at the boat shop, and his voice mail on his cell phone. I left messages describing the e-mail request from Rachel Schrader both places. Then I tried city hall. He wasn't usually there on a Monday, but he might have dropped by. He hadn't.

I gnawed my knuckles a minute, then called the police dispatcher. No, she couldn't get hold of Chief Jones, and Jerry Cherry was tied up with a three-car wreck down the street from the Superette. "Nobody's hurt," she said, "but he'll be over there for a while."

By then Lindy was in the shop, champing at the bit, ready to head out to the Schrader property. "I don't understand why you're dragging your heels," she said.

"After you've survived two attempts on your life, Lindy, I don't understand why you're so eager to go off to a lonely house in the woods." I sighed. "Let me tell Aunt Nettie that I'm leaving."

For once Aunt Nettie wasn't standing over a hot vat of chocolate. I found her in the break room. She has a desk there, though I've never known her to sit down at it and do any work. She uses it merely to stack papers and letters on. Anything private or important I file in my office, because once a paper hits Aunt Nettie's desk, it's lost until the odd moment when she loses something she really needs and decides to sort things out.

This happens maybe once a year, and this seemed to be the day. She had moved her pile of papers to one of the break room tables, and she was walking back and forth arranging things into stacks. I was pleased to see that she was also filling a black plastic trash bag.

I told her about Rachel Schrader's e-mail. "I've called her cell phone, and I talked to her assistant," I said. "I guess it's on the level."

Aunt Nettie frowned. "If you don't feel right about it, Lee, you shouldn't go."

"It's like Lindy says. How can we refuse a request from Rachel Schrader?"

"That reminds me." Aunt Nettie searched through one of the piles on the break room table. "I found this. It's that prayer for the working woman that Julie Singletree sent right before she died." She pulled out a stack of papers printed with Julie's distinctive rose background. "I read the poem, but I quit without reading the rest of the message."

"Julie's messages always had lots of junk at the bottom. Nobody ever read all of them. You can toss it out."

"Before you go, did you straighten out the Nordstrom order?"

We chatted about business matters for a minute. I reassured her about the Nordstrom order, and she explained a problem with an Easter bunny mold to me. Then I went around and gave her a hug before I left. "I shouldn't be too late," I said.

But I still felt uneasy, so when I got back to my office I ignored Lindy's pacing and insisted on one more check. I called the land line for the Schrader house.

"Hellooo!" It was Hilda VanTil again.

"It's Lee McKinney," I said. "We got held up, but we're on our way."

"I hope so. Mrs. Schrader is getting impatient."

Lindy was, too. I couldn't put her off any longer. We got into her rental car and headed out Lake Shore Drive. It was almost dark.

# CHOCOLATE CHAT
## CHOCOLATE AND ROMANCE

". . . The taste of chocolate is a sensual pleasure in itself, existing in the same world as sex. . . . For myself, I can enjoy the wicked pleasure of chocolate . . . entirely by myself. Furtiveness makes it better."
                                        —Dr. Ruth Westheimer

" 'Twill make old women young and fresh;
Create new motions of the flesh.
And cause them long for you know what,
If they but taste of chocolate."
                                        —James Wadworth (1768–1844)

(Description of lovelorn nobleman in seventeenth-century France) "His love for her was such that he shut himself in his room for months on end . . . without eating, drinking barely enough cups of chocolate to sustain him."
                    —Primi Visconti, quoted by Sophie D. Coe and
                        Michael D. Coe in *The True History of Chocolate*

"It's not that chocolates are a substitute for love. Love is a substitute for chocolate. Chocolate is, let's face it, far more reliable than a man."
                                        —Miranda Ingram

# Chapter 21

Lindy was excited as we drove along through the gathering gloom. She seemed to be anticipating an adventure. But I was glum. I still felt nervous about being asked to meet Rachel Schrader.

I guess it was nerves that made me turn around to see if there was a car behind us. There was, but it was turning left. It didn't look threatening.

I guess I'd reminded Lindy of our brush with death, because she spoke. "I don't think anybody is following us."

"It'll be a long time before I stop checking to see who's behind me."

"Me, too." Then she turned her compact rental car toward West Street, rather than toward the Orchard Street Bridge. "Let's go the long way around," she said. "I'm not all that excited about driving past that drop-off on Lake Shore Drive."

"Fine with me." I faced forward again, and in the process I somehow dumped my big leather satchel onto the floor. All my belongings landed under my feet.

"Dad gum! I just had everything out of that bag earlier this afternoon," I said. "Don't make any sudden stops while I gather it all up."

"I'll have to slow down when I get on the Interstate."

I began to pick up my stuff and stow it back in the tote bag. It's not easy for a six-foot person to pick up things off the floor of a Neon, but I pushed the seat all the way back and tried. Sunglasses, billfold, keys—that was just the start. I carried far too much junk around with me. There was even a big sheaf of papers.

"I thought I got rid of all these papers back at the office," I said.

I picked the papers up and realized I was holding the printout of the long message from Julie, the one Aunt Nettie had had on her desk. It was the message that had caused me to request that Julie leave me off the list for inspirational items.

"I thought I tossed this into Aunt Nettie's trash," I said. The big print size Julie had used to send e-mail made the thing easy to read, even in a dim light. I thumbed though the pages as we drove. "Julie never killed anything," I said. "Here's that recipe for cookies Diane Denham sent out way before Christmas."

"How about the punch recipe that Carolyn sent? I meant to print that one out."

I looked further. "Looks as if it's not here," I said. The car swerved, and I looked up. Lindy was turning into the Schrader property.

"I guess that's Brad's house," Lindy said.

"Yes, just follow the road on around to the right. It makes a circle, and the main house is at the opposite end of the loop, on the lake shore." I looked back at the papers in my lap. "I'm pretty sure the punch recipe isn't here, Lindy. I'm down to the last page and it's . . ." My voice trailed off as I read what was on the last page. As I took it in, I began to feel almost dizzy with surprise.

Then Lindy threw on the brakes, and I almost hit the windshield.

"Lee!" She screamed my name. "Look!"

The car was completely stopped. Ahead of us, parked beside the road and plainly visible in our headlights, was an old, ragtop Jeep.

"Lindy!" I was screaming, too. "Drive on! It's too narrow to turn around and go back! Brad put that Jeep there as a trap! He wants us to get out and investigate! He's the murderer! Drive like hell!"

Lindy may have paused a second, but she didn't argue. She floored the Neon's accelerator, and the little car leaped forward. I craned my neck around, and I saw a figure run out of the woods, toward the Jeep.

Lindy yelled. "Are you sure that was a trap? What about Mrs. Schrader?"

"She's not here! That e-mail was a trap, too! And Brad must have imitated Ms. VanTil's voice when I called."

"How do you know?"

"It's in this e-mail. Brad told Julie what he was up to. He's planning to kill Martin! Julie thought he was kidding."

Ahead, the bulk of the flying saucer mansion became visible. As we reached the turnaround area in front of it, I yelled. "Stop!"

"What now?" Lindy hit the brakes and the Neon skidded to a halt.

"Listen," I said, "there's a road that cuts through the middle of the big circle drive. If we go on, Brad can cut us off. He's got us trapped if we go forward."

"What should we do?"

I took a deep breath. "Cut your lights."

Lindy complied. "Okay," I said, "I'm going to get out. You turn the car around facing the way we came in. Can you do it without lights?"

"Sure. What are you going to do?"

"Break a window."

I didn't stop to explain. I jumped out of the car and headed for the flower bed. I knelt and dug through the snow until I got hold of one of the ostrich-egg-sized beach stones that filled it. Then I staggered up the broad stairs, and hurled the rock at the window on the right side of the door. Nothing happened, except that the stone bounced back and nearly hit my foot. I picked it up and threw it again, tossing it as hard as I could.

This time the security system activated an alarm, and a deafening clanging noise began. I ran back down the steps, circled the car, and jumped in. Lindy's mouth was hanging open, but when I pointed forward she took off. There was just enough light to see the road without headlights.

I was terrified. Would my trick work? Had Brad taken the shortcut across the circle drive? Would he hear the alarm and think we'd tried to get into the house? Would he go there, looking for us? Or was he waiting for us right where we'd seen the Jeep, ready to ram into us?

Lindy was speaking, but I still couldn't hear a word. She didn't hurry; it was simply too dark. But she drove on steadily. Soon I saw the roof of Brad's cabin, a straight line against the twisted tree limbs.

The siren was far enough away now that I could yell and be heard.

"Get out onto Lake Shore Drive. If Brad's waiting for us at the entrance, it's too late anyway! Then head for Aunt Nettie's."

Lindy flipped on her lights. "Okay, Lee," she said. "But you'd better be right about all this, or we're in a lot of trouble for breaking Mrs. Schrader's window."

I pulled the e-mail printout from behind me—I'd wound up sitting on it after I jumped back in the car—and tapped it. "It's all in here! As good as a confession. I've got to get this to Chief Jones."

Lindy wheeled onto Lake Shore Drive and floored the Neon. A blue truck loomed up, coming toward us. Its horn blasted, but we didn't stop.

Maybe we were in the clear. But no, behind us I saw lights bouncing off the trees, and a car turned into the road. Again the pickup's horn blasted, but the lights careened around the truck and came speeding toward us.

Lindy saw the lights. "Oh, god! It's the same lights I saw the other night!"

"He's not two blocks behind us." That meant we couldn't take the evasive action we had before, such as turning into a drive and hiding behind a hedge. If there had been a hedge anywhere.

Neither of us spoke. The Neon wasn't a fast car. But the Jeep was old. Could we outrun Brad? Could we get to Aunt Nettie's before he caught up with us? Was he armed? If we got to Aunt Nettie's would he shoot the place up?

I tried to think logically. Brad hadn't used a gun on Carolyn, and he hadn't used one when he chased Lindy and me. He'd killed Julie with his bare hands. He was into ecology, not hunting. The chance of his having a gun didn't seem large.

"We're going to have to pass that drop-off." Lindy muttered the words, but I knew what she said. I'd been thinking about the drop-off, too.

"We're going the other direction. He can't shove us toward the drop-off unless he gets on the right-hand side of the road."

Lindy's chin was grim. Her lips barely moved, but I heard her. "Damn it! He's not going to push us off this time!"

But as we got near the place where the bank had been eaten away, I realized that the Jeep was going to try just that. He pulled up close behind us, then swung right, as if he was going to pull around on our right-hand side.

"No, you don't!" Lindy yelled. She edged the Neon closer to the edge of the road, resisting the natural impulse to pull to the left and move away from the Jeep. The Jeep bumped our rear end, but Lindy squeezed a few more miles per hour out of the Neon, and we stayed on the road. The Jeep fell back, but I knew he would try again.

It was a nightmare—not only because we knew we were close to death, but because of the lighting. Our headlights were hitting the road ahead, and the Jeep's headlights were stabbing into the Neon's rear window with a harsh, brilliant light. It gave the whole chase a nightmare quality, as if it weren't really happening.

And then I realized that there was another set of headlights involved. They were high and bright, and they were behind the Jeep. A third vehicle was in the race.

I saw the Jeep shudder and veer across the road. But it hadn't hit us. What had happened?

It shuddered again.

"It's that truck!" I yelled it out. "It's behind the Jeep! It's bumping the Jeep the way the Jeep bumped us."

"That's *his* problem!" Lindy's voice was grim. She looked straight ahead, her hands gripping the steering wheel as if it were a life preserver and she had been tossed off a boat in the middle of Lake Michigan.

I watched out the back window. The Jeep shuddered again. It jumped ahead and nearly hit us. But the Jeep's driver—I was sure it was Brad—was worried about the truck behind him. Brad was weaving back and forth across the narrow blacktop.

Then it happened. The Jeep driver must have thrown his brakes on. The old car veered across the road.

Then the Jeep hit a patch of ice. It spun around like an out-of-control merry-go-round.

The Jeep went through the orange tape alongside the washed-out area, clipped the edge of one of the concrete barriers, and plunged over the edge and down to Lake Michigan without ever slowing down.

# Chapter 22

I yelled, "He's gone over!"

Lindy slammed on the brakes and pulled the Neon to the edge of the road, almost ramming its nose into a bank of piled-up snow. The truck stopped behind us. Its driver jumped out. Lindy jumped out. I crawled out, since I had to go out the driver's side because my door was jammed shut by snow. But it was only seconds before the three of us were in a group hug.

The driver of the truck, of course, was Joe. I think I was crying. I hope I told him how glad I was to see him.

The three of us ran back down the road to the spot where Brad had gone over. We could see the lights of the Jeep at the foot of the bank.

"I'll go down," Joe said. His voice was grim. "I already called the cops on my cell phone, and I've got a good flashlight in the truck."

"I can come, too," I said.

"I'll yell if I need help, Lee. Wait and wave the cops down when they get here."

Lindy moved the Neon so that its headlights gave a little illumination to the area, and I used my cell phone to call the dispatcher, telling her we needed an ambulance, as well as law enforcement. Joe didn't come back up until the police were there. "It was Brad Schrader," he said. "Just the way you thought. He was thrown out halfway down. I don't think the EMTs will be able to help him."

Joe put an arm around both Lindy and me, and we stood at the top of the bank, looking down. "Maybe it's all for the best," I said. "Poor Mrs. Schrader."

"But why?" Lindy said. "Why would Brad try to kill us?"

"Because he killed Julie, Lindy," I said. "And he must have killed Carolyn, too."

"But why were we next on the list? We didn't know that."

"I think you did, Lindy. While we were standing around here, I remembered something. You went by Julie's the night she was killed."

"But I didn't see anything."

"You said there was a car—you called it 'a bug-eyed car'—in Julie's parking lot, right? You said you stumbled and fell into it."

"Yes, but—Lee, you know me. Unless the car was some odd color, I wouldn't know it again."

"But you also said it was parked backward."

"Right. It had been backed into its slot."

"It only just now occurred to me, but Brad parked his car backward in the shed out beside his house. And he drove a Prius, which is a rather unusual car. If he was inside Julie's apartment . . . if he looked out and saw you stumble and fall into his car . . . he'd find it hard to believe that you wouldn't remember it. And maybe you would have, eventually."

Warner Pier and Michigan State police were gathering, and Joe got permission for us to leave. The Neon and Joe's pickup had to stay there for the moment, so Aunt Nettie came to get us. It was at her house that the others read the message from Brad to Julie, the message I'd read in the car, the message I believed had caused her death.

It was far at the bottom of the long list of e-mails I had printed out and given to Aunt Nettie. I hadn't read it until that afternoon, and I'm sure none of the other members of the Seventh Major Food Group had read it either.

"Julie," it read. "Last night Uncle Martin admitted to me that he intends to develop the Warner Pier property as a resort. I could kill him! That land absolutely must be saved! The only hope is to give it to the Lake Michigan Conservation Society."

Brad and Julie had exchanged several other messages on the topic. Julie had tried to calm Brad down. But he had been adamant. "A louse who would treat the lake this way isn't even fit to live," Brad had written. "And Grandmother won't DO ANYTHING." He had put the words in all caps, the e-mail equivalent of shouting.

Julie, bless her heart, had replied with some stupid poem about good coming out of evil. She had later forwarded the same poem to the Seventh Food Group, with Brad's irate messages trailing along at the end.

Hogan Jones, who'd been informed about Brad's crash on his way back from Lansing, came by the house as soon as he could. Hogan read the printout and shook his head. "Sounds like Martin might have been meant to be the real victim. Brad obviously killed Julie, but I doubt it was premeditated. Julie just got in the way, sent this message on. He probably got mad about that and hit her."

"She was such a little thing," I said.

Hogan nodded solemnly. "Yes, Brad probably panicked when he discovered he'd killed her. And then Carolyn Rose, Lindy, and Lee stumbled into the mess."

It was right at that moment that a car pulled into Aunt Nettie's drive. It crawled up to the house, paused, then inched into the parking area behind the house.

"Who can that be?" Aunt Nettie said.

"More cops?" I looked out the window. "Oh, golly! It's a big white Cadillac, and I think Rachel Schrader is in it!"

I was already feeling sorry for Mrs. Schrader, and as I watched Martin help her out of the car, I felt terrible. We all ran out to greet them, of course. We were all talking at once, offering to help with the wheelchair, to carry Mrs. Schrader, to do anything she needed done.

But she waved us aside. "I can walk as far as Mrs. TenHuis's door," she said. "It's only vanity that makes me use the chair."

She crept down the walk, leaning on Martin's arm, and I saw what she meant. Her limp was pronounced and unattractive. But she made it into the house. There she sank into a rocking chair and turned to me and Lindy.

"I've come to ask you young women to forgive me. To forgive Martin. If we'd acted on our suspicions you wouldn't have had this terrible experience."

I didn't know what to say, but Aunt Nettie saved the day. "Oh, Mrs. Schrader," she said. "It must have been awful to suspect your own grandson. No one can blame you for believing in him as long as you could."

Martin sank into a chair, his face gray. "Brad has nearly driven Mother crazy, ever since his parents died." He looked up at Hogan. "I guess you found out about the trouble he got into over hacking."

Hogan nodded, but I was mystified. "I thought Brad never touched computers," I said. I held up the computer printout. "I was surprised when I saw these messages to Julie."

Martin looked at his feet. "Brad was forbidden to touch a computer as part of his plea agreement," he said. "He was involved in the Ecoterror case. It took a lot of lawyers, but in the end the prosecutors couldn't prove that he'd actually been one of the hackers Ecoterror used, and he agreed to a plea bargain that avoided jail time. We had a hard time finding him a job that didn't involve computers. That's how he wound up in public relations. He only had to use a computer as—well, a typewriter. And he could be imaginative. He came up with the design for that new white pen.

"Mother and I have been frantic since Julie died. We knew Brad had a bad record, but we couldn't figure out any reason he would have killed Julie! He was closer to her than he was to anybody else. I kept telling myself I must be wrong, that Julie must have been killed by a burglar. Or a stalker."

He turned to me. "That's why I quizzed you, Lee. I hoped Julie had mentioned some threat. An odd phone call. Something."

Mrs. Schrader spoke. "And I had much the same idea, Lee. When I heard that your e-mail group had been hit by a computer virus of course I suspected Brad. But I couldn't understand why he would do such a thing. If he'd been caught, it would have meant prison."

I didn't say anything. Brad had gone far beyond sending a computer virus to the Seventh Food Group. He'd burglarized House of Roses, he'd knocked Lindy out and stolen her laptop, and apparently he'd even managed to get into my computer while he was waiting in my office.

Martin went on. "I kept hoping that Brad wasn't involved until today, when I took a look at the old Jeep. Brad had put it back up on blocks, but a look under the hood convinced me he'd juiced it up so that it would run. I headed back to Grand Rapids to talk to Mother. I thought we could get a lawyer, then convince Brad he had to give himself up. But I was too late. Brad made one more attempt at getting you and Mrs. Herrera out of the way. Thank God you escaped!"

"Thank God Joe listened to his answering machine," I said.

"Thank God Lee was suspicious about the e-mail from Mrs. Schrader," Lindy said.

"But I called to check on that," I said. "Brad must have answered the phone imitating Ms. VanTil's voice. He fooled me completely."

"I'm sorry to say that the young people have made fun of poor Hilda's odd voice for years," Mrs. Schrader said. "Brad was particularly good at imitating her, because his own voice had a rather whiny sound."

Until then Mrs. Schrader had displayed an iron control, but now tears began to fill her eyes. "I'll always blame myself. I didn't get along with Brad's father. As a result, I didn't see much of either Brad or my son while Brad was small. I didn't realize what an unstable person Brad's mother was. I didn't step in when Brad was young; I did nothing to help a bad situation."

"Mother! Anything you had suggested would only have been seen as interference!" Martin shook his head. "Without his parents' cooperation, I don't think anyone could have helped Brad."

"I could have done more after they died, Martin. When Brad moved back here, I shouldn't have let him move out to the cabin. He was alone too much. He sulked and felt sorry for himself. And he got back into computers, despite agreeing not to do that. We should have done something to take him out of himself. I failed him."

"Julie tried to help him," Martin said. That comment seemed to end the discussion.

Brad's house was searched that night, of course, and we found out later that the final evidence turned up there. Julie's Macintosh computer and Lindy's laptop were hidden in a closet, along with a laptop that Brad apparently owned himself. Brad, of course, had never kept his agreement not to touch a computer.

Since Julie died, he'd been hooking into all the Seventh Food Group e-mails. Stupidly, none of us had taken Julie's address off the master list, so anything we sent to each other had gone to her address as well. And like most of us Julie kept her e-mail access code stored in her computer, so getting into her messages was no problem.

Brad had used Julie's e-mail when he pretended to be his grandmother and enticed Lindy and me out to the Schrader estate. If I hadn't disobeyed instructions and left a message for Joe, telling him where we were going, Brad might have trapped us. Joe had saved our lives.

No one understood exactly how Carolyn Rose got into the deal, but her phone record did show a call to the Schrader house in Warner Pier. As Joe and I pieced it together, she must have realized that someone from Schrader Labs had dropped the white ballpoint in her shop, and that—because she found the pen near the window the burglar had used—that someone had been involved in the break-in. She must have called Martin at Schrader Labs to tell him about it. Was she hoping to reestablish her connection with Martin? Maybe.

Carolyn left a message with Martin's secretary, but she then called the Schrader house at Warner Pier. Brad must have answered the phone. Carolyn would have had no idea that the white pens were a new item that only a few people had access to, so she probably mentioned the pen. Whatever she said to Brad, it caused him to come to her shop and kill her.

But Brad wasn't entirely cruel, I guess. The searchers also found a cage of pet mice in his house. There was a brown one, which Martin Schrader identified as Brad's. But there was also a white one which Martin identified as the mouse taken from Julie's apartment. All we could figure was that Brad hadn't wanted to leave it there unfed. That was the best we could discover to say about Brad.

One of the things that really mystified me was, why had Julie been afraid of Jason? It took me a day to realize that she hadn't been afraid of him at all. Brad had merely claimed she was, possibly trying to keep the police interested in Jason. He lied.

That night I felt truly sorry for both Martin and Rachel Schrader. I took a little comfort from seeing the tender way Martin handed his mother into her car. Now that she had only Martin to turn to, maybe they could comfort each other.

The Schraders had barely left when another car came up Aunt Nettie's drive. It was a compact car, not a law enforcement vehicle.

"Who can that be?" Aunt Nettie said.

The compact pulled around the house and stopped. A short, round guy—wearing a down jacket that made him look even shorter and rounder—got out.

Aunt Nettie gasped and ran out the back door. "Bobby! We've had so much excitement I nearly forgot you were coming!"

Bob came in rather nervously, as if uncertain of his welcome, but when he saw that Aunt Nettie was really glad to see him, he agreed to stay overnight, rather than driving three or four hours back to the Detroit area in the dark.

Bobby turned out to be well-scrubbed, with the square Dutch face so typical of Michigan. Once out of his down jacket, he wasn't as round or short as he'd looked getting out of his car. He was just a couple of inches shorter than I am.

Of course, he had to be introduced to Joe and to hear all about our excitement, so it was after ten o'clock and we were all eating pizza before he and Aunt Nettie began to talk about his job prospects.

"Did you bring us a résumé?" Aunt Nettie asked.

"No, I didn't," Bob said. "I appreciate your asking for one, but I'd really rather stay in the Detroit area."

I admit that I felt a weight lift from my shoulders.

Bob grinned in a way that looked a little like Aunt Nettie. "See, my girlfriend has another year in college. So, even if I don't find a real good job right away, I want to stay over there for now. I think maybe my girl—Lisa—is one reason Mom is pushing me to ask you for a job. She likes Lisa okay, but she thinks we're too young to settle down."

"Mothers are like that," Aunt Nettie said. "And she's got a point. You don't want to make lifetime commitments too early."

Bob nodded. "Oh, we're not rushing into anything. Besides— well, I've always worked in food service. I'd like to try something else, if I can."

Aunt Nettie smiled. "That makes sense, Bobby."

"Plus, I'm not sure I want to get involved with family—I mean in a business way. I want to—you know—prove I don't need to get any special treatment from relatives. Prove that I can make it in the real world."

Aunt Nettie looked at me. "Is TenHuis Chocolade part of the real world, Lee?"

I laughed. "It is during the weeks before Valentine's Day. The chocolate business doesn't get any more real than that. But Bob has a good point. Chocolate is a very specialized business. I can understand his wanting more general experience in a first job out of college."

Bob looked apologetic. "It's not that family isn't important, Aunt Nettie. It's just that I don't want to be too tied up with family. Unless it's with Lisa."

I thought about what Bob had said as I finished my pizza. Bob didn't want to be "too tied up" with family, except with his girlfriend, whom he obviously saw as his future wife.

I felt the same way about Joe. When I thought of family, he was the most important person who came to mind.

But there was more to it than that. Look at the Schraders. Mrs. Schrader hadn't gotten along with Brad's father. So she'd seen very little of Brad while he was growing up. Now she blamed herself for not making more of an effort to help him.

Maybe it wouldn't have made any difference. On the other hand, fifteen years earlier Aunt Nettie had taken in a difficult teenaged niece for the summer. Her kindness had laid the basis for a lifelong friendship between us. Plus, the example of a good marriage I'd seen as I lived in the same house with her and Uncle Phil—well, it had sure given me a better pattern than the one I'd gotten from my parents.

But my parents were still my parents, I realized, even if I got impatient with them. If one of them was sick, I'd be on the next plane to Texas. But what would we have to talk about after I got there? We'd grown so far apart. . . .

Before Joe left that night, I took him in the kitchen for a private talk.

"You're right," I said. "We do need to have a real wedding."

Joe looked amazed. Then he gave me a bear hug. And a big kiss. Then he spoke. "Wow! I'd given up on that. What brought about this change of heart?"

"Oh, I was thinking about how Mrs. Schrader regrets not making peace with Brad's father. I don't want to have that kind of regret when my parents are gone. Having them at the wedding won't be easy! They may refuse to come. But at least I can invite both of them. And Annie. And Brenda. But I think we should hold the wedding up here. Not in Texas. I'll gather my courage and do this, but I want them on my turf. Not me on theirs."

I agreed to call my dad the next day and to talk to my mother as soon as she came back from her current trip. Then Joe and I made a date to talk about all the details the next evening.

Then he went home. His truck had been released by the police, so I walked him out to it. I even sat in it with him for a while.

All the best stories end with a clinch.

## CHOCOLATE CHAT
## REFRIGERATOR MAGNET CHOCOLATE

"Hand over the chocolate and nobody gets hurt."

"Save the Earth. It's the only planet with chocolate."

"If there is no God, who created chocolate?"

"Money talks. Chocolate sings."[1]

"The four essential elements: Means, Motive, Opportunity and Chocolate!"[2]

1. Contributed by Nancy Lebovitz
2. © Instant Attitudes

## About the Author

**JoAnna Carl** is the pseudonym for a multipublished mystery writer. She spent more than twenty-five years in the newspaper business as a reporter, feature writer, editor, and columnist. She holds a degree in journalism from the University of Oklahoma and also studied in the OU Professional Writing Program. She lives in Oklahoma but summers in Michigan, where the Chocoholic Mystery series is set.